CONFESSIONS FROM A FARMER'S WIFE

A Novel

CONFESSIONS FROM A FARMER'S WIFE

BY CAROLINE WAY

Greenbrier Book Company, New Bern, NC

CONFESSIONS FROM A FARMER'S WIFE

Greenbrier Book Company
P.O. Box 12721
New Bern, NC 28561
Visit our Website at www.greenbrierbooks.com

Cover design by Anton Khodakovsky

ISBN: 978-1-937573-08-9

First Print Edition

To my parents, **Cliff** and **Betty.**
Thanks for always being there,
even when I didn't make it easy.
I know how fortunate I am to
have you both. I love you guys.

In memory of my grandparents: **George** and **Jessie.**
The older I get, the more I realize what a
blessing it continues to be for me to
have had them in my life. I am richer for it.

Aubrey and **Caroline.**
The older I get, the more I wish I had been
granted the opportunity to get to know you.

ACKNOWLEDGMENTS

The idea for this story was conceived while on my way to have lunch with my friend Beth. It was just a picture and a few opening lines, but the urge to write the images and dialogue down was so strong I almost turned around and left her sitting in Chili's all by herself. Fortunately I opted to keep the lunch date with Beth and, as we munched our way through chips and salsa, she listened while I bounced ideas and dialogue off her.

Since then, many more have become a part of this story as it made the journey to the page making the writing process a less solitary one. These are those people:

Linda Johnson, Pam Lungociu Lagoc. Thanks for also being there in the beginning.

Linda Pickrell—Thanks for getting the typing started and for caring enough to ask, "Wait, who gets this?"

Michelle Roswell—Now you can finally read the second half!

Colleen Patterson—Thanks for your friendship and honest critique!

Ken Whitmell—Thanks for not saying, "You're terrible, get back to work!"

Adela Rodriguez Whitmell—Thank you for getting it–all of it! Next time we road trip together, I won't drive by the Tim's!

Janice Dick—I feel like this story belongs in part to you! Thank you for mentoring me through the process .

Cheryl McKay Price—Thank you for sharing the gift of your friendship and the benefit of your experience.

Ron and Janet Benrey—Thank you for believing from the very beginning, even when others didn't.

Even though she is not here to see the completion of this story, I will never forget her enthusiasm or support at the genesis of this adventure, so in part, this book is dedicated to **Beth Bridges** and her own personal journey of courage.

PART ONE

Job was a man who lived in Uz.
He was honest inside and out,
a man of his word,
who was totally devoted to God
and hated evil with a passion.
Job 1:1 (*The Message*)

Prologue

I am the last one. Of those whose lives I will speak of here, I alone remain. Parts of my story have been heard before—amusing anecdotes spoken around tables filled with laughter; or while sitting beside a warm wood stove on a cold, autumn evening scented with the hint of snow—but I now feel the need to unburden myself of all that I remember, good and otherwise.

The good comes quickly with lightness to my heart. The other, not so. Not even the passage of decades makes it possible to understand what was gained through those trials, nor does time give purpose to speaking the memories aloud, and yet, I will. I will tell it all, the good and the other. There is no reason left not to tell it.

My name is Jessie.

This is my story.

One

Spring 1928

I was six, he was eight. We met down by Miller's Creek, named for the young woman, Cora Miller, who drowned in its crystal waters. It was never certain if the drowning was by accident or not, but suspicion floated in the lore of our town.

I sat with my feet hanging, toes barely dancing along the glistening water's surface. I remember I was contemplating—exactly what I cannot, or will not, recall. I know my thoughts were heavy for my young mind, but they would not be the heaviest I would contemplate during my life. Many, no most, of those thoughts sprung from this meeting with him.

It might have been anger sustaining the impulse that carried me to this place beyond sight of my house. Perhaps my older brothers, of whom there were two, had served as catalyst. It was not uncommon for them to do so, for tormenting their younger sister was a task they took seriously, but whatever the reason, it mattered only then and only to me. It is inconsequential, except that it launched a journey that began that afternoon with a one-mile walk down a hard- packed gravel road which lead to the meeting.

A pair of boy's legs joined mine on the bank. They were longer than mine. The feet attached to their ankles, dipped below the surface of the water with a gentleness that belied their maleness. Really, I knew they belonged to a boy because they were dirty. I was six.

I did not jump in surprise at this stranger's presence. Even then it felt right. My eyes jumped from muscles bound in skin decorated with the scabs of an eight-year-old's war wounds, to eyes that were brown, like the drying mud which gloved his ankles. The eyes were liquid and bright. Bruises ringed each dark pool and spanned the crooked bridge of his nose. Though I did not understand the sensation until much later, I drowned.

I smiled. He did not. He looked at me. I smiled again, unfazed, and stuck out my tongue. I was six. He stuck his tongue out and crossed his eyes. He was eight. I laughed in delight.

"What's your name?" I asked.

"Job, like the Bible," he told me, delivering it as one, five syllable word.

"Well, *Joblikethebible,*" I mimicked his speech pattern, "what happened to your nose?"

"It broke."

"Why?"

He paused to consider his answer, his eyes never leaving mine. With a shrug of his bare shoulders, and the brightest of smiles, he proudly stated the five words that would serve as his answer to most things, "The good Lord willed it."

I accepted his answer without question. "I'm Jessie."

He took me to his father's dairy barns. The first structure, a large airy space, surprisingly pristine and orderly considering the number of livestock in it, housed two new automatic milking devices. Each one hung in readiness for the cows that entered the barn and lined up in nose-to-nose rows. Dozens of gleaming silver milk cans lined the walls waiting to be filled.

With a casual confidence, he showed me how to milk a cow, sending a stream of warm milk into the open mouth of a waiting barn cat. I was fascinated as I connected the milk from the enormous beast before me, to the milk my mother poured over my much-hated cream of wheat on cold winter mornings.

I tried to emulate his confidence as I took teat in hand, but my efforts proved ineffectual. The only thing earned from my tug was a disdainful stare from a pair of very large black eyes. He placed his hand over mine, guiding it in the required manner, until finally I managed victory.

"They have four stomachs, you know." He pulled me away by the sleeve of my shirt in the direction of the door at the far end.

"Cows?"

"Yep."

"Do not."

"Do so."

"Who says?"

"My dad." That settled it as far as he was concerned.

I shrugged, intrigued by the idea. "Y'sure could eat lots."

My attention span, being as short as my age was young, was soon diverted by another wonder as he led me out of that great hall into the second less formal one.

The Cottage. It was called that because the warmth in that structure invited one to explore the possibilities hidden beneath its protective beams. In Sunday school I learned about baby Jesus being born in a stable and that the cows had been lowing. I did not know what lowing meant, but this place had cows too, and it felt good to be there. Any baby would like to be born in this place, and they were. Not the human kind, or the divine, but the bovine.

He led me down the short walkway of the Cottage and past the "rooms" with their reddish brown guests, to the last one on the end. He climbed the bale of hay nestled up against the wall and peered over to what lay beyond. I quickly scrambled up after him. Peering over was another matter, for he was a good head taller than I.

I levered myself up into position with my arms resting on the edge of the stall and my chin resting on my arms. I looked down and gasped. Standing on four spindly legs was a calf. He looked like a sundae; all creamy and white like ice cream on the bottom with sweet golden caramel on top. A Jersey, I learned.

"What's his name?" I whispered with the most reverence I had ever shown up to that point in my life.

"Doesn't have one."

"Why not?"

He opened his mouth to answer but paused. I waited so long as he watched me with those eyes.

"Well?" I demanded.

"You name him," he told me. His look was serious.

"Really?"

"Yeah."

I turned to look back at the young creature before me and thought very seriously about the privilege I had been granted. The calf looked up at me with deep dark eyes reflecting the solemnity of the emotion I had witnessed in Job's. I had my answer.

"Job."

"Yeah?"

"Job."

"Yeah?"

"That's his name!"

"What is?"

"Job."

"Oh."

I swung my leg up and hooked it over the wall with total disregard for the fact that once over I would have almost twice my height to drop before landing on the bed of straw below. I got no farther. A hand grabbed hold of the back of my shirt and held me in place. I struggled to free myself, intent on my prize.

"You shouldn't go in there," he stated.

"Why not?"

"Y'might get kicked."

I hesitated and looked at his swollen nose. "Did it hurt?"

"Yep."

For a boy of eight to admit to a girl of six that it hurt? Well, let us just say I believed. My brothers constantly denied the fact that they had any pain receptors in their bodies even when my teeth left marks on their legs and arms while they sat on me in retribution for something, I must confess, I often started. From them I learned the importance of bearing up proudly under pain. I shed tears as sparingly as possible, not wanting to appear weaker than the boys.

Those few drops that did slip between my lids in the presence of my brothers were often of the alligator kind; cold blooded and ruthless. Only my mother knew when I was bearing false witness and when the need for an outlet was real. She would do one of two things; hold me outside the presence of the prying eyes of my brothers allowing me to save my pride; or send me to my father who would heft me onto his broad shoulders, march the quarter mile from our front step on Third Avenue to the corner of Main Street and into Millie's Ice Cream Parlor. All the while we walked he would sing songs of whimsy and nonsense at the top of his lungs. Neighbors would shake their heads and he, uncaring, would sing louder.

My father never once asked me the source of my problems on our journeys to Millie's, nor did he ask when seated and diving into a sundae covered in pink sprinkles. Sometimes, when I was older, I wished he would have. Perhaps then, I would have learned to share more of myself with my husband.

So it was with a mournful sigh of resignation and a last look at Job's nose, I swung my leg back down onto my side of the wall and left the four-legged Job on his side. My Job had said I *should* not go in. If he had said I *could* not go in, I might have had to prove otherwise.

Summer 1930

In the year that passed quickly, the outside world changed drastically. Banks closed, businesses closed, and people who did not have much, seemed to have less. Vermont was not a rich state so most people already knew poor. Bartering and trading goods for services became a growing practice.

To work off property taxes, some folks worked on the roads which were still being rebuilt after the flood of 1927. My father, Benjamin Bingham, managed the bank in Grand River Junction. It was part of the Chittenden County Trust out of Burlington, which managed to survive the October 29, 1929, crash and ensuing financial chaos—barely, but that was enough. It seemed as though barely surviving became the norm. For the most part, life in our little glen continued much the same as it always had, at least it seemed that way to me, but I was eight, and my world was small. I did not care if someone came to school wearing clothes made from grain bags that had been bleached and re-dyed, as long as they could play jacks.

In that same year, Job and I spent many afternoons after school and on weekends at Nightingale Farm. In the summer months we swam in Miller's Creek and we played baseball, at least my brothers played baseball. They played with Job and the other boys in the large flat yard behind the big yellow farmhouse where Job lived. I wanted to play. They would not let me. I was too young.

For some mystical reason, the age to play had been set at eight. It probably had to do more with the fact that, last summer when we first moved to the Junction, and I met Job, he had been eight; and last summer, my oldest brother and his friends needed a place to play baseball. Job's father's farm had the best yard. So there was no earth shaking magical significance surrounding the determining age of eight, but eight it was.

Now the time had come. I was eight and ready to play ball with the big boys. The big boys, however, decided the rules of play had changed. Now, it seemed, I was too small. I was small in comparison to them, but not as they put it *too* small. I would prove them wrong. They had told me I could not play. *They* were my brothers.

If you take a critical letter out of brothers, it becomes *bothers*. That is often how I viewed Michael and David. Michael was twelve, and David was ten, the same age as Job. The day school let out for the summer, the two of them grabbed their gloves and bats and headed off on their Sears Roebuck bikes, the mile down the road to the farm. They thought Job was more their friend than mine. I knew the truth. I met him first.

I watched my brothers riding down the street and fought back tears of anger. My mother opened the front door of our house and sat next to me on the top step of the porch. She let me brood until the boys were well on their way and my anger fully stoked. My face burned and I clenched my hands inside the pockets of the shorts that had belonged to David just the summer before. My whole body trembled in outrage.

My mother reached over and redid the ponytail on my head. I had a head full of unruly curls the color of wet cinnamon inherited from my father. The ponytail was my mother's way of avoiding long and loud battles in the morning before school since I refused to let her cut it in the shorter style other girls wore. Once she had my hair contained, she placed her arm across my shoulders.

"Why are you angry?" she asked, knowing the answer.

"They told me I couldn't play."

"Ah."

We both sat there for a little while longer, each with our own thoughts. What hers were I cannot say. Mine, however, centered on visions of the boys picking their teams and starting to play without me.

"Is your bike broken?" she asked.

"No," I answered all my resentment funneled into that one word.

"Why don't you go for a ride?"

"Where?"

My mother turned me to face her. "Wherever you would like."

My mother's name was Claire. At that moment she was the most beautiful person I had ever seen. Her black hair shimmered in the sun and her blue eyes sparkled at me. Suddenly we were grinning at each other, co-conspirators in some great game. Without actually saying it, for to do so would betray my brothers who, while boys, were still her children, my mother was granting me permission to follow them.

I hugged her briefly and mightily before leaping the four steps down to the walk that took me around to the side of our house to the garage that was too full of other treasures to hold the car.

"Where are you going, Jessie?" she called to my retreating back, laughter lurking at the edges of her voice.

"For a ride!"

Two

I made it to Nightingale Farm in record time. The game was already underway.

I jumped off my bike, letting it fall where it would and raced around the big yellow farmhouse to the yard in the back.

Michael was at bat and, therefore, the first brother of mine I set eye upon. He saw me coming and immediately held up one hand, and with the other, let the tip of the bat fall to the ground.

"Hold up, Job! My sister's here," he called to Job on the pitcher's mound.

Michael's disgust was evident in the way he stressed our family tie, but undaunted, I marched up to him and made my intentions known.

"I'm playing."

The declaration was met with a chorus of groans from the other boys, but it did not lessen my resolve. I reached for the bat.

Michael was quick and twisted it out of my way.

"No, Jessie!"

"Yes I am!"

"No you're not!"

I cocked my right arm to bash his nose right off his smug face. I might have succeeded too if it were not for the hand that grabbed hold of my wrist.

"Jes." Job's voice held a note of caution.

"Job, I want to play," I explained. "Why can't I?"

"Cause you're a girl," spoke David, from among the group of boys that had gathered around us.

I shot him a glare that had him hiding behind Michael. We were at an impasse. Neither the bothers nor I were going to back down from our positions.

"She can play on my team," Job spoke softly. All eyes including my own turned to regard him with surprise.

"But the teams are already picked!" chimed in Kenny Martin.

"Yeah, an' we're ahead." added Andy Simms.

He threw them all a look that clearly stated he had made up his mind. Some shook their heads in total disbelief, but none argued.

"Next at bats, she hits." he said.

I did not. Oh, I got up to swing the bat as he had promised, but I did not hit. Three times at bat, and three times out. It was no consolation that our team won without my insisted upon help. I was humiliated and angry. When the game was over I left without speaking to anyone. I rode my bike the longest mile home ever.

Dinner that night was a quiet affair, on my part anyway. Michael and David snickered amongst themselves, a humiliation which proved to distracting for me to eat. My mother finally excused me from the table without having to eat my carrots and ignored my brothers' pleas for early clemency. This eased my anguish slightly.

I left the house and cut through the neighbor's yard, not even stopping to pat Duke, the one-eyed, one-eared, old tomcat that belonged to nosey Mr. Lawhead across the street. I was headed to Miller's Creek and sanctuary.

I was not surprised when those legs, long, muscled and lightly dusted with the early signs of manhood, appeared next to mine. I was grateful that my tears of shame had dried and he would not see them. It was some time before he finally broke the silence.

"If you're going to play, Jessie, you're going to have to learn how to hit."

He took my hand in one of his long fingered hands and pulled me to my feet. Maintaining his grip on my hand, he led me down the path to the farm and into his back yard. I loved his hands.

That evening my batting lessons began. For three weeks they continued. He taught me how to stand, and how to grip and swing the bat. Catching and throwing lessons followed. Sometimes my efforts met with failure and sometimes I succeeded in knocking the ball a few feet forward or foul. At the end of each lesson, my arms hurt.

The morning of what would prove to be my final lesson, he appeared with a shiny new wooden bat, purchased with the money he had been saving to buy a new glove.

The bat was lighter, and the grip settled more firmly into my hands. It felt more balanced. I took my stance at home plate, a battered grain sack stuffed with straw and nailed into the ground through the centre, and I waited. He pitched. I swung. The impact, when it came, shot down the bat and up my arms to the shoulders.

I looked up in surprise and watched the small white projectile sail over his head. I looked at him, then down at my hands, noticed briefly that I had ripped open a blister, and then looked back at him.

His entire face smiled, revealing a slightly crooked front tooth in the row of white. I jumped up and down, whooping my delight and started to go to where he stood on the pitcher's mound. The look on his face changed, the smile turned calculating. I stopped puzzled. He looked over his shoulder to where the ball lay at the end of the yard.

"What?" I asked suspicious.

"You better run," he grinned.

"What?"

"Run!"

With a speed any Olympic sprinter would envy, he raced for the ball.

The instant it took my mind to register what he wanted me to do, was my undoing. I only made it to third base before he tagged me out. I did not care. I had hit the stupid ball!

My arrival at that afternoon's game would come as a great surprise, especially to my brothers. Timing would be everything.

Michael and David left on their bikes as I watched through the screen door, waiting. My mother came up behind me, and I jumped guiltily when she placed her hands on my shoulders.

"What are you doing Jes?" she asked sensing I was not merely seeing my brothers off to their game.

"Nothing."

"Uh huh."

My brothers reached the corner. It was now or never. I stepped forward, opening the screen door. My mother's grip tightened. I hoped beyond anything I had ever hoped, she would not have something in mind for me to do this afternoon as she sometimes did when the bothers left to play ball.

"Where are you going?" She leaned against the wall, oh so casually.

"For a ride." I tried to match her tone.

She paused a moment, her blue eyes searching my green. I held my gaze steady. She raised an eyebrow and tilted her head to one side.

"Have fun."

I burst out the front door, grabbed my bike and raced off.

I timed it perfectly. By the time my brothers reached the yard, all the boys were gathered. I rode my bike up to where the others lay discarded to the side, and dropped it to the ground. A few of them heard the clatter and turned.

A chorus of groans and a "Not again!" from David greeted my approach.

I strode right up to them as if I did it everyday.

"Jessie, go home!" Michael implored.

I ignored him.

"Let's pick teams," Job intervened as if nothing unusual were happening. He turned to Michael. "You go first."

Going second meant Job had last pick. We both knew I would be last.

We had first at bat. My first two teammates were out; one by strike out and the other by pop fly. Job was on first base, having hit a single.

I approached the pile of bats—there were only three—and selected the smaller one. My heart raced and my stomach churned. I feared I would be sick, or wet my pants. I walked over to home plate wiping sweaty palms on my shorts and took up the stance. I batted right-handed.

"Easy out, Kenny!" someone called.

Kenny Martin was pitching. He was only eight too, but he was taller than me.

"One, two, three!" called someone else from the field.

Kenny nodded once to the back catcher, checked over his shoulder to make sure Job was not going to steal second and pitched.

I swung and missed.

My hands were too slippery on the bat. I wiped them off on my shorts again and looked down the base line to first where he waited. He bent down as if to tighten his shoelace and grabbed a handful of the dry dirt that surrounded the base. He rubbed the dirt between his hands and then looked back at me.

Kenny was ready to pitch again, but I stepped back from the plate and placed my bat down.

Kenny waited while I picked up a handful of dirt and used it to absorb the moisture from my palms. "Like that's gonna help!" he jeered and the others agreed.

I looked back to first base, got an encouraging nod, picked up my bat, and resumed my stance. Kenny shook his head once, twice, then the nod. He settled in to pitch. I waited. The windup came, followed quickly by the release.

I watched the ball come closer, closer and swung. The smack of wood against leather followed by the smack of leather upon flesh was met with a stunned silence.

Kenny Martin lay flat on his back on the pitcher's mound, blood gushing from his upper lip. On the ground, three feet away and covered in blood and dirt, was the baseball.

Pandemonium erupted as everyone rushed to Kenny. He got to his knees, his hands pressed to his mouth. Blood oozed from between his fingers, a lot of blood.

Voices jockeyed to be heard with cries of "Wow!" and "Hey Kenny, you all right?"

"Go get my mom." Job gave me a light push in the direction of the house.

I ran up to the back door of the farmhouse and knocked frantically. Mrs. Nightingale arrived carrying a small bundle of clean towels. I adored May Nightingale. Sometimes even though I went to visit Job, I would insist we just sit in the kitchen and keep his mom company.

"Good hit, Jessie," May said as she passed and headed toward the gathered group of boys.

I followed her and stood on the edge of the circle surrounding Kenny and Mrs. Nightingale. I was mortified. They would never let me play again after this.

May lifted the towel she pressed against his face for a closer examination of Kenny's ballooning purple lip. "It'll need stitches probably, and it looks like you lost a tooth." I heard a sense of justice in her tone.

"It wath looth anyway," Kenny lisped. He looked up and his eyes found mine. He smiled succeeding in sending a fresh streak of blood across his already spattered shirt. "Nith one, Jeth!"

I was shocked. The condemnation I expected was not forthcoming. Several of the other boys echoed Kenny's sentiments.

My brother, David, clapped me on the back. "You really smacked that one, Jes!" He seemed almost proud.

"Thanks," I replied somewhat unsure. This newfound respect from a brother who took great delight in being a bane of my existence was unsettling.

Job's mother went to get the truck to take Kenny home. Before getting in the vehicle, Kenny marched over to me and grabbed one of my hands in his still very bloody ones. He pressed something small and hard into my palm and closed my fingers around it before jogging back to the car.

I looked down into my hand and saw the lost tooth that Mrs. Nightingale had spoken of.

"What's this for?" I called.

"Luck!" He grinned and blood dripped down his chin. "Thee ya tomorrow!"

I regarded the tooth with great pride. "See ya tomorrow," he had said.

The smile I directed at Job was victorious.

The implications of the slightly guarded smile I received in return, I did not understand. And if that smile tightened into a grimace as we watched the truck pull away, I pushed it to the back of my mind. I was eight. The subtleties of subtext were lost to me.

That day marked my acceptance into the realm of the boys. I played ball with them regularly. I was one of them. Only as the inevitability of my approaching womanhood drew near, did being one of the guys lose some of its appeal.

Three

Summer 1935

Although much of my time was spent with the boys, I did have a best friend of my own gender, Laura White. She was what I was not. Feminine.

Laura's hair was the shade of pale honey and her eyes were a lighter blue than my mother's. Her skin would capture the sun and turn a wonderful gold during our swimming sessions in Miller's Creek. My skin would redden and freckle. Laura giggled. I guffawed, a trait that often earned me a stern look and a scolding from the school librarian, Mr. Carpenter, when Laura and I, instead of doing the work assigned, would sit and write the last names of boys behind our own and imagine ourselves married to them.

"Oh look, Jes," she would coo. "There's William Pitt. You could be Jessie Pitt. If you had a son you could name him Armand, Arm for short. Arm Pitt."

Snicker.

"Or a daughter," she continued without mercy. "You could call her Cherry."

Another snicker.

"Or better still, Peach!"

Guffaw and a scolding.

Considering the depth of the feeling that grew for him, it seems strange now that Nightingale never followed my name. Most often than not, and usually in private, it was Martin. I thought Kenny was cute.

Most of the girls did. I still had his tooth hidden safely in a small felt pouch in my jewelry box on my bedroom dresser.

It was the end of the summer we were fourteen. Laura had just returned home from a rather long visit with her grandparents in Maine, something she did several weeks of every summer. She telephoned to say I should grab my bathing suit and meet her at Miller's Creek. I changed quickly, throwing a faded shirt from Michael's discards and my cut off overalls on over my suit. I yelled to my mom where I was headed and left without my shoes.

The day was beautiful. It was the last Saturday before school started and I intended to enjoy it immensely. After the swim, there would be another ball game followed by a town cookout at Nightingale Farm. I looked forward to catching up with Laura whose sporadic letters told of a boy she had met.

As I approached the clearing beside the creek, I heard Laura's lilting laugh. I hurried my pace and arrived at the edge of the clearing only to stop short at what I saw.

Laura, her skin glowing from a summer by the sea, was resting on her elbows as she reclined on a brightly colored blanket. She wore the same modest one-piece swimsuit that I wore. The top half of the suit was a red tank top. It was attached to black shorts that had a small figure of a diving girl in a red swimsuit embroidered on the hem of the left leg.

Her pink lips were parted in a smile as her head tilted back listening. He was there. He stood tall and straight. The tan on his arms was only slightly darker than that of his chest and back. Water ran in rivulets from the hair on his head only to be caught in the hair that now shadowed the developing muscles of his sixteen-year-old chest.

I could not hear what was said from where I stood, but Laura laughed again. He shook his head like a wet dog after a bath, causing Laura to squeal in flirtatious protest. Flirting is an art I never mastered much to Laura's and my chagrin.

When he saw me, his manner changed. The mood of the wide friendly smile he shared with Laura shifted, an almost imperceptible difference, perhaps only noticed because of the heightened state of self-consciousness I suddenly found myself in. There was so much I did not understand.

Laura turned to see what had captured his attention. She squealed and ran to meet me as I approached. "Jessie!" She hugged me tight. " I missed you so much!"

"I missed you too," I said, and meant it. With Laura I could be myself.

"Hi, Jes." His voice had deepened. It resonated warmly from deep within. I shivered. I loved his voice.

"Hey, Job." I responded overcome with a shyness never before experienced in his presence.

"You going swimming?"

I looked at Laura with her curves that filled out the suit and compared them with my own. I now understand fully the feelings of inadequacy that flooded my heart, but not then. Having successfully garnered my position as one of the guys, this new self-awareness was confusing. Frightening.

"Uh, yeah, I guess," I mumbled.

I love Laura for what happened next. She was always more sensitive to the intricate currents between a man and a woman. I was in many ways what Laura often accused me of being—dense.

"Girls only, Job." Laura turned and pushed him in the direction of the path. "Go play with your cows."

"At least they appreciate me." He offered only token resistance to Laura's pushing. "See ya, Jes."

A cheeky wave and wink and he was gone.

I breathed easier and Laura flopped herself down on her towel with a melodramatic sigh. "Gosh, Jes, he is so handsome."

I looked at her like she had two heads.

She rolled her eyes. "Don't you think so?"

"I don't know."

I sat down next to her and plucked at the grass. It was true. Mostly. I never really gave Job's looks much thought. He was Job. His looks had never been a determining factor in our friendship. In comparison to some, he was not as obviously good-looking; I mean Kenny Martin was beautiful almost to the point of pretty. But, I guess if Laura was going to make me evaluate his looks right then, when compared to most he was handsome.

"Never really thought about it," I said.

Laura's sigh dripped with exasperation. "Maybe you should!"

"Why?"

She looked at me like I had two heads before smiling with calculation. That smile always made me suspicious. "What?"

"Nothing." She lay down and closed her eyes as if to bake the day away.

I threw grass in her face. Laura laughed, which allowed some of the grass to slip into her mouth. She sat up and spit it out good-naturedly.

"It's just that with the way he looks at you…" she trailed off for dramatic effect, pausing to delicately pluck a non-existent piece of left over grass from her lips.

I was reluctant to ask but had to anyway.

"What are you talking about?"

"You're like this team, y'know? Like Bonnie and Clyde. Inseparable."

"Laura, Bonnie and Clyde were bank robbers." Last spring, the papers had been full of their exploits and we played endless games of cops and robbers ending in dramatic make-believe shootouts. Laura was always Bonnie Parker.

"I know."

"They shot them."

"I know that too." She waved dismissively. "But they were a team right up to the end. It was so romantic."

"You're crazy!"

She patted my hand like I was the crazy one, then rose to her feet. "Let's just swim and I'll tell you all about my summer. It was great!"

She entered the creek at a run. My earlier self-consciousness forgotten, I tore off my outer clothes and scrambled after her.

We floated and talked. Laura told me of the boy, Mark, she had met and how, when her grandparents found out he was eighteen, they had forbidden her to see him. This did not stop Laura though. Some afternoons she would say she was going to the beach or for an ice cream, then she would sneak off and meet her boy. I say boy, but his eighteen compared to her fourteen, made him more of a man.

"All we did was hold hands," Laura informed me with great regret. She had been hoping for a kiss. "But when I confessed I was really only fourteen, he got pretty angry. Told me to do a lot of growing up between now and eighteen."

She smiled a cat ate the bird and the cream smile.

"You look happy about that." I was confused.

"I am." She ducked under the water and reappeared with a spray of water from her mouth. "Mean's he's considering waiting."

When Laura wanted something, she usually got it.

We finished our swim and lay on our towels, faces turned to the sun.

"Jessie?"

She sounded half asleep. She did not fool me.

"Yeah?"

"What's wrong with Job?"

"Nothing, I guess."

"Well then?"

"Laura, besides you, he's my best friend," I stated as if that explained it all.

"So?" she came back.

"So," I echoed, "I can't think of him that way."

"Can't or won't?"

I had to think about that. Over the years, I had always loved spending time with Job. He let me be myself without ever making me feel small or stupid like my brothers sometimes did. Job was like a brother without the bother.

"I *don't* see him that way," I finally answered, although inexplicably my heart rate had increased slightly.

"Huh," Her grunt indicated that she had her own thoughts on the matter.

"Drop it."

"Okay, okay." She sat up and looked down at me. "So who do you like in that way?"

I sighed in resignation, but could not stop the grin I felt spread across my face. She was correct in her thinking that I did view someone that way. He had a thin white scar on his upper lip that gave his mouth the look that it was perpetually grinning. I had his little white tooth in my jewelry box.

Laura grabbed my hand and urged me to sit up, excited now by the prospect of learning what young man had caught my eye. "Who is it?" she demanded in anticipation.

I blushed, unexpectedly shy about voicing my answer. I had never revealed to anyone the true depths of my crush.

"You like Kenny Martin!" Laura blurted verging on a wail.

I dropped my head to rest on my knees.

"But Jes, all the girls like Kenny."

As Kenny had matured, he had become the object of many admiring glances from the young ladies. While two years younger than Job, he was not as tall, but he was broad and muscular and a graceful athlete. The fact that his features were fine and combined nicely to form a face that bordered on pretty, did not hurt.

"Does he like you?" Laura wanted to know.

I shrugged without lifting my head. "I think he just sees me as one of the guys."

"We'll have to change that," she said finally.

I groaned inwardly.

"Tonight after the ball game."

I groaned outwardly.

"There's a dance tonight after the cook out, right?"

"Yes," I dragged the word out slowly and cautiously.

"Good," Laura patted my hand as if I was a small child in need of assurance. "You don't worry. I'll take care of everything."

That made me worry.

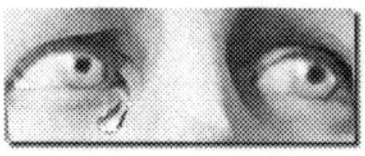

The farmhouse sat on a hill at the end of a long drive. It had a wrap around veranda complete with porch swing and a couple of rocking chairs. Everything about it, including the pale yellow paint was warm and inviting. The rooms were furnished lovingly with furniture built for living. The house had been expanded from the original two bedroom structure that had been Rand's home as a child with the hopes of filling it with children. And, while the dream of many children had gone unfilled, the house was not empty.

Upstairs there were four bedrooms and a bathroom. The huge claw foot tub rested in an alcove, shielded by a flowered homemade curtain that hung from a rod suspended from the ceiling. A gentle breeze ruffled the matching cloth hung over the window, opened for ventilation.

I stared at the reflected image of the girl in the mirror above the sink and wondered how she came to be in there. The evening had started out innocuously enough.

I had arrived at the farm with my parents and brothers. My mother went to find May, my father to find Randall Nightingale, Job's father, and the three of us children went to find out when the baseball game would get underway. People gathered in small and large groups, laughing, talking or huddling together seriously. Children ran amok chasing one another or being chased by frustrated parents. Those wishing to play baseball gathered around home plate, and a coin was tossed into the air to decide who got to select team members first.

Kenny won the coin toss and picked first. He chose me. This was not out of the ordinary as Job or Kenny, depending on who won the toss, often chose me first. Perhaps I should have given this practice more consideration since, even though I had improved drastically, I was by no means the best player. Laura gave me a sly wink from the sidelines which I ignored.

The game proved energetic and entertaining for all. The score was tied and it was the bottom of the ninth inning. I waited on third base for the opportunity to score the winning run. Kenny came up to bat. Job pitched and Kenny's bat connected, sending the ball flying high over center field. He took off running for first base but I waited. Michael was in center field. He would make the catch.

When he did, I took off for home at a flat out run. Michael's throwing arm was good. He easily got the ball to Job, who fired it off to Phillip Ross, the back catcher. Phillip braced himself for the catch and I began my slide.

It was close. Phillip and I both knew it. He stood above me, grinning, the glove on his left hand pressed against my shoulder. I refused to budge in case I lifted my foot off the stuffed grain sack that was home plate.

We waited for Mr. Carpenter, the librarian and umpire of the annual community game, to make the call.

"Safe!" Mr. Carpenter called throwing his arms out in the gesture to match the words.

I lay in the dirt as pandemonium from my team broke out. Kenny was the first to come running over to where I lay. He grabbed me by the hands and pulled me to my feet only to nearly knock me over again with his exuberance.

"Way to run, Jes!" he cried. "That was fantastic. You won the game!"

He scooped me up in a huge bear hug. When the rest of my team came running up to join in, I once again found myself on the ground, this time underneath a pile of bodies.

"Let me breathe!" I pleaded. "Let me up!"

One by one, like monkeys in a barrel, bodies were pulled off the pile. I lay there taking in great gulps of air. Above me, with his deep brown eyes and shy smile, Job stood, hand extended.

"Nice play."

I grinned. "Thanks."

I extended my hand to accept his help getting up, only to find myself swept to my feet by Kenny. He threw a cocky arm across my shoulder and turned to face an unsmiling Job.

"Isn't she great?" Kenny boasted on my behalf. "What a play! Too bad, Farmer, you lost this time."

Job looked at me, an expression in those eyes I could not define, but which still made my stomach lurch. I felt guilty, and that confused me. What had I done to feel guilty about?

"Yeah, Kenny, you won," he agreed. "This time."

"That was so great!" Laura grabbed my hand and pulled me away from the two of them. "Come on, we've got some things to do. See you in a little while, boys."

Oh yes, Laura. That is how I came to be standing in front of a mirror in the Nightingale bathroom.

"Where are we going?" I had asked my captor.

"Inside to get you cleaned up," she answered innocently enough.

"Why?"

Laura had rolled her eyes in disgust and dragged me to the house.

Now, I shifted my gaze slightly and pinned her with a glare. It was all horrifyingly clear.

She sighed impatiently. "Look, if you want Kenny or any other boy to be interested in you, you have to get their attention."

"No, I don't!"

"Yes, you do! Come on Jes. Just this once. If it doesn't work, I promise you'll never have to do it again."

I turned around and took hold of the dress I wore. I shook the skirt for emphasis.

"Laura, I wear a dress to church. They all see me there," I reasoned.

"That's church. This is different."

"How?"

"It's not church!"

Oh sure, that explained it.

"Besides, it's either wear the dress or go out there half naked because I'm not giving you back your clothes."

"Laura!"

"Jessie!"

I capitulated. I had no choice really. She would not be moved, and I found myself turning to face my reflection again. The print of the dress was small and feminine. The soft blue, yellow, and green flowers added to the cool, fresh feel of the fabric against my skin. It had capped sleeves and the skirt fell in soft folds against my bare legs. My heart knocked against my ribs. It was the first time I almost considered myself pretty.

"I can't do this," I protested and started to pull the dress over my head.

Laura stopped me.

"Yes, you can," she assured me. "You look great."

"I feel stupid."

"Don't." Laura stepped back surveying. "Now, I thought about shoes, but my feet are bigger than yours so you'll just have to go barefoot, not that you care. I'm just glad it's long enough to hide that scrape on your knee. There's only one more thing."

"No more!" I cried.

"Hush, just turn around."

"Why?"

"Turn around!"

She gripped me by the shoulders and took the choice away. With my back to her, Laura reached up and tugged, releasing my hair to fall around my shoulders.

With the eyes of one who now understands the power of femininity, I can look back and know the effect was great. At fourteen, I merely felt vulnerable.

My father was on his way up the back steps as we were passing through the back door. He wiped at a smear of something on his shirt. When he heard the door slam behind us, he paused, looked up, and forgot about the stain. His jaw went slack.

For just a moment something shimmered in his eyes. He reached out and ran a hand over my hair. Inexplicably I wanted to cry. I think we both realized with a sense of loss, I was too big to ride his shoulders to Millie's Parlor.

"Ben? What's taking you so long?" My mother arrived to stand behind my father. She looked up. "Jessie you look beautiful."

Her recovery time from the surprise was quicker than my father's.

"Thanks," I mumbled more than a little embarrassed.

"Go and eat before there's nothing left. I'm sure you're hungry after that game." She reached out and squeezed my hand before turning to my father. "Now, let's get you cleaned up. Honestly Ben, I don't know who's worse, you or David."

We let them pass and enter the house before Laura and I headed off to stand in line at the barbeque. I fidgeted with my paper plate while trying to avoid direct eye contact with anyone. Laura searched the crowd for something or someone. When she grabbed my arm abruptly, I had to scramble to keep hold of the plate.

"Here he comes," she whispered.

I looked around. The only person heading our way was Job.

He walked up to me and looked through me with those dark, direct, brown eyes of his. I looked away, ardently willing the flush I knew threatened to rise beyond the back of my neck to subside.

"Laura. Jessie," he greeted.

"Job," Laura returned.

"You both look really nice tonight," he said, not looking at Laura.

"Thank you," Laura replied. I think she may even have snickered.

"Hey, Jes." Kenny appeared from nowhere. I found myself incapable of responding to anyone or anything. "A bunch of us saved you a seat by the tree. Come on over when you get your food. By the way, nice dress."

"Thanks." My gaze kept returning to those eyes that never left my face. I was conflicted. Why, or about what, I could not adequately define.

Job followed Kenny's progress across the lawn, his pulse beat visibly at his temple.

"Well, you ladies have a good evening," he said before departing to join his father at the grill.

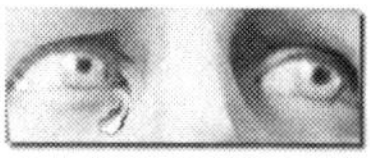

I watched Kenny return from discarding our plates. My breath caught in my throat. He was so handsome, with his sun-streaked hair and turned up lip. Realizing I was staring I glanced away hoping no one noticed. Jennifer Abbott gave me a small smile, the expression in her eye unreadable. I looked away quickly. I did not know Jennifer well, and what I did know—or thought I knew—had been gleaned from the rumor mill. It was not favorable.

She was a pretty girl, taller than me, with dark brown hair and blue eyes. Her hair was always perfect—her mother owned the hair salon in town—and she wore makeup. Jennifer's mother was divorced. Girls tended to avoid Jennifer, while boys tended to flock to her.

Kenny stopped in front of me. "May I have this dance?"

I did not know if I was ready for this, but I knew I wanted to be. I reached out to take Kenny's extended hand.

"Not this time, son," came a deep baritone from behind me.

I turned around startled. It was Mr. Nightingale.

Randall Nightingale was a large man, tall and barrel-chested with hands that easily spanned his wife's waist. On more than one occasion, Rand had picked me up with one hand, Job with the other, and tossed us over his shoulders for a bumpy laugh filled ride up to the house. While Job had his father's height, and hair color, his eyes and lean build were more like May's.

I looked up into the face of the man that loved me as the daughter he would never have. "Miss Bingham," he said formally with a bow. "May I have the honor of this dance?"

He did not wait for my reply but swept me off to the area cleared for dancing. Soon I was laughing, my bare feet resting on top of his as they stepped around the lawn.

The rest of the night followed in a haze of conspiracy. When the dance with Mr. Nightingale finished, my father pulled me out to dance. His deliberately awkward moves kept the laughter flowing.

One dance moved into the next until finally, as the buttery smooth tones of Bing Crosby floated out into the night, my father took my hand and led me in search of refreshments.

After a brief rest, the dancing continued, first with Mr. White, Laura's father then another with Mr. Nightingale, and so it went. Even Doc Fisher got in on the game. All of it, I would later learn from Rand, orchestrated from the start. No way was Kenny Martin getting close to me that night. Unfortunately, these gallant men could not protect me every day.

I was weary and footsore by the time my family began the trek home.

Michael, who was eighteen and now grown as tall as my father, came over to me and stopped. He turned around and crouched slightly with his hands on his knees. "Climb up, Jes," he said.

Too tired to argue, I climbed up on his back and he, apparently without effort, piggy backed me home. I hugged him around the neck as he walked and talked to me about nothing and everything.

Michael was leaving after Christmas. He was going to university to study architecture. I began to comprehend how much I would miss him.

It was strange really, the mood of the walk that evening. I guess I have always known that even when they were a bother, my brothers loved me; indeed, they would have fought fiercely to protect me if there had ever been a point that I truly needed their protection. They were becoming young men, and I, against my better judgment, was becoming a young woman.

Four

Fall 1935

School started after that weekend, and brought big changes. I was now in high school. The school was fifteen miles away, between Grand River Junction and Baldwin. This meant riding the school bus, something my brothers and Job already did.

The bus had been new almost ten years before I rode it, and was just a step up from the tarpaulin-covered truck that used to service the district. It had benches around the inside, which meant we all sat facing each other. It was a tight squeeze sometimes, but in winter the extra body heat was a welcome thing. The rumor around the Junction was that the town was intent on purchasing a new bus for next year: a great long steel machine with glass windows. The lack of drafts would be wonderful, but until then we would continue to huddle close and wear our woollen hats and mittens.

Laura and I always sat together in the middle of one of the side benches. Job and David sat to one side of us, on the bench behind the driver, and seated in his usual spot by the back entrance was Kenny Martin. It was not the warmest location to sit in winter but I think he sat there because it allowed him to stick out his feet and trip unsuspecting or forgetful riders. I confess, I laughed along with the others when Kenny succeeded in catching some poor person off guard.

During those bus rides, I began to envy the girls at the back of the bus, the ones like Jennifer Abbot, who was always with Kenny. They knew the art of flirtatious looks and gestures. I did not. I sat on the bus listening to the giggles and whispers, and watched the furtive glances and smiles, and envied. Most of the attention was directed at Kenny, but other boys, including Job and David, received their fair share of looks and smiles.

David sometimes smiled and joked back but usually found something interesting in the passing scenery to watch. Job was either oblivious to—or ignored the efforts of—several young women who tried consistently to gain his attention. After an initial smile in acknowledgement or greeting, he would put his head back, close his eyes and, for all appearances, would sleep. The less notice he gave those girls, the more effort they applied to their methods. It was futile however, and gradually, as the winter passed, I became aware of the occasional whisper about Job thinking he was too good for them.

Kenny had no problem soaking up the adoration of those who batted their eyelashes and giggled at his wit. Almost with regret, I thought that Laura had abandoned her plot to have me noticed as more than one of the guys. I was wrong.

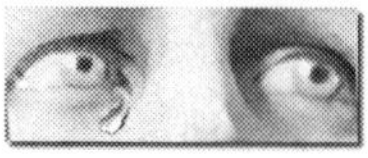

Spring 1936

It was just before the spring dance of my freshman year. On the bus, Laura and I sat together as usual. She was particularly chatty. I discovered why when the bus stopped in front of the Martin home and Kenny climbed up the steps. He was greeted by his friends at the back and waited while they made room for him in his usual seat. He looked about the bus, nodding greetings to other friends.

"Hey, Kenny!" Laura called.

"Hi, Laura." He smiled and leaned forward resting his elbows on his knees.

"Buck Rogers was great last night, don't you think?"

I stared at Laura in disbelief. She never listened to the radio program most of us listened to faithfully. She said it was just too much to ask her to believe that things like suspended animation for five hundred years, death rays, and gamma bombs were possible. A giant ape falling in love with Fay Ray and climbing the Empire State Building only to be struck down in a hail of bullets was much more realistic.

"Yeah, it was pretty good. I didn't think you listened to it."

"A girl can change her mind, can't she?"

"About a lot of things, I'm sure."

General laughter from the guys.

"You got me there." Laura laughed unfazed. "You going to the dance Friday?"

It was asked innocently enough but I did not trust it.

"You bet." Kenny leaned back and stretched out his legs. "I wouldn't miss it. Are you?"

"Jessie and I were thinking about it."

We were?

"Are you going with anyone?" Laura continued, seemingly guileless. She knew most people went to dances in groups, preferring to meet up there. Only big dances like the one held at graduation required a date. She was playing a game for Kenny's benefit and it worked.

"No." Kenny tilted his head and looked at Laura with consideration. I think he began to suspect her line of questioning had ulterior motives. I knew it did, I just did not know what they were. "There's a group of us going together. Why don't you two meet us there?"

"You would do that?" Laura fluttered her eyelashes. "You would let us meet up with you?"

"Sure!" he puffed out this chest with pride at his generous offer. "Then Jessie and I can finally have that dance she owes me. Right, Jes?"

His wink made me blush.

"Yeah, sure."

I do not know if a sound or movement, or something even more elemental caused it, but I glanced in Job's direction. His posture had not changed. He still looked as though he were sleeping, but I suspected he was not. The sun reflected off his eyes confirming my suspicion. Although his eyes were barely open, he was looking directly at me. David observed the interplay between us all with open curiosity.

"What are you doing?" I quickly turned back to Laura and whispered in her ear. Originally we planned to spend the Friday night at her house and go with her parents to see a movie in Baldwin.

"Change of plans," she said.

"Come here and hold still," Laura commanded as she poked around in her small clutch purse.

We stood on the path that led to the two storey brick schoolhouse. The evening was cool and damp. The overcast sky threatened to open up and rain on us at any moment. As if I was not frazzled enough already, I was certain I could actually hear my hair frizzing.

Laura came up with a small compact I regarded with more than a little suspicion.

"What is that?"

"It's lipstick."

"Yes. Why are you pointing it at me?"

"Don't ask questions. Just wear it," Laura huffed in exasperation.

Reluctantly I submitted and allowed her to apply the color.

"Now press your lips together like this."

Laura demonstrated and I mimicked pressing my lips together and moving them back and forth. I stuck my tongue out to run it over my coated lips.

"Don't lick it!" Laura wailed with such dismay, I stopped.

The offending substance felt greasy and foreign on my lips. I desperately wanted to run a fist over my mouth and remove the lipstick but refrained, afraid of how Laura would react to that. I tugged on my brassier instead. I was not used to wearing one. This was my first. Talk about trying to make mountains out of mole hills.

"Don't do that." Laura pulled my hands away. "It's not ladylike."

"It's not comfortable."

Neither was the moment my mother presented me with the small paper bag suspiciously similar to the ones from the store Laura's parents owned and operated.

"Jessie?" I heard my mother's voice faintly followed by a knock. My bedroom door creaked open and I heard her voice again, clearer. "Are you in here?"

"Yes." Unfortunately. "In the closet."

"Why are you doing in the closet?"

"Looking for a dress." I had spent at least an hour hiding in my bedroom closet with only my dismay for comfort. I could not decide what to wear.

There was a brief pause.

"Why are you looking for a dress in your closet?" she asked dryly. "They're all out here."

She was correct. I had removed every dress from the hanger it called home and given it a new home on the floor, or the bed, or the chair. Whatever surface was closest really.

"I can't decide what to wear," I moaned trying not to whine too much. I deemed nothing to be suitable. This was a momentous event, at least it seemed that way. It should have a matching ensemble, and I was running out of time to decide which one it would be. Laura and her parents would be here shortly to take us to the dance.

"Don't go anywhere," my mother said after another short silence. "I think I have just the thing.

Where did she think I would go? Moments later she returned and ordered me out of my dark sanctuary. "Tell me what you think," she said. "I bought it for your birthday but now seems like a good time to give it to you."

My mother pushed aside a pile of clothing from the bed and laid out a slim knitted skirt and sweater set in charcoal grey. The outfit would make Laura drool.

"It's perfect." I clapped my hands together suddenly looking forward to the night ahead.

"There's just one other thing." My mother nervously extended the bag from the clothing store.

"What is it?" I took the bag from her.

"Open it.

I opened the bag and peeked inside, then promptly shut it and shoved it back at my mother. I wanted to crawl back into my closet.

"Jes, it's time." My mother opened the bag herself and pulled out the small scrap of fabric. "And you can't really wear that outfit without one."

Reluctantly I took the brassier from her. It really was very pretty.

"It should fit. Evelyn has a good eye for these things."

Evelyn was Laura's mother. The former catalogue model had combined her flare for fashion with her husband's business acumen. They owned an apparel and fabric shop which drew patrons from neighboring towns.

I turned the bra over in my hands. I only had one question.

"How?"

My mother laughed with relief and pulled me towards the bed where she sat and I stood in front of her. The next few minutes were spent laughing at my attempts to get the garment on properly. Finally I had it right and stood before her, uncomfortable but grinning. When my mother's eyes glistened with tears, my confidence failed. I crossed my arms over my chest.

"Don't." She sniffed and tenderly pulled my arms down by my sides. "You're so beautiful. Inside and out. I'm so proud of you."

"Jessie? Come on!" Laura shouted from downstairs, preventing the moment from becoming maudlin. I had dressed quickly and enjoyed the boost to my ego generated by the dropped jaws of my brother and Laura.

I tugged again at my bra.

"How can you stand it?" I asked Laura as she swatted my hands away for the second time. She had been wearing one for over a year.

"You'll get used to it."

I doubted that, but I could not take it off now.

"Let's get this over with."

I took a deep breath and marched up the path to the school.

Five

Spring 1936

Paper flowers and streamers in spring colors bloomed along the walls of the second story room, an ineffectual weapon against the cloying scents of too-sweet perfumes and sweat. A band played on the stage at one end of the rectangular room while people danced in front or gathered around the long table laid out with refreshments at the other end. I wanted to turn back around.

Laura pulled me into the room and we headed for a group of people standing in a darkened corner. I was too nervous to register the owner of the broad suit clad shoulders in front of me and when he tuned around at Laura's tap, I stopped breathing.

Kenny.

Light reflected off the sleek pelt of his cream slicked blonde hair. The white of his shirt accented the tanned features of his face. He smiled down at me with that crooked grin. His teeth were just about as white as his shirt.

"You made it!" he smiled.

Kenny introduced Laura and I to the group, although we knew most of them, and we stood around making small talk. Some of the group paired off and went to dance. This left Laura, Kenny, Jennifer Abbott and me.

Kenny asked if we would like some punch and left to get several glasses. The three of us remaining, stood awkwardly until Jennifer broke the silence.

"You look very nice tonight, Jessie," she spoke quietly.

"Thanks, Jennifer." I was polite, but not overly.

Pause.

"Is this your first spring dance?"

"Yes."

Another pause.

"Well," she said finally. "I hope you have fun."

"Thanks."

Kenny returned that moment balancing three glasses of punch. "Did you ladies miss me?"

"Desperately." Jennifer's dry tone and roll of the eyes, earned her a mock scowl from Kenny as she took her glass from him.

Laura, who had not said much up to this point, had been keeping her eye on the door. Whoever she was hoping to see must have arrived for she suddenly excused herself.

As she left, a young man approached Jennifer and asked her to dance. When she agreed, he quickly shot a triumphant look across the room to his friends. I saw Jennifer's jaw clench. Her smile appeared forced as she allowed the young man to take her arm. I was now alone with Kenny. Suddenly my heart pounded, my palms sweat, and my breathing grew uneven.

"Alone at last," Kenny leered with a melodramatic twirl of an imaginary moustache. It made me laugh and alleviated some of my tension.

"That's better. You have a great smile, Jes."

I blushed, thankful for the dimness of the lighting.

"You look very pretty tonight," he complimented. "But then you always do."

Had the boy gone crazy? Always? I would give him tonight certainly, but usually I was dressed in trousers, overalls, or loose jumpers.

I searched frantically for my moral support. She could deal with this better than I. Laura however, was across the room in deep conversation with David and Job. Job did not look happy.

"Would you like to dance?" Kenny's words interrupted my observations.

"Hm?"

Kenny glanced over to where I looked. He took the cup of punch from my hands.

"A dance." He laughed. "You still owe me one, remember?"

"Yes, I remember."

As he led me out onto the floor, I glanced over my shoulder. Job was glowering. He shook off the hand Laura placed on his arm and walked away. Kenny spun me around with a twirl and all thoughts of Job spun away.

I was stiff. Kenny held me respectfully, but my hand was cold in his. He must have sensed my nervousness for he set about making me laugh. He began a sly commentary on fellow dancers that soon had me relaxed, laughing, and a little shocked at the outrageous nature of it. I looked up at something he said about Mr. Carpenter, one of the chaperones for this event who was nervously frowning at his charges on the dance floor. My eyes connected with Kenny's and the laughter stuck in my throat. Nervous excitement—and something else—did battle just below my rib cage.

The music ended.

"Thanks for the dance." Kenny smiled and squeezed my waist with the hand that rested there.

I stammered a suitable response. I felt hot and flushed.

We walked back to where we had left our drinks on the bleachers. Laura sat waiting. Kenny thanked me for the dance, excused himself so he could go and talk to someone else, and with a wave to Laura he left.

"Well?" prompted Laura once Kenny was out of earshot.

"Well what?" I grinned. I could not help it.

"Do you think he likes you?" she grinned back.

"Maybe," I shrugged. Then, with more excitement, "Maybe. What were you and David and Job talking about?"

"Not much," she waved dismissively and dragged me to the ladies room.

I did not dance with Kenny again, but both Laura and I were kept on our feet by a number of partners. During the times I danced with other boys, I never felt the same emotions as I had with Kenny, but sometimes I would catch him watching me as I danced.

When Kenny disappeared near the end of the night, I felt a certain disappointment, but it was time for Laura and I to meet her parents anyway. We were headed down the path to the curb, when a loud burst of laughter made me turn.

Over in the bushes, a group of people leaned against the school wall. It was hard to tell who was there, but in the dark the red glowing dots of burning cigarettes could be seen. The smoke wafted over on the night breeze. Light bounced off something silver as the object was raised to a waiting set of lips and someone drank from it before passing it to the next person. I realize it was a flask. I could not be sure, but I thought I saw Kenny among the group. I looked again but it was too dark. I dismissed my concerns as being part of my imagination and climbed into the car with Laura.

The Cottage was dim, compared to the brightness of the outside. I stopped inside the door, waiting for my eyes to adjust. "Mr. Nightingale?" I called.

"Down here, Jes." His voice came from the end of the row and to the left. The same stall I had been ready to climb into when I had been six. I walked down that way, climbed the bale of hay that rested outside and peered over. It was easier now that I was fourteen.

Mr. Nightingale had one hand raising the tail of a cow while the other arm was buried almost up the shoulder inside the animal.

"Feet first?" I asked.

He smiled pulling his arm out with a great sucking noise. "Feet first. How are you doing?"

"Okay." I shrugged.

Mr. Nightingale exited the stall and dipped his arm in the bucket of water resting next to the bale, rinsing it clean. "The boys have gone to the school."

"I know."

David mentioned going out there earlier; something about meeting with Mr. Carpenter about options for college. David and Job had one more year of high school left and of course would be thinking of what they would do after. I had not thought about Job leaving. I just sort of figured he would be staying on the farm to take over after his father. I knew David was considering studying business. For myself, I was not thinking that far ahead.

Mr. Nightingale gave me a shrewd look with his warm hazel eyes. "What's on your mind?" he said.

I shrugged again and sat on the bale. He sat next to me and threw his clean arm around my shoulders. He smelled of barn and cows. It was not unpleasant.

"Can I ask you a question?" I said.

He nodded in assent. "You just did. Didn't you?"

I smiled.

"That's not the question."

"It isn't?" He shook his head in apparent confusion. "But it was a question, right?"

"Yes."

"But not *the* question?"

"No."

"Okay, so what is the question?"

"How can you tell if a boy likes a girl?" I muttered under my breath.

"How can you tell what?"

I took a deep breath and spoke more clearly. "How can you tell if a boy likes a girl? I mean, really likes her. Not just as friends."

He took his arm from around my shoulders and ran his hand over his face. "That is a question, isn't it?"

I nodded and picked at the hem of my fraying shorts.

"Maybe you should ask a woman, like Mrs. Nightingale, or your mom."

"I thought of that," I said trying to stave off discouragement. "But then I thought maybe a guy would know better, what sort of things a guy does when he likes a girl."

"I see." He nodded his understanding. "Are we talking specifically or generally?"

"Generally specific."

"That helps." His soft laugh was rueful. "Leave it to a woman to be vaguely specific."

"Please." I was begging now. "Can you help me? I'm sort of confused by the whole thing."

"I can see that." He leaned back against the stall behind us. There was a thoughtful pause while I waited hopefully. "Well, I suppose a young man might give a girl little gifts like flowers and such, if he liked her. Then he might make it a point to talk to her. Tell her she looks pretty."

My heart leapt a little. Kenny talked to me quite often and had said I always looked nice.

"Go on."

"He might take her out for ice cream or to a dance."

While Kenny had not actually asked me to the dance, he did dance with me.

"Jessie?" Mr. Nightingale covered my clenched hands with one of his large calloused ones. "Are we talking about a certain young man here? I sort of need to know to give you adequate information."

"You won't tell anyone?"

"On my honor." He held up his free hand in sign of his pledge.

"It's Kenny Martin," I blurted finally and went on to tell about the dance and all that had transpired there. How, even when I was dancing with other boys, Kenny had been watching me. Of course I left out the part about how having his arms around me had made me feel. I did not even tell Laura that part.

"Oh. I thought…had hoped you…" His eyes narrowed as he trailed off and just stared at me for a few moments. I could tell he wanted to say something but was considering his words very carefully. Perhaps if he had said what was on his mind it might have saved me a lot of heartache—might have, but doubtful. Instead he sat back against the stall, filled his cheeks with air and released the pressure with a little "pfff."

"Well, Jessie, I don't know Kenny really well, except for what I've seen with my own eyes, so I'm not really certain what to tell you about what he might do to show he likes a girl."

Deflated, I leaned back against the wall.

"There is one thing I can tell you, however." He squeezed my hands. "If a young man truly cares for a young woman, he'll have no eyes or thoughts for any other. He'll hate to see her cry, love to see her laugh and want nothing but the best for her."

"Is that how you feel about Mrs. Nightingale?"

His smile was beautiful. "From the moment I first set eyes on her."

"Why?"

"Because the Good Lord willed it," he replied simply. "Jessie, if a man and a woman are looking for the best, they'll want what He wants for them."

Though I later came to doubt the truth of those words, I believed them then.

Six

Spring 1936

The next morning my mother's only comment about my early readiness for church was a raised eyebrow. Most Sunday mornings we fought a small war of wills over my attendance. I always lost.

It was not the actual attending of church that I resisted but rather the having to dress up. I still did not enjoy wearing a dress, but after Friday's dance, I appreciated the effect it could have. Besides, that morning I was on a mission. If I was going to determine if Kenny was what the good Lord willed, I would have to find out exactly how to obtain that information.

The little white church, with its tall steeple stood in the center of town. Friends and family filled the oak pews to either side of the red-carpeted aisle that led up to the raised dais. The organ on the right, and the piano to the left, flanked the platform and the choir seating like sturdy sentinels always alert and poised for duty.

Behind and above the choir seating hung an oak cross. Oak wall hangings mounted to either side of the dais held the black and white numbers of the hymns for the morning, as well as the attendance records from the previous week.

My family sat in our regular pew, next to Laura and her parents. It was not too close to the middle, yet not in the back. Laura and her family were already seated and I slipped into the pew next to her. The Nightingales sat a few pews up and to the left.

"Can you meet me at the creek, after church?" I whispered to Laura.

"I think so," she responded and turned to check with her mother before confirming her answer. "I have to eat and change first."

We agreed on a time and waited for the service to start. I was anxious, not because I was eager for the message Reverend Pike would deliver, but rather because I wanted it to be over.

I went through the motions of standing for the opening hymn and prayer, and then slouched in the pew as the head deacon declared the weekly announcements. I only remember he was as boring as his voice. There was one more hymn and then Reverend Pike took the pulpit and began his sermon in a deep voice slightly accented as though he hailed from somewhere south of the Mason-Dixon Line instead of just over the New Hampshire state line.

"The Lord knows the desires of your heart."

I sat up straight in the pew. It seemed as though the sermon was going to be right on topic.

Was this a sign?

"If you delight yourself in the Lord, he will grant you those desires." The reverend carefully and with great deliberation opened his black leather bound King James Bible and looked over the congregation. "What then, should those desires be? Hmm?"

It seemed like his eyes bored into mine a lot longer than anyone else's. I was positive Reverend Pike could see into my heart and knew what I desired. I swallowed reflexively, looked down at my folded hands and tried to slow my pounding heart.

Did Reverend Pike really know what was in my heart? Had God somehow informed him of what I wanted? Was I wrong in what I desired?

If I wanted God to give me what I desired in my heart—Kenny—then I had to delight myself in the Lord, and I most definitely needed help trying to understand what that meant. I listened intently to the rest of the sermon and tried with all my being to discern by what manner I would be able to obtain my desire.

The flaw in my thinking was that it should have been less about what I wanted, and more about how I could serve God with my desires. But, at almost fifteen, my world had only grown marginally bigger than it had been at eight. I only gleaned what I wanted; in order to know what God wanted for me, I had to pray about it. I had to pray about desiring the right thing, and I had to tell God I wanted Kenny and let the matter be handled by Him.

I just knew He wanted what I wanted. After all, Reverend Pike said that God only wants the best for us.

Laura was not there when I arrived but the little clearing was not empty. Job and my brother sat on the bank. Their heads were bent close together and they appeared to be in earnest conversation. I knew David had gone with Job after church, I just did not expect to see them here. David saw me and elbowed Job, indicating they were no longer alone. When Job saw me approaching, he rose to his feet but avoided looking directly at me.

"Hi," I said with hesitance. Obviously I was intruding, interrupting a serious discussion. Job bobbed his head by way of greeting.

"I saw you at the dance Friday. You left early, before I could speak to you."

He looked at his feet and kicked at the dirt. "Something came up."

I thought he seemed angry and was hiding something from me. This was the first time he was anything but open and forthcoming. Usually he would offer the information of what had drawn him from the dance, especially if it was something to do with the farm. I spent so much time there with him that I felt a part of things, and he included me in them.

"Is everything all right?" I asked when he did not volunteer anything more.

He kept his face partially averted when he glanced at me from beneath half-lowered eyelids. "Why wouldn't it be?" he said quietly.

David spoke up then saying they were headed to work on Job's truck and they departed leaving me puzzled. Laura found me standing in the same spot when she arrived.

"Hey," she said, "you okay?"

I nodded despite the uneasy feeling that I was not. I felt as though in some way I had hurt him. I thought over everything that I had done or said recently and could not figure out what it might be. I shook off my uneasiness and explained to Laura why I asked her to meet.

"Let me get this straight," she interrupted my rambling, "You want to pray about Kenny?"

"Yes. Is that silly?"

Laura looked at me in consideration, a slow private smile spreading across her face. "No, it's not silly," she finally answered. "It's actually pretty smart. I'm surprised I didn't think of it sooner."

Laura always was more concerned about spiritual matters. Considering the often calculating way she dealt with things, boys in particular, it amazed me. She was extremely wise about divine workings, as wise as one could be at fifteen.

Laura continued on the topic of prayer, "Do you want to pray or do you want me to?"

"You do it," I determined, suddenly intimidated by the importance I was placing on this moment.

She took my hand as we sat on the bank and bowed our heads. Her words, when they came, were carefully chosen. The importance of them, I understood only on one level.

"God," she prayed, "We learned this morning that You know the desires of our hearts better than we do ourselves. I'm not sure I understand how that all works but I believe it's true. I also believe You know things about us that we don't know yet. I ask for Jessie, that You would reveal to her what the true desire of her heart is so that she can do what You want her to do. Amen."

"Amen." I repeated and looked up at Laura. "Now what?"

"Now we wait."

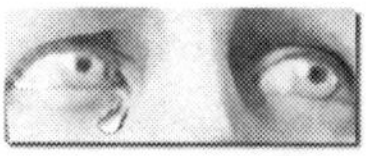

Summer 1936

I waited and watched for a sign, any sign, and I only saw what I wanted to see. I turned fifteen a week before school finished. Kenny remembered to wish me a happy birthday at lunch. That was a sign. The day school let out, he said he would see me at the ball game that afternoon, another sign. He lost the coin toss but still, I ended up on his team. Yet another sign. For all my intense scrutiny, however, there were other signs I missed.

Job no longer smiled as openly when he greeted me. He no longer chose me to play on his team. His words of congratulations for a good play were sparse. There was an unspoken tension between him and Kenny. Our friendship was changing, and I was too caught up in myself to pay attention. By the time August rolled around I was no longer making casual visits to the Nightingale farm. I only went for the games. Most of my time had been spent hanging out with Laura before she went to Maine. We often waited together at Millie's Parlor for Kenny and some of the others to show up after their summer jobs or chores. But Laura left for her visit with her grandparents and I often found myself waiting for Kenny with Jennifer once she finished working in her mother's salon for the day. Without Laura's breezy personality pushing things along, conversation often stalled. Ours was an uneasy friendship. Frankly, I found Jennifer intimidating. I envied the comfortable back and forth she had with Kenny.

I did not see as much of David that summer either. He started working as a farm hand for Mr. Nightingale and did not come home in the evening until after the last milking. It was strange really how my attention had been refocused on matters of a more feminine nature.

My parents were not exempt from my exclusionary behavior. This year, I was not making the traditional walk to the Nightingale farm with them. Kenny was picking me up any time now. This had come about the previous evening as we were all leaving Millie's. We had been kicked out after becoming too loud.

"Good night," I called as I started down the street in the direction of home. "I'll see you tomorrow at that farm."

Amidst the answering good nights, Kenny called my name. I turned and waited while he jogged up to me.

"Why don't we pick you up tomorrow, on the way to the game?" he said with a twinkle in his eye. The corner of his mouth with the thin scar turned up even more as he smiled.

"I usually walk with my parents," I blurted too surprised to say anything else, like "That would be lovely, Kenny," or "Thanks, Kenny. I would like that very much."

"So? What do you say?" He reached out and squeezed my shoulder. "We drive right by your house."

"Um. Yeah. Okay," I managed. My mind was still zeroed in on where his hand had squeezed my arm. "That would be nice."

"Tomorrow, then." He squeezed one last time and ran to catch up with the rest of the group.

A sun kissed Laura was waiting on my front step when I arrived home. The sight of my confidant was what I needed in that moment.

"You're back!" I cried and raced up the walk.

"I'm back!" She gave me a big hug. "My parents are annoyed but I'm staying here tonight. I just know I missed something good and I want you to catch me up on everything."

"Come on." I hauled Laura up to my room and filled her in on the lasted turn of events.

"You," she jabbed me with a finger in the arm, "have a date with Kenny Martin tomorrow!"

We were seated side by side on the floor, our backs resting against the side of my bed.

"No, I don't," I poked her back. "He said '*we'll* pick you up,' not '*I*.'"

"He's picking you up though?"

"Yes."

"Oh, I wish I could be in the car."

I begged her to come, but she refused. Instead, the next day I waited by myself for the car to pull up to the curb in front my house. When it arrived, there were three other people in it. Phillip Ross was driving. He was Kenny's best friend, mostly I think because he could drive and Kenny did not, at least not legally.

Jennifer sat beside Phillip. That meant the back seat next to Kenny was free. My heart beat faster. A sign?

"Hey Jes!" Kenny called through the window and leaned over to open the door, "Get in!"

I did, greeting the two in the front as I did so. Phillip turned to peer over his shoulder. "Playing with the big boys tonight?" the underlying sarcasm of his tone was not lost on me, although the reason for it was.

"Shut up, Phil," Kenny said and pushed the other boy's head back around. "He's just jealous because I get to sit in the back with you."

I smiled uncertainly and sat back as Phillip pointed the car down the street.

Jennifer turned sideways in her seat. "Tonight should be fun. Don't you think?"

"Of course it will," Kenny interjected before I could respond, dismissing Jennifer's question. He tossed his arm across my shoulders and I forgot how to think. "This night is always fun. Good food, good friends. What more could you want?"

There was a strain between these two that I had not sensed before. For everything that Kenny was and became, he had always treated Jennifer with more respect than the other boys. I was never sure why.

We arrived at the farm and Phillip parked with a flourish, stirring up gravel and causing several people to jump out of the way and many heads to turn. Phillip and Kenny laughed openly as we climbed out of the car heading for the yard.

"You two play nice," Kenny called over his shoulder as he and Phillip ran ahead to the waiting group of our peers.

I watched as Kenny greeted the guys with manly handshakes and back slaps. To a few of the girls he leaned in and whispered in their ears. What he said, I do not know but they giggled and fluttered their eyelashes. I envied their easy manner with him.

"He's such a crumb sometimes," Jennifer whispered under her breath.

I was not certain if she meant for me to hear, but I had. Her statement made me angry. I realize now that my judgement where Kenny was concerned was a little cloudy around the edges but then, at fifteen, I was experiencing feelings for this boy that blinded me to certain character traits. They also made me behave toward Jennifer in a manner I would, and do regret.

"Why would you say that?" I demanded, ready for a confrontation.

I could see by the way her eyes narrowed that she was deciding if she should say more. She opened her mouth and closed it. I took a step away from her, intending to leave her behind.

She reached out and grabbed my arm.

"Kenny's not always what he seems to be."

"What does that mean?" I was trying for indifference but do not know if I achieved it fully. I did not want to hear anything negative from her. "Are you jealous?"

The chuckle she released hinted at scoffing. "No. I just know Kenny."

"I know what I'm doing," I told her and yanked my arm free of her grip.

When the dancing started Laura and I spent much time on the floor dancing with the different boys in the group. When Kenny finally asked me to partner him, I was ecstatic. He maneuvered it so we were in the shadows, away from most of the others. We did not talk at first and this was fine by me. I was not certain I could have said anything intelligent.

"It was a great game tonight, wasn't it?" I finally worked up enough nerve to ask.

"Yes. Too bad we lost to your pal, Job."

"It was close though. And there's always next year."

Kenny nodded agreement and pulled me closer than perhaps decorum dictated. The proximity of his body was enticing and discomfiting.

"You sure are growing up nice, Jes," Kenny whispered in my ear. The heat of his breath warmed the skin of my neck. I could feel the fine hairs on my body stand up and take notice.

Over the course of the summer I had filled out a little more in certain places. My hips lost some of their boyishness and my breasts—well I was starting to have some hope for them.

I rested my head on his shoulder like some of the other girls did with their escorts, and I believe I would have stayed like that for the rest of the night if the music had not ended signaling the dancing was done. All of us, Phillip, Jennifer, Laura, Kenny, and I piled into the car for the drive home. The night was cool but I was not. With Laura in the back, I was sandwiched between her and Kenny, who had his arm draped across the back of the seat behind me. Laura gave me an "ah ha" look. I gave her a knock-it-off pinch.

Since Phillip had to drive past my house to get to Laura's, he dropped me off first. Kenny got out of the car to walk me to my door, something he had never done before. I waved good bye to Laura and the others. Jennifer glared at Kenny from the passenger window..

"It's been a great summer." He took my arm and guided me up the path I could walk in my sleep. I knew every crack and raised stone and certainly did not need his help, but still, his hand on my arm felt nice.

"Yes" I agreed.

Then he said the words I had waited to hear, the words that eliminated the need to look for any more signs.

"I like you, Jes. Why don't we go out sometime, just you and me?"

"I'd like that." I could barely breathe and had to concentrate on what he said next. The blood was rushing through my ears at such a rate, it made hearing difficult.

"Great! I'll call you."

"Great." He would call me. I threw a smug smile in Jennifer's direction.

Kenny moved down the steps. "See you at school!"

It was a long time before I had my date with Kenny. Mr. Nightingale saw to that.

Seven

Fall 1936

Mr. Nightingale waited on the front porch in his usual overalls and work shirt. "How are you, Jes?"

"Fine," I answered then opened the door wider. "Come on in. I'll get my dad."

"Actually, it's you I've come to see."

"Me?"

He nodded and moved away a few feet to the top step. "Come on out here for a minute. I've got something I'd like to ask you."

I was a little worried about what he wanted to know. To open the door and find Rand Nightingale standing there that Sunday afternoon was out of the ordinary. Not that it was unusual for him to be at our house, he and May were regular visitors, even on the occasional Sunday, but that day, I knew he was not expected. I knew because, my mother was standing watch as I sorted through my closet in an effort to determine which clothes I would keep for school and which could be given away.

My boredom was reaching epic proportions when the doorbell had chimed and I cheerily volunteered to get it before anyone could stop me.

I stepped out and closed the door behind me. Once I was seated next to him on the top step, Mr. Nightingale got down to business quickly.

"Jessie, I'd like to offer you a job."

"A job?"

"It's like this," he explained, "Job and David are going to be leaving after this year for college. That's going to leave me a little short handed.

Now I know you've been busy with other things lately, and haven't been around to see us much."

I hung my head but did not say anything. I did not know if he knew the reason for my absence, but I could guess that he did. He was the one I had gone to about the whole business in the first place.

"I always thought you loved the farm as much as anybody there did." He didn't say it but I know he meant Job.

"I did," I agreed.

"Did?"

"I do, it's just that, well, other things came up." Given more time and some serious thought, I am sure I could have come up with a lamer excuse, but I was put on the spot.

Mr. Nightingale nodded. "Anyway, I just thought since you were already a little familiar with how things worked, maybe you could help me out and come and work for me. It would give you some money for when you go away to college."

"I'm not going to college," I said.

"Why not?" he seemed surprised. "You're a bright girl."

"What would I study?" I shrugged.

"I don't know. What do you like to do?"

What did I like to do? I liked baseball, but being a girl, I could not make a career out of that. While I was okay at math, numbers did not hold the interest for me that they did for my father or David. I had enjoyed working at Mrs. White's store the few occasions Laura and I had "worked" there to help out during the holidays, but while I could ring up purchases without any problems, I cared only mildly about fashion. I guess the only thing I really enjoyed and, if I was to believe my teachers, was any good at, was writing. I loved the possibility of words. I spent what time I kept free from other concerns, lost in them, transported through the emotion of them, trying to put them together in similar patterns. I wrote stories about the things I experienced. I chronicled the wants of my life in a small leather journal hidden under my mattress. I was too insecure to ever let anyone read any but the occasional story I felt was worthy of being read.

"I would like to write." I voiced the thought out loud.

"Do they have schools to teach that?" Mr. Nightingale asked intrigued.

"I don't know?"

"It'd be worth looking into," he suggested.

My head filled with thoughts of where to begin.

"I'd have to ask my parents," I told him. "About the job."

I would have to ask about school too, no doubt, but I was still considering that idea.

"Already did," he seemed pleased to have removed that object. "They said it was your decision."

"Well then I guess I could."

"Before you totally commit yourself," he held up a hand in caution, "I have to be honest with you. It's a hard job. Before and after school. All day on Saturdays, but you'd have Sundays off. You'll have to keep up your grades too. If you don't, I'll have to find someone else. That's the same deal I made with David. Do you think you're up to it?"

Mr. Nightingale knew what buttons to push. If David could do it I certainly could. "When would I start?"

The appeal of having my own money in hand was at the forefront of my mind. It would allow me to purchase an outfit for a date. I did not realize the impact a job would have on my blossoming social life.

"Tomorrow morning. You can bring a change of clothes for school."

"Okay."

"You're sure now, Jes?" he gave me one last chance to change my mind.

"Yes," I nodded. "I'll see you tomorrow."

Mr. Nightingale shook my hand to seal the deal before rising to leave.

"Oh, one more thing," he turned back, "wear boots."

Four thirty came early. David stood over my bed shaking me.

"Jes, come on," he said harshly. "We're going to be late if you don't get up now."

"I'm up." I rubbed eyes that felt like they had a whole beach worth of sand in them, and swung my legs over the edge.

"Here." David dropped a pair of his old work boots on the floor. "They'll probably be a little big, so wear two pairs of socks."

I nodded and yawned.

"I'll meet you downstairs," he said shaking his head as he left.

With my eyes half closed, I stepped into the overalls that I had laid out the night before, pulled on two pairs of socks and grabbed the satchel containing my school clothes. As I went, I thumped down the stairs. If I had to be awake at this hour, I would make sure my parents were too.

David had a glass of milk and some toast waiting for me and I shoved it down without tasting as we headed out the door to get our bikes. The sun was barely awake itself at that hour, which I remember thinking was a good thing. It would probably have burned the eyes right out of my head.

When we arrived at the farm, David took me into the main milking barn where we met up with Job, Mr. Nightingale, and three other men; John, Mitch, and Pops. John was bulky, about thirty years of age, with a round sweaty face that smiled but hardly ever spoke. Mitch was shorter and stocky, what teeth remained in his mouth were stained yellow from chewing tobacco. Pops, who had no teeth that I could tell, was my favorite of the three.

He was lean and wiry, with gnarled hands, a weathered face, and white hair that stood on end in every direction. Pops owned a comb, but I do not think he ever used it. It was hard to determine his exact age, and once, when I dared to ask, he merely grouched out, "Old."

In the early years, when I hung around the farm more, Pops griped about my being underfoot, but then I would find a peppermint slipped magically into my pocket. I knew it was from Pops because he always carried a brown paper bag of the small pink candy. He was also a marginally reformed pickpocket.

"Well, look who's graced us with her presence this morning," Pops grumped. "Think you can do a man's job do ya? Why yer such a tiny thing the wind from a cow's arse'll blow ya right over on yer own."

I glared and stuck out my tongue. Pops was not much bigger than I.

Mitch hooted with laughter, "Watch out Pops," he warned, "You're more likely to end up on your arse after a look like that!"

Mr. Nightingale stepped in at that point calling a halt to the teasing and divided up the work for the morning. It was a regular happening, and most of them knew their roles. I was the only one unsure of what I would be doing.

"Pops," Mr. Nightingale said, "take Jessie into the birthing barn and set her up cleaning stalls and feeding."

"Birthin' barn," Pops muttered, "Women's work."

"Try to keep up," I groused back and turned for the barn as Mitch hooted again.

In the end it was I who struggled to keep up. Bales of straw and hay grew heavier, and my blisters bigger as the morning wore on. By the time I was done and headed into the house to wash and change, I could not lift my arms. They flapped like loose rubber bands at my side. As I walked, I gingerly placed my hands in my pockets to keep from looking too obviously uncomfortable. My right hand came in contact with a small round object. I didn't have to pull it out to know what it was, or who had put it there; I just wondered how he got it there.

I turned to see where Pops was and found him leaning against the barn watching me. I smiled. He winked then shouted at me to quit staring at him and get to school since I could use some smartening up.

I knocked, then entered through the back door of the house into the kitchen. May Nightingale was at the stove. She turned and smiled. Something about her always made me feel at home. Her eyes were deep brown, like Job's. She was tall and slender. Her dark blonde hair was long and straight and kept in a bun or a braid depending on the day. I could not count the number of times her hand had rested on my head. It was a possessive caress. It was the same way she touched Job.

"How'd it go?" she asked and squeezed me in the tight hugs that were uniquely her.

"It went," was all I could manage through the protest of my body.

She laughed and pointed to my satchel on the table saying Mr. Nightingale had brought it in. I looked at it and groaned. Something else to lift. Another chuckle from Mrs. Nightingale resonated in the room, but with sympathy she carried the bag upstairs and into the bathroom for me.

"I've filled the tub. The water is hot." She gave me a pat on the back causing me to whimper. "It'll help take some of the soreness out."

"Thanks," I managed as she shut the door herself.

I could do no more than close my eyes and let the heat of the water seep into my body. Even that hurt. Finally after a knock on the door and a warning to hurry or I would miss the bus, I emerged. The soak had helped, a little.

I entered the kitchen amidst the smells of eggs, toast and ham. My mouth watered and my stomach growled with the realization I was ravenous. It seemed like yesterday since the meager breakfast David had fixed for me. I wondered how I would make it to lunch without passing out. Fortunately, Mrs. Nightingale's culinary efforts were on my behalf. She stood at the backdoor with a cloth sack in hand.

"Here you go Jes." She gave me the bag. "There's something in here to eat while you're waiting. I put Job's and David's in there too."

I hugged her in an effort to communicate my heartfelt gratitude.

"You're welcome, love." She returned the hug then pushed me gently out the screen door. "See you this afternoon."

I groaned.

"It'll get easier, Jes."

"Promise?"

The soft clap of the door closing was followed by May's laughter.

They were waiting for me. Without a word David took the bag from my hand and opening it, he pulled out two small packages wrapped in butcher paper. He handed one to Job and kept one for himself and then handed the bag back to me. I pulled out a matching package and opened it to find heaven.

Inside was a warm toasted sandwich of egg, ham and cheese. I started to sit to eat.

"Don't," David said around a mouthful of food.

"What?" There was no way I was not eating.

"Don't sit," Job answered.

"I will if I want to."

"Suit yourself," Job said and bit into his sandwich. He may have done so to hide a smile.

"I will." I did.

He and David looked at each other with a shrug and continued to eat. We finished and without a word Job took the garbage, shoved that into the cloth bag and shoved the bag into the mailbox.

I sat in silence with my eyes closed. I did not know about them, but I was too tired to say anything.

"Come on Jes," David said. "Bus is here."

I could hear it approaching. It was the new bus the town had purchased with the help of the surrounding communities. The all-enclosed, steel-body Wayne Works vehicle was a big step up from the canvas covered truck of the previous years.

"I can't." I could not get up. My body had turned to stone.

He shook his head, reached down and grabbed my arm. With a strong tug, he pulled me to my feet.

"Ow!" I protested. "That hurts!"

"I told you not to sit."

I hit his arm. It was worth the effort.

He smirked in Job's direction and headed for the bus. I looked at Job. He looked at me all innocence. I hit him too.

"What was that for?" He took an affronted posture.

"You were laughing."

His jaw dropped and he sputtered in offense. "I was not."

"Yes, you were."

"Did you see me laugh?"

"Inside. You were laughing on the inside."

He "harrumphed" and stuck his nose up in the air before marching onto the shiny new steel bus that had arrived two weeks before the school year begun.

I watched him go with an undefined emotion. I missed him even though he was right here. I rubbed at the pang in the center of my chest and climbed onto the bus behind him.

I slid into the seat Laura had saved for me. Forestalling anything she may have said, I told her to wake me when we got to school, propped my knees on the seat in front of me and fell asleep. Thirty minutes later she nudged me awake and in fact spent most of the time nudging me awake throughout the day and many that followed.

Eight

Spring 1937

Before I knew it Christmas had come and gone and a new year started. The winter had been harsh and made working difficult. Wading through several feet of snow was a trial for both four and two legged creatures.

I saw a fair amount of Kenny when I was at school, as Laura and I ate lunch with that group daily. Occasionally he would make a comment about going out, but the suggested date never seemed to materialize.

I enjoyed working on the farm but it kept me from doing anything else. The seed of resentment was growing, making me restless. I was anxious as talk of getting away from small town life began to fill more and more conversations.

Most just wanted out, but some, a select few, spoke of going to university. Even Laura was anxious for time to pass so she could head to Maine and pursue what she knew was meant for her, at least for the summer.

I began to question the stability of my security. Everyone I knew was eager to leave and move on with the business of life. David and Job would be graduating and leaving for college: David to business school in Philadelphia, and Job to an agricultural university in Burlington. It was just the northern part of the state, but as far as I was concerned, it may as well have been California. I wondered what there would be in Grand River Junction for me. Would I still be working on the farm? I was still considering the possibility of university and decided I needed to pursue it further.

One afternoon in April, after our composition class, I decided the time was right. My latest story had received an "A plus."

I told Laura to go and save me a seat on the bus. I needed to ask Mrs. Wilkins a question. Mrs. Wilkins was our grammar and composition teacher. She was a good teacher, tough but fair.

I approached her desk and waited while she tidied the scarred surface of the large wooden piece.

"Miss Bingham," she smiled. "Is something on your mind?"

"Did you mean it?" I asked, afraid I would cry if she answered "no."

"Did I mean what?"

I opened my composition book to the last page with writing. At the end of my story, in her precise handwriting, was the comment, "You have a wonderful gift. You should pursue this further."

"Yes." She accompanied the simple answer with a direct look.

I let out a breath I had not been aware of holding.

"Where do they come from, your ideas?"

I shrugged. "My head."

Mrs. Wilkins laughed. "And from your heart, also?"

I looked down at the floor and shrugged unsure how to respond.

"Your stories are good, Jessie."

I decided to trust her. "Are there schools that teach writing?"

"Yes, there are." she leaned over and scribbled something on a small square of paper.

I took the paper when she held it out to me and read what she had written: Barnard College, New York City.

I looked up at her. "New York?"

"Manhattan, actually."

"It's pretty far." The thought of going to such a big city was more than a little daunting.

"It's a women's college, small, but with a good reputation."

She directed me toward the door of the classroom.

"You have plenty of time to think about it." Mrs. Wilkins placed a hand on my shoulder. "Let me know what you decide when you decide it. I'll help in whatever way I can."

I stuck the paper in between the pages of my textbook. "I will. Thanks."

I left the room smiling. In my heart was a new hope. I now had an objective to pursue that would make me fit in with everyone else. I could now talk about going away to school even if I was not exactly certain it was what I wanted. I was still smiling when I heard my name called. I turned around to see Kenny running to catch up.

"Hey!" he greeted. "You're awfully smiley today. What's up?"

"Mrs. Wilkins was just telling me about a school in New York she thinks I should attend," I told him proudly.

"That's great!" He threw an arm around my shoulder and squeezed. "Congratulations."

"Thanks."

"What would you study?"

"Maybe writing," I told him shyly. Not even Job knew of my desire to pursue it seriously. While our friendship was finding a more even footing, and I was spending more time in his company than I ever had, I no longer felt like I could talk to him that way. It bothered me but I did not know what to do about it.

Kenny interrupted the flow of my thoughts. "Well, that will give you something to do until you get married and settle down."

I found his words dismissive and disturbing. I was undecided about how to respond, so I gave a non-committal nod. We walked outside and towards the waiting bus.

The day was warm for April, and the snow was melting rapidly. I breathed in the damp air that carried the slight scent of rotting vegetation previously hidden by the snow, and I started thinking about getting to work. The Cottage was awaiting the arrival of several new guests. I would get to be a part of welcoming them this year and I waited eagerly.

With these thoughts and the others concerning future plans taking up space in my head, I had almost forgotten Kenny's presence, until he placed a hand on my elbow preventing me from climbing on the bus.

"Say Jes," he said with a too charming smile. "Is there any chance Farmer Job could do without you Saturday? A bunch of us are going out to the lake for the day and I wondered if you would like to go with me. We still have a date to go on."

My heart beat fast. It had been months since Kenny had done any more than suggest such an outing, and now he was suggesting a trip to Sparrow Lake. I wanted to go desperately. I heard the talk, and if it was remotely accurate, there was a lot of kissing done at Sparrow Lake.

My mind worked fast. It was only Tuesday. If I asked Mr. Nightingale this far in advance he would let me off on Saturday. I had never missed any work yet. Surely he would make an exception. I looked up at Kenny to tell him my thoughts and noticed he was looking over my shoulder. I turned my head and discovered Job standing behind me, waiting to get on the bus. He looked angry.

"Oh, hey there Farmer Job," Kenny said.

"Kenny," Job squeezed out through clenched teeth.

"Jessie," Kenny said, "Why don't you ask him now."

"I don't think the time is appropriate." I tried to drag him onto the bus.

He shook off my hand. "Why not, Jes?" he asked. "Don't you want to go?"

I wondered what had happened to shift the mood suddenly.

"What do you want to ask me?" Job's calm was deceiving.

"She wants Saturday off to go out with me." Underneath Kenny's statement was a not so hidden challenge.

"Is that true?" Job's gaze pinned me in place.

I stood overcome by guilt. It made me angry. Why should I feel guilty? I did not owe Job any explanations about who I liked or wanted to date.

"Do you want to go out with Kenny?" Job asked again rephrasing his question.

Suddenly empowered by a sense of outrage at being made to feel guilty for something I did not understand, I threw my shoulders back defiantly.

"Yes," I stated firmly.

I thought I recognized hurt as one of the myriad of emotions which crossed Job's face in a matter of seconds.

"So," Kenny put in. "What do you say?"

Job looked at me long and hard before he replied.

"I'm not her boss." He shrugged with apparent indifference. "She'll have to ask my father." He shoved past us and climbed onto the bus without another word.

Kenny turned to me with a cocky grin. "Well?"

"Well what?" I was trembling with left over anger and something else I did not want to examine too closely.

"Are you going to ask Mr. Nightingale for the day off?"

"I'll try."

"Great! Let me know tomorrow at lunch." He gestured for me to precede him onto the bus.

I climbed up slowly and headed to where Laura sat wide-eyed and waiting. Before I sat, I took one last look at Job. He looked at me briefly, sharply, then deliberately turned away to look out the window. His snub made me angry all over, and I flopped down with a huff next to Laura.

"What just happened?" Laura leaned in and whispered.

I explained to her the details of the brief incident concluding with Job's final dismissal.

"Wow." Laura exclaimed softly. "Job was right there when Kenny asked you out?"

I nodded.

"And you told him straight out that you wanted to go with Kenny on Saturday?"

Again I nodded.

"When we prayed, I never imagined things turning out like this."

"Me either," I said. "I finally get what I wanted and now I don't know if I want it."

"What?" Laura exclaimed in disbelief. "You are going to ask for the day off aren't you? You are going to go?"

"I don't know anymore. I'm so confused about the whole situation now."

"Why?"

"Because."

"Because why?"

"Just because!"

"Jessie," Laura sighed in frustration, "Do you still like Kenny?"

"You know I do."

"Then why do you feel guilty?"

"I don't know. Job just seemed so angry."

"Does that matter to you?"

I gave her my best "what do you think?" look.

"Why?" she asked. "You're just friends right?"

"Yes," I answered although a part of me was no longer certain of the fact.

"Then it shouldn't matter if Job is angry. You haven't done anything wrong."

I thought about what she had said. It was true. I had not done anything wrong. I had merely indicated to him that I would like to go on a date. Why that raised the hackles of one of my friends, I did not know.

"You're right, Laura. It's his problem."

"Okay then! You'll ask for Saturday off?"

"I'll ask for Saturday off."

I would have too, if I had gotten the chance.

When I emerged from the bathroom wearing my coveralls, and the boots I had purchased with my first paycheck, Mrs. Nightingale was waiting for me in the kitchen. "Jessie," she headed off my progress to the door. "Rand stopped in. He said to tell you that you could have Saturday off if you wanted it."

"He did?"

"Yes."

"How did he know I wanted it off?"

She shrugged too casually.

"Job." I punched my leg with a clenched fist.

"Is something wrong, Jes?"

"No. Yes." I could not make up my mind. "It's just that it's none of his business."

Mrs. Nightingale turned from the sink and the dishes she was washing to wipe her hands on her apron. "What isn't Job's business?"

"My life," I declared and marched out the door towards the main milking barn where I knew Job would be. Mrs. Nightingale called after me but I ignored her.

He wasn't in the main barn when I arrived so I demanded his whereabouts from Pops.

Pops paused in the act of dumping feed into a bin. "Does this have anything to do with that young man you're so keen on going out with on Saturday?" he asked slowly. "Though I don't know why you do Jes. He ain't got nothin' more'n a pretty face. Course I guess that's reason nuff for some. Didn't think you were one of em though."

"Does everyone know my business?" I exploded.

"Now hold on. He don't want to see you hurt, is all. None of us do."

"I know what I'm doing. Why can't everyone just let things alone!" I wailed.

"By everyone you mean Job?" Pop flipped a peppermint into his mouth.

"I could knock his nose straight for sticking it in where it doesn't belong. Where is he?"

"He's in the birthing barn."

"Jessie?" Pops called me back.

"What?" I didn't turn around.

"Don't be too hard on him."

I paused inside the Cottage to let my eyes adjust. Hearing a commotion a few stalls down and on the right I headed that way.

"Is it bad?" It was David's voice.

"Yeah." That was Job's. "Real bad."

I marched over to the stall and flung the door open. "Job, I need to talk to you," I stated firmly.

He turned from examining a cow, his arm inside the birth canal. "Not now Jes," he dismissed me and turned back to the animal.

"Yes, now!"

"Jessie!"

"Job!"

The cow chose that moment to release an agonizing bellow, the likes of which I had never heard before. She stepped to the side twisting Job's arm. He cried out.

"David," he grimaced and pulled his arm out slowly. "Go get my dad." He turned to me and began stripping off his shirt. "Jessie, whatever it is will have to wait. I need you to go up to the house and call the vet right away."

The urgency of the situation finally set in. "What do you want me to tell him?"

"Tell him we've got a cow in trouble. She might not make it."

"What's wrong?"

"I don't know. Just go."

I turned and ran to the house with my heart pounding and legs burning. Mrs. Nightingale was waiting.

"I saw you coming. What's happened?" Her no-nonsense tone calmed me somewhat.

"Cow." I puffed. "In trouble. Call vet."

Without so much as a nod, she disappeared inside. I collapsed for a moment on the steps trying to catch my breath.

When Mrs. Nightingale reappeared, she was wearing boots and coveralls. "The vet's on his way. Let's go."

Back inside the barn, the men gathered outside the stall. From inside the cow groaned in agony.

Mr. Nightingale was just rinsing off his arm. Like Job, he had stripped to his undershirt to examine the cow.

"Big calf. Breach," he turned to his son. "She's in trouble."

"The vet's on his way, Rand," Mrs. Nightingale informed him. "What can we do?"

"May, you and Jessie go help the boys finish the chores. Pops go grab some clean gunny sacks for when the vet gets here." He shook his head and ran a hand over his sweating face. "Let's pray we can save them both."

Everyone sprang into action at that point and rushed to complete the evening milking and feeding. By mutual consent we all returned to the Cottage. The news there was not good. Dr. Roland Case, the veterinarian, arrived twenty minutes after the call had been made to him. He was a short, barrel-chested man with thinning, straw colored hair, ice blue eyes behind wire rimmed spectacles, and large steady hands. The vet was a man more comfortable around animals than people.

Mr. Nightingale looked at his wife, a grim sadness in his eyes.

Mrs. Nightingale nodded then turned to me.

"Jessie," she spoke quietly and firmly, "Let's go make some coffee and sandwiches."

Reluctantly I followed. I wanted to stay. I hoped that perhaps my presence would in some way help but knew that it would not.

As we walked Mrs. Nightingale placed an arm around my shoulders and pulled me close.

"It will be all right, wont it? Now that the vets here?"

At that moment a loud shot rang out.

I froze looking up into her face.

"Jessie," Mrs. Nightingale held onto me tightly, "There's nothing more we could do."

"I know," I squeezed back the tears, grateful that I did not have to witness what happened.

Mrs. Nightingale led me back up to the house. I felt as safe in her presence as I did in that of my own mother. I needed the comfort only she could provide in that moment. I could not know we would again find ourselves at this place, or that the sorrow of the future would take longer to heal than the grief of the moment.

Mr. Nightingale entered as May and I finished making coffee and sandwiches. He looked weary. His wife went to him and they held each other for a few brief moments.

I wondered if I would ever have that, someone with whom to take solace, and tried to picture who it might be. The picture floated in my mind but the figure remained faceless.

"The calf is alive for now," Mr. Nightingale spoke softly. "It's a big male."

I looked up, distressed anew, as that meant in three days the calf would be gone too. Mr. Nightingale came over to where I stood.

"Jes," he said. "The little fellow's alive for now but he needs a lot of care."

"All right." I waited for his instructions.

"I'm going to set you up in the barn tonight. You'll have to feed him every few hours. If he makes it through till morning he'll be all right."

I nodded but said nothing. I was unsure of whether or not I wanted to be the one responsible for this life. If he survived, the calf would most likely be taken and sold in a few days. Although I had accepted that as the way things had to be, it was generally something I tried not to be a part of.

Mr. Nightingale must have known the direction of my thoughts, but when he spoke, his words brought a spark of hope.

"If you keep this calf alive, he's yours to do with as you wish."

I held my breath hardly believing my ears. "He'd be mine?"

"Yep."

"Could he stay on the farm?"

"On one condition," Mr. Nightingale stated.

"Anything," I quickly promised.

"When he's old enough, we work out a breeding deal. That guy's going to be a big bull. He'll make fine milk calves."

I agreed. Although I had not even met the calf, already I felt that he belonged to me.

"All right then," Mr. Nightingale placed a hand on my shoulder. "Get on down to the barn. May will call your mother."

All was quiet as I entered the smaller barn and made my way to the stall. I hesitated a moment, afraid of what I might see. A soft rustling removed that fear. A new creature was in there, one that I was responsible for.

On a fresh bed of straw, rested a large bull calf. He was lighter in color than the others I had seen. "You're beautiful." I whispered to him.

"Hi." Job spoke quietly from the corner of the stall where he was sitting. I had not noticed him before then.

"Hi." I answered back.

The young calf struggled to his feet. On legs unsteady, he made his way over to me.

"Hi, fella." I crouched to greet him so that we were on eye level.

We remained that way for several moments just looking at each other. He took a few cautious steps toward me as I continued to make soothing noises at him. When he was close enough, I carefully stroked his nose. He quickly sucked my fingers into his mouth.

"Hey!" I tried to pull my hand away.

"He's hungry." Job laughed. "David will bring a bottle in a minute."

I rubbed his nose with my free hand and let him suck the fingers of the other. I decided to call him Blizzard.

"Jes?" Job came over and stroked Blizzard's neck.

"Yeah?"

"You wanted to talk earlier."

I ran down through my memory and suddenly recalled the Kenny thing.

"I know about what, and I'm sorry I made you mad."

"Why did you go to your dad when it wasn't any of your business?" There was no anger left, just a hurt. He stood and wiped his hands on his jeans as I waited for him to answer.

"There's something I need to tell you, and I don't know if the time's right."

"Just tell me." My heart began to beat a little faster.

"I don't want you to go out with Kenny," his words tumbled out in a rush.

"Why?" I had started to guess at that, I just did not expect him to say it straight out.

His eyes drew me in. They seemed to say I should know why.

"Why don't you like Kenny?" As Laura would have noted, it was not one of my brighter moments.

"It's not just because I don't like Kenny," Job said. He took a deep breath and expelled it on a puff that expanded his cheeks. "I don't want you to go out with him because I—"

"Hey! How's the little guy doing?" David's entrance interrupted Job.

I felt my shoulders let go of some of the tension that had been building in them. It was as though I understood, somewhere in my subconscious, that the words he had been about to speak would have asked for more than I was ready to answer.

"Blizzard's hungry," I blurted both with relief and to stop Job, just in case David's presence was not enough to deter him from the topic of conversation.

"Blizzard, huh?" David held up a large glass bottle with the finger of a rubber glove stretched over the opening. "That's who this is for,"

After demonstrating how I was to feed my new charge, the two of them left, and I settled in for the night.

Those next few days were a blur of hard work and fun. I refused to leave Blizzard in the stall all day. He just made too much noise. Everywhere I went he would follow. If I went up to the main house to bathe, Blizzard tagged along like a large puppy and waited noisily outside. On the Friday morning of that week, I unintentionally lingered in the bath. I fell asleep.

A frantic knocking on the door startled me awake. In the background I could hear Blizzard bellowing.

"Jessie," May shouted through the door. She sounded angry. "Get out here now!"

Yes, definitely angry.

I dressed frantically and ran out to the kitchen. Somehow Blizzard had managed to climb his way onto the back porch and halfway into the kitchen before getting stuck in the screen door.

"Blizzard," I said more calmly than I felt. Mrs. Nightingale did not look at all pleased. "Come on pal, back up."

Blizzard quieted upon hearing my voice, I approached his shoulders and placed my hands upon them. "Come on big guy, back up." I pushed and Blizzard took a few tentative steps backward. Slowly he came lose from the door. I crawled out after him and he turned to nuzzle his head into my belly.

"Did you miss me, huh?" I crooned.

"Jessie," Mrs. Nightingale's tone indicated her annoyance.

"Yes. Ma'am?"

"A calf is not a house pet."

"Yes, Ma'am"

"In the future, Blizzard will remain in his stall when you come up to the house."

"Yes, ma'am"

She turned and went back into the house, the screen door swinging awkwardly after her. I pulled Blizzard down the steps one at a time. Making sure the animal was not following, I made my way back up. Blizzard watched closely but dared not make the climb again.

"Mrs. Nightingale?" I spoke hesitantly through what remained of the door.

"Yes, Jessie?"

"I'll pay for it."

"I know, honey." She came out and gave me a tight hug. "Now get to the barn and see to that calf. I don't know how he'll manage tomorrow when you're off."

"What? Oh!" I had forgotten about Saturday and Kenny. "But I didn't think…What with everything that's happened—"

"Jessie."

"Yes, ma'am?"

"Sometimes it's good to just be a girl."

"Yes, ma'am," I blushed.

"Now go!" she pushed me gently toward the door.

That next morning, I was bleary-eyed and exhausted. I forgot about what the day meant, even when my mother arrived. She leaned over the stall as I finished feeding my charge.

"So, this is the boy who stole my daughter," she spoke softly so as not to startle Blizzard. "He's a handsome fellow."

"Hi, Mom." It struck me how much I had missed her.

"Hi, yourself."

"This is Blizzard."

Slowly my mother opened the stall door and entered. She crouched in front of Blizzard and gently stroked his white face. "Hello, Blizzard. Aren't you a gorgeous fellow," she crooned. "Is Jessie taking good care of you?"

"For the most part," Another female voice carried over the stall door.

"Hello, May," my mother spoke. "Thanks for taking care of my daughter this past week."

"Thanks for letting me."

I yawned.

"Get that tired girl home," Mrs. Nightingale laughed.

My mother hugged me. "Phew! And into a bath."

We left the Cottage and my mother and I climbed into the car. "I missed you this week," she smiled softly.

"I missed you too."

"Are you hungry?"

I shook my head. "I just want my bed."

"That's easy enough," she said. "Come on let's go."

My father met us on the top of the porch steps. "It's good to have you home." He greeted me with a hug.

A car pulled up as we were getting ready to enter the house.

Kenny. I wanted to cry. I did not tell him I had the day off. I had not been to school to see him the whole week, so the only way he would know was if someone else told him. I could guess who. Maybe he thought that by interfering now, he was making up for interfering in the first place.

"Is that Kenny Martin?" my father asked. "Why is he here?"

"Shush, Ben." My mother turned him around. "Come inside. I'll run you a bath, Jes."

I waited until she had my father inside the house before going to meet Kenny who was now leaning against the car. Jennifer was in the front seat with Phillip.

"Hey, Jes!" Kenny smiled looking extremely handsome in the morning sun. Even the golden hair that furred his arms glittered. It hurt, not just my eyes because they were so tired, but my heart too. "Are you ready to go?"

"No."

"Oh. Well we can wait."

"You guys go without me. I just got home and haven't cleaned up yet."

"It's no problem. Really," he assured me. "We'll wait. Won't we Jen?"

Jennifer leaned out the open window. "Kenny, get in the car," she told him.

"Jen," his tone held a warning. "We're not in a rush."

"Kenny, if you just looked at her, you'd see she's dead on her feet." Jennifer turned and smiled at me. "How did things go? David told me you had a crazy week."

"Yeah. Things went fine though."

"Good," she smiled again. "You must be exhausted after sleeping in the barn and all."

Kenny became solicitous. "I wasn't thinking. Of course you must be tired. Do you want us to come and get you in a few hours?"

Maybe, if I thought I would be awake.

Jennifer saved me from a reply, and I wondered if her motives were not ulterior in nature. "Of course she doesn't want us to come back. Let the girl go inside and get some rest. Let's go Kenny, the others are waiting."

"Jes?" Kenny asked. "Is that what you want?"

I nodded. "Sorry I didn't let you know."

"Hey, don't worry. You get some sleep. We'll see you at school."

With a wave he was gone, and I figured Jennifer had won that round. She had Kenny all to herself, and I had blown any chance I may have had. I might have cared more if I was not asleep on my feet.

Nine

Spring 1937

"Has anyone asked you to the formal dance yet?" Laura asked out of the blue as she rubbed a hand over Blizzard's neck.

"You would know if they had," I pointed out to her while I scratched the bull's ears.

It was weeks after the day I watched Kenny drive away with Jennifer and Phillip. My mood had matched the weather that followed, rainy and gray. Even at school things were different. It felt as though Kenny was avoiding me. Laura and I had switched to sitting with David and Job at lunch, something that had gone a long way to restoring my friendship with Job. Laura's advice to me was to just hang on. She was certain there would be other opportunities coming my way. So far, that had not proved to be true in the way I wanted it to be.

I kept busy on the farm. Blizzard had grown immensely and was penned in a paddock alone. I had to be careful to avoid that area during the main part of the day, as any close proximity of mine to Blizzard set him to bawling loudly. Today's visit with Laura was an exception. To me he was like a three hundred pound dog, demanding to be scratched around his big black eyes and ears, but Mr. Nightingale was insisting that I wean him from his attachment to me. Pops was particularly adamant about the matter.

"Like all fellers, he's meant to be territorial. Don't go forgettin' that," he said one day as I finished up my visit and Blizzard looked like he was going to follow me right through the fence that surrounded him. Keeping that in mind, I stepped down off the fence rail and pulled Laura after me.

"I don't understand it," Laura said, throwing an arm across my shoulders. "I see the way the boys look at you now."

I looped my arm around her waist and we turned in the direction of the path down to the creek. What Laura said was true. Over the year, I had grown another inch or two so that I was now among the average. My curves had filled out more, not enough to be in the same class as Laura, but enough that I could no longer be mistaken for a boy when wearing my coveralls. It left me unsettled. I could sense the growing interest of the young men in my circle, and more were making an attempt to catch my attention. Laura was certain any one of them would ask me to the prom at any minute.

Unlike the regular spring dance, this dance was for those like Job and David who were graduating, although everyone was welcome to attend. This was the dance where most people took a specific escort, and talk of who might ask whom, and who was wearing what, flooded the halls of school. Class pictures were taken, a moment captured forever of friends soon to be departing for colleges or jobs, and destinations outside our little haven.

David and Job were among the departing for college category. David was ecstatic to have been accepted to the college of his choice, and while Job was also pleased to have obtained the college goal he had selected, he did not overtly jump for joy. I was ambivalent about the whole thing.

If David was anything like Michael, once he left for College, I would scarcely see him. Michael's visits were sporadic, reserved usually for Christmas or some other holiday. This year we hardly saw him at all because he was visiting the home of certain young lady named Catherine. Though David was still my brother, he had become less of a bother. Somewhere along the way we had become friends.

As for Job's departure, I was more undecided about that. What would the distance do to our newly restored relationship? I was enjoying having him back in my life. I did not want him to go away again. I had Laura, but I did not want to lose that which I had just regained.

I shook off the heavy thoughts, and returned to the issue at hand,

"Who else asked you?" I pinched Laura's waist and took the focus off of me.

"Tommy Watts and Will Pitt."

"And you turned them both down."

"Yes."

"So, I have to turn them both down," I concluded then qualified, "if they ask."

"Correct."

Laura felt I should not accept an invitation from any boy whose first choice was not me. She was refusing invitations from all boys because none of them were her first choice. No sense in letting them believe they might stand a chance with her. I also did not have to deal with the "who to go with" issue, due in a large part to Job.

Anytime a potential suitor dared more than a friendly "Hello," a calculated stare from him would shoot down the unsuspecting, causing an abruptly aborted assault. I laugh now, but if I had been aware of it then, it would not have been so amusing. It might have irreparably damaged our newly restored relationship.

"I'll probably just go with David since he doesn't want to ask any of the girls he knows and he is aware of Mark."

David and Laura had a strange friendship. I did not try to understand it.

"So, how is Mark?" I switched topics to one that Laura loved to dwell on.

"His letters are always very proper and reserved, but I can sense he's coming around." Laura flopped onto the grass near the edge of the creek. "I have to be careful not to push, though. He has to believe that changing the rules to start dating, now that I'm sixteen, is his idea."

I reclined next to her

"How are you going to do that?"

And just like that Laura was explaining her convoluted plans for the future.

She was sixteen, and it was indeed sweet.

"Where's he going?" I asked Job around a mouthful of food as David took his sandwich and wandered, apparently aimlessly, down the road.

He shrugged and bit into his breakfast. I opened my mouth offering him a glance at the chewed contents. It was a game we had played, a contest of sorts to see who could make the other lose their appetite first. It usually ended in a draw. A second later, I caught a glimpse of what my breakfast must have looked like. We grinned at each other and continued to eat.

After a moment of companionable silence, he spoke. "Hey Jes?"

"Umm?"

"Are you going to the prom?"

"Dunno," I said around a mouthful of food before swallowing. David had asked me the same question earlier, on our way to the farm. "Haven't really thought about it."

I was not about to confess to him how much time I had actually spent obsessing over it, no matter how close we were again.

"If someone asks I might. Why?"

He shrugged. "Are you waiting for anyone in particular to ask you?"

I shrugged. "Why?"

"No reason, really," he paused to take a breath. "I just wondered if—" Job never finished his question as the bus rounded the bend and caught his attention. Spying the oncoming vehicle I immediately began gathering my things.

"What were you saying?" I asked as soon as I had everything in hand.

"Nothing. It'll keep."

When Laura and I climbed off the bus at the school, I heard my name called. It was Kenny pushing past others on the way out of the bus in a hurry to catch up to us.

"What does he want?" Laura muttered earning a raised eyebrow from me for her tone.

"Jessie!" Kenny slid to a stop in front of me.

"Hey, Kenny," I laughed as he gave a courtly bow.

"Give us a minute would you, Laura?" he smiled.

Laura turned to me with a look that said she would only go if I said it was okay. I gave her a "why not," shrug and she moved a distance away to wait.I turned to Kenny. "What's going on?"

"Are you going to the prom with anyone?"

"No." What was with everyone this morning?

"Well then," he grew solemn. "I would be very honored if you would attend with me."

My mouth opened but nothing came out. I do not know what I expected him to say, but that was not it, especially since we rarely hung out any more.

"Jessie?" He leaned his head in to look at my face closer. "Are you all right?"

I nodded.

"Is that a yes, you'll go? Or a yes, I'm all right?"

I nodded again.

"Which one?"

"Both," I finally managed.

"Yes?" He smiled hopefully.

"Yes," I smiled back.

"Swell!" He grabbed my hand and kissed it earning a few good-natured jeers from passersby. "I'll call you and work out the time and everything."

With a wave, he strode away.

As he passed Job, who had joined Laura, Kenny reached out and slapped him on the back. Job's face went dark and his body stiff. Laura placed a hand on his arm and whispered something to him. His body slowly relaxed but the coldness on his face stayed. With a shake of his head he stalked away.

"What's up with him?" I asked Laura as I arrived where she stood.

"More importantly," she grabbed my arm and started leading me toward the school. "What's up with you?"

I stopped dead in my tracks. I was going to the prom! Kenny Martin had asked me to the prom. I tried the words out loud to see how they would feel: "I'm going to the prom with Kenny Martin."

I watched Laura's mouth open, close.

Open.

Close.

"You look like a fish," I noted and earned a slap on the hand.

"Kenny?" she said although it was more of a question. "Kenny asked you to the prom?"

"Yes."

"And you said 'yes'?"

"Yes."

She turned to watch as Job entered the school building. "But didn't? Aren't you –?" She gave an arms open plea heavenward before taking my hand and dragging me toward the same door. "I don't think I'll ever understand anything again."

"What are you talking about?"

"I don't know." She plastered a smile on her face. "So, you're going to the prom with Kenny."

"Uh, huh."

"Do you know what you're going to wear?"

I groaned.

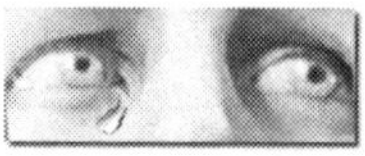

With great care I took the dress off its hanger and laid it on my bed. The first order of business was the stockings—a horrid affair with garters et al. Next was the slip. A delicate bit of silk and lace I was sure I would rip before all was said and done, and finally the *piece de resistance*, the dress.

It was a dream.

The pale gray sheath did not look like much on the hanger but once on, it clung to my form from neck to ankles. The sleeves were short, baring my arms and there were three glittering clips, one on either side of my neck and one at my waist. There were folds at the knees designed to make dancing possible and the back was slashed deeply, which had required the purchase of the appropriate undergarments. Standing there observing the ensemble in the mirror I wanted to put a sweater over the whole thing. I was afraid my father was not going to let me out of the house, for although completely covered, I felt more exposed than ever before.

A knock on the door had my heart skipping a few beats. "Come in."

It was David, looking unbelievably handsome in his formal suit. His hair was freshly cut and slicked back off his head. I caught a faint whiff of the cologne he had obviously borrowed from my father.

I gaped. "You look great."

"Thanks," he puffed up his chest and preened, making me laugh. "You look incredible. Like a woman."

I blushed. Now I really wanted my sweater.

"Dad's downstairs with the camera. He wants a picture before we leave." He rolled his eyes.

My father's camera.

A newly purchased item, it had become the most annoying gadget in existence. It seemed that everyday since he purchased it, we were forced to sit still for photographs and then sit still and exclaim over the pictures once they came back from being developed. My mother had finally forbidden its use except on special occasions. I guess this qualified.

I made a face at David and grabbed my lipstick, a glorious red Laura insisted I buy, and after observing the effects, I was glad I did. I snagged the lace shawl that had been my grandmother's and went downstairs to face the music.

My mother had to elbow my father hard to get him into action. I made sure the shawl did not slip and reveal the back of the dress as David and I posed at the bottom of the front steps to the house. My father snapped away, first David and me, then David, then me, then David, then Mom and the two of us.

I had just asked David to calculate mathematically how many more options there were in the pattern when Job arrived in his truck. From here they were going to pick up Laura.

"Good evening Mr. Bingham, Mrs. Bingham," Job called from the truck and they returned his greeting. He nodded his head in my direction but said nothing as he drove away.

The part of my consciousness responsible for feminine vanity was irked. My own brother had been more impressed with how I looked.

Kenny's car came down the road and stopped before our house. I have used beautiful to describe Kenny before, and I know beautiful is not a word often attributed to masculinity, but in this case it fit. He looked beautiful in his white dinner jacket and black slacks. His hair was slicked back like David's and only served to accent his fine facial features. My palms began to sweat as he approached.

"Jessie, you look lovely tonight." He held out a perfect red rose framed by white baby's breath. "This is for you."

"Thank you," I replied with a nervous smile and glanced to my mother who nodded. "Would you pin it on, Kenny?" I asked as she had schooled me.

As Kenny moved closer to pin the corsage on the left side of my dress, near my shoulder, I caught a movement out of the corner of my eye.

My father.

The only thing holding him back was my mother's firm grip on his arm. Kenny's head was bent close to mine. I could smell soap, hair cream and the underlying scent of something else. Something I would not identify until later.

The combination was intoxicating—either that or I was hyperventilating. I felt his fingers through my dress as they brushed against my collarbone.

"There," he exclaimed triumphantly and stepped back breaking the spell. "That's got it. Are you ready to go?"

I took his proffered arm and, with a last wave at my parents, we were off.

The first indication that the night would not be what I expected came during the drive to the school. As soon as we were out of sight of my house, Kenny reached into the inside pocket of his jacket and took out a slim silver flask. He handed it to me and asked that I unscrew the lid. The sharp sweet smell of alcohol floated up to my nose. It was that *something else* I noticed earlier when Kenny pinned the corsage to my dress. My heart sank. No one I knew drank anything stronger than soda pop.

Kenny took the flask from my hand with a muttered, "Thanks." As he was about to drink, he noticed me staring and held the flask out. "Want some?"

I could only shake my head in disbelief that he would even ask. I turned my gaze to the road ahead and tried to subdue the sick feeling in the pit of my stomach.

When we arrived at the school, Kenny came around to my side of the car and opened the door to help me out. As soon as the door shut behind me, he spotted a group of his friends standing just outside the school door. Most of them I knew, but there were a few dates among the group that I had not met, boys or girls from the neighboring town of Baldwin. Jennifer was there as well.

"Hey!" Kenny called to them and headed off in their direction.

I followed, unsure of what I should do. One of Kenny's pals noticed and joked that Kenny forgot something. Kenny turned around and spotted me standing outside the circle. He swore and grabbed my hand pulling me next to him.

"Sorry." He turned to the group. "Everyone, this is Jes. Jes, you know most everyone."

That was the extent of the introductions.

"You look very nice," Jennifer said and placed her hand on my arm.

"So do you."

And she did indeed look lovely. Her long blonde hair had been twisted on top of her head so not a strand was loose and her pale peach dress accented the creamy tone of her skin.

The discussion among the group turned to the future and how glad they would all be to finish school, some even if it was only for the summer. Another flask or two appeared and were shared along with a few cigarettes. Some of the girls in the group took their turn at each but Jennifer's refusal to partake gave me the courage to do the same. Her quiet support that night only made what I would say to her later that much more hurtful.

We went inside, and I searched the room for Laura. I spotted her standing with David and Job on the far side of the gymnasium and waved. Kenny caught the gesture and immediately took my hand in his. The band started to play and he hauled me onto the dance floor.

Every time I tried to get close to Laura, David, or Job, Kenny would find a reason to dance, get some punch, or visit his friends outside in the bushes.

I was numb with disbelief and disillusionment. I was not having fun and as ten o'clock rolled around I was having less and less. That is when it all came crashing to a halt.

As Kenny's visits outside had become more frequent, his hold on me on the dance floor became tighter. His mouth began to graze my ear, then my neck. His breath was moist and hot and smelled of stale cigarettes and spirits. It made me more than uncomfortable. I was definitely out of my element.

"Kenny," I whispered embarrassed and tried to pull back when his lips grazed my cheek.

He pulled me closer, and looked blearily into my eyes.

"Come on Jes. Jus' havin' some fun. You like to have fun don't ya?"

His face began to descend to mine and try as I did, I could not avoid him.

His mouth closed on mine and I froze. My mind went blank. When he tried to deepen the kiss I recoiled in horror. With a shove I managed to disengage myself. People stopped dancing to gape.

"What are you doing?" With one arm I fended him off while with the other I wiped my mouth.

"I'm just trying to show you a good time." He tried to kiss me again and what happened next was instinctive.

I smacked him in the face as hard as I could. The resounding crack caused even more of those around us to stop and stare. I was mortified. I watched as Kenny's cheek went from white to red in the shape of my hand.

From out of nowhere, or so it seemed, Job arrived.

"Is everything all right?" The steel of his voice emphasized the danger lighting his eyes.

Kenny whirled drunkenly to face Job. He no longer looked golden, the shine was replaced by disheveled hair and red cheeks.

"It's fine." He grabbed my arm and I knew there would be bruises. "Isn't it Jes? Tell him it's fine."

"Is it Jes?" Job's eyes never left Kenny's swaying form.

It was not, but I could not bring myself to tell him that. I was afraid I might succumb to the overwhelming urge to cry. That embarrassment would be too much.

"You see?" Spittle flew in Job's face as Kenny went nose to nose with him. "She doesn't want to be with you. She wants to be with me."

He turned a cocky glance my way. In stunned amazement I watched as his expression shifted to one of sickly surprise. The air filled with the cloying stench of alcohol as Kenny, in a most ungentlemanly fashion, emptied the contents of his stomach onto the arm he still held and down my dress. No one moved in the stunned silence that overtook the room as the band finished playing their song.

Despite his inebriated state, Kenny had the wherewithal to be apologetic. He cursed several times as he tried ineffectively to wipe the vomit off my arm.

"Jessie, I'm sorry."

I heard the first snickers begin in the crowd nearest to us. I needed to flee, to go anywhere and be anywhere but there. I tried to pull my arm free.

"It's okay Kenny. Just let go."

"No. I'm sorry, really." His grasp on my arm was firm.

I pulled harder. "Let go!"

"You heard her." Job stepped up.

"Get lost, Farmer." Kenny turned on him, "She's with me. I asked her first."

"Why?" My whole body trembled. I did not want to know why he had asked me to the dance, I wanted to know why things were going the way they were. "Why, Kenny?"

"Because, Jessie," the emphasis on my name made it sound dirty. "I knew Farmer Boy wanted to go with you."

Job's fist came up with such lightning speed that Kenny was an unconscious heap on the floor before he knew he had even been hit. David jumped in quickly and bent over Kenny. He felt for a pulse.

"Well, he's not dead," David said with a certain degree of disappointment.

Laura was at my side, a comforting hand on my back.

"Come on." Job turned and took my arm. "I'll take you home."

I had been grabbed enough for one night. With a fierceness driven by outrage, I pulled my arm free and ran. I found myself in the ladies room staring at a pale shaking stranger. The door opened behind me and Jennifer stepped from a stall into my line of sight. It was unjustified, but my anger now had a focal point.

"Did you know?" I asked coolly.

"Know what? What's happened?"

"Did you know that Kenny only asked me because he thought Job was going to?"

I took her silence for ascent. With an outward calm that belied my inner turmoil, I began to wash my arm. I wanted to tear the skin off, as though it were the offense and not Kenny's stomach contents.

"I wanted to tell you," Jennifer said.

"I'll bet you did," I scoffed. The hurt on her face almost looked genuine. "You would have loved that."

"It's not what you think."

"How do you know what I'm thinking?"

"Kenny is my friend. Nothing more," she began firmly. "I was furious when he told me what he'd done. For some reason I don't understand, Kenny resents Job. Maybe it's because he knows Job is ten times the man he'll ever be. I don't know. On the bus he overheard David asking Job if he'd asked you yet. When Kenny realized Job hadn't, he needed to beat him to it. I knew you would be hurt because I knew you liked him."

"You would know all about that," I interrupted.

Jennifer ignored my comment and continued.

"I tried to get him to change his mind. To think of you, but he wouldn't listen. And then he started drinking again." She paused unsure of what to say next.

"You didn't even try to warn me."

"Would you have listened? I knew what you thought even if it was wrong."

The fact that she was right did not sit well with me at that moment.

"Oh please," I sneered. "I know what you're like. Everyone does."

She paled visibly and an unreadable mask closed over her face.

"I'm sorry, this happened," was all she said before leaving.

I wanted to go home. I nearly knocked Laura over. I did not see her come in. How long had she been there?

"That was pretty hurtful, Jes."

Long enough.

"That's not like you." Her tone and look held reproach.

If she was not going to be sympathetic, I did not want to be around her. I brushed by her and out the door.

"Where are you going?" she called.

"Home!"

The engine rumble was familiar. The approaching headlights illuminated the road in front of me, and I watched my shadow appear and shrink the closer they drew. I picked up my pace, an easier task since I left my shoes and stockings on the side of the road a mile back. I did not want to face him. I was sweaty, smelled like alcohol vomit, and my feet hurt. If anyone could get me out of my mad, it was him and I was not quite ready to give it up. I heard my name called and started running.

With a roar, the truck pulled past then halted abruptly. It was either stop or hit it.

"Get in," he ordered.

"Leave me alone!"

I headed around the truck. A big mistake as that took me past the driver's side. The door opened and he jumped out to block my way.

"Get in the truck."

"Don't' tell me what to do."

"You cannot walk home."

"Just watch me!"

I dodged him and headed down the road. He climbed back into the vehicle and followed. We continued that way for another half mile before he spoke again.

"Jessie, please let me drive you home. It's not safe."

I stopped, drained and defeated. My feet were raw and cold. I knew my hair had lost most of its style, and I questioned the sanity of what I was doing. Wearily I climbed onto the seat beside him.

"Please Job, don't talk. Just drive."

Ten

Spring 1937

He turned off the truck and then the headlights. We sat in silence. When enough time had passed so that our eyes adjusted to the dark, he got out, came around to my door and opened it. He held out his hand, and I placed mine in his. It looked small and fragile, in contract to his, but it was safe.

We walked hand in hand to the creek bank and sat as we had when I was six and he was eight. Ten years I had known this boy, now a man by rights.

He took off his socks and shoes and rolled up his pant legs and together we dipped our feet in the soothing coolness of the water. The chirping of crickets and the croaking of the frogs enveloped us. I looked at the hand that held mine and noticed the split knuckle. Suddenly I was six again.

"What happened to your hand?"

"It broke."

He remembered too.

"Why?"

A shrug.

"The good Lord willed it."

But, I was no longer six, and I could not accept the answer without question.

"Did He, Job? Why? Why would God will this?"

"God wills a lot of things for a lot of reasons. Sometimes we know the answer right away. Sometimes we don't." There was a conviction in his voice. "There is a reason things happened tonight the way they did and someday, I believe, He'll show it to you. When you're ready."

"You really believe that?"

He took my hand in both of his and pressed it against his chest.

"With all my heart."

The intensity of his eyes disturbed me, so I moved on to another confusing subject.

"You hit him pretty hard."

"Not hard enough."

He released my hand to flex his and examine the split on his knuckles.

"David said he was still alive. That's probably a good thing."

"Probably." Despite his agreement, he sounded doubtful. "It took a while for David and me to get him into his car. David was going to drive it to Kenny's house and leave him out front to sleep it off."

Without warning I was crying. I found myself wrapped in Jobs arms as he murmured soothing words of comfort.

"Feel better?" he asked when I pulled back to drag my arm across my face.

"A little," I nodded. "I'm such a fool."

"Why?"

"Because the good Lord willed it?" I hiccupped on a weak laugh. "Imagine, I thought Kenny actually liked me."

"He's the fool," Job declared, more than a tiny bit of anger surfacing.

"Maybe." But he was not the only one.

During my flight from the school, I realized a few important truths. I understood that if I had every really been in love with Kenny, I was no longer so. That feeling had disappeared as quickly as the whiskey in Kenny's flask. Without a doubt my feelings were greatly hurt, after all, I had been emotionally invested; and, to a sixteen-year-old girl, rejection of any kind strikes a blow to self worth. It somehow validates the little voice inside that whispers to her, "You're not good enough," when she is alone at night with nothing or no one counter it. I also concluded the mistake had been mine from the beginning, and that hurt my pride more than my heart.

"Jes," he took my hands again, "I know someday you'll find the man who loves you more than anything."

I made some sort of noncommittal sound and lay back on the grass letting the music of the night wash over and soothe me. A frog croaked from somewhere very nearby, and I smiled. Something Mrs. Abbott, Jennifer's mother, had said while doing my hair came back to me.

Somehow, the woman had conquered the mass that was my hair and arranged it in a smooth sophisticated style with large loose bouncing curls just below my shoulders.

"Wow," I whispered when she had finished.

"I'll say," Mrs. Abbott agreed in her soft drawl not from any local region. "Kenny won't know what hit him."

My eyes flew to hers in the mirror. How did she know? She winked.

"You just remember, Jes, the first frog you kiss isn't likely to be a prince."

I managed a small smile. What was she talking about?

"Don't worry, hon." She patted my shoulder before removing the protective cape I wore. "You'll understand soon enough, I'm afraid. Now go, and enjoy your evening."

"You're smiling," Job observed softly, as he leaned over me. His words pulled me from my musings.

I looked up at his face as he gazed down at me. It was hard to read with only the moon for light. His eyes were hidden in shadow, but in my mind I could see the warmth of their brown. "Have you ever kissed a girl?"

I had not meant to give voice to the mildly curious thought that ran through my head, but since it was now out there, I wanted to know the answer.

He turned away without acknowledging he heard the question. Picking up a stone he tossed it into the creek.

Now I was very curious. I knew my brother Michael had kissed a girl. I would have been remiss in my duties as a little sister if I had not caught him doing so. And while I did not have the proof, I suspected David had too. I even suspected he had kissed Laura, but she would neither confirm nor deny my suspicions. I did not want to ask David.

I sat up. "Have you?"

He shook his head. "Not like you mean."

"Why? Isn't there a girl you wanted to?"

"I don't want to kiss just any girl," he shrugged, answering but not answering my question.

"Me neither. I mean I don't want to kiss just any boy." I had thought I wanted to kiss Kenny.

"What about Kenny?" he asked as if he read my mind. "You kissed him."

I felt myself grimace in distaste. If kissing were anything like what I had experienced this night, it would be a while before I tried it again.

"He kissed me. I did not kiss him." I smiled again. "Besides, he was a frog."

"Huh?"

"Definitely a frog."

"What are you talking about?"

"It's like in that story. The one about the princess and the frog."

"Ah. And Kenny was not a prince?"

"Nope."

"A frog?"

"Uh huh," I emphasized my agreement with a firm nod of my head.

There was a thoughtful pause. The frog croaked again.

"Jessie?"

"Yeah?"

"How many frogs do you think you'll have to kiss before you find a prince?"

It was my turn for a thoughtful pause. I started to laugh my sense of humor fully restored. "An awful lot."

"Well in that case," his eyes began to scan the creek bank near his feet. With lightning speed his hand disappeared under the water's surface and quickly reappeared holding a wriggling slimy, wet, bullfrog. He turned and pinned me down dangling the dripping creature over my face. "Maybe you should start now!"

I squealed in protest and tried to wiggle free. "Come on Jes," he goaded. "I dare you."

"Job!" I cried and grabbed his arm to prevent the frog from coming any closer.

"Who knows? This could be the one." The frog inched closer. "Give him a kiss."

I glared into his laughing face and with deliberate care I lowered the creature and puckered up. I kissed the frog on its sticky nose and managed a crest fallen expression when nothing happened.

"Nope," I sighed dramatically. "Just a frog. What's a girl to do?"

Job laughed and released the animal back into the creek. "Be careful Jes. Don't kiss too many."

"Oh? Why?"

"Warts."

"Warts?" I sat up.

"Yeah," he nodded seriously. "Just think. How many guys would want to kiss a girl with warts all over her face."

I pushed myself off the bank and stood thigh deep in the water, not caring that my dress floated around my legs. It was ruined anyway. "I'll give you warts." I declared and began scouring the depths.

"What are you doing?"

"He's got to have a brother right?" I reasoned. "Who's to say he's not a prince? Here froggy, froggy."

I spied one and grabbed. With a cry of triumph I closed my eyes and kissed the frog with a big smack.

"Nothing." I tossed the frog over my shoulder and began another search.

Job laughed. He tossed his suit jacket aside and entered the creek. "Here!" he cried a moment later. "Try this one."

I waded over and grabbed the frog to kiss it. It went the way of previous kin, as did several of its successors. It didn't take long until both of us were soaked to the skin and laughing so hard we could hardly stand up.

"Enough!" I finally cried. I clambered out of the creek and stood dripping in the moonlight. I felt carefree, the events of the evening securely locked away in my memory.

Job waded his way over to the bank. "Are you sure? I think there are still a few more."

"I think I've kissed them all, and more than once."

Job turned his back to me and grabbed his jacket. He held it out behind him. "Here put this on. It's cold."

"No it's not." I squeezed water out of my hair. "I'm fine."

"Just put it on."

"Seriously, I'm fine."

Keeping his eyes averted he climbed out of the creek and draped the jacket around my shoulders. I was in the process of shrugging it off when I glanced down. If I thought my dress had been figure hugging before, it was nothing compared to what it did when it was wet. I quickly shut the jacket and looked up into his face. His eyes locked on mine and I felt myself being drawn into that gaze, drowning again. I shivered.

He stepped back.

My teeth began to chatter and I realized I was cold but not from the air. This was Job. What was this new and frightening element that had suddenly entered our relationship? I tried to conjure up a picture of us as children, how he looked, how he laughed. Relentlessly the images turned into the man standing before me. I denied it.

"It's really late." He passed his hands threw his hair, pushing it off his face. "What time are you supposed to be home?"

I evaded his gaze. "Now, would probably be good."

No one else was awake, and the sun was just beginning to peak over the horizon, but the milk would be delivered by now.

Sure enough, the four bottles sat on the top step. I sat down next to them, pulled the lid off one and poured myself a glass. I should have felt angry, upset, hurt, or any combination of the emotions, but I did not. I cried all that out last night with him. And he let me. He had not patronized, made light of, or tried to talk me out of my tears but accepted them. He accepted me. I spent the remainder of night thinking about that instead of sleeping.

I drained my glass and stretched. That is when I heard it, a "croak" from behind me. Next to the door were my shoes. Job must have found them on the way home from the school. He would have had to come back sometime during the night and left them for me. He left something else as well.

My right shoe wobbled and fell. Out hopped a green frog. I bent down to pick the little fellow up.

"Hey there handsome," I crooned as I looked into its bulging black eyes. It croaked. "All right, but just a little one."

I kissed the frog and received another deep chirp for my efforts.

"Jessie, is that you?" My mother called quietly from inside the door. "Who are you talking to?"

I carefully placed the frog into the front pocket of my shorts. "No one. Just myself."

"What are you doing up? Is everything okay?" She came through the door and stood before me a worried expression on her face. In her hands she held a damp gray mass. My dress. I had dumped it in a heap inside my bedroom door and left it there.

"What happened last night?" She opened the screen door and stepped out onto the porch.

"What do you mean?" I played dumb.

She held up my dress and waited.

"There was a little accident at the dance, and my dress got ruined. Since it was already that way, we decided to go for a swim." It was not exactly a lie, I told myself.

"An accident?" She immediately became concerned and began to look for any signs of injury. Before she could roll up the sleeve of the shirt I had carefully chosen to hide the bruises on my arm, I pulled back.

"It was nothing." I assured her. "Kenny wasn't feeling well. He got sick on my dress. David took him home early. I went swimming, and Job brought me home."

"Swimming?"

"At Miller's Creek."

"In your dress?"

I could see she wanted to believe what I was saying, but suspicion narrowed her eyes. I shrugged.

"It seemed like the thing to do at the time."

"I know you're not telling me—was that a frog?" Her gazed zeroed in on the vicinity of my shorts.

"G'morning." Laura's decidedly sleepy and grumpy voice sounded behind me.

"Laura!" I leaped the steps to the walk and hugged her. "I'm so glad to see you." She had no idea how glad.

"What are you doing here?"

"Looking for you. Good morning, Mrs. Bingham."

"Good morning, Laura." My mother turned and opened the screen door to go back into the house. She held the sodden mass of dress in my direction. The gesture and her pointed look said in no uncertain terms she was not done with me yet.

"I was afraid you might end up at the creek or something," Laura said to me and smothered a yawn. "I didn't want to miss you."

"The creek sounds like a perfect idea. Stay right here," I told Laura. "I'll be right back."

"I came to see you, remember? I'm not going anywhere."

"Don't be late for church," my mother charged as I dashed by her and up the stairs.

I snatched Job's jacket from the chair in my room where I had left it, retrieved the frog from its hiding place, said a brief prayer of thanks that he was in one piece, and returned downstairs.

"Come on," I pulled Laura along behind me.

Halfway there, I paused and carefully placed the frog into one of the pockets of the jacket.

"Is that a frog?" Laura asked with a disgusted glare.

"Yes."

"Ick, and is that Job's suit coat?

"Yes."

"So, he did find you?" It was more of a declaration than a question and I realized her bad mood was probably a result of worry.

"Yes." I paused to make sure I had her attention. "I'm sorry for the way I ran out on you last night."

"Fine. But I'm not the only one you need to apologize to."

I hung my head and acknowledge the truth of her statement. "This afternoon, I will find Jennifer and apologize. I promise. Will you come with me?"

"Only if you tell me why you're putting a frog in the pocket of Job's suit coat."

"I need to return it."

"The frog or the coat?"

"Both." I laughed and started walking again.

"I'm just glad you're all right." She looked at me. "You are all right aren't you?"

"My feet hurt still, but not so you'd notice. And there is this." I lifted up my sleeve and showed her the dark purple bruises that circled my arm where Kenny had grabbed me."But really? I'm all right. I didn't think I would be, but I am. Talking with Job helped."

"He's a good man."

"I'm lucky to have friends like you and him."

Laura stopped and huffed.

"What?"

"Nothing."

"Not 'nothing.' What?"

"Job's just a great guy. That's all."

"Agreed."

She touched the bruises. "I'm sorry Kenny turned out to be such a greaseball," she said softly.

"Me too."I found myself on the verge of tears again; the kind of tears that result in the face of sincere concern. "I'll tell you about it later, after I return this."

Laura waited out of sight at the corner of the house. As I approached the back door of the farmhouse, I sensed movement inside. Not wishing to be discovered, I hung the jacket on the handle of the screen door and started down the steps. The third one creaked under my weight and I froze as the inside door opened. So much for a clean getaway. Maybe if I had gotten to play Bonnie Parker once, I would have been better at evading detection.

"Jessie?" It was Mrs. Nightingale.

"Good morning." I tried for a casual posture.

"What are you doing here?" She opened the screen door and the jacket along with the frog fell to the floor.

"I just came to return that," I explained as she bent to pick it up. I winced slightly as she folded it and sent up a brief prayer for Mr. Frog's health.

"Why did you have this?" she asked puzzled.

"It's a long story. I'm sure Job will tell you." I was pretty certain he would not. "I'll see you later, Mrs. Nightingale."

"Sure." She turned to go in but then had a thought that made her turn back. "Jessie?"

"Yeah?" I paused my hoped for clean extrication gone.

"How did it go last night?"

"Um. Fine."

"Was it what you expected?"

I could not help the slow grin that stretched across my face.

"Not at all."

With a wave, I turned away, leaving her to try and figure out what I meant. When I heard a yelp of disgust and my name called out with the same tone, I broke into a run and grabbed Laura as I passed her.

It marked a turning point that day. It was the first time I had ever kept anything back from my mother or Mrs. Nightingale. Those two women profoundly shaped my life, but now there were things I would keep to myself. I was breaking away, growing up, becoming a woman of my own. It would be a long process, but it had begun.

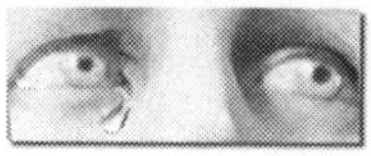

The high emotion of the previous night, combined with a lack of sleep, caught up to me even before the service began. I found myself unable to refrain from rubbing eyes that were hot and gritty. It was during the singing of the first hymn, as I stood next to my mother and yawned for fifth time, that I caught the glance from Job. My energy level picked up just a bit.

He was with his folks, two pews ahead and to the left. He turned ever so slightly as though to offer his mother a better view of the hymnal they were sharing. He raised his eyebrows, his expression hopeful, asking in silent shorthand, *That one?*

I shook my head sadly. *No.*

He shrugged. *Maybe next time.*

I was about to nod my response when I realized Mrs. Nightingale had turned to see with whom Job was interacting. She sent a look of her own. I bit the inside of my cheeks. To have even the slightest facial twitch at that moment would be pure folly. My peripheral vision told me Job was enjoying the moment.

It was a subtle thing, but I believe somewhere deep inside, floating at the edge of my denial was a recognition that, despite my statements about us being just friends, more was happening. He had begun his courtship, but it would take a while for the realization to surface. I did say I was often behind the grind in these matters.

Eleven

Fall 1937

Summer's end—I greeted it with a certain degree of sadness. The foundations of my world were shifting, expanding as I began to perceive with greater awareness, life outside the familiarity of the Junction. David's bags were packed and waiting by the door in readiness for the trip to the train station tomorrow. With a pang I realized a similar set of bags would be waiting by another door. Even Laura was eager for more of life away from here. I found myself considering, with uncertainty, what lay ahead for me.

I picked up the hideous green and yellow porcelain frog that rested on my dresser. A sixteenth birthday present from Job, it still made me smile every time I looked at it. Mrs. Nightingale had snorted with disgust when I pulled it out of the box. She had asked her son the timeless question, "What were you thinking?"

"It's perfect," I assured her before kissing the frog on the nose. "Almost," I then clarified as Job snickered.

Another frog, its front left leg painted white as though in a cast, brought other memories flooding back.

I broke my wrist trying to jump over Andy Simms. As soon as I hit the ground, I knew that something had gone terribly wrong. I remember telling myself not to cry along with all the *it-hurts-too-much-to-breath* writhing I was doing.

"I broke my wrist," I finally managed to communicate to those standing around.

"Can you move your fingers?" Job tried to move my good hand so he could have a look.

"No." I turned my back protectively.

"You haven't even tried."

"I don't care."

"Let me see it."

"Don't touch it."

"Let me see it!"

"Not if you're going to touch it!"

"I won't."

"Promise?"

"Jessie!" He spoke my name as an order.

I had showed him my wrist and true to his word, he had not touched it. He and David had driven me to the hospital in Grand River and waited until I emerged with a heavy plaster cast on my arm. I must have fallen asleep on the ride home because it was not until I was getting ready for bed that I had noticed the drawing on my cast: A chubby frog sitting on a lily pad, wistful expression on his face. "Could I be the one?" was scribbled in a balloon over its head. I kissed it and whispered, "Not you either," before falling asleep.

A grumpy week at home was enough for my mother to put me on the bus to Maine for a visit with Laura. When the small package arrived for me, I headed down to the beach to open it in private. There was no letter, just the frog with the painted cast and note that asked, "Do I get the lucky break?" I mailed a postcard the next day. The only words written on it were, "Sorry, you're out of luck."

I returned from Maine in time to have the cast removed. I could hardly wait. It was itchy, smelly, and I was pretty sure I had a piece of a twig stuck in it. I wanted to get back to the farm, to baseball, to him.

There were two things I noticed as I walked up the drive into the main yard. Behind the main house, the framework for a new building was underway.

"What's that?" I pointed and asked David. He had made the walk with me to find out why none of the Nightingales were in church that morning. I had expected to see them, him, there.

"It's a house."

"I can see that," I rolled my eyes. "But whose is it?"

"Mr. and Mrs. Nightingale's. They're going to move into it when Job gets back from school and takes over the farm.

Why the Nightingales' would move out of a house that was perfectly big enough for all to live in, I did not understand. David said nothing more on the matter and I did not ask. The second thing I noticed was proving too great a concern.

Everyone was over by the bullpen. They were hot and sweaty and there was evidence that a fair sized portion of the fence surrounding the pen had just been rebuilt. The boards were unpainted and a couple of hammers lay on the ground.

"What's going on?" David asked Job as we approached. "We missed you this morning."

"We had a little problem." He stepped around David and gave me a one armed squeeze. "Welcome home! How was your trip? How's the arm?"

"Fine and almost as good as new." I spotted Blizzard at the end of the pen. He was lathered in sweat and breathing heavily. "What's the matter with him?"

"He went crazy. That's what's wrong." Pop spat on the ground in disgust. I looked to Job for confirmation.

"It took all morning to get him back here." Job said.

"Why?"

"He's a full grown animal, Jes," Mr. Nightingale came and rested his hand on my shoulder. "He's a big animal and felt it was time to stake his claim on things."

I moved with disbelief to the fence. I had one foot on the bottom rail when Blizzard lowered his head and squared his shoulders. His nostril's flared as he snorted.

"It's best you don't get too close anymore." Mr. Nightingale pulled me back.

"We'll just keep him away from the other bull for now," Job said. "And make sure the fence is reinforced. That'll come out of your pay."

"Of course it will." I sighed heavily. First a door, now a fence. How much more would this animal cost me?

Since I could not lift anything heavy for a little while yet, I learned to drive the hay wagon and took perverse pleasure in starting abruptly and dumping David off the end. All the while, little frogs kept appearing in the most peculiar places. Sometimes it was a pocket, or a milk bucket. One even landed outside my bedroom windowsill. Each frog was different than the last, many of them hand carved and painted, and I kissed each one faithfully.

Now, I wondered how many more frogs my future held, especially since Job was leaving in the morning.

I swallowed a sudden compulsion to cry and put my dress into my satchel. My ball and glove went into the canvas bag along side the dress and the gift for him. I did not use the smaller bat anymore but there would be younger kids playing that day who might need it, so I picked it up to take with me. Once I was sure I had everything, I headed downstairs to meet my parents and David for the walk to the farm.

At the Nightingale farm, I eagerly went off in search of Laura who had arrived home earlier that day. I found her talking to Job near the barbecue. He was working to get it lit.

"Hey!" I cried and ran to hug Laura. "Welcome back!"

"Thanks!" she hugged me back.

I made a face at Job to acknowledge his presence. He returned in kind.

"How was the rest of your time in Maine?" I turned back to Laura. I didn't say "with Mark," but she knew.

"It was great!" she glowed with excitement. "We set a date."

"For what?" I asked stupidly thinking the wrong thing. "You haven't even gone out with him yet!"

At least not officially. My presence in Maine had allowed for Laura to spend more time with Mark than would otherwise have been possible. I was a built-in chaperone, and the three of us had toured the countryside together.

She knocked lightly on my head. "That's what we set the date for."

"Oh, right," I laughed at my mistake. "Sorry."

"Don't be. That will come soon enough." She turned a sly glance my way and directed me until we were out of hearing range from Job. "So?"

"So?" I dragged the word out as she had.

"So, what about you?"

"What about me?"

"And Job," she whispered under her breath.

"Me? And Job?" I whispered back. "What are you talking about?"

She stomped her foot in exasperation. "I know he sent you something in Maine, and," she added with emphasis, "he hasn't taken his eyes off you since you got here. Why do you think he hasn't been able to get that fire started?"

I glanced over. He did not appear to be looking at me or having trouble with the fire.

"Laura," I said with great patience, "He couldn't get the fire started because you were distracting him. As for what he sent me in Maine, it was a joke. Between *friends.*" My stress on the last word had her pouting but she did not get to say anything further as David joined us and we all went to get the ball game started.

I was on Job's team that year. He picked me first. Kenny did not put in an appearance. By the end of the eleventh inning when neither team had scored, it was declared a tie. People were hungry.

If they ate more than usual or laughed louder than they normally did, perhaps it was because somewhere inside was the knowledge that many of our group would not be returning for some time to come, if at all. War was marching across Europe and while it appeared to be far from our town, there were some who feared it was not far enough. We wanted to hold on to the moment, to freeze it in our minds in order to be recalled in times that required a touch of innocence, and the innocence of many would be taken in the coming years, but it would not be the warring of nations that would take mine.

The dancing began and I went from partner to partner. My father, Mr. Nightingale, Mr. White and even David all took me for a turn around the makeshift floor. There were a few classmates thrown into the mix, but one partner was conspicuous by his absence. It was not until late into the evening that he approached me. I believe on a certain level, I had been avoiding the moment. I knew my life would change. What would I do without my best friend? What could I say to him?

As he placed his hand on my waist and I placed my hand in his I noticed the scent of soap and hay. It was familiar, comforting. I relaxed and we danced in silence for several moments. I tried to remember dancing with him like this before. I could not.

"I like what you've done with your hair," he complimented softly with a smile.

"Thanks," I blushed slightly and felt the need to say more. "Laura did it."

After I had cleaned up, Laura had demanded entry into the bathroom as had become her usual custom. With an approving nod at my dress choice she had stood back with a calculating look at my hair. "Up," she stated and then proceeded to scrounge in her purse for a ribbon she had stashed there for such an occasion.

"I like what Laura's done with your hair." There was laughter in his voice.

"Thanks," I returned as we continued dancing. "I guess you're all packed."

"Yes."

"Are you excited?"

"Yes. A little sad too."

"Sad?" I was surprised by the admission. "Why?"

"It's going to be hard to be away from everyone, the farm." He paused and looked at me. "My heart is here."

"It will be here waiting for you," I said misunderstanding as was my way.

"If the good Lord wills it."

I smiled at just how much he sounded like his father.

"I'll miss you."

"Will you?"

His smile irked me. He didn't have to sound so happy about it.

"Yeah," I said testily. "But don't let it go to your head."

His burst of laughter had a few heads turning in curiosity.

"With enthusiasm like that, how could I?"

Sheepishly, my laugher joined his.

When the music ended we stepped apart. "Thanks for the dance," I offered with a certain degree of self-consciousness.

He bowed slightly. "Come on, its time to say goodbye to your folks."

"Before we do, I have something for you."

"For me?"

"A present. A sort of graduation and going away gift." I was wringing my hands. Inexplicably I was having an attack of nerves.

"Where is it?" Job asked. He motioned for me to take the lead. "Let's go get it."

His eagerness relaxed me enough to laugh at him as he pushed me to move faster. I raced him up the back steps and into the kitchen. My satchel was sitting where I left it, on a chair at the table. I opened it and before I could change my mind, extended the plain brown paper package.

Slowly, to tease me, Job began to undo the string that tied the package together.

"Just open it!" I tried to take it back and do the job myself.

He was faster and moved out of my reach, leaving me nothing to do but wait.

I had deliberated for some time over what to do about a gift for him.

I could buy any number of things, but I wanted it to be something I knew he would find value in. The careful way he was running his hands over the soft black calfskin of the Bible, let me know I had succeeded. The pages of his old one were worn and loose. The binding was giving way after many years of opening and closing. I knew he treasured it and spent much time perusing the words found inside. I wanted him to have one that he could once again read through without fear of causing any more damage.

"Job, may you always use this as the good Lord wills it. Jessie," he read the inscription out loud. "I will do my best. Thank you."

"You're welcome." I kept my head lowered while I swallowed the lump of emotion that threatened.

We walked together through the house and out the front door. My parents and David were standing with the Nightingales. Mrs. Nightingale was hugging David and telling him to write home occasionally. Only when he had promised to write faithfully did she release him so he could be wished well with a handshake and a slap on the back from Mr. Nightingale.

The ritual repeated itself with Job and my parents. When David and Job said their good-byes it was with enthusiastic words of encouragement and a hearty backslapping hug.

He turned to me and I looked at the button in the center of his shirt. I could not meet his eyes. "Good bye, Jes."

"Bye, Job." I tried a smile. "Be safe."

"You too. There'll be a lot of slack to pick up around here."

I groaned. "Don't remind me."

"Well, see ya."

"Yeah. See ya."

My parents began to move down the driveway. Reluctantly, I followed.

"Jessie?" He called making me pause and turn around. "Keep an eye out for frogs while I'm gone."

I ran up the stairs with a tearful laugh and gave him a quick, fierce hug.

"I will," I whispered. "I will."

As I held my father's hand and walked down the long driveway to the road, I was almost positive I heard a frog croaking from the vicinity of the front porch of that big yellow farmhouse.

Twelve

Spring 1939

Laura was getting married, David was not coming home, I was accepted to Barnard, I was eighteen, and Job had not responded to my last letter. What else could make me miserable?

I lay back in the grass and let my feet dangle in the water of the creek. I watched the clouds overhead as they drifted by. One looked like a woman's dress blown off the line by the wind. Which reminded me, it was my prom, and no one had asked me to go, well Jimmy had, but I knew he just felt sorry for me, so I took pity on him and told him to ask a girl he really wanted to take. He asked Veronica Drew. She was smart. She said yes.

His name was James Gordon. He preferred Jimmy or Jim. Some boys managed to get through those first awkward years of puberty pretty easily, not so Jimmy. When we first met, he was a skinny fourteen year old with stringy brown curls, more than the occasional facial blemish, and a voice that struggled to find a comfortable pitch; and he was my saving grace for two years. Rand—I could call him that now—hired Jimmy right after Job left, and besides being company, Jimmy had a genuine fondness for the guests of the Cottage. He did his job with a care and fastidiousness that soon had him earning my respect. Of course, it did not hurt that he could run like the wind and had a throwing arm that earned him the local title of, "The Righty Lefty Grove." With Jimmy, I experienced what it might have been like to have a younger bother.

I still smile every time I remember his first morning of work. At the bus stop I saw him about to sit to eat his breakfast sandwich. "Don't sit," I said.

"I just hafta. I ain't used to that kinda work this early."

I shrugged and leaned against the mailbox to eat my breakfast.

When the bus arrived, Jimmy groaned and struggled to stand.

"Please, kill me," he begged of no one in particular. "It ain't right to let an animal suffer so."

"It gets better," I told him and held out a hand to pull him up.

"It can't get any worse." His voice cracked on the last word making him sound like a puppy with a pulled tail. I pretended not to notice the red creeping up his neck as I stuffed the cloth sack into the mailbox.

"Walk around some at lunch. It will help work out some of the stiffness."

He smiled thanks and slowly climbed onto the bus.

Now Jimmy was a sixteen-year-old young man, with less stringy but still curly brown hair, fewer blemishes and a voice that had found a surprisingly deep note. He also had a date to the prom.

It was unfair, but I blamed Kenny Martin for my mood. While the two of us took great pains to avoid each other, and Kenny had lost some of his shine for many people, I could not help but think of him on an evening such as this. The events of two years ago had soured me on the whole idea of prom, and last year, Laura and I opted to go to a movie, thereby eliminating the need to fuss about it all. Tonight Laura was going with her fiancé.

In January, on her eighteenth birthday, Laura got her first official date with her Mark from Maine. Like a scene worthy of *Gone with the Wind*, only without the Civil War and Atlanta burning, Mark descended from the train, swept Laura up into his arms, and twirled her around as she squealed in delight. Even I appreciated the romantic drama of it all. The wedding was set for after graduation. I was genuinely excited for her, I just wanted to be excited about so much more.

I wanted to be excited about graduation and going away to school, and a small part of me was. It would be new, something that was just mine. I would have a chance to discover things about myself away from the watchful eyes of those who knew me so well. There would be no preconceived notions about who I was or how I had to be. However, another part of me wondered if I felt that way because everyone else felt that way. I was not confident that leaving would be the right thing. I liked living in the Junction. I did not know what I would do with myself if I left. I was even less certain about what the future would hold if I stayed.

I had hoped to hear what his impressions were on the subject of my leaving. I had written weeks ago, when I received my letter confirming my entrance into Barnard. I told him that I was excited about getting to see a big city and leaving home. I told him how I was looking forward to finding out what life was like outside Grand River Junction. After all, that was what people wanted to hear, what they expected to hear, was it not? Now, I wished I had told him the truth. I wanted to hear what he thought about it all, but he had not responded. Not a word.

For two years, our only source of communication had been letter writing. I had not seen him except for once. He did not come home for Christmas, choosing to stay at school and look after various projects so his classmates could enjoy the break. The Nightingales had taken Christmas to him. During the summer break, he chose to go to Wisconsin and learn about making cheese and creamery operations. The only break he took was for Michael's wedding in Philadelphia.

Last summer, the whole family had gone for the big event. Michael's wife, Catherine, was a warm and generous girl who reminded me of May Nightingale. She was willowy, with light brown hair and hazel eyes that sparkled when she smiled.

I was kept so busy with last minute dress alterations, the first chance I had to see him was as I walked down the aisle behind Catherine's sister and matron of honor. He was standing next to David, Michael's best man. He looked broader in the shoulders and chest. The planes and shadows of his face were stronger; less boyish. The same thing had happened to Michael and David. Even their topics of conversation were shifting, becoming more centered on politics, policies, and philosophies about the war and if America should become involved.

I wondered if Job took part in similar conversations and what his opinions might be, but found I was inexplicably nervous. I could hardly look directly at him, and when the opportunity to talk was lost in the business of the wedding, I had a sick feeling that I had lost a moment which could not be returned. But, his letters continued to arrive with faithful regularity and with each passing day, week, and month, I grew more eager for them.

I would strive to be the first to reach the mailbox in hopes of finding an envelope addressed to me, in a handwriting that had become as familiar as my own. The letters were entertaining, filled with talk of things he was learning, and people he was meeting. Occasionally a little frog would appear in the upper right corner of one and I would kiss it. When the hoped for prince failed to appear, I would fold the letter carefully, place it back into the envelope, and store them in my jewelry box right next to the little white tooth.

A glance at my watch, an early graduation and birthday present from Michael and Catherine, told me I had now been sitting by the creek long enough for my parents to wonder where I was. Maybe a letter would arrive tomorrow. With a sigh I stood and turned to leave. A movement in the shadows caught my attention.

A man was watching me. The sun was low in the sky and the dark of the woods obscured his features. I felt a scream rise in my throat as he stepped toward me. When I recognized him, I almost cried with relief.

"Hey, Jes," he came closer a smile on his lips. "I didn't mean to startle you."

"What are you doing here?" I asked still not believing he was there.

"I went by your house, but your father said you hadn't come home yet," he shrugged. "I figured you'd be here."

"No, I mean what are you doing here?" I gestured all inclusively. "When did you get here?"

"About an hour ago."

"Are you home to stay?"

"Yes."

I could feel the smile grow on my face. With a little skip I covered the ground to give him a huge hug. I pulled back to look at him.

"You look great!" I declared and looked at him again. His hair was slicked back off his face. I caught a pleasant whiff of aftershave. He really did look quite wonderful, all dressed up the way he was.

"Why are you wearing a suit?" I stood back to take in the dark clothing. It was striking in contrast to the white of his shirt.

"Do you like it?" He straightened his jacket and smoothed his tie. "It's the latest in fashion, or so I'm told."

I laughed. Job did not care about fashion. I took a few steps around him.

"It's beautiful, but why are you wearing it?"

"It's prom night." His tone suggested more of a comment on the status of my IQ than the imparting of information.

I waited for him to elaborate.

"I'm going to prom. At least I think, or hope, I'm going to prom."

"You are?"

I mentally sifted through the people we both knew. He had not mentioned anyone in his letters except in the most casual sense.

"Who is she?" I tried to appear nonchalant.

"Who is she, who?"

"The girl."

"What girl?"

"Who is the girl you are going to prom with?" I practically shouted at him.

"I can't tell you that," he laughed.

"Why?"

"I haven't asked her yet."

Now I was totally confused.

"You came home to go to the prom, with some girl you haven't even asked yet?"

He grinned and nodded. I couldn't believe what I was hearing.

"How do you know she isn't going with someone else?"

"Are you?"

"Am I what?"

"Going to the prom with anyone?"

"No."

"Well then?"

"Are you asking me to prom?"

"Yes."

"Why?"

"Why? You're asking me why I'm asking you to prom?"

I nodded waiting for an answer.

"Jessie, when I got your letter about going away—"

"You got my letter?"

"Yes and—"

"You never wrote back."

"I know and—"

"Not even to congratulate me."

"Would you let me finish, please?" He threw his arms out and looked to heaven for help. I threw him a glare and nodded for him to continue.

"I wasn't going to come home until the end of the summer. I was going back to Wisconsin for a couple of months, but when I got your letter," he paused here to make certain I would not interrupt again. "I was excited and sad. I knew if you left before I came home, it might be a long time before I saw you again, if ever. I didn't want that to happen, but didn't know if I could change things so it wouldn't. I'd given my word that I would be there."

I knew how important Job's word was to him.

"I had to pray long and hard about what God wanted me to do. Then things in Wisconsin fell apart, and I knew God was telling me to come home. I was so glad. I started thinking about what I could do to show you how much I –" here he hesitated briefly, "appreciate you and what your friendship means to me. I thought, if I could get home in time, I could take you to the prom. Neither of us got much out of the last one. Maybe I could put a better memory in place. So I came home. For you. For me."

I was speechless.

"So, please Jessie," he said. "Would you do me the honor of going to the prom with me?"

I answered with the first thing that came to my mind.

"I don't have anything to wear!"

"I'm not swimming in this dress," I warned him.

"Your suit's in the back," he said with a laugh. "I had your mom get it while you cleaned up."

I glanced behind us to the headlights of the car that followed. "Mark's pretty great isn't he?"

"I just met him a couple of hours ago."

"Yes, but you liked him."

"Yes. I liked him."

Our appearance at the prom had been greeted by a squeal of delight from Laura, who had planted a kiss on Job's cheek leaving a lipstick print behind. She had thrown her head back with a laugh and demanded Mark's handkerchief in order to wipe it off. I watched Job as he sized up the young man behind Laura, waiting to see how Mark would react. Job's manner, while not quite proprietary, was definitely protective; and it dawned on me then, how much Job cared for Laura. It was a side of him I had not considered before, but one I appreciated.

Mark took back the soiled handkerchief and stuck it into his pocket with a resigned shake of his head and amused sparkle in his eye, before extending his hand to Job.

"Mark Newcomb," he introduced himself.

Job relaxed and accepted the open greeting in Mark's gesture.

"Job Nightingale."

"It's nice to finally put a face to the name. Laura's told me so much about you."

"You should know, she exaggerates," Job deadpanned receiving a friendly shove from Laura and an open laugh of agreement from Mark.

Job relaxed at Mark's friendly manner and the two started to bond over talk of school and work.

"Talk later." Laura grabbed Job's arm when she had finally had enough. "Let's dance and you can tell me all about whatever it was that kept you away from here for so long."

We traded partners on and off again throughout the night. For the first time in a long time, I found my my life comfortable—even if it was only for another week. Laura would soon be married and gone. If I thought about it too long, I feared I would start to cry, and I was grateful when we finally pulled into the driveway of the farm.

By the time Laura and I changed and made our way from the farmhouse to the clearing, Job and Mark had several lanterns lit. I watched with enthusiasm as Mark grabbed up Laura and jumped into the creek with her. When I saw the speculative gleam in Job's eye, I jumped in before the choice was made for me. He followed with a huge splash that we cheered with approval. I then spent the next several minutes laughing at his subtle attempts to entice me to kiss a frog he caught.

The darkness was retreating when Laura yawned, causing the rest of us to follow likewise. It was time to go. The night was over. Job drove me home in spite of Mark's offer to see me safely home. He pulled up outside my house and got out to walk me to the door.

"I believe Laura and Mark will be very happy," he said as I took my wet towel and swimsuit from him.

"Yes," I agreed sincerely.

"What about you, Jes?" he looked me in the eyes. "Are you happy?"

At that moment it was easy to smile up at him and nod. At that moment, I was happy.

"Good," he continued. "It's important to me."

"It is? Why?"

He looked away for a moment, thinking about how to phrase his next words.

"Because you matter to me," he stated solemnly. "Whatever God has in store for each of us, I know it will be for our best. That's what I want for you. It's what I pray for you. If going to New York is what God wants for you, then it's what I want for you."

I was not sure how to respond. My faith in God was not mature, not like the faith of this man who stood before me. I had not given God much of a place in my decision. I do not think I would have known how to do so if I had thought to do so. How could I know what God wanted of me when I did not even know what I wanted of myself? I changed the subject.

"Thanks for tonight," I smiled up at him. "It was the best prom I've ever been to."

He laughed quietly. "It was my pleasure," he said and squeezed my hand.

I watched him walk to his truck before calling out softly, "Job?

"Yeah?" he paused to turn.

"Welcome home."

Thirteen

September 1939

If I had known it would be the last time I walked with my parents down the road to the farm, perhaps I might have taken care to appreciate it just that little bit more.

It was hard to reconcile that I would be leaving in the morning. The end of this summer saw my bags packed and waiting at the front door for the train ride into New York. Every time I thought about it, thought about leaving, I felt more than a little sick. I observed my parents as we walked. I saw the touch of gray at my father's temples and the slight lines of age and laughter around my mother's eyes. They were growing older. I was growing up.

Everything whispered this was home.

My team lost the baseball game that year despite Jimmy's best efforts, and I cut my shin on a slide into second for which I was called out. It stung as I cleaned it. It would leave a scar. That would teach me to try and steal a base. When I emerged from the bathroom and entered the kitchen I found Mrs. Nightingale making more root beer.

"Can I help?" I offered.

"Yes you can. Here, stir this." She handed me the long wooden spoon with a sigh of relief

I looked out the window at everyone as they danced, or sat grouped together in fellowship. A feeling of disconnect settled around me. I did not want to dance. I carried the pitcher of root beer out to a table, and before I realized my destination, my feet had carried me to the Cottage.

The moon was bright and full, so I left the door open in lieu of turning on the overhead light and began to wander down the row of stalls. Most were empty but in several I found new arrivals nestled next to their mothers for comfort. They were safe here. I felt safe here. I always had, and perhaps that is what had drawn me to the place.

"Hello? Anyone in here?" A voice called warily.

"It's me, Pops. Jessie." I saw his wiry form silhouetted in the door.

Pops came and sat next to me. He smelled of soap and peppermints. "I saw the door open as I was makin' the last rounds for the night. I shoulda knowed it was you sittin' in here. You always did love this place, right from the start."

I smiled. "That was a long time ago."

"Not so long," he said and sat next to me. "Why ain't you up at the house dancin' with some handsome feller."

"I didn't feel much like dancing," I shrugged.

He nodded as though he understood.

And I think he did, for we sat together in companionable silence listening to the sounds of the night and sucking on pink peppermints. Crickets chirped and added their song to the music that floated down from the house. The constant chewing of cuds was a soothing rhythm underlying it all, punctuated by an occasional bleat or lowing.

I thought back over the summer and how much had changed. Job was different, I was different, and our friendship was different. After Laura's wedding, I felt a bit lost. It was not like other summers where she would return full of tales about what had filled her summer. This time she was leaving as a married woman. She would not be back. I felt at loose ends and Job knew it.

When work ended for the day, we would head to the creek for a swim, or walk into town for ice cream or penny candy. We entered livestock in county fairs and won ribbons. We went to movies and afterward sat in his truck outside my house and talked for hours, sometimes until the sun came up, which made the next day very difficult and sometimes hilarious as we battled the need to sleep on our feet. Laura would have chided me for not seeing the pattern that was developing, and she would have been right. I may have been blind to that, but not to everything.

I began to see in full, how deeply his life was governed by his desire to serve his Lord. He began to challenge my complacency with the status quo demanding to know what I believed and why. We debated and discussed back and forth.

Sometimes it turned heated as we argued over one point or another, and other times we laughed or sat in awe of something we had read in the Scriptures. If for no other reason than these talks forced me to read my Bible more, I am grateful.

We did something else that I had not done by myself, or outside of Sunday school, in quite a while. We prayed together. It was a fragile beginning, but I found a desire growing within me to know my God and what His plans for me were, and it was in seeking those plans that I began to feel an increase in the nagging doubt that surrounded my imminent departure.

I ignored it.

I ignored the small voice inside me as God speaking, and chose to believe I was just anxious. This would be the first time I would have to stand on my own.

"You know Jes," Pops spoke after a while, bringing me back from my mental wandering. "You don't have to go."

"I know," I sighed, and tried to keep the tremble out of my voice. "But if I don't, I'd feel like I was letting everyone down."

"Folks would understand."

"Maybe."

What would I do if I stayed? What opportunity for writers was there here? All the great writers went to New York, did they not? And I had convinced myself I wanted to be a great writer. A voice inside fighting to make itself heard as it cried out that I could write anywhere. I was going to New York, I told it firmly, struggling to hold back tears of doubt and fear. Everyone wanted me to go.

Pops stood and made his way silently down the aisle. He paused and turned at the door. "You can always come home, Jes," he said before walking out into the night.

My hand bumped something as I shifted restlessly. There on the hay next to me was a wrinkled brown paper bag. As I opened it, the perfume of pink peppermints teased my nostrils, and I cried until I fell asleep.

When I woke it was to a gentle touch on my cheek. I sat up feeling drained and disoriented, as I looked into the worried face of Job. "What are you doing here?" I asked in confusion.

"Looking for you," he answered softly. "What are you doing here? Everyone's been looking for you."

"What time is it?"

He glanced at his watch. "It's nearly eleven. The party's finished."

"I fell asleep," I said stating the obvious as I rubbed my eyes.

He held out his hand. "Come, I'll take you home."

I let him pull me to my feet but stepped away to retrieve the little brown bag. "Where are my parents?"

"They went home to see if you were there."

"They must be worried," I started to panic.

"I ran into Pops and he said he thought you were down here," he said calmly. "My mother called your house to let them know I would get you home."

He fell into step beside me as I walked down the aisle of the barn. "Jes, are you all right?"

"I just needed a little time to myself."

I did not offer any further information and was relieved when he did not push the issue.

The brief ride home was quiet. I sniffled all the way and Job let me. His only reference to my high state of emotion was the silent offering of his handkerchief. At the door I blew my nose one last time and held out the crumpled piece of wet cotton in order to return it to him.

"You can't think I want that back now?" His expression was so comical it had the desired effect. I gave a watery chuckle and balled up the bit of cloth in my fist.

"I have something for you," he said, and I watched as he pulled a slim velvet box from the pocket of his trousers. "It's a kind of going away and don't-forget-me gift."

My heart had started to race. I could not guess at what was in the box. I nervously pulled the ribbon off the small oblong case and lifted the lid. Nestled on a layer of green velvet was a beautiful silver chain. Suspended from the chain was a delicate charm of a preening frog prince. After a breathless moment, I felt laughter release itself from my chest.

"I love it!" It was truly lovely. And perfect.

He lifted the box from my hands and carefully took the necklace out.

"Turn around," he said.

I turned and waited while he fastened it around my neck. I ran my fingers over the little frog where it rested against my skin. The metal was cool and hard but warmed quickly under my touch.

"Thank you," I whispered through my tears, and held the crowned amphibian out. "For more than just this."

I am uncertain which one of us moved first, but it was rather abruptly that I found myself unable to breathe as we stood holding each other.

There were no words, no good-byes. A soft kiss on my forehead and he was gone.

If only he had asked me to stay.

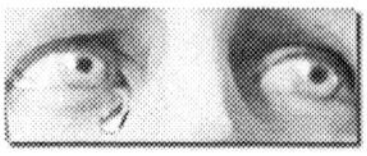

December 1939

"Miss Bingham, isn't it?" A cheery voice interrupted my brooding, and I was brooding. I hated New York. It was not what I thought it would be. I wanted to go home.

"Yes, Professor Williamson." I stood as my Romantic Poetry teacher, and the only professor I liked, approached. "How are you today?"

"Much better than you, by the look of things. Please, sit." He sat next to me. "What are you doing sitting out here in this nasty cold?"

It was the first week of December. The ground was frozen and the walkways covered with a layer of slush and ice. Everything was dull grey, even the sky.

Before I could think about it, I handed him my paper, the one for which I had received a less than stellar grade and even worse comments. "Quaint, but where is the relevance outside New England?" my literary writing professor had written, echoing the sentiment I had received from several other professors. Not all life happens in Vermont, was the overriding implication. The problem was, for me it had.

I watched as Professor Williamson began to read. He was a gentleman of indeterminate age with an amazing head of salt and pepper hair that sprang out from his head in coils of rebellious disarray. His moustache was thick and full and grew down either side of his mouth. The only way one could tell he was speaking was when the white fur moved slightly and the smooth tenor of his voice filled the lecture hall. His accent marked him as British, and he smelled of pipe tobacco.

Now the professor held my paper in one hand and unwound the blue wool scarf from around his neck with the other. "Put this on," he instructed me and continued reading. I obeyed, as he was my professor, and was immediately engulfed in the scent of sweet tobacco.

I valued this man's opinion. His class was the only bright spot in the three dark months I had spent in New York.

I found the city fascinating with its tall buildings and throngs of people. It was an organism, a living entity that breathed a life of its own. There was so much to see and do, but all of it left me feeling slightly empty. I found myself disoriented by the fast pace to survive and succeed. The atmosphere at the school was no different.

Staying in the dormitory had been mandatory. The other girls in the dorm were nice enough, but each was concerned with her own life. The loneliness of a "Wheaty" from Vermont was not a high priority, and though I tried, I did not find a confidante among them. I felt small and insignificant next to their apparent worldly sophistication and experience. I did find that tales of their exploits and habits made interesting filler in the letters I sent home regularly. However, in those letters I was reluctant to reveal my unhappiness. I did not want to appear ungrateful for the opportunity given to me, and I did not want to admit that I was a failure.

"Arrogant dog!" Professor Williamson barked pulling me violently from my musings. "Barrington wouldn't know relevance if it ran stark naked through the hallowed halls of academia shouting, 'I'm Relevance! I'm Relevance!'"

Professor Williamson referred to the maligned Professor Barrington's elegant scrawl at the bottom of the last sheet of my paper. We had been asked to write about an incident in our lives through which we had gained a deeper understanding of something, someone, or ourselves. I had written about my experience with Blizzard, and how despite my desires to do so I could not make him into something other than what he was.

I had gotten a "D". It was the first time I had ever gotten a grade that poor. I did not know what a "D" meant, except it was not the usual "A" I was accustomed to, and it was humiliating.

"Miss Bingham," the professor handed back my paper and pulled out a pipe and a small leather pouch. "Not only is this paper well written, it is very revealing. There's its relevance."

I could only listen and watch with fascination as he stuffed the end of the pipe with a wad of tobacco, struck a match and held it to the bowl of the pipe, then puffed deeply. A cloud of blue smoke hung in the air around his head.

"What I mean is this. The story is not about a bull, and that is obvious. It is about a young girl's maturing into a young woman, and the realization that life cannot always be what we desire to make it. It will be what it is intended to be. It is written from the heart, and to say it is not relevant, is to say that *you* are not relevant; and you, Miss Bingham, most certainly *are* relevant."

Tears of gratitude sprang to my eyes. I blinked them back and tried to say thank you to him.

"No, my dear, thank you." he patted my hand. His gray eyes twinkled. "Thank you for being honest in a place where honesty is often overshadowed by the need to write what is expected, in the manner that is expected. Honesty and truth cannot be contained by structure, although they may be found in structure. They must be allowed to be what they are. You must be allowed to be what you are and who you are."

A gentle snow began to fall and cover the ground. Professor Williamson shivered. "Blasted snow," he grumbled. I began to unwind the scarf to return it. "Keep it," he dismissed. "My wife, dear heart, insists on knitting me a new one every time I insist on losing one."

His wink made me smile inside and out for the first time in a long time.

"Are you happy here?" His eyes caught and pinned mine, demanding nothing but honesty.

I shook my head and dropped my eyes. It was the first time I openly acknowledged the fact. I took several deep breaths, trying to maintain a hold on the tears that threatened.

"Don't be ashamed, Miss Bingham. There is nothing shameful in your answer."

I lifted my head meeting his eyes once again.

"That's better," he nodded. "Now, if you are not happy here, then why are you still here?"

"I beg your pardon?"

"Pack your bags and go home."

"Excuse me?"

He laughed at my confusion but took pity on me and explained. "Your writing is very good, if somewhat unpolished. It will only get better if it is allowed to mature and be what it will be—if you are allowed to mature and be what you will be. I fear if you stay here, that will not happen. Oh, I have no doubt that you would continue to be an excellent writer, but I fear the price of that. Even if no one outside these walls recognizes your talent, or reads your work, or knows your name, you are meant to write the stories that mean something to you. Go home, Miss Bingham. You can write anywhere, but you will write best there."

I made my decision in that moment. It felt right. There were no doubts. Oh, there was a certain amount of regret and disappointment, a feeling that I had failed somehow, but there was also some peace in it.

"I think I will," I said quietly. "Thank you."

Professor Williamson wrapped an arm about my shoulders and gave it a reassuring squeeze. "Keep in touch, will you? And send me more of what you write. I would like very much to read it."

The semester concluded a few short days later, and I did what would make the parents of any college student proud: I dropped out of school, took what was left of my tuition money and bought a car and a map.

Fourteen

December 1939

"It's beautiful," Laura observed coming up behind me. I had been waiting for her to come out of the bakery across the street.

"Yes, it is." I took a last look at the cream cable knit sweater in the shop window and relieved her of some of her packages. "All set?"

"It would look wonderful on him. Are you going to get it?"

"No," I turned to look at the street with its busy shoppers. Lights were winking on with the fading of the afternoon sun.

"Why not?"

I shook my head as unexpected tears sprang to my eyes. I knew when I made the detour to Maine before going home, that I would have to answer some questions I was reluctant to face. And yet, I think knowing that, was the reason I made the choice in the first place. Laura would provide the sounding board and the support I needed to make some difficult decisions, or so I thought.

"He's in love with you, but you know that."

"Maybe." I started down the sidewalk towards Laura's house.

If he loved me, then why had he not asked me to stay? Why had he never given any indication that he felt that way? If everyone else could see it, why did I not?

"*Definitely*. I think deep down you know it." Laura followed behind me.

There had been moments I thought it might be true, like when he kissed me on the forehead that night before I left, but most of the time,

I felt he treated me the same as he always had—nothing beyond friendship.

"And you obviously care about him a great deal."

"Yes, I do." I stopped abruptly causing her to bump into me, and forcing several other passersby to take evasive measures. "I love him, Laura. I do. But, how do I know if it's the kind of love you need to have to spend your life with someone? How did you know it was Mark for you? I mean the absolutely-without-a-doubt-till-death kind of love?"

"I don't know." She threw her arms out and shrugged at the same time. "I just sort of knew it. I know I told you I was going to marry Mark the instant I saw him, but I didn't really know it, not for certain, not until there was this one day when I looked at him. I got all hot inside, like someone set my chest on fire. We weren't doing anything out of the ordinary. We weren't even officially courting. We were in my grandmother's kitchen, and he spilled something on his shirt. He laughed about it, and it just hit me that I was going to marry him. I don't even think I was completely in love with him. I just knew it."

"Well, I've been looking at Job since I was six years old, and not once have I felt like my chest was on fire."

"Well maybe you've been looking at *him* for too long!"

"What does that mean?"

"Maybe you need to look at someone else."

"Like who?"

"Like yourself!"

We had raised our voices to a level that might be considered shouting to some, including a few of those who were glaring at us with obvious disapproval. Laura groaned and shook her head with a wry laugh.

"Come on." She grabbed my arm and pulled me along the sidewalk. "There are enough people in this community who think hiring such a young preacher was too risky. As it is, Mark will no doubt hear about his young bride making a scene in public and how he better get control of his personal affairs. Wait until they find out I'm pregnant."

One of the first things shared between us when I arrived was the wonderful news that Laura and Mark were expecting.

She had blushed and glowed at the same time when she informed me of the news. "In June," she sighed. "I hope she has her Aunt Jessie's birthday." The trip to town on this afternoon had been because, it seemed for Laura, pregnancy and the compulsion for baked goods went hand in hand.

Laura also filled me in on some of the struggles Mark was having with being accepted in the area. Most people were enthusiastic about his presence, but Mark's age, and the age of his very young wife, had raised more than one eyebrow. Now she took my arm and dragged me down the street after her.

"Ruth Lunnie Donaghy Flynn will surely faint dead away. If anything could drop her, it would be the thought of the young preacher having Biblical knowledge of more than just scripture."

Mark was in the kitchen heating the kettle when we arrived at the house. Laura greeted him with a quick kiss.

"Hi," she said. "We're going to need your office for a bit."

"All right." Mark's eyes widened in surprise and he looked from his wife to me and back to his wife again. "Is there something I can help with?"

"No. Thanks." She smiled at him and picked up the bakery box I had set on the counter. "I've got it covered. Jessie, grab the milk."

She left the room, taking it for granted that I would do as she commanded.

"Your father called," Mark said as he took the whistling kettle off the stove.

"Great." I sighed. I would have to deal with that later.

"He sounded worried. He wanted to know when you were coming home."

"What did you tell him?"

"That you were fine, and that you were leaving here tomorrow." Mark added half a teaspoon of sugar to his tea. "I told him I would have you call him but he said that as long as you were doing okay he would wait until he saw you."

"Thanks."

He smiled and sipped his tea. "And Jessie?"

"Yes?"

"Good luck in there." He nodded in the direction of his study.

She sat at Mark's desk. Her shoeless feet were propped on the glossy surface and she leaned back in his chair, a look of sublime happiness on her face—that and a lot of confectioner's sugar.

I set the milk and glasses on the desk, and Laura put her feet down.

"Mm, mm, mm. Those were good." She poured a glass of milk for herself. "You made it just in time though. I saved you a couple. Never say 'I don't love you.'"

I looked at the two pastries left in the box. They did look appealing, but I was nervous about what Laura had to say. I pushed the box across the desk to her. "Never say 'I don't love you.'"

Like a bird on a worm, Laura dove for the box.

"You can put it on my grave stone," she held up a pastry and used it to punctuate the air, "She never said, 'I don't love you.'"

I laughed at her dramatic antics and sat in the chair across the desk from her. I waited while she chewed and swallowed, and captured the last pastry from the box. She pointed it at me.

"Now, about that." She took a bite.

"About what? Your gravestone?"

She made a face. "No. Love."

Here it was.

"I was thinking while I was waiting for you to bring the milk." She took a gulp.

"That long?"

"Don't interrupt." She put the last bite of pastry into her mouth and chewed slowly before swallowing.

"People are different, Jess. They love differently. Job's known for years that he wants you." Laura got up from the chair and came around to sit on the desk in front of me. "For some reason that scares you, but right now you need to look at yourself and the way you think of him. If you can't love him the way he loves you, then you need to walk away. He deserves to have someone love him in the absolutely-without-a-doubt-'til-death kind of way."

"I know he does." I felt my stomach sink.

"You do too. But if you can't be the one who loves him that way, then you need to stay away. It's selfish if you don't, and it's not fair to him. If you can't walk away then you need to ask yourself why. But to do that, you need to stop looking at him with eyes that are still six years old."

"I'm not sure I know how," I confessed. "Or even if I can."

"You said you love him."

"And I do, but—"

"No! That man is not your brother. You need to make the choice to love him, or to let him go."

She was right. I would have to choose and pretty soon. I knew Job would not wait much longer. I could feel it in his letters. It was a subtle intangible thing, but I knew it was there. It was why I had kept every one.

I knew also, there would be very little room for error in the conclusions I came to or in the choices I made. Too much lay at stake. I had finally stopped fooling myself about that.

To say my life would have been *less,* if I had not met him on the bank of Miller's Creek, is an impossibility. I cannot know what my life would have become. I only know it would have been different. The degrees of better or worse were immeasurable for their lack of existence. I would be changed if he were to be gone from my life, and yet, to go home and not return to him what was in his heart, would change us both.

"I feel sick," I finally said.

"Me too." Laura groaned softly.

I looked up. She looked sick. She had gone pale and a faint sheen of perspiration had appeared on her forehead. I saw her throat work as she swallowed reflexively. Without thinking, I picked up the decorative metal tin that served as a wastebasket and handed it to her.

She smiled weakly but gratefully and sent a longing look at the empty pastry box.

"What a shame." She sighed.

The entire incident was over quickly and after wiping her face Laura turned to me.

"Well, I won't do that again," she said.

"Eat that many?"

Her smile was slow but I could see the sparkle in her eyes.

"Eat them that fast."

Thick, wet snow started to fall and dusted the car as I sat there. The lamp in the living room cast a warm yellow glow on the snow that already covered the lawn. One or both of my parents were still up. A small orange cat paused in the midst of crossing the lawn to sniff curiously at something hidden beneath the surface of the snow. It was one of one-eyed, one-eared Duke's progeny, no doubt. It had been quite some years since I last paused to scratch his chin. I could not even remember the last time I saw him. The porch light flicked on and the little cat scooted away. Curiosity would not get it tonight.

The front door opened and my father stepped out onto the porch. He peered into the night to see who was there. Slowly I emerged from the warmth of the car and stood in the cold air. It was refreshing. I inhaled deeply and waited.

"Jessie?" My father moved closer to the steps. "Is that you?"

"Hi Dad." I stepped up onto the sidewalk and waited, for what, I did not know exactly.

My father took his time coming down the walkway. He paused as he looked over the car.

"It's a Nash." I said inanely.

"It's nice." He kicked a tire. "New?"

"Almost."

He wrapped his arms around me then. "I'm glad you're home safe and sound," he whispered softly and kissed my hair.

"Me too," I agreed and squeezed my eyes tight to hold back threatening tears.

"Ben?" My mother called from inside the house. "Who's there?"

"Someone you've been waiting for," he called to her.

"Jessie?" She appeared in the doorway.

"Hi, Mom." She moved down the walkway at a quicker pace than my father and without any small talk hugged me tight for a minute. She then held me at arms length and took inventory.

"You look pale. Are you feeling well?" She pressed a hand to my forehead.

I took her hand in mine and squeezed reassuringly. "I'm fine. Really. Just tired. And I have a headache."

"Of course you do." She tucked my arm in hers and led me toward the house. "Ben, just leave her stuff for tomorrow."

"Is there anything you need tonight, Jes?" My father asked before following.

After I assured him there was nothing I would need before the next day, we went inside.

For the next two hours I talked. They listened, with only the occasional question for clarification. When I was done, they knew everything from what had happened at school to Laura's baby news. They knew it all except that part which concerned him.

My father brought up his name first "So, what are your plans now?" He crossed his ankles where they rested on the footstool and leaned back in his chair.

"I find a job."

"What about going back to the farm?" he suggested. "I'm sure Job could use you."

"No." I shook my head firmly.

"Why not?" my mother asked. She was seated on the sofa next to me. "You've always enjoyed it there."

"Yes I have."

"Then—"

"No." I cut her off more sharply than I meant to and took a deep breath to get hold of my emotions. I was too tired to control them properly but my mother was not the cause of my exasperation. It was me. I was causing it myself. I tried to explain without revealing too much. "I just want to try something different. I need to."

There was a long moment where I pleaded silently for them to understand. I could not tell them that I had made a choice to put some distance between Job and myself. They would not understand and I was definitely too tired to explain that and maintain control of my emotions.

"If that's what you want," my father finally said, still a little puzzled.

"It is, Dad," I assured him and felt myself relax.

"We just want you to be happy." My mother wrapped her arm around my shoulders and pulled me close.

"I know." I closed my eyes and tried to pull into my heart as much as I could of the comfort she offered.

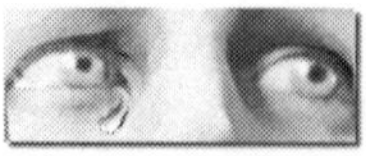

I stood at the back door and look out into the yard. There was a path of footprints leading to the back shed but other than that, and a few animal prints, the snow was untouched. In winters past, there had not been an inch left unmarked by the activities of my brothers and me.

"When does David arrive?" I asked.

"They'll be here Christmas Eve."

"They?"

"He's bringing Sarah with him. She's a lovely girl." My mother paused in the middle of returning plates to their cupboard. "A bit shy at first, but I think you'll like her."

"Dad and David could move Michael's old bed into my room. We could share."

It would be different. David's girlfriend would add an unknown dynamic to the group.

"I had the same thought." My mom came and took the brush from my hands. She ran it over my hair. "It's nice that you would make the offer though."

We stood quietly together, each of us keeping our own thoughts inside as she brushed and braided my hair.

"What are you going to do with the rest of the day?" she asked as she unwound the hair ribbon that I had wrapped around the handle of the brush.

It was well past noon. I had slept late then taken the opportunity to soak in a hot bath. It was nice not to share a bathroom with anyone but family. It was nice not to have the day planned out ahead of time.

"I think I'll take a walk into town." I held the end of my braid while she tied the ribbon around it.

"Why don't you let Job know you're back? I'm sure he'd love to go with you."

"Maybe later." I took back the brush and started out of the kitchen. I did not want to discuss Job. I was still trying to decide what I was going to do about him. "Thanks for doing my hair."

I ran the brush back up to my room and pulled a warm sweater over my blouse. I grabbed an old navy pea coat of Michael's that still hung in the front hall closet. My work boots were stiff and tight from lack of use, but I tied them up and stepped outside.

It was cold but there was no wind. It was the kind of day where the sun was so bright it hurt the eyes, and nostrils stuck together as nose hairs froze. The snow squeaked underfoot like cheese curds on teeth. Invigorated, I skipped down the front walk and headed for Main Street.

It looked like a postcard. Bright ribbons of red and green adorned shop windows and lampposts. Familiar faces smiled in greeting and stopped to ask how I had been, or to comment that it was good to see me home for Christmas. So different from New York where it seemed a rare occurrence if eye contact was made by anything other than accident. It was good to be home.

A bell tinkled as I opened the door and stepped inside. The shop was busy. Christmas was just a week away. Mothers were buying presents for their daughters, and a few sons sifted awkwardly through the sale racks for gifts for their mothers. Mrs. White stood behind the cash register, a smile on her face. Despite the smile, she wore a slightly harried air.

She finished ringing in a young woman's purchase and looked up to see who had come in. "Jessie! Praise God," she exclaimed and came to give me a hug. "You're just in time."

She dragged me behind the counter and pointed me so I was facing the cash register. A new addition just before I left for New York. "Just punch in the price on the tag and hit this button here. Then, when everything is rung in, hit this one here. It will give you the total."

I started pushing buttons. There were a couple of incidents that required Mrs. White to step in, but pretty soon I caught on and found I was enjoying myself.

It was an hour before the store cleared out enough for me to take off my outerwear, and Mrs. White and I could sit in the back room over a cup of tea. I was grateful to see cookies on the tray.

"You saved my life just now," Mrs. White slipped off her shoes and sighed. "I thought I was going to break. This is the busiest Christmas season in a long time. How can I repay you?"

"You could hire me," I told her seriously.

"Done," she said before taking a moment to study me. "Laura called and told me everything. I'm sorry New York wasn't what you expected."

"Me too," I agreed and trusted that Laura had only talked about New York. "But I'm where I want to be now."

"Then that's all that matters." She leaned forward with excitement. "Imagine. I'm going to be a grandmother! Do I look like I could be a grandmother?"

"No." I laughed at her good-natured outrage. The statuesque woman with the cool gray eyes was the furthest thing from any grandmother I could picture. Always impeccably dressed, with not a hair out of place, Evelyn White never looked flustered, even when she was. She projected a manner of smooth sophistication which belied a down to earth warmth and a rather sharp sense of humor she often directed at herself.

"Well, good." She stood and took my hand. "While we still have some peace and quiet, let me explain where things are and how they run, although not much has changed since you were last here."

The final hours of the afternoon had disappeared rapidly. At five o'clock I was told to run and lock the door or we would never get home. Half an hour later the store was restored to a more orderly state, and I said good night to Mrs. White with the promise that I would see her at nine o'clock sharp the next morning.

There was more bite in the cold now the sun was gone, and I hunched my shoulders in an effort to keep the chill from my neck. I heard the rumble behind me before I saw the truck drive by then stop at the curb. My stomach dropped. I had not decided what to do about Laura's advice.

I did not want to admit to myself that she was right. I had begun to question her assessment of Job's feelings towards me, after all, he never did anything to indicate that he felt more than friendly.

Now, he hopped out of the truck and ran around the front of the vehicle to where I stood. With a "whoop" he picked me up off my feet and swung me around.

"You are home!" He set me down and stepped back. "My mom said you were but I didn't believe her at first. When did you get in?"

"Late last night." I stepped back.

"Why didn't you call me?" He opened the passenger door and indicated I should get into the truck.

I did not want to get in, but the memory of the looks Laura and I had received during our little public outburst was still fresh in my mind. Maine Street was still busy with people closing up shops or heading home for dinner. "It was too late to call." I climbed in the truck.

"Not last night. Today. Why didn't you come on by the farm?"

"I don't know. I just…" I saw him looking at me and there was nothing but friendly curiosity in his gaze. I looked away.

"You just what?" He moved his body so his face was in front of mine again. This time there was more then just curiosity in his eyes. "Did something happen?"

"No. Yes. Sort of."

"Hang on." He closed my door and then went around and climbed in the driver's side of the truck.

I did not say a word as we made the very short trip to Third Street and my house. After he pulled up behind my car and parked, he turned sideways in his seat to look at me. "Okay, so what did not, but did, sort of happen that you didn't tell me about?"

"I'm not going back to New York."

"You're not going back?" He leaned forward. "Why? When did you decide this? Why didn't you tell me?"

"I hated it. I tried to like it, truly I did, but I didn't want to be there." I looked directly at him so he would know I meant what I said next. "I don't think I ever really wanted to go."

"Then why did you?"

Because you did not ask me to stay. I battled strong feelings of resentment.

"Everyone was so excited for me. I felt like I had to go," I finally said with a shrug.

He ran his hand through his hair. "I'm sorry if I ever made you feel that."

I said nothing.

"You never mentioned any of this in your letters." His brows drew together in a frown. I could see him going over them in his mind.

"I didn't know how to tell you."

"You say, 'Dear Job, How are you? I'm fine, but I hate New York and I'm coming home for good.'"

"It wasn't that simple."

"It's not complicated either, Jes. You know you can tell me anything."

"Yes, but I don't always have to tell you everything."

"That's not what I'm saying."

"I didn't want to tell you!" I shouted. "I was embarrassed. I felt stupid."

I could feel my heart pounding in my chest as we sat in the aftermath of my outburst. I could hear the blood rushing in my ears. It was only moments that we sat there but it felt like hours.

It was his turn to stare out the front windshield. "What are you going to do now?"

"I got a job." I watched for his reaction from the corner of my eye.

"When? Where?" He fired the questions with a sharp jerk of his head in my direction.

"Today. For Mrs. White."

"Just for Christmas or for good?"

"For good."

"Really? I was hoping…I thought…I just assumed you'd want to work on the farm."

"Laura's pregnant."

"That's wonderful," he smiled broadly. "Tell her I said congratulations. But what has that to do with you working for her mother?"

"Since she'll be going to Maine quite a bit over the next months, Mrs. White wants someone she can count on to run things here."

"Is that what you want?"

"I don't know what I want."

For long moments the only sound in the truck was the running engine. I met his scrutiny head on. His eyes were dark glittering pools almost lost in the shadows. My head felt as though it would explode.

He shifted in his seat, not saying anything. I could see him chewing the inside of his bottom lip. I had never noticed him do that before.

"I hope you find what you want," he said and indicated the conversation was over by slipping the truck into gear.

I opened the door and slid out quietly.

"Good night."

"Bye, Jes. Tell Laura and Mark congratulations for me."

The truck door had barely closed before he started down the street. I shivered, and not because of the cold.

Fifteen

December 24, 1939

Joseph was more than a little embarrassed by having to put his arm around Mary; the angel kicked his younger brother, the shepherd, in a not so peace-on-earth-good-will-toward-men kind of way; and we lit our candles and sang Joy to the World. It was a perfect Christmas Eve, at least for an hour or two.

Inside the church, hot cocoa and cookies were served, and I could no longer ignore the Nightingales. They were genuinely happy to see me, but I could see the question in their eyes. I told them how much I missed them. It was true. I felt contrite that I was avoiding them, even if it was not them I was really avoiding.

I did see him briefly that night. David was laughing with him about something as they helped to herd the sheep from the manger scene back onto a truck. I fought the impulse to go over and join them. This was what I wanted after all, some space to figure out what I was going to do. I knew with one apology I could have it all back the way it was, at least on the surface. Under it, I would still be uncertain. He would still be certain.

I turned and hurried to catch up with my parents and Sarah before he saw me. I knew I was not quick enough when David caught up and held me back from the rest of the group.

"What's going on with you and Job?" he demanded.

"Nothing's going on." I tried to pull my arm free.

"Don't lie, Jes. You're not very good at it."

He was angry. "If there's nothing going on, why didn't you come and say hello? It wasn't so long ago that you spent every spare minute out at the farm. Now he says you haven't been out there since you've been home. Why is that?"

"I've been busy working at the store. It's the busiest time of the year," I informed him. "I didn't say hello just now because I didn't see him."

"Lie."

He was right, so I ignored that point.

"I said I've been busy."

"Not good enough."

"It will have to do."

"We are not moving from this spot until you tell me why you've been avoiding him." When he got that look in his eye I knew he meant what he said.

"Has he done something? Is that it? Did he hurt you somehow?"

His protective concern brought tears to my eyes, and I blinked frantically to get them to dry up without falling.

"He hasn't hurt me. He hasn't done anything." That was the problem. I had done it, but how did I explain the constant need to stop and catch my breath whenever I thought about not seeing him again? How did I explain the persistent urge to cry that I could not allow myself for fear I would not stop?

"He loves you Jess."

"So everyone says."

"You don't believe it?"

"Why would I?"

David, being the gentle, kind, sensitive, caring brother he was, laughed. "I've asked myself that question many times and still haven't found a good reason." He tried to pull me in for a brotherly hug. I pushed away and punched him, which made him laugh more. I tried to stalk away but he held on.

"What are you afraid of?"

To have this conversation on Christmas Eve with my brother of all people, was not what I would have expected, but there we were, and I needed someone to say the words aloud to.

"I know he loves me. We're friends. But, why would he *love* me?"

This time David thought better of making a smart remark. He wrapped his arm across my shoulders and we began to follow my parents and Sarah at a slower pace.

"Why wouldn't he? You are a beautiful loving woman. The way you put Sarah at ease so quickly proves that. I've never heard her laugh like she did tonight with anyone but me."

When I met Sarah earlier in the day, I was struck by how much she looked like my mother. She had shoulder length black hair and blue eyes that sparkled when she smiled. Where my mother's skin was like fine porcelain, Sarah's had more gold tones. She was shy, but not a doormat, and immediately I could see what must have drawn David to her. I spent most of the afternoon sharing the most embarrassing stories about him that I could recall.

"Today made me so thankful that I had a sister as funny, and precious, and as generous in spirit you. He sees that about you. That's why he loves you."

"He's so confident and patient. I'm not" I argued. "He knows what he wants. He always seems to do the right thing, and I don't. It's like he's perfect. I've never seen him really lose his temper. Except when he punched Kenny, but even then he did it for me."

"Don't fool yourself." David laughed. "Job hit Kenny because he wanted to hit Kenny. You were doing a pretty good job of defending yourself and Job knew it. He just recognized an opportunity to get away with what he'd been itching to do for a long time, and he took it. Punching that greaseball was a purely selfish moment on his part."

If what David was saying was true, and being Job's friend he probably knew the inside and out of it, I had something entirely new to mull over.

"He's a good man, Jessie. I'd trust him with my life." David stopped and looked down at me. "Even more importantly, I'd trust him with yours. But he's just a man."

Something about the uncertainty I was feeling must have been reflected on my face. David grew really serious.

"So do him a favor. Don't start something you're not prepared to finish."

"I don't know what there is to start, or if I want to start it!" I could hear the defensiveness in my own voice. Why did it seem as though everyone was more concerned with Job's getting hurt, than with mine?

"I know you don't. And that's okay. For now. But you will have to decide."

The street was deserted by then, my parents and Sarah having entered the house quite a few minutes before David and I arrived at the end of the front walk. I could see Sarah through the front window as she curled up in the wingback chair and watched while my father crouched to start a fire in the fireplace.

"Until I went to Philadelphia," David continued quietly. "I didn't realize how woven together we were. Everywhere we went, everything we did, we moved as a unit, you and Job in particular. So I can guess there are a lot of expectations out there that the two of you will just always be together. Falling in love and getting married would be the next step. There are quite a number of people that just expect it to be Jessie and Job forever. I'm guilty of thinking that myself. And, while I know it would make quite a few people happy, it has to be your choice. Whatever you decide, I'll be with you."

I could feel the mild nausea lifting from the pit of my stomach. David really understood, perhaps even better than I did. Everyone just assumed I would want to be with Job. I was certain even Job felt that way in some small part of him, and it irked me. No one had any business thinking anything for me. I went to New York because it was what I felt was expected of me and I was unhappy. I did not want to make such a life altering choice based on anyone's expectations but my own.

It was time to change the subject. I hugged David and thanked him for his support.

"I really like her." I said with a gesture towards Sarah. We climbed the steps and watched as she smiled at something my father said.

David paused at the door and reached into his pocket. He pulled out a small square velvet box. "Do you think she'll like this?"

I stared down at the simple gold band with its solitary diamond that was revealed when David opened the lid. I shrieked and clapped my hands.

"Sh!" David covered my mouth

"When are you going to ask her?" I whispered with barely contained excitement.

"Tomorrow morning when we open the gifts." He smiled sheepishly. "It's corny I know, but Sarah doesn't have a family. I wanted her to know that we would be her family now. That she'd never be alone again."

"It is corny," I sniffed through tears of joy and hugged him. "But it's beautiful, absolutely beautiful, but there better be an impressive present from you to me under that tree or your secret will be no more."

David, like the good bother he was, dragged me over to the porch rail and proceeded to shove snow down the back of my neck.

Sixteen

December 31, 1939

Sarah stepped out of the fitting room in a simple white suit. The skirt was long, almost to her ankles and the jacket fit snug in the bodice. "What do you think?" she asked with nervous excitement.

"It's beautiful," I said. "I still can't believe you're getting married tomorrow."

"I know," Sarah giggled and wriggled in delight. "But David and I discussed it and the only people we want to invite are all right here, and with neither of us wanting a big fuss made, we decided tomorrow would be perfect."

New Year's Day. I could not think of a better way to start the New Year. Well, I could think of one, but that was not going to be, especially after the previous week and the events that occurred on the afternoon of Christmas Day.

It had been our turn to go the Nightingale farm for Christmas dinner. There was a large group gathered. Pops, John, Mitch, along with Jimmy, Jimmy's older sister Agnes and their parents, and the Whites were all there. With the excitement over David and Sarah's early morning engagement, it was easy for Job and me to avoid direct contact. The problem had occurred after dinner, when Job offered to show Sarah the barns and explain to David his plans for expanding the dairy to include a creamery. Jimmy and Agnes piped up that they wanted to go as well. Despite a strong desire to hear what his plans were, I decided to stay and help tidy up.

"You go, Jes," my mother said as she picked up my plate. "We can manage without you."

I chanced a peek across the table at Job. He was not looking at me, but I sensed he waited for my answer. Other than a perfunctory "Merry Christmas," we had not exchanged a word with each other.

"No. I'll stay and help out." I stood and picked up the bowl of leftover potatoes. Another glance at Job and I saw the slight negative shake of his head, the same kind of shake someone gives when they are displeased about something

He pushed back his chair and stood. "I'll meet you in the main barn," Job said to the room in general before marching out. There was a brief shocked silence in the wake of his abrupt departure. I heard his steps as he crossed the kitchen followed by the soft thump of the kitchen door and the sharp bang of the screen door as it swung back on its hinges.

I carried the potatoes into the kitchen and found May staring after the door, a look of puzzlement on her face.

"Is something wrong with Job?" May turned to look me.

"You'll have to ask him," I shrugged and placed the bowl on the counter.

That had earned me a don't-take-that-tone-with-me look from May, and a don't-you-speak-to-her-like-that look from my mother. I left to gather more dishes.

Later, I wrote in my diary about how disgusted my mother had been with my behavior and about how big a pill Job had been. Especially by the way he laughed and concentrated on Agnes for the rest of the evening. She was amusing, but not *that* amusing. Besides, I had heard she was practically engaged to some guy from Baldwin, and if she was not, then she should have been.

"Here you go Jes." Mrs. White entered the fitting room and pulled me back to the moment. She carried a box which she handed to me. In the box was a suit similar to the one Sarah wore, only in a beautiful coppery brown, a little lighter than my hair color. "As soon as Sarah changes I'll wrap hers up and you can take them with you."

"Thank you, Mrs. White, for this," Sarah said with an encompassing gesture.

"It was an absolute pleasure. I'm looking forward to tomorrow." Mrs. White hugged her. "And please, call me Evelyn."

There must be something about getting married that made you mature enough to call someone you barely knew by her first name. I had known the woman most of my entire life and had yet to be granted that privilege.

Soon, Sarah and I were on our way home with our precious bundles. We walked in companionable silence a few minutes before Sarah slipped her arm through mine.

"Jessie, are you sure you're all right with this? I mean with standing up for us with Job."

"Tomorrow is not about me and Job. It's about you and David. I wouldn't miss standing up for you for any reason."

"You're sure?"

"Positive." I gave a little shrug. "Besides, I already have the suit."

David was not around when we arrived home.

"Job called and needed his help with something." My mother informed Sarah. "He didn't know how long he would be, but we have much to do without him anyway."

Five hours had since passed my mother's explanation. My first instinct was to run right out to the farm and see what was going on, but it was not until Sarah looked at the clock for the one hundredth time in the last hour that I finally gave in.

"What time did you say he left?" I asked my mother again.

"Six." She frowned as the clock gave a short chime signaling the half hour. The next chime would signal the New Year.

"I'm going to see what's taking so long."

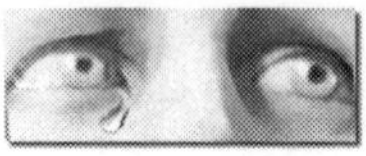

I drove as fast as was safely possible on the snow-encrusted roads and pulled in next to the Cottage. David was there, about to climb into my father's car.

He looked tired and dirty and as my headlights illuminated his face, I saw him glance at the little barn then back at me. With a shake of his head, he approached the car as I opened the door and stepped out.

"What are you doing here?"

"I came to see if I could help."

"It's too late." He grabbed my arm as I headed for the small barn. "Go home."

"But—"

"No, Jes. Leave it alone."

David's grip tightened as I tried to get free. "Leave him alone. Tonight, just let it go."

David's attitude told me there was something else going on in that barn besides just a bad dropping of a calf. I averted my eyes from David's in silent refusal to do as he wished.

Without a word, he released my arm and left.

Inside the Cottage, the warm glow of the overhead light illuminated Job on his knees, head bowed. Lying on the ground before him, steam still rose from the bodies of what looked to be a sleeping cow and her calf. It was an illusion for although the heat rose from the bodies, there was no rising of the chests. The only movement was the long slow stroke of a blood-covered hand over a wet, lifeless body.

I stood transfixed just inside the doorway. Every feeling and experience I had that centered around this man flooded my mind in waves of memory.

"I'm sorry," I said. For so many things, I realized.

When he finally looked over his shoulder at me it was with the same deep brown eyes that I had fallen into when I was six and he was eight. At least the colour was the same. The unguarded trust was no longer there and it was my fault.

"Some things aren't meant to be, I guess." He stood.

We both knew we were talking about more than a dead cow and calf. He looked defeated, something I had never seen in his posture before.

"I—"

"Go home, Jes."

"But—"

"Go home!" he yelled. "Leave me alone!"

I pushed open the door, desperately fighting the tears that threatened. The cold blast from the outside doubled me over, and I slipped off balance. I landed on hands and knees. The pain radiated outward from my knee caps and made my whole body weak. I gave an inarticulate growl as tears of frustration blurred my vision. I rolled onto my side and stayed that way, afraid I could not stand up.

My palms burned from the scrape of the icy ground. Something cold slid along the side of my neck down to the ground. The little frog prince on my chain.

Carefully I rolled over and tested the ability of my legs to hold me up. They were wobbly, but strong enough to get me inside the little barn once more.

Job had moved. He was now seated on a hay bale, his head in hands. Dried blood crusted between his fingers and on his shirt. Mindless of that, he pulled up the hem of his shirt and wiped his face.

"I need to ask you something."

"Please, Jessie. Go home." He was crying.

"Was hitting Kenny something you wanted to do for a long time?"

"What?" He wiped at his face again and turned to me with a look of complete confusion.

"Why did you hit Kenny? Did you hit him because you wanted to hit him, or because you were defending me?"

"Jes—"

"Just answer the question!"

He looked like he was going to protest because he did not understand where the question was coming from. I waited, silently demanding an answer.

"I hit Kenny because I wanted to hit Kenny," he confessed begrudgingly. "I'd wanted to hit him for years. *Years!* Now, go away and leave me alone."

"I have something to say."

"I don't want to hear anything you have to say right now."

"I love you."

My original plan upon re-entering the barn did not include the blurting out of those words, but things were not going as expected, not that I really new what my expectations were or should have been. Well, penny or pound, dime or dollar—whatever the saying—I was in, and with a calm born of a deep conviction, I knew it was the truth. Saying the words felt more like coming home than pulling up outside my parents' house the night I returned from New York.

I waited for Job's response.

His head slowly tilted to one side and his shoulders shifted in a small shrug. "What would you like me to do about that?"

I swallowed convulsively. "I want you to tell me you love me."

"No."

His rebuff hit like a punch to the gut. My knees gave way and I landed hard on the bale of hay beside me. I sucked in badly needed air.

"I'm not going to say it."

"Why?"

He walked over and sat on a bale across the aisle from me. "Because not too long ago, you told me you didn't know what you wanted."

I felt the heat of anger from him as he stared at me. I saw the hurt, and did not back away.

"I know, and I know I hurt you because of that. I'm sorry. But it's different now."

"Why?"

Why was I ready now? What had changed? I tossed these questions around in my head, searching for an answer that would let him know that I meant it. That I was ready.

Job gave a derisive snort. "I'm going to get the tractor," he said. "I'd appreciate it if you're gone when I get back."

"Wait!" I cried, suddenly calm again. "I know why I'm ready now."

The answer had come to me. It was the only answer that would do and I believed it was right one.

"Because, Job-like-the-Bible," I said and I felt myself smile, "The good Lord willed it."

Seventeen

December 31, 1939

I watched his face closely and waited. And waited. His skin had just a hint of windburn where it stretched across his cheeks and the slight bump and crook of his nose. A shadow of stubble darkened his jaw.

My eyes moved to his mouth. I wanted it to smile and form the words I desperately needed to hear. I could tell he was worrying the inside of his bottom lip with his teeth.

"Please, Job." I could feel my smile wobble, could hear it in my voice as I struggled to maintain my composure. "I need to know that it's not too late."

"What if I say it is?" He watched me intently.

"I don't know." I pressed my hand against my chest and rubbed against the pain of that thought. It was necessary to concentrate on my breathing to keep from passing out.

"What if I say it's not?"

"I don't know."

I shrugged helplessly. I had not thought beyond the moment we were in. Any illusions I may have held that everything else would fall into place in an orderly fashion once the words had been spoken, were quickly disintegrating.

"Well, I need to know," I said.

He stood and made his way over to the door. He rested his hand on the lever that would open it. "I can't decide one way or the other until I know you've thought about it more."

"I can think about it from now until next year, but it won't change anything."

"It will make you more certain of what you want."

"Don't you mean it would make *you* more certain of what I want?"

I went over and grabbed his shirtsleeve, as it looked like he was about to make an exit. Now that I had started this, I was not going to let him finish it. Not that way.

"If you want to know what I'll do if you tell me it's too late, I don't know. Tell me and I'll find out." My temper threatened to get away from me so I took a deep breath before continuing. "I don't know what will happen either, if you tell me it's not too late. I'd like to think I do, but I don't. Not really, and neither can you, but if you tell me, then we'll find out together. Just don't make this about me not knowing what I want, when I'm finally here telling you I love you!"

I shoved him and stepped back. I was fuming now.

"What is it about then, if it's not that?" He looked away, staring at some spot high on the wall in front of him.

"This is about you refusing to trust that you finally have what you want." I do not know where that revelation came from, but this was turning out to be a night for revelations, so I was willing to run with it. I found it comforting somehow, that he should find himself in a big whoop-de-do. That he would be as crazy with the same insecurity I found in myself. "Sooner or later you're going to have to trust me. Trust that I mean it. Trust that it's real."

"I trust you." He said the words but he did not turn to face me.

"No you don't. Not really."

"Are you calling me a liar?"

"You've never been one before, so I'm not sure why you would start now."

That had his attention. He turned and looked at me finally. Okay, so it was more of a glower really, but at least he was facing me. "That's the problem. I don't think you know what I have or haven't been."

"Fair enough. I'll tell you what I know then." I took a deep breath and began, "I know you've been a better friend to me over the years than I've deserved at times or than I've been to you. I know you care about the things that are important; your parents, the farm, your friends and God, and I know you have them in the right priority. I know that you think things over, maybe way too much before making a decision, but that you're usually right, and I know that makes me nuts sometimes because when I disagree with you, I'll probably be wrong and I really don't like that. But, I know that you've never made me, and will never make me, feel stupid for it."

Here is where I took another deep breath, and put some space between us. The next part would probably be as big a revelation to Job as I found it was to me.

"And I also know that a good portion of the blame for this situation is your own fault."

"My fault?" He scoffed. He stepped towards me, closing the recently created distance. "How did this get to be my fault when you're the one that took forever to realize her feelings?"

"Because you're the one who's never acted on his feelings!"

He looked like I had smacked him, but I refused to back down or be intimidated. His eyebrows went so high they disappeared under his bangs, and his mouth opened but nothing came out. I took advantage of the moment to verbally strike him again.

"Maybe if you had, I wouldn't have wasted so much time on Kenny. Maybe if you'd asked me to the prom in time, I wouldn't have gone with him, but no, you had to think about it—forever. And maybe, just maybe, if you'd kissed me that night down at the creek, we could have saved ourselves a lot of time. You never once, in all the years that we've known each other told me what you wanted. Everyone else seems to know how you feel, but not me, the person you're feeling about. Not even when I left for New York. Why didn't you ask me to stay? Maybe you were right in thinking I wasn't ready to hear it, but we'll never know because you never trusted me with your feelings. You never acted on them."

It was my turn to move to the door. I was just about done, as I had already said more than I ever imagined I would on a subject that I had never been completely comfortable with in the first place.

"I know that's a lot of maybes and yet here we are, once more," I said as I turned to face him, "with you not trusting me, not acting, even though I'm telling you how I feel and asking to know that you feel the same way. I realize I've already taken long enough for both of us, so why don't you save us more time. Just tell me that you love me, or tell me to go."

It hurt that he let me stand there for quite some time without saying a word, and I refused to let him see me cry. I turned my back and prepared to walk out of the barn. I took that first step and grabbed hold of the door lever.

"All right!" he shouted.

I did not dare turn around.

"I love you."

He sounded so annoyed, I almost laughed. I felt the smile and the tears of relief at the same time.

"All right," I whispered. I could not let go of the lever. My tenuous grip on that handle was the only thing keeping me upright.

"Now what?" he asked quietly.

I managed to turn my head enough to look over my shoulder. He sighed and ran his hands through his hair, not caring that he was matting it with dirt and blood.

I shrugged. Like Job, I had never been here before. Perhaps I thought there would be music that would swell with emotion and fill the barn, or fireworks to light the clear night sky with vibrant colors of red and green, or legions of angels singing halleluiahs that would cause the earth to tremble, but there was none of that. There was a dead cow and calf in a barn as the chimes from the Catholic Church on the other side of town struck the hour for the New Year.

I did feel warm inside. Peaceful. And lighter, definitely lighter in my heart and mind, like the right key had slid into the lock and opened it. And it was scary, like the summer I was ten and Job convinced me to jump out of the hayloft. It had taken every nerve of courage I had to make the leap, but I had done it. The freefall into the hay below had been both terrifying and exhilarating. I was in a freefall again. *Now what?*

"I don't know." I offered a smile. I saw one flirting with the corners of Job's mouth. "I guess I'll see you tomorrow."

I heard him laugh as I closed the barn door behind me. I think I heard it all the way home.

Sarah was awake when I crept into my room.

"Is everything all right?" she whispered in the dark.

"Yes. Sorry if I woke you." I felt my way along my bed to where my nightgown lay hidden under my pillow. "Go back to sleep."

"I can't." The sound of rustling bedclothes indicated she was in the process of sitting up. "I'm too excited."

I understood the heightened state of emotion she found herself in. I doubted I would be sleeping much either. Like an over-inflated tire tube, I was ready to burst, and yet I could not bring myself to share my news. It was too new. I wanted to take it out, turn it over in my hands, feel it and explore it without any comment from another as to what shape or form it should take. There were only two people who could decide that, and one of them was not here.

"It's an exciting day," I said and sat on the edge of my bed to change. For more than the sake of modesty I was glad for the dark. I could still feel plastered on my face, the silly grin that had appeared as I made my way home and realized what had just happened.

"Did you see Job tonight?"

"Yes."

"And?"

"We reached an understanding."

"Good. I'm glad."

"Me too."

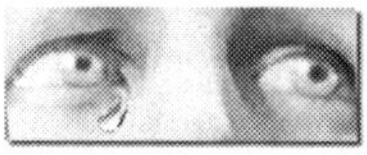

January 1, 1940

The ceremony was a small, simple affair with family and those who were considered family. Although their numbers did not fill the pews, the little white church with its tall steeple was filled to overflowing.

Until the moment I was to step out and walk down the aisle ahead of Sarah, I had not been nervous, but suddenly I found myself taking quick shallow gulps of air. I could not wait to see him. I was giddy with anticipation.

As I walked down the aisle, I could not prevent my eyes from seeking out Job's. He stood tall and straight next to David.

I could not look at him enough. It was a new development, and I took the time to let myself absorb it, to absorb him. I saw reflected on his face the same feelings I knew shone from mine. If all eyes had not turned to the radiant bride as she entered, the moment might have given up our secret.

Both bride and groom said their vows clearly and without wavering. They were pronounced husband and wife and they kissed. I could not help myself. I snuck a look at Job from beneath lowered lashes. He was looking at me.

Heat, slow and steady crept up the back of my neck and into my ears. My cheeks grew warm. I could not help but recall the words I had tossed out at him the previous evening, the ones about what might have happened if he had kissed me down by the creek. Was he thinking the same thing?

I had thought about kissing before, especially the night that Kenny had attempted to navigate the route unsuccessfully. And maybe, once, or twice, but just ever so briefly, in order to dismiss it as nonsense, I had thought about kissing Job.

Now that one thought was at the forefront of my mind and I did not dismiss it as nonsense. But what if I did not like it? I had not liked what Kenny had tried to do. How would kissing Job be different, other than the fact that I now wanted to try kissing Job?

Filled with a jittery energy, I fiddled with the frog pendant hanging from my neck. Two thoughts entered my mind at that point. The first was that I had never, in jest or otherwise, kissed this particular frog. The second thought was: I was done with kissing frogs.

I was disoriented to find Job standing directly in front of me.

"Is something wrong?" he whispered softly and offered his arm. Somehow I had missed the presentation of the bride and groom and their walk down the aisle.

I shook my head slightly, a simultaneous answer to his question and clearing of the distracting thoughts. I took his arm and avoided looking directly at him.

"You had this funny look on your face," Job continued.

If only he knew. I pasted a smile on my face and together we walked down the aisle.

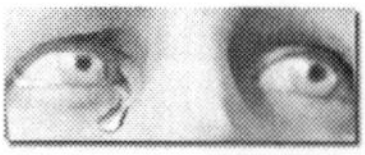

The reception lunch was held at the Nightingale farm, as the house was the biggest. It was Job's wedding gift to David, that and a good price on a small piece of land at the edge of the property closest to town. I believe Job would have given it to him for nothing, had he felt David would have accepted it. Instead, a fair deal was struck, and after a brief trip back to Philadelphia to pack up their belongings, Sarah and David would be returning to Little River Junction to begin their life together. They had rented a small apartment in town over Martin's General Store, which was owned and operated by Kenny's father. They would live there until their new house could be built.

"Grab your coat," David said to Sarah after the main festivities had been seen to. "I'll show you where our house will be. Then we'll get ready and go."

"I still can't believe it." Sarah shook her head and laughed. "I never would have imagined."

"Soon there'll be no need for imagination." My mother gave her a hug and a gentle push to the door. "In the meantime, go and dream while we clean up."

"I'm so happy for them." I said to my mom as I waited for her to shut the door.

"Me too." She took my arm as though to turn and walk with me to the kitchen. I knew, from the way my mother smiled, who had entered the front hall behind me.

"Job," my mother said and gave him the kind of hug she would give Michael or David. "I just can't thank you enough for this afternoon."

"It was my pleasure, Mrs. Bingham. I was happy to be able to do it." He stepped back after returning the embrace and turned to me. "Are you busy at the moment? There's something I'd like to show you."

I told myself not to react out of the ordinary. After letting my imagination run away for that brief moment in the church, I was careful to keep a tight watch over it, lest I give something away. In a silent game played by unspoken mutual consent, we walked in friendly circles around each other all afternoon, enjoying the brief moments of close proximity that circumstances, such as posing for pictures, provided.

On those occasions the lingering touch or pressure of his hand on my back or at my waist told me what he would not reveal to anyone else. And in response, if I leaned in a little closer than usual, no one noticed, except Job. Inside I was jubilant while outwardly I smiled and laughed and carried on as though my life had not changed in any manner whatsoever.

"I have to help clean up." I answered his question, trying for a mildly disappointed look, before turning to my mother. "I'll have time before we go right?"

"Why don't you just go now," my mother said as I was hoping she would. "There are more than enough hands to help here."

"Really?"

"Have fun."

"Thanks mom." I kissed her cheek.

"Yes. Thank you, Mrs. Bingham." Job smiled at her. "Let's get your coat Jessie, and your boots."

"Where are we going?" I asked a few minutes later as I slipped out of my shoes and stepped into my boots.

"The Cottage."

I looked up in surprise.

"It's all right," he said. "It's something good. Something that happened after you left last night."

Was it just last night? I felt myself grin and pulled my upper lip between my teeth to keep the smile from taking over. He grinned back.

"Let's go." I opened the front door and stepped out onto the front veranda.

It was strange to be with him without a number of other people present. I found that I was a little tongue-tied. I think he was too, for when I did sneak a peek up at him, I caught him sneaking a peek at me and we both looked away, and then back, and then away. It became a game that made for precarious walking through knee-deep snow, and yet allowed for much amusement. We were still laughing in the barn when Job took my hand and led me to a stall half way down.

"Look inside," he said and waited for me to peek over the wall.

My eyes widened in amazement. Inside was a cow and her calf, just hours old. The calf lying on the straw in the corner was the spitting image of Blizzard.

"Is it his?" I asked.

"Yes."

"It's a girl!" I realized with excitement when the calf stood.

The protective mother watched us warily from the stall as her young one peeked cautiously out from behind.

"They're beautiful."

"So are you."

Just like that, the atmosphere in the barn changed. I became aware of the fact that he still held my hand. It was not the first time he had taken my hand; it just felt like it. The nerve endings in my hand had come alive. He shifted his grip so that our fingers were intertwined. I returned the squeeze of his fingers and looked up into his face. He was smiling but there was a hint of self-consciousness or uncertainty, maybe both, in his eyes.

"I've been waiting for a quiet moment with you all day," he said. "So I could tell you that, without anyone else around to interrupt. And to tell you again that I love you. I still find it hard to believe that I can say those words to you. You did say them too, right? I wasn't just imagining that?"

"No." I smiled. "I love you too."

I laughed with him as he made a big show of sighing with relief. There was an awkward moment once the laughter had died down where it seemed as though both of us wanted to do or say something, anything, but did not know quite what would be appropriate.

"Did you tell your mom?" he asked.

"I didn't tell anyone. You?"

"No."

"I didn't want to share it yet." I shrugged. "I wanted to keep it all for me. For us."

"Yeah, me too."

"And I didn't want to take anything away from Sarah and David." I hesitated because the idea I was about to express was just forming. I needed to make sure I said it correctly. "The thing is…."

"What?"

"I don't think I want to tell anyone yet." I looked at him to see if I could gauge what he was thinking. I took his nod as an indication he was listening and rushed on. "I just want it to be you and me for a little longer. Everyone will be so happy for us and they'll start asking questions we haven't even asked ourselves. Or they'll make comments and feel like they have the right too. All I want is for us to be the ones in control of this right now, so that when the comments and the questions come we can answer them together."

"I understand."

"You do? I mean, I don't want you to think that I'm afraid to let people know. I'm not, at least not for any other reason than I don't want them to step into it."

"I was thinking the same thing," he said. "There's been enough meddling in our relationship already. I could see it happening, but I let it because it suited what I wanted. That's my fault, and I don't want it to happen again. I won't let it."

"I like what I'm feeling." I looked into his face and embraced the warm rush that filled my heart. "I like how I feel knowing you feel the same way about me. Everyone knows so much about us and our lives. Except this." I raised our clasped hands. "This is just ours."

"They won't be happy if we keep it from them. You have to know that." His eyes searched mine to confirm I understood the ramifications of what we were discussing.

"Is it wrong if I say, 'I don't care'?"

"Probably." He smiled slowly. "But it could be fun."

"When the time is right, when we're ready, we will tell them." I felt myself return his smile. "But only when we're ready."

"Agreed." He bent his head slightly, pulled our linked hands closer and pressed a kiss against the back of my hand.

My heart kicked into a higher rate with a *kagung* I thought for certain could be heard outside my body. My free hand sought out the little frog that hung around my neck, my fingers running over the familiar ridges and points like a blind person gathering information from a pattern of Braille dots on a page.

"Do you know I've never actually kissed this frog?" I waited a beat before checking his reaction.

His smile was gone and his eyes narrowed in intensity as he scrutinized the charm I twirled between my fingers.

"Why not?" His gaze found and held mine.

"Maybe I was afraid of being disappointed again."

"And now?"

"Now, I'm thinking I should take the chance. What do you think?"

"You might as well see where it takes you."

My hand was trembling. I raised the little charm, slowly. If what I thought, and what I hoped would happen did happen, there would be no turning back. No undoing it. It was already too late for that. Words had been said.

I kept my eyes on his but when he did not move, I hesitated. He was supposed to move right? That was how I saw it work in the movies.

"Second thoughts?" he said. The look in his eyes said he too realized there would be no turning back. The slight smirk he wore issued a challenge. He knew what strings to pull.

I closed my eyes and continued the little frog's journey to my lips. That is when it happened; instead of contacting hard metal, I felt the tender brush of his lips against mine. Every thought, every sound, every smell faded from consciousness. My whole being was fixed on that point of contact.

His lips were warm and softer than I expected, but then I had not really known what to expect. Certainly the overwhelming rush of blood through my body was a surprise. I opened my eyes slowly and met his. He was so serious I could not help but smile. Whatever this feeling was inside me, I wanted more.

"Hello," I said. "I've been looking for you."

"I've been waiting for you," he replied.

I laughed and threw my arms around his neck and squeezed. He laughed too. It was just contagious, this thing inside me.

I felt myself lifted off my feet as he hugged me tight. On impulse I placed a hand on either side of his face and pressed my lips against his. That was it. It made sense suddenly. All awareness of time was gone as we explored new tastes and textures. The more I kissed him, the more I wanted to kiss him. I lost myself in it willingly.

That is where David and Sarah found us; standing in the middle of the Cottage, arms wrapped around each other and lips locked together.

I believe David's words went something like: "I'm sorry Sarah. When I said there was something you might like to see in here, this wasn't exactly what I'm meant."

Job and I sprang apart with matching expressions of surprise, embarrassment and guilt. I felt my face flame and pressed my hands to hot cheeks. Red crept up the back of Job's neck, a sure sign that he too was uncomfortable. David and Sarah on the other hand, stood before us grinning like two cats discovering an entire flock of cream covered canaries.

"I wanted to show Sarah the calf," David explained calmly. "I see you two have managed to put things right between you."

"You might say that," Job nodded and despite my mortification, I fought a giggle.

The four of us stood there staring at each other for a minute in an absurd snapshot of social awkwardness. What was the proper thing to say in such a situation? And, so much for our secret.

"Last night when you said you two had reached an understanding, I had no idea you meant this." Sarah finally broke the tension and gave me a quick hug. "I think it's wonderful. David we should be going."

David nodded without looking at her. He stared hard at Job. "But, that's my sister he was kissing."

"It didn't look like she minded," Sarah said then blushed as she gave me an apologetic look.

"It's not her I'm worried about." David turned his look on me. "How do you feel about him, Jessie?"

I knew the reason for his blunt question. He wanted assurances that I was not starting something I had no intentions of finishing. He wanted to know that it was real and not something I was trying on for size. I could not return it, if it did not fit.

"I love him," I told him simply and in spite of the discomfort of being caught as we were, I could not help but smile. I know we were not going to tell anyone, but I felt that anything less than the truth, considering the circumstances, might prove detrimental in some manner. I also knew that if there was a person I could trust to help us and not hinder in anyway, it was David.

"And I love her." Job spoke up and placed his arm around my waist.

"If I thought otherwise, this would be going differently." David smiled at his friend and extended his hand. "I'm happy for you."

Job shook David's hand. "Thanks. It means a lot."

"Okay, so now we know where they stand with each other," Sarah said and took hold of David's arm, "Why don't we leave them and go back up to the house? I'm sure everyone is waiting to say goodbye to us."

"Why don't we all go back together?" David gave Job a look I did not understand. "We can share the good news with everyone."

"No!" Job and I said in unison and with identical panic. We looked at each other and started to laugh.

"You can't tell anyone." I said a little calmer.

"Why not?" Sarah asked. "It's great news."

"We want to keep it to ourselves for awhile." Job answered. "We want to get used to it all without any interference from anyone."

"David, you know what we're talking about," I said.

We waited while we watched David think. Finally with a shake of his head he sighed. "I can see how there might be certain expectations placed on you now."

"It would be nice if we had our own before we took on anyone else's," Job stated. He smiled down at me and took my hand.

"Well, it won't stay quiet for long if you keep looking at each other in that way." Sarah observed.

Eighteen

Winter and Spring 1940

It had been easier than we expected, keeping our secret. It was, at first, a game we enjoyed. Job and I would make no attempt to hide the fact that we were spending time together or going out, expecting at every turn to be called to account for it, and surprised each time we were not. I do not know why we were surprised, for on the surface we were not behaving any differently than we had for most of our lives.

It was beneath the surface that things had changed. It was there that the current pulled us along together. Neither one of us could have escaped should we have wanted to. The more time that passed, it became less of a game and more of a treasure that we hoarded between us. It was a time of growing together and learning about each other in new ways that included, but went beyond, the original boundaries of our friendship, and were unfettered by the expectations and pressures of others. If I found myself thinking I could not feel any more for the man I was discovering than I did in that moment, then the next would prove me wrong. It started on our first official date.

He took my hand in his. Even that most innocent of contact was enough to increase the rate at which my heart beat and cause my breath to catch in my chest. I wondered at this new awareness and how quickly it had taken hold. I wondered if he felt it also, and what we would do about it.

"Tell me about New York." He squeezed my fingers and I realized I had been staring at our joined hands. We were on our way out to dinner and a show, the first time in almost a week we were actually able to sit down and have a private conversation.

Talking over the phone was just too much of a risk, especially since it was possible the telephone operator might be listening. If the operator in question should be Margie Walters, and chances were good it would be, it was highly probable she was listening, and Margie was a gossip. She took pride in knowing about things before they were printed in The Grand River Junction Gazette, and spread them about freely. People only read the paper to confirm what they already knew from Margie's accounts.

I told him about my arrival and my first impressions of the city. I described the awe I felt at seeing the Empire State Building and standing on its observation deck high above the city and the world. I mentioned the frantic energy I felt standing in Times Square for the first time and how amazed I was at the number of people there were. I wondered where they were all going in such a hurry. I talked about how it all made me feel lost and made me long for the view of the mountains we constantly took for granted day after day. I entertained him with tales of the exploits of the girls in the dorm, exaggerating eccentricities only slightly for effect.

I spoke more solemnly about my difficulties at school, and with great affection, I talked of Professor Williamson. I explained how it was through his words of encouragement that the professor had given me the courage to come home. By the time it was all told, we had arrived at the restaurant. It was not one I had been to before, and it was not in Grand River Junction.

"Miss Bellows Falls Diner," I read the sign. "Are we in Bellows Falls?"

I had become so engrossed in our conversation that I had failed to notice the direction we were going in or the time it was taking us to get there. Bellow's Falls was two hours from Grand River Junction.

"Yes." Job shut the passenger door behind me. He placed his hand on the small of my back and guided me to the door of the diner. "I figured there would be less chance that we would run into people we know here."

Over dinner, I asked him when had learned to draw so well. I referred to the amusing illustrations of frogs that had appeared in many of his letters that he had written to me over the years he was at school and which became especially detailed during the time I was in New York.

With a modest shrug, he admitted that it was something that as a boy, he discovered he could do. He revealed that he sometimes painted to relax.

"Water colors mostly," he said and ducked his chin. "Just for myself. I don't show them to anyone."

"Did you ever want to do more with it?" After all the time we had spent together over the years, the fact that I did not know about this part of his life humbled me. Perhaps I had been a little too self-absorbed.

"There are only two things that I've ever really dreamed of. Owning the farm and hearing you say that you love me. I have both now, and I am very content."

Content. I briefly wondered when I would begin to feel that way. What exactly did it mean to feel that way?

The color was high across his cheeks and neck. He stared intently into my eyes. The pulse in his temple beat erratically. It was this that made me understand being vulnerable was not easy for him either. I had the power to hurt him beyond anything I had yet done, and he had given it to me.

"I'm glad." I smiled with a shake of my head. "I just find it hard to comprehend that I've known you longer than not, and I never knew you could draw."

"Stick around, Doll Face." He said in his best Bogey imitation, which was not that good. "There's a lot about me you don't know. See?"

"Doll Face?" I chuckled. "What am I, your moll?"

"That's right. You got a problem with that?" His eyes were twinkling with merriment. With a flourish he tossed the money for the bill on the table.

"Come on Pally," I just laughed again. "We'll be late for the movie."

"Stick with me Doll Face. Everything will come out aces, you'll see."

"Jeepers, that's swell, Pally."

A few heads turned at our laughter as we left the restaurant but we did not care.

We also did not care that we were the last to leave the theatre. If the owner had not come along and asked us to leave, we would have sat there all night long.

We were doing nothing more than sitting and holding hands, but we were together and it felt right. Neither one of us had wanted to bring the night to a close.

Inside the truck, I leaned into Job for warmth. Frost glazed the outer edges of the windshield and my breath was visible as it escaped between chattering teeth. I sniffed a nose that ran from cold.

"Tonight was swell. Thank you."

"What did I tell you, Doll Face? Aces. Everything was Aces." He pulled the vehicle onto the highway and headed for home.

I chuckled and leaned my head on his shoulder. We settled into a companionable silence and I closed my eyes just thinking about how we were the same together, and yet completely different. The rumble of the engine, together with the whir of rubber tires on asphalt combined to lull me into a doze where my thoughts wandered. The roads had been paved several years before as part of the state's effort to create jobs for many of the unemployed. Michael had done it for a summer, and I wondered if he had worked on this section. They had yet to get to the road that led to Job's farm, but the accounts in the paper said it would happen this coming summer.

"You asleep?" he asked softly.

"Not quite." I yawned and snuggled closer to him. "Why?"

"There's something I need to talk to you about. I don't know how to say it except to be blunt, so if what I have to say makes you uncomfortable you need to let me know."

"All right." I sat up and turned so I could look at him. The darkness made it difficult to read his face.

"There's never been anyone for me but you." He squeezed my hand. "I've never even kissed another girl."

"Not even when you were away at school?"

"Not even then." He turned to look at me. "I took a couple of girls out once or twice, and I thought about it."

I did not comment, needing a moment to absorb the idea of Job out with another girl.

"I just always, ever, only, wanted you."

I sensed his internal debate over what I presume was the choice of his next words. "Kissing you is dangerous."

The thought was so absurd to me I just about laughed out loud.

"It makes me want to do more than kiss you."

I stopped laughing and gave thanks for the darkness that hid his discomfort from me. It meant that my own was hidden from him. His words had provided me with the means to define the edgy feeling that had been there since the night in the barn. It had been buzzing just beneath the surface layer of my skin the entire week, making it difficult to think of anything except being with him again and filling my senses with him. It was a craving. It was desire, and it was the first time I had ever felt it.

I did not know how to respond, so I sat staring mutely out at the darkness. I heard his heavy exhale. He let go of my hand to run his through his hair and over his face—a sure indication there was more to come.

"That night, after David and Sarah found us, David reminded me of something I was very close to forgetting."

"I thought we weren't going to let other people interfere?" I was annoyed that David would comment on our relationship considering his understanding of our concerns.

"We aren't." He took my hand again. "But in this case, I'm glad he did."

He turned to me again and made sure I was listening attentively before he continued. "While you and I might love each other, we are not man and wife. Do you understand what I'm saying?"

I could only nod. I believed, as he did, certain intimacies were reserved for marriage. My parents had raised me to believe it. I had been taught the Bible says that is how God meant for it to be. I also understood the world was changing. More and more, people believed they knew better where the boundaries of morality should lie, choosing to ignore those laid out by God.

In New York, I had been in the room on occasion when the subject was being discussed among my peers. The knowledgeable and sophisticated air with which the girls spoke had contributed to my feelings of awkwardness and alienation. They talked about sex so casually; as though it were just the latest dance crave sweeping the nation, like the samba introduced at the World's Fair the year before. For them it was the natural progression of a relationship. I kept silent in my corner of the room and listened as my sense of inadequacy grew. My experience was limited to the offensive incident with Kenny Martin. Fear of ridicule kept me too intimidated to ask them what all the fuss was about, but I was starting to gain a measure of comprehension.

I had only kissed Job, and it had only been that one time, but immediately I had wanted to do it again. I found it extremely intriguing that particular want could lead to something more, and here was Job, admitting to me that he was feeling the temptation. It did not help me that I knew I made him feel that way.

I concentrated on the sensation of his thumb rubbing over the back of my hand and pondered the best way to bring up my newest concern. I had tasted sweet fruit, and while I understood the consequences of overindulgence were more severe than an upset tummy, I did want to see if it was as sweet as memory held.

"Does that mean you're not going to kiss me again?" I asked.

There was a beat of silence.

"Goodness, no!" He shook his head and chuckled. The intensity of the moment diffused. I found myself sharing his laughter.

He stopped the truck in the middle of the road and thoroughly answered my question, just in case I still held any doubt.

"I love you." He said releasing me slowly. "But we're going to have to help each other keep our heads on straight. One day at a time."

A short time later we were parked in front of my house. Out of the corner of my eye I caught a movement in the window of the house across the street. Seconds later the outside porch light of the house came on, casting a glow that fell short of the truck, and with an inward sigh, I knew there would be nothing to keep our heads about tonight. Mr. Lawhead, the owner of the porch light, had brought more than one youthful indiscretion of Michael's, David's, or mine to my father's attention. Michael said on several occasions that he still tasted soap every time he saw the man.

I pulled away from Job and scooted over to the door. Before I opened it, I held out my hand. "Thanks for the lovely evening."

"You're welcome." He played along, unaware of our potential audience, and shook my hand. With a grin he started to lean closer. With much regret, I freed my hand, opened the door and popped out of the truck.

"I love you," I whispered. "And nosey Mr. Lawhead is watching."

I closed the door on his very surprised face and gave a cheeky wave as I backed up the walk to my house. It was hard to be certain in the dark, but I believe, before I spun away, I saw him banging his head against the steering wheel.

After that, most of our outings were evenings spent at David and Sarah's, where we were chaperoned while we played games and listened to the radio or, every now and then, danced to a gramophone recording. Occasionally Job and I slipped away to Baldwin and occasionally back to Bellows Falls for the opportunity to sit in the back of a dark theatre and hold hands or share a sweet kiss or two, or three, or more.

We dealt with that area of our relationship in our own way. By agreement, and after one late night of doing nothing more than talking at the kitchen table—well almost nothing more—I did not step into the farmhouse alone with Job again. The allure and opportunity that privacy provided was dangerous, and we both recognized it. In response, prayer became a vital aid in our determination to keep things honorable before God—prayer and the ever present and watchful eye of Mr. Lawhead.

Gradually, the urgency that had gripped us so fiercely in the beginning abated over the weeks. Passion and desire remained and, in fact, deepened in direct correlation to our becoming more intimate on levels of spirit and intellect. It was the desperateness of having to be with each other that lessened.

We found a rhythm that we could both keep time with, and so we followed it, but with each passing day and week, I found myself wanting to change the tempo, to speed it up. I was questioning our choice of keeping things a secret for so long, and I was being questioned about our relationship.

June 1940

It was the end of June, almost my birthday, which meant for over six months we had managed to continue without discovery. I thought about how unaware I had been of the rate at which time had passed, and just how easy it had actually been to pass it undetected. Certainly there had been a few raised eyebrows from Mrs. White, but she never asked for information and I never volunteered any. Besides as the time grew closer for Laura to have her baby, Mrs. White was too preoccupied to care about what Job and I were up to. She would be leaving for Maine shortly and I would run the store, with Sarah's help.

My mother had, on occasion, suggested I might want to spend less time with Job and focus on trying to meet someone else, but when I pointed out that I already knew everyone my age and none of them appealed to me, she let the subject drop, except that one night.

My mother was still in the living room tidying up when I let myself in through the front door. It was after a trip to Bellows Falls for a movie with Job.

We had left much earlier in the day as Job wanted to stop and check out the creamery complex in the town.

I paused and pressed a hand to my still tingling lips, hoping against hope there was not some way for her to know by looking at me that I had been, and not too long ago, just saying a pleasant good night to Job.

I tried to appear casual as I stepped into the archway that opened into the living room.

"Hi. What are you still doing up?" I asked.

"I'm not quite ready to go upstairs yet. I thought I would tidy up a bit." She hesitated briefly then turned to face me. "I thought you and Job were going to a movie?"

"We did. Why?" I used hanging up my sweater as a reason to keep my face partially averted. I could feel my heart pound in my chest. Had we been discovered? Did she know? Was she angry?

"Your father and I decided we would go too. We looked, but didn't see you anywhere at the theatre."

Uh oh.

"In Baldwin?" I asked and waited while she nodded an affirmative response before plumping a pillow.

I could tell something more than just not seeing us at the theatre was bothering her but I stuck to the topic at hand, relieved they had not been in the same movie house that we had been.

"Job and I decided to go to Bellows Falls," I said and walked to the bottom of the stairs. "We went to Baldwin last week. Besides, Job wanted to check out the creamery there."

"You didn't mention that when you talked about your plans."

"You didn't mention you might want to join us." I put a hand on the newel at the bottom of the stairs hoping to put an end to any further talk. "Maybe next time we can go together. Good night."

"Jessie, wait." My heart sank. I had only made it up one stair.

"Come. Sit." My mother patted the cushion of the sofa. "There's something I want to talk to you about."

"Can it wait? I'm pretty tired." I reluctantly backed down the step I had climbed.

"Do you think spending so much time with Job is fair to him." She approached me instead of waiting to see if I would sit.

"Why wouldn't it be?"

She shrugged and leaned against the archway wall in a casual manner that was not at all as it seemed. "I guess because of how he feels about you."

"We've had this discussion." She had plucked a very sensitive nerve and I reacted with a mental jerk.

"No we haven't. Not this one." She jerked back. "We've talked about you finding someone else. Now we're talking about you letting Job find someone else."

"Okay, but why are we talking about it?"

I wanted to scream what was really in my head, that he was not going to find someone else. He had who he wanted, and so did I, but I kept it to myself. If my mother was this bothered by the idea that I would be interfering in Job's future happiness, how much more bothered would she be when it was revealed that we had kept our happiness from them. I should have told her then, but it was not solely my decision to make.

"I've told you before, Job and I have an understanding. We like what our relationship is and we're keeping it that way."

"But Jessie—"

"No, Mom! He's a grown man. He makes his own decisions. If he wants to spend time with me, that's his choice."

I climbed two steps at once, hoping to leave it at that.

"What about the future?" She raised her voice to match mine.

"What about it?" I turned and looked down at her from where I stood.

"I just don't think either one of you is thinking about it."

The argument had ended almost immediately, when my father had appeared at the top of the steps to find out what the raised voices were all about.

She had been right though, my mother, I had not really considered anything beyond one day at a time, and he never broached the subject of the future with me. I had not yet brought the subject up with Job. I was not positive I knew how to without seeming to be fishing for answers to questions neither of us had asked.

Frustration and annoyance stirred. I decided to clean my room.

Nineteen

June 1940

I went through my room, putting aside clothing no longer worn. I found myself smiling when I realized just how many items had previously belonged to Michael or David. I still wore things that were considered tomboyish, it was more practical on certain occasions, but I began to realize how much working for Mrs. White had done for my sense of style. In my next letter to Laura, I would have to tell her of my observation. She would be so proud.

I sorted through old high school papers, pulling out stories and reading with a critical revisionist eye. I added the stories to the collection of essays written in New York and promptly knocked them over as I turned away too quickly.

Among the scattered papers, I found a letter from Job. Somehow I had missed it in the sorting. I smiled at the little frog arched backward in a dive off his lily pad. I realized that it looked like a question mark, and the longer I examined the sketch, the more certain I became that it was exactly that.

Intrigued, I collected all the other letters Job had written to me while I was in New York. I separated those with frogs from those without. I was left with seven. I gave intense scrutiny to those drawings which had previously received only a cursory, albeit appreciative glance.

One frog raised a top hat and looked like the letter Y. Another had been drawn in a forward hopping motion indicated by a double arched line. An M. So far I had the word, 'my.'

"My what?" I wondered out loud. Other frogs formed letters that would fall in no discernable order until my mind registered the date of each letter. I arranged them on the floor before me in chronological order.

My vision wavered between dancing frogs and the darkness of unconsciousness. If I had not been sitting down, I would have fallen into a lump on the floor. I shook my head, forced myself to empty my lungs, filled them again, and then repeated the instructions. In. Out. I looked at the letters once more.

Marry me?

In. Out.

He had asked me to be his wife before ever being certain of how I felt about him. Considering my emotional state at the time it was probably just as well I had not discovered the hidden message, but now things were different. Now he knew how I felt about him and how he felt about me, yet not once in the past few months had he broached the subject of marriage or hinted at that type of commitment. There was no careless tossing about of phrases like, "When we're married…" or "When our children…" Why?

I did not think he had changed his mind, so I considered everything I had learned about him and drew this conclusion. He was waiting again, biding his time until he thought I was ready. Immediately I was angry and wanted to confront him about holding back. Then I had to think about myself. Was I ready?

There were still times when the fact that I was in love with Job Nightingale left me dazed and amazed, times when the power of my feelings almost dropped me to my knees. Now I had to add marriage to the pot. Yes, I thought about what it might be like to be married to Job, but they were distant passing thoughts that floated in the realm of possibility. Now they had substance in the realm of reality, solid form on the floor right in front of me.

I made my way over to the window. I opened it to let the cool spring breeze slide over my face and neck, and inhaled air scented with rain and pine trees. Sudden but brief spring and summer storms were common in the area. They arrived with a dramatic but cleansing flash and bang before moving on over the mountains.

For me New York had not been the answer. I did not feel at home there. But here, in Grand River Junction I knew what my life was. This was my home.

I also knew that I loved Job with every fiber of my just about nineteen-year-old self. If I married Job, Little River Junction, Vermont, would be my home forever. Yet, without him, I would not feel at home anywhere, not even here.

I had to marry Job.

With a deep sense of peace layered with a dusting of nervous anticipation, I determined that I did not want to wait another moment without telling him. But, how to do that?

A plan was already formulating in my mind as I changed my clothes quickly and crept downstairs. It was not quite half past three in the morning. I needed to catch Job before he went to the barns. If I got to the farm in time, he should still be sleeping, or at least in the house.

I left the road and cut through a hay field hoping to avoid detection by Pops, or one of the others, should they be up and about. It would be difficult to explain what I was doing sneaking up the drive at that early hour. The house was still dark when I entered the back yard, but that did not mean that Job was inside. I could hear the stirring of animals waiting to be let into the barns. He could already be there.

Job's bedroom window was at the back and was open. I panicked momentarily when I questioned whether or not Job still slept in that room. With his parents in their own house across the way, I wondered if he had moved into their old room. It was larger, but at the front of the house. The topic had just never come up, and I was reluctant to head around the front.

I took a chance and picked up a pebble. After a quick prayer of thanks for the years spent playing baseball, I tossed the small stone at the window. With a "clink" it bounced harmlessly off the glass pane.

I waited.

Nothing.

"Clink." Another stone and another wait.

Maybe he had moved around to the front? Or maybe he was down in the barn? I picked up a bigger pebble this time, about twice the size of my thumbnail, and tossed it upwards toward the open part of the window. Unfortunately Job chose that moment to place his sleepy face in that exact spot.

I winced when the small stone connected with his forehead, grateful that it had been a gentle toss and not a throw. I snickered a little too. I blame it on nerves, and not the comical look of confusion as Job shook his head and rubbed the spot where the pebble had connected.

"Psst." I whispered.

He frowned and looked around the yard.

I stepped to the edge of the shadows. "Down here!"

"Jes?"

"Yeah. Sorry about that."

"What are –?"

I held a finger to my lips.

"What are you doing here?" He said softer this time.

"I needed to tell you something."

"What?"

I stepped back as the light came on in his parents' kitchen. "At the creek."

"Give me fifteen minutes?"

I nodded and waited until his head disappeared inside before I snuck around the house and back through the field. It would take me close to fifteen minutes to get there the way I was going, but I really did not want to be discovered.

He had not arrived yet by the time I entered the clearing, so I sat in the grass, not caring that the dew was soaking my behind. I grew more nervous by the minute. It had been much more than fifteen minutes. I was headed back toward the farmhouse when I saw him.

He strode down the path with a carefree gate. He wore a sleeveless undershirt beneath faded denim overalls. His arms swung easily at his sides. They were long and well muscled. His hair was damp around his face and clung to his forehead in pieces while the rest bounced slightly with each step. He lifted a hand in greeting when he saw me waiting. The smile that lit his face banished any prepared speech I might have made.

I ran to meet him and wrapped my arms around his waist. He was warm and solid and smelled of something that was uniquely him.

"Good morning to you too." He laughed and squeezed me tight. "Is everything all right?"

"Yes." I snuggled closer.

"Good. I just stopped by the barns so nobody would come looking for me." He kept his arms about me as he walked us to the edge of the creek bank. He sat and pulled me down so I sat across his lap. He pressed a kiss to the top of my head. "What are you doing up this early?"

"I haven't been to bed yet."

"Why not?"

I swallowed hard. Now that the moment had arrived, it felt like a hundred frogs were leaping around inside of me and one was stuck in my throat.

"Yes." I could not get out more than a whisper as I found myself unexpectedly shy.

He bent his head to see my face better. "Yes? What does that mean?"

"Yes." I managed a little louder. "I said, yes."

"Yes, what?"

"Yes." I looked directly into his eyes for emphasis.

He raised his eyebrows in a gesture that said he still did not understand.

And I thought I was slow on the uptake at times. With a heavy sigh, I extricated myself from his arms and carefully stepped into the creek. It was cold, almost painfully so.

I began to search the shallower water at the edge of the bank.

"What are you doing?" He pulled off his boots and socks and slipped his feet into the water.

"Shhh." I held a finger to my lips as I spied what I was searching for. My pounce was successful.

I held the little frog up and being careful not to hurt the creature, I spread his forelegs apart and let his hind legs dangle straight below.

"Y." I said and waited for his reaction.

His eyes narrowed slightly.

"E." Without much success I tried to shape the little creature.

Job had grown absolutely still. I think he was holding his breath.

"S!" I exclaimed as the frog gained his hard fought for freedom and landed with a plop in front of me.

He remained motionless, looking like he wanted to believe that I was referring to what he thought I was, but could not quite accept it. I flicked water at him. The drops landed along his upper body and face. The look in his eyes shifted, daring me to do it again.

"Yes! Yes! Yes!" I punctuated each word with a shower of water in his direction.

With a loud whoop, he pushed off the bank. Too late, I tried to dodge his attack and we both went under the water. I surfaced coughing and sputtering through laughter. I attempted to push the hair out of my face. He laughed and dove at me again. This time he pulled me tight against him.

"Say it again." He whispered against my ear.

"Yes." My arms wrapped tightly around his neck. "I'll marry you."

His kiss was different. Yet another layer to savor. Laughing and breathless, we made our way back to the shore. With our faces turned skyward, we collapsed side by side.

"I didn't think you'd figure out what I was doing with the letters." He laced his fingers with mine and brought my hand to his lips.

"I probably would not have, if my mom and I hadn't argued, making me angry enough to clean my room," I confessed. "She was concerned that neither one of us were thinking about the future. It made me start thinking about things like marriage and how you never talked about the subject. I was angry because I thought you were holding back again."

I turned my head in his direction to see how he reacted to that. He had the grace to look sheepish. I pushed myself up on my elbows and leaned over him. "I'm ready for this, Job. I want this."

I lay back down searching for the right words to tell him what I felt then, and what I was feeling now. "I stayed up all night thinking about how everything has led to this moment. Any way I looked at it, I discovered that to be the truth. And so I took my certainty and came to tell you."

"When you first came home from New York," he started as he rolled onto his side and ran his index finger across my eyebrows and down my nose. "I thought you didn't tell me you were back right away because you'd found the message and didn't know how to tell me, no. And after we talked in the truck, I really thought that was it."

His finger traced the outline of my lips I caught his hand with mine and kissed his palm before burying my cheek in it.

"I had to keep them all," I said. "I'm so glad I did."

"I am too, except I didn't think you'd ever figure out what I did, so I was planning on asking you again. Only in person this time."

"You can ask me any way you want and the answer will still be the same."

He lay back down and pulled me over so my head lay on his chest. His fingers smoothed the hair at my temples in a slow rhythm so soothing I found my eyelids growing heavy. My heartbeat settled into the same easy tempo as his. I was so content where I was, I never wanted to move. My thoughts were as lazy as my body as they drifted from the present to the future.

"My mother is going to be so angry when she finds out." I said with a yawn. "So is yours."

"You can't tell them yet." His voice rumbled in his chest.

"Why not? Don't you want them to know?"

"Not yet."

"Why?" I propped myself up so I could look down at him.

"Please, Jessie?" His smile was pleading and hopeful all at once. "Just a little longer?"

"Okay, but how long?"

"You'll know." He lifted his head and kissed me softly. "Trust me?"

I acquiesced despite the urge inside to take out a full page advertisement in the New York Times. I was going to be Jessie Nightingale. Mrs. Job Nightingale.

My birthday came and went, and still, no announcement. I received a large flat rectangular gift instead of the small box I had started hoping for.

With great care, I untied the ribbon and peeled back the cloth wrapped protectively around the object. I covered my open mouth with a hand that trembled more than slightly. The painting was a watercolor in a simple wooden frame. It portrayed a little red haired girl seated on the bank of a creek. In her hands, she held a large bullfrog up to lips gently pursed in a kiss. In the bottom right corner it was signed "J. Nightingale."

"It's absolutely remarkable," my mother said examining the piece for the third time. "I had no idea you were an artist."

"There's a lot you don't know." Job quipped with a wink. I nearly choked on my root beer. He thumped me on the back. "Careful, Jes."

"Again with the frogs," was Mrs. Nightingale's only comment.

Mrs. White called at that moment with the news that her granddaughter, Andrea Jessie, had arrived that afternoon weighing in at a healthy seven pounds. I finally had a reason to let out the emotions swirling inside me, and have no one question the reason for tears.

Later, I found myself lying in bed and wishing there had been a way for me to find a moment alone with Job. I did not have the opportunity to thank him properly for his gift, or to ask about other things, and I was running out of patience. In a few more days it would be July. How much longer would he insist on waiting?

A 'tap-tap-tap' on the window pulled me out of my reverie. Cautiously I crept over and pulled back the curtain. It took a fright filled moment for me to realize that the gruesome face mashed up against the glass belonged to my dearest. With one hand I clutched my chest to ensure my heart was still inside it. With the other hand, I shook a fist at him. He pulled back in silent laughter.

I eased the window open with the temptation of pushing him off the roof in the forefront of my mind. When he captured my lips with his however, all thoughts of bodily harm fled.

"I just wanted to say goodnight." He beamed revealing both rows of teeth.

"How did you get up here?" I leaned out looking for a ladder but found none.

"It was easy." He pointed to the large maple that hung over the roof of the garage. Its branches were strong and thick with age. From there he had stepped across the short distance to the roof of the house and worked his way along the overhang to my window.

"You're nuts."

"About you." He kissed the tip of my nose.

I felt myself grinning stupidly.

"About the painting," I said. "I love it. I love you. Thank you."

"You're welcome."

"Job, I—"

He placed a finger on my lips.

"Soon, Jes." His lips replaced his finger. "Soon."

I watched as he dropped from the tree to the ground. I blew him a kiss and he waved before disappearing into the night. I left the window open with the thought that it was probably a good thing I had not known, when I was younger, how easy the route of escape could be.

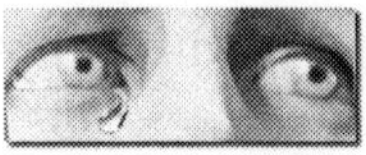

July 4, 1940

After that, the first break we had to really be together came on the Fourth of July.

Everyone eagerly consumed ham sandwiches and lemonade on the back veranda of the big house. Jimmy and a few of his friends joined us that day. They had spent the morning helping with some of the final construction details of David and Sarah's house. Now they talked about going into Baldwin for the parade and fair but lamented the fact that none of them owned a vehicle to get them there. Job offered to take them.

There were cheers all around.

"Hey Jessie," Jimmy piped up. 'Why don't you come?"

A few of the others agreed to his suggestion.

"I don't know. It looks like a boys only thing." I was dying to go, but I was supposed to help with preparing the picnic supper for after the fireworks. It was hot, and we were going to meet down at the creek for a swim by lantern light.

"Nah." Jimmy dismissed my comment with a wave and shrug. "Besides, you're one of us."

"The story of my life." I rolled my eyes and punched him lightly in the shoulder.

"Why don't you come, Jes?" Job's tone suggested total innocence. "It'll be much more fun than watching eggs boil."

His mother pinched his waist. "You'll be wanting to eat those eggs later."

"Yes m'am." He bowed his head with the proper amount of penitence and then proceeded to ruin the effect by winking at me. "What do you say, Jessie?"

I turned pleading eyes to my mother. "May I?"

"Why not?" She threw up her hands. "If I say 'no,' you'll just mope around here all afternoon anyway."

We all raced to the truck and I climbed in front with Job. Jimmy and his friends clambered into the back and with a racket of horn blowing and cheers we left the rest of the group in our dust.

"He's sweet on you." Job commented after Jimmy's failed attempt to stick a wet finger in my ear through the open window.

"Who, Jimmy?" I wiped the side of my face. "He is not."

"Didn't you notice how he invited you to come along before I could?"

"You're not serious?"

"I am." He snuck a quick squeeze of my hand. "And I can't say I blame him."

I looked out the back window of the truck and pointed a threatening finger at Jimmy who tossed his head back and laughed along with the others.

"A girl could do a lot worse than Jimmy."

"Really? What about you? How did you do?"

"Me? Worse. Definitely worse."

His eyes narrowed with mock menace. "You'll pay for that," he growled before ruining the effect with a grin.

With a carefree laugh I stuck my head out the window and let out a shout of unadulterated joy echoed by voices from the back.

The day passed in a haze of too much popcorn and soda pop. We rode the Ferris Wheel, got lost in the house of mirrors and played games of chance until the sun was low in the sky and people began to make their way over to the field for the fireworks display.

We waved to our parents in the stands and convinced Jimmy and his gang that the group of young girls they recognized should not go unescorted. This left us alone at last, in a sea of hundreds.

With a spectacle of color and sound the fireworks began. Job and I leaned back on bent elbows. Occasionally our shoulders would bump and our fingers touch, but we were all too aware of those around us. For the finale, the national anthem boomed out in distorted patriotism from the speakers of the stadium sound system. Red, white and blue explosions from above accompanied the song as we all stood. The carefree smiles I saw on many faces that night are etched in my memory.

The anthem ended, followed by a moment of silence then a unified cheer. When it was over, I made to leave with the departing crowd but Job placed a hand on my arm. "Let's wait for the crowd to leave first." He sat down and patted the blanket next to him.

"It was a good day, wasn't it?" I stretched my legs out before me.

"It certainly was."

We sat in comfortable companionship as the crowds passed around us and Job called an occasional "good night" to someone he recognized.

"Look, Jes!" Job pointed to the sky so suddenly he startled me. "I don't think the show is over."

I looked up and around. The sky was clear and so were the grounds, almost. "What are you talking about? We're just about the last ones here."

"No," he argued. "Look up. What do you see?"

"The stars." I humoured him and looked up. "And a beautiful crescent moon."

"Huh. I thought I saw something in the sky." He scratched his head in confusion. With a jerk, his arm lifted and he pointed upward. "Look! Over there!"

"More stars."

"What about over there?" He changed directions. "I thought I saw more fireworks."

"Job, we're too far from anywhere else to see any other fireworks." I felt his forehead. "Do you have a fever?"

He brushed my hand aside and pulled me closer. He extended his arm directly in front of me in order that I could sight down it. "There! What do you see there?"

I tilted my head to get a better angle. Sure enough I thought I saw something glitter only it wasn't in the sky. It was on the end of his finger. "What was that?"

"You did see it!"

"Job, what is that?"

"Fireworks."

I grabbed for his hand and he tucked it close to his body for protection. "Let me see!" I captured his hand in mine and pulled it free only because he let me. He kept it fisted tightly and, with much laughter, I tried to pry his fingers open.

I glanced at him expecting to see him laughing with me, and while amusement lit his eyes, something else in his look had me releasing his hand as though burned. My mouth went dry. I could not hear anything except the pounding of my heart. It was louder than any percussion from the fireworks had been.

"What's in your hand?" I forced the husky words past the paralysis of my throat.

"Fireworks."

He tilted his head to one side and smiled. It bordered on smug. With a slow and measured pace, he uncurled his fingers. Lying on his palm was a ring. I had before and since, seen fancier rings, but none as beautiful. A rectangular ruby flanked on either side by two small diamonds was set in a band of white gold wide enough to be solid, yet narrow enough to still be considered dainty. The image blurred and shimmered as tears obstructed my vision.

"It belonged to my grandmother."

"It's beautiful."

"Jessie Bingham, I know you've already said yes, but I'm asking again." He took my hand in his and placed the ring on my finger. "I love you more than anything on this earth. Will you marry me?"

Unable to speak, I could only nod, and there in front of anyone who cared to watch, he cradled my face in his hands and placed a soft kiss on my lips. When he pulled back, there were tears threatening in his eyes.

I threw my arms around his neck and hugged him.

"I love you," I finally managed before laughing. Over his shoulder I checked out the ring on my hand. "Fireworks, huh?"

"Oh don't you worry." He hugged me back. "When people catch sight of that ring, there will be quite a show."

I leaned back to look at him. Now that it was time to bring our relationship out into the light, I felt a pang of panic. There would certainly be explosions of a sort.

"But for now," Job took my hand and pulled me to my feet. "Let's see how long it takes them to notice."

I let him gather up the blanket and took another opportunity to examine the ring. "I think they'll notice this."

"Maybe." He had the blanket folded and tucked under his arm. "But as we both know, sometimes people see only what they expect to see. Come on." He took hold of my left hand and we began to walk.

As we rounded the stands, he pulled up short and pushed me behind him. "Our folks are still there. They're talking to someone." He gave my hand a squeeze. "Are you ready?"

I nodded.

He took a deep, steadying breath before leading us out from our hiding spot.

My mother saw us approaching first. "Oh, Jessie, I just..." Her voice trailed off as her jaw went slack at the same time her eyes locked on our linked hands.

"Hi, folks." Job nodded casually. "We'll see you back at the farm."

"All right." His mother turned to see what mine was gaping at. "David and Sarah went ahead to..."

"Shall we go and meet them, Doll Face?" Job smiled down at me a gleam of mischief in his eye.

"Okay, Pally."

I regarded him with a suspicion that was well founded when he bent his head and planted a quick kiss on my lips. If our parents had not drawn the correct conclusion about our joined hands, the sharp intake of breath I heard from my mother let me know there would be no doubt about it now.

We walked away leaving four agog adults in the parking lot of the high school.

Inside the truck we shook with childish glee. "Did you see their faces?" I wiped at tears of merriment that spilled down my cheeks.

"I know!" Job mopped up a few of his own tears.

In unison we turned to wide eyes on each other dropped our jaws. This sent us into another fit of hysteria.

"I can't believe you kissed me in front of them." I pressed my hands against cheeks that grew warm all over again at the memory.

"You didn't mind did you?"

I laughed and launched myself at him, seeking a longer, deeper kiss. "Let's get out of here before they realize what just happened."

Twenty

July 4, 1940

We had changed into swimsuits at the big house and were making our way to the path leading to Miller's Creek when the headlights from my father's car turned up the drive to the farm. As one, we took off at a dead run through the woods. We could see the lanterns flickering at our destination.

David and Sarah were on their feet waiting as we burst into the clearing "What's wrong?" David demanded as Job and I struggled to catch our breath. "We could hear you guys running almost all the way from the house."

"Cat's out of the bag." Job panted.

David groaned. "Quick. Everyone get in the water!"

Like deer trying to outrun a raging forest fire, we dove into the creek. The timing was perfect. Angry voices carried on the night air. They were drawing closer. We began a not so spontaneous game of splash the other person.

David and Job called a greeting to the parents as they entered the clearing. At the same time Sarah leaned close and whispered her congratulations. She had seen the ring.

In the mad dash I had completely forgotten to take it off at the house. I was not yet accustomed to its presence on my finger. I clenched my fist to ensure it would not come off and thanked Sarah quietly with a promise of a better look in the near future. She mumbled something about the uncertainty of there being a future.

"Job Nightingale!" May's voice rang out. "Get over here right now."

"Uh, oh." I muttered as he swam past. I sunk low in the water and hid behind Sarah.

"You too, Jessie." My mother's tone allowed for no argument.

"Uh, oh." Job mimicked over his shoulder. I stuck my tongue out at the back of his head.

We climbed out of the creek and stood, hands behind our backs and heads hanging. I snuck a look at Job out of the corner of my eye and snorted when he made a face.

"Don't you laugh, young lady." My mother bore down on me.

Wisely, I nodded and said nothing. Job tried to hide a snicker with a cough.

"You'd better not either, young man." May's angry tone was one I had never heard before.

"Yes, m'am." Job snapped to attention.

Now that they had us where they wanted us, it seemed they did not know quite what to do with us. They stood and stared. The silence grew until it became comical. I felt myself beginning to loose the battle against nervous laughter. The low clearing of my father's throat had me in check once again, although, the quick peek I took in Mr. Nightingale's direction was almost my undoing. His sly wink undermined my control considerably.

"How long?" It was my mother who finally spoke. She had come to stand directly in front of me. Her outrage was palpable. I knew nothing but the truth would be acceptable.

"January." I said waited for the reaction.

"January?" My mother's voice was soft. The tone terrified me. It meant I had really crossed a line with her.

"I believe it was December." Job leaned over and said to me.

Had he lost his mind? Did he not realize the peril he was in?

"Don't you remember Jes?" he continued like we were not facing an immediate and painful death. "It was New Year's Eve."

Mrs. Nightingale took a threatening step towards her son. He stepped back and covered his head with his arms. He peeked at me from underneath and, from the grin he was trying to hide, I knew he was not afraid his mother would strike him. I felt he should have looked more closely at her face, but she was his mother.

"New Year's Eve?" His mother's voice was much louder than my mother's had been.

In an extremely rare and grave lack of judgment, he laughed. "Yes."

When his mother took another ominous step toward him he tried to edge behind me. I however did not want to get caught in the middle and sidestepped to save myself. Mr. Nightingale adroitly took his wife by the arms and pulled her back a safe distance.

"Is this true, Jessie?" My mother turned on me.

It was my turn to try and hide behind Job. He could sidestep with as much agility as I could. I would have hugged my father as he in turn took my mother back a few steps, except for that fact that he looked unhappy as well—just not so much as my mother.

"Claire, let them explain." He spoke to his wife before facing my intended. "I trust you do have an explanation, son?"

"I do, Sir."

"It better be good." May's voice promised dire consequences should she deem his answer lacking in any way.

"We're waiting, son." Rand's voice was less threatening but still commanded a response.

Job stood straight. I saw the look he sent me out of the corner of his eye and warning bells went off in my brain. "It was all Jessie's idea."

He had thrown me to the lions.

"Rat!" I cried. "You went along with it! In fact, if I recall, I wanted to tell them back in June when –"

"Yes." Job interrupted before I could continue and dig a deeper hole than the one we were already in. He placed an arm around my shoulders and squeezed. "I did go along with it without argument. We just wanted to keep it to ourselves for a while."

"Why?" My mother threw up her hands. "Did you think we wouldn't approve? Because if you did –"

"No." I shook my head. "Just the opposite. We knew you would approve, too much."

"That's ridiculous," Mrs. Nightingale declared. "How could we approve too much?"

"Easily." Job answered and flashed a look of thanks at his father who maintained a firm grip on Mrs. Nightingale. "We both knew this is what you all wanted for us. Had wanted from day one. We began to talk and realized that every time we turned around, you all were manipulating things to that end."

"Manipulating?" I did not know my mother's voice could reach such an octave.

"Claire," my father cautioned.

"Ben, we did not manipulate." She was vehement in her denial.

"Claire," he tried again.

"We may have nudged a little." She huffed. "But we did not manipulate.

"I don't know about you all," Mr. Nightingale spoke up. "But I manipulated."

"Me too." My father shrugged.

I learned a lesson in the fine art of blame shifting in the next instant as May focused her attention on me.

"Well, if we did, you have no one to blame but yourself," she accused.

"Me?" I squawked.

"That's right. My poor boy has loved you forever but you couldn't see it. You had to set your sights on that silly Kenny Martin."

"Hey!" It was my mother's turn to redirect blame. "You're *poor boy* had fourteen years to make his feelings known. Dead turtles move faster!"

Job and I looked at each other in wide-eyed disbelief. This was something we certainly had not counted on. A startling outburst of male laughter interrupted the blame debate.

"This is not funny, Rand." My mother turned to him. "They've deceived us. For six months they have snuck around and lied to us."

"Can you blame them?" My father was still chuckling. "With all of us poking around in business that should have been left to them, I certainly do not. I think we got what we deserved."

"But –"

"Claire, he's right." May's capitulation was reluctant but resigned. "As much as I hate to admit it. Who knows? If we had left well enough alone, they might not have had to lie to us."

"We never lied." I volunteered the information not really expecting it to be pacifying.

"That's true." Job stepped forward to provide support. "We always told you where we were going and who we were going with. You only saw what you wanted to see."

"You could have been upfront with your intentions, Job." My father was not laughing now.

"Sir, I believe I made my intentions clear to you quite some time ago." Job was firm but respectful. "I believe you gave me your blessing."

"You did?" I looked from one to the other. "He did?"

The measuring look my father gave Job would have intimidated a lesser man. Job did not waver in resolution. "Yes, son, I believe you're right." Satisfied with what he had seen in Job, his attention turned to me. "Jessie, do you love this man?"

I was then the focus of everyone's attention. I looked from my mother to his, and from his father to mine. Each was silent, waiting for my answer. I tried to keep a straight face as the importance of the moment would seem to warrant, but failed miserably. I could not stop the smile that spread across my face. "Yes Dad." I took Job's hand in mine. "I love him."

The mothers cried. The fathers shook hands. Job and I found ourselves enveloped in a mighty group hug. I had a thought about another shoe needing to drop but it was pushed out of my mind as a sheet of water doused us all. We had forgotten about David and Sarah floating in the water behind us.

"Finally!" David's proclamation was followed by a yelp as Sarah pinched him "What was that for?"

"You knew?" My mother turned on her son. "You knew and didn't say anything?"

"It wasn't our place to say anything." David defended himself.

"And it was too much fun." Sarah's shy confession had all eyes pointed in her direction. She quickly ducked behind David.

By the time the ensuing water battle was declared a draw, we were all weary and wet. I hauled myself up onto the bank and left the others to float and talk. As I wrung the water out of my hair, my mother joined me and administered the same twisting treatment to her own hair.

"Are you very mad?" I threw her an appraising glance.

"It's a happy mad." She threw an arm around my neck and pulled me close for a one armed hug. "I am very happy for you. He's a good man, Jes."

"I know." But was I a good enough woman?

Where had that thought come from?

The lantern lights threw long shadows over the rippling surface of the water. I looked to where Job was smiling at something Sarah was saying. He was listening intently and nodding at various breaks in the story, one half of his face lit brightly, the other in shadow. The depth of my feelings for him caused an ache in the center of my chest.

"I wanted to talk to you about it, but I just couldn't." I said quietly. "I'm not sure why really. I think fear mostly."

"Fear of what?"

"Everything." I shrugged. "Of how intense what I feel is. I didn't expect it. I didn't know what to do with it. I wanted to shout it to everyone who would listen, while at the same time keep it hidden and safe. Crazy, huh?" I looked at her then and was mortified to see her crying.

"It's nothing." She waved in dismissal of her tears and took a bracing sniff and turned to me. "Jessie, I'm sorry for doing anything that made you feel you couldn't come to me about this."

"You didn't do anything. Not really anyway." I realized that I must have hurt her more than I had ever given any thought to. I owed her an explanation but was not sure I had one that was adequate.

"I'm not a little girl anymore." I wrapped my arms around my knees and rested my chin on them. "I needed to know that I could think and act as an adult. I didn't want to run to my mother at the first sign of trouble. I knew I loved him. I just didn't know if I was in love with him, and you couldn't tell me that. "

"Jessie, even adults need someone to talk to." My mother rubbed a comforting hand over my back.

"I know. I did talk to someone." I explained to her how helpful David and Sarah had been and about them finding us in the barn. I did not tell her what they had found us doing in the barn. There are some things you just do not need to tell you mother.

"Well, I am glad you had someone, but you know I'm always here for you." She kissed my temple.

"I know." I leaned into her familiar comfort.

"Come on." My mother stood and held out her hand. "Let's get the food out. I'm starved."

Without thinking, I placed my left hand in hers. She squeezed and pulled me to my feet but refused to let go of my hand. How could I have forgotten again?

I felt her fingers moving over mine, one finger in particular. "Is that what I think it is?" she whispered.

"I don't know," I said. "What do you think it is?"

By the time my mother stopped crying I felt as though I had experienced just about every emotion I could. I had never been hugged so much before.

It was a relief to finally have everything out in the open, although it did take some adjustment. It was not just having to undo six months of programming and getting used to the idea of everyone knowing we were a couple that had me stiffening a little awkwardly every time Job's hand or arm brushed up against me, it was something on a more subconscious level. There was an awareness of each other as man and woman that I was still becoming accustomed to. Just thinking of myself as a woman, not a girl, was still a relatively new and probably premature concept. Add to that the mystifying awakening of the sexuality that inherently belongs to a woman and not a girl, it was no wonder that I was uncomfortable with the idea that others—specifically my parents - should see me in that light.

But, as talk of engagements turned to talk of weddings, my mild discomfort was forgetten. Before I knew what was happening, my mother and soon-to-be mother-in-law, were off on a discussion of dates, guest lists and colors. As I listened, my appetite for food waned in direct correlation to the growing feeling of shrinking into insignificance. This was why we had kept our relationship a secret for so long. I was wishing it had remained so. With each passing minute the list of things that I was being consulted on diminished. It was not long before I was no longer a part of the conversation.

"Excuse me." I stood abruptly. "Since you don't need me, I'm going to change."

Conversation stopped. I felt every eye on me as I headed briskly up the path to the house. I was out of the woods and starting across the yard before Job caught up with me.

His long strides enabled him to get in front of me where he stopped and turned. I tried to step around him but was blocked. "What's wrong?" he asked.

"I'm cold."

He took of the shirt he had thrown on but not buttoned, and placed it around my shoulders. "What's really wrong?"

"Nothing. I just want to change." I ducked around him and continued on my march.

He allowed me to get as far as the veranda steps before taking hold of my arms and forcing me to look at him. "Jessie, tell me what's really wrong. Please?"

"I don't want a wedding."

The complete lack of movement from him other than the ever increasing firmness of his grip made me realize he had misunderstood my blunt outburst. I clarified for him, "I want to get married. I just don't want a wedding."

I found myself crushed against his bare chest and barely able to breath. “Don’t ever scare me like that again,” he scolded.

“Sorry.” My apology was muffled as my face was mashed into his sternum. I wiggled uncomfortably and he relaxed his hold enough for me to turn my face and pull in a deep breath.

“What do you mean you don’t want a wedding?”

“I don’t want a wedding.” I wrapped my arms around his waist. “Not if it means that our parents make all the decisions.”

“You mean our mothers.” It was a statement and not a question.

“Did you hear them down there? Not once did they include us in any of the discussion. You’d think it was them getting married and not us.”

“They’re just excited for us. Give them a little time to calm down.”

“By then we’ll have a dozen kids.”

I felt his soft chuckle through his chest wall. “Probably.”

Voices floated to us from the direction of the path. The others were returning to the house.

“Go inside and change.” Job kissed the top of my head. “Then I’ll take you home.”

I scurried inside, grateful that he was willing to take on the task of talking to our parents. I admit I rushed through the changing process to eavesdrop on the conversation outside. I managed to catch the last little bit from my spot beside the screen door.

“There was no harm meant.” It was my father speaking.

“I know that Mr. Bingham, sir.” Job’s voice was firm and clear. “I also know I promised that I would not deny you the honor of walking your only daughter down the aisle.”

When had he promised that?

“I will do my best to keep that promise.”

“You will do your best?” My father did not sound pleased that the specified promise might not take place. “What does that mean?”

“Right now, Jessie doesn’t want a wedding.”

“Doesn’t want a wedding?” My mother sounded incredulous. “That’s ridiculous.”

“What exactly does that mean?” Rand’s tone was calmer than my parents’, especially my mother’s.

“It means exactly what it sounds like it means.” I stepped through the door and moved to the edge of the veranda. There were a lot of vague meanings being bandied about but in a moment of pique, there was one I intended to make clear. “I understand that everyone is excited for us. We are too. But there are a lot of things that Job and I have yet to talk about. When we have, we'll let you know. Until then, there will be no wedding planning."

I believe it was steam I saw drifting out of my mother's ears. It may have been smoke. Whatever it was, she was hot, and so was I. In her face I saw the look that said, "We will discuss this at home and alone." I shot her one that said, "We will not."

My mother and I had not had many confrontations of wills up to this point, but then I had never really attempted to assert mine in such a manner, at least not with her. I realize now that it was not so much a battle of wills as it was a battle for independence motivated in no small part by selfishness on my end.

I marched down the steps and handed Job his shirt. "Will you please take me home?"

He put his shirt on and began to button it up at the same time he sent me a puzzled frown. "Don't you want to stay and work this out?"

The knot in the middle of my diaphragm told me I probably should. I shook my head and walked toward his truck at the same time I mumbled a general goodnight.

We were on the main road before he spoke. "What was that about?"

"What was what about?"

"You know what."

"No I don't."

"Jessie."

"Job."

He pulled the truck over. "Don't do that."

"Don't do what?"

Since we had begun our courtship, Job and I had never really had a fight. We had disagreed and debated, but never really shouted. Part of me was terrified at the thought of it. Another part was strangely curious and exhilarated. I wanted to yell and I did not want to do it alone.

I set out to see how much goading it would take before Job would break. I found his is propensity for calm rational thought exasperating at times, as it was a character trait that I had not developed—and never really would—and I was in no mood to be reasonable. However, I do admit I was caught off guard at how little baiting it took.

"Don't feign ignorance!" Job's voice filled the small cab of the truck.

"Feign? Who uses a word like feign?" It was not one of my more pleasant moments.

"I just did and don't change the subject!" He turned to face me. I stared in fascination at the vein that bulged in his temple. "You were rude and high-handed back there. I want to know why?"

"My mother called me ridiculous!"

"No Jessie, she did not. She called the idea of there not being a wedding ridiculous."

"It's the same thing."

"It is not and you know it." He sighed heavily.

"You don't understand." I turned to look out the window, surprised by the sudden appearance of tears.

"I'm trying to."

"They listen to you. I just wanted them to listen to me."

"You didn't give them a chance. You walked away before we could make them understand."

He was right and with a nod I acknowledged that.

"Besides," he continued. "I don't know why you're surprised by their reaction. One of the reasons we kept things a secret is because we both acknowledged the rather enthusiastic way they tend to approach matters where you and I are concerned. Let's be fair and remember that they were pitched low and inside tonight. All things considered, I think they handled it pretty well."

"I know." I nodded again. "I think I just didn't realize how difficult I was going to find it when they did know everything."

"I need you to promise me something." He took my hands in his.

"If I can."

"Promise you'll tell me if things ever get to be too difficult or crazy for you? Anything, the wedding plans, our parents…if something worries you or frightens you, you'll trust me enough to tell me before it gets too big. Don't back away from it."

"I promise."

"Because whatever it is we'll work it out together."

"I promise."

I said the words, never counting the cost they would demand.

Thunder rumbled in the distance as he pulled the truck back onto the road.

"You really promised my dad he would walk me down the aisle?" I asked when his earlier words came to mind.

He grinned.

"When?"

"Awhile ago."

"When?"

"I was twelve." I shook my head to make sure there was nothing in my ears that may have affected my hearing. He laughed before continuing. "I don't think he took me seriously."

"I'm sure he didn't. What changed his mind?"

"Tonight."

It was my turn to laugh. We were just pulling up in front of my house and rain had begun falling in earnest. Laughter turned to a sigh as I saw the light on in the living room. I don't remember them doing so, but my parents must have passed us when we were stopped at the side of the road.

"Right now, I wish you hadn't made that promise to my dad." I said.

"I know. Do you want me to come in with you?" He put the truck into park.

"No. I have to face this one myself."

"Okay. I'll pray for you." He kissed my forehead.

"Thanks. I'll need it."

On impulse I checked over his shoulder for movement in the window across the street. Sure enough, the curtains were moving. I was still feeling a defiant, so I gave Mr. Lawhead something to report to my mother, or anyone else who cared to listen.

Twenty-one

July 1940

"The more I think about it, the more I like the idea of eloping," I confessed with a purpose in mind.

"I promised your father." Job shook his head and chucked a small stone at some invisible target across the creek.

"What if there was a way to do both, elope and have my dad walk me down the aisle?"

"I'm listening." I shifted on the blanket to face him and began to explain my thoughts on the matter. By the time I was finished, the angle of the sun cast sharp evening shadows, and Job was as excited as I was.

"I think it just might work." He grinned broadly.

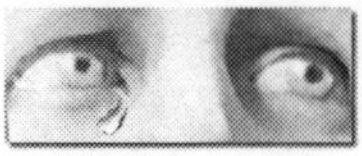

August 1940

Over the next several weeks, all the plans fell into place. With the help of my mother I picked out a dress. I dragged Job into the men's side of the store and helped him pick out a beautiful soft grey summer suit and shirt. We accomplished that just before Mr. and Mrs. White returned from Maine and figured out what were up to. They brought with them the something I was waiting for.

"Welcome back!" I hugged Mrs. White warmly when she appeared from the back room one Monday morning. "When did you get in? How was it? Tell me everything! Is she as beautiful as her grandmother?"

"Thanks. Late last night. It was wonderful, but not long enough. There's a lot to tell, and it's unfair but she far outshines the beauty of any mortal on the face of the earth," Mrs. White answered all in one breath.

"And mother and father?"

"Doing well. Which reminds me." Mrs. White pulled an envelope from her purse. "Would you mind telling me why my son-in-law is writing to my daughter's dearest friend?"

"Yes I would." I took the envelope and tore it open. There was only one line and it made me smile. When Mrs. White tried to look over my shoulder, I quickly stuffed it back in the envelope.

"So how have things been since I left?" She looked at me with suspicion.

"Fine."

"Your parents?"

"Doing well."

"You and Job?"

"Also doing well."

"How well?" She leaned forward searching my eyes with hers.

"Same as before you left." I returned her gaze.

"Huh." She pursed her lips thoughtfully. The chimes over the door sounded indicating a customer had arrived. "Well I guess it's back to work."

Despite some of my most creative hand gesturing that morning, it had been Mr. White who had noticed the ring first. He arrived in our side of the shop and told us to put up the "Closed for lunch" sign.

"We've just finished lunch," Mrs. White responded.

"Then make it an out for ice cream sign." Mr. White returned. "I'm taking you both out for a treat."

"He's been like this ever since he became a grandpa." Mrs. White shook her head and rolled her eyes. "There's nothing to do but go along with it."

Off we went to Millie's. It was when I looked up from the first taste of my ice cream that I found Mr. White smiling shyly at me.

"Congratulations, Jessie." He nodded toward my hand. "Job?"

I smiled and nodded before throwing a glance at Mrs. White.

"What's Job?" She licked at her spoon.

For the first time, I really noticed Mr. White's eyes. They were dark, somewhere between green and brown and at the moment a delicious merriment danced in them.

"Nothing, Dear." He took a bite of his sundae.

"Excuse me." I reached across for a napkin with my left hand even though the right was closer.

Mrs. White's spoon clattered to the table.

"Jessie Bingham, you little liar!" She grabbed my wrist. "I can't believe you looked me right in the eye and lied. 'Same as before you left,' you said."

"I didn't lie." I shook my head enjoying the moment.

"But—Oh my, oh my, oh my! When?"

"Since New Year's."

"I knew something was different!" she cried. "I just couldn't quite figure it out."

"We got engaged in June, but I didn't get the ring until three weeks ago."

"Oh my goodness!" Mrs. White examined the ring more closely. "It's lovely. Does Laura know?

"Some, but not about this. And you can't tell her yet. I have a surprise for her."

"She and Mark and the baby are coming here at the end of the month," Mrs. White said still distracted by the ring and its implications.

"Yes," I extricated my hand from her grip. "I'll tell her when she gets here."

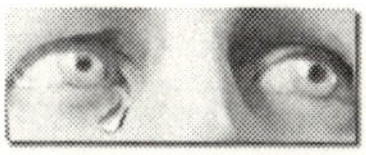

SEPTEMBER 2, 1940

I thought I would be more nervous, and inside there were a few butterflies, but they were more about my concerns over getting everything and everyone in place. When I thought about what the day would mean for me on the larger scale, I only felt a calmness that this was how it was supposed to be.

I passed the morning helping my mother around the house. I had to stop smiling at her as I helped hang the sheets because she began to look at me funny, but other than that, it was a pretty normal morning. Michael and Catherine arrived shortly before noon. Catherine was one of only two people, beside Job and I, who actually knew what was going on. I had to tell her, to get her to strongly encourage Michael to visit his parents. She finally convinced him with the excuse of her newly discovered pregnancy.

After lunch, I drove over to Job's and entered the house. Our house. That I was hanging my wedding dress in the closet next to Job's shirts, solidified the monumental importance of the day.

I had seen the room before, in passing, as I traipsed up and down the stairs after Job when we were children, or on the mornings when I needed to get ready for school. But this was the first time I had ever really been in it. Our room.

My favorite feature of the room was the low window with the bench seat built in. I had always wanted to sneak in and sit and stare out over the yards below. I daydreamed about the stories I could imagine from that spot. The furniture in the room, bureau, and bedside tables, were solid wood, heirlooms from generations previous. The bed was new, moved in several days ago. It was a wedding present from Pops and the others. They had painstakingly labored over its construction from the day they learned of the engagement.

"Your intentions had better be honorable if you're kissin' my love like that." Pops had groused with a certain amount of humor upon catching Job and I behind the barn.

"They are." Job laughed as I squawked in embarrassment. "I'm going to marry her."

"That's fine then." Pops tossed a peppermint to me. "Carry on."

They had worked quickly, afraid of it not being ready for the big day since they did not know when that day would be, but they had not sacrificed workmanship. The wood was as warm as it looked. I ran a hand over the delicate carving of vines curving across the arching headboard. The motif ran along the side rails to the footboard of the sleigh bed. Thinking about what would soon take place in that bed was unavoidable and I was hit by a wave of uncertainty.

The passion we shared for each other had been strong but innocent. We focused so much energy on not doing what God had made our bodies for that it was difficult to believe soon there would be no need for restraint.

Would I please him? Would he please me? What did that even mean? They were vague, general phrases tossed about so casually by some of the girls in New York. The bold frankness with which they spoke seemed, to me, to diminish the meaning of it all. Then there had been the talk with my mother.

Not since I had been thirteen and she had sat down to explain to me the ins and outs of what it meant to become a young woman, had I been so excruciatingly embarrassed, and yet, when she led me into the living room one evening, I looked forward to what was to come with more than a little curiosity.

As I washed dishes with my mother one evening, I noticed there was none of her usual chatter about what the neighbors were up to in their gardens or about what she had read in the newspaper that day. It made me nervous. When she took the last dish out of my hand before I finished drying it completely, I knew I was about to find out what was on her mind.

"We need to talk," she said and took my hand.

My mouth went dry and my mind began to spin through possible topics of conversation. I sat quietly and clasped my hands in my lap, not quite able to meet my mother's eyes. The last thing I wanted was a discussion with her about the intimacy between a man and a woman; and yet, I wanted it more than anything else. I had some information. What good was having a married best friend if you could not press her for some details, but I was curious about what my mother would say.

She took a big breath and let it out slowly. Her hand trembled slightly as she pushed a strand of dark hair behind her ear and a faint pink crept up her neck and high into her cheeks. "I'm not sure why this was easier with Sarah, but it was." She laughed ruefully and took another fortifying breath. "Jessie, my mother wasn't around to have this talk with me when I married, and even if she were, I'm not sure she would have said much. The wife of the minister who married your father and I took it upon herself to explain what would be expected of me as a wife. She meant well, but there was no joy in her advice. As a result your father and I almost didn't make it beyond the first few months of our marriage."

I was taken aback to learn my parents' marriage had almost ended before it began. The love between them was clearly evident in the affection they had never hidden from my brothers and me.

"She talked about duty and obligation," she continued. "What I should and should not expect. What was proper and what was not. I vowed that if and when I had a daughter, I would not pass on the same misinformation."

My mother's hand waved dismissively.

"It was all very lifeless and incomplete."

"Incomplete?"

My mother nodded and the blush in her cheeks deepened. "She explained the physical aspects of intimacy but nothing more."

"I know that stuff already." I spoke without thinking and the sharp look my mother directed my way along with her raised eyebrows was a good indicator that clarification was need and quickly. "Not that way!" I felt the heat rising in my own face. "I mean, I can guess, because of working on the farm. Not because…Job and I haven't…I mean there was kissing but…"

I stopped my stammering explanation and gathered my thoughts.

"We have been very careful not to do anything that would disappoint you and Dad, or his parents, or God."

She relaxed visibly. "Jes, there's so much more to it than just the physical side of it. My hope is for you to find that for yourself."

She squeezed my hands in hers. "As for the physical, well, don't be disappointed if it's not what you expect at first. You and Job will learn together if you trust each other and listen to each other. He loves you. So very much."

"I know he does."

"Be honest with him about how you're feeling." She pulled me tight for a hug and one last word of advice whispered in my ear. "Most importantly, relax."

Oh sure, at the time it had sounded possible. But standing here now, I found there were so many questions I wished I had asked.

"Hi."

I started at his voice. I turned to see him watching me from the doorway.

"Hi, yourself."

How long had he been standing there? I fought to suppress the blush I knew was filling my face. Could he know what I had been thinking?

His sudden and intense scrutiny of some flaw in the wood of the doorframe, told me I was not the only nervous person in the room.

"People will be arriving soon," he said and picked at the wood.

I looked at my watch. "Is it really that time?"

"Yes. Are you ready?"

I felt my face split into a wide smile. I waited to speak until he looked at me.

"Yes," I said softly. "I'm ready."

The boyish grin that took over his face was full of anticipation and relief. I took his extended hand and we made our way to the back yard where the end of summer gathering—and our wedding—were about to get underway.

The yard was filling up. Rand worked at getting the barbeques lit while May filled pitchers with iced tea or lemonade. It was not long before my parents arrived and went to work themselves. I kept searching the crowd for the Whites. Laura, Mark and the baby were arriving with them. I was really looking forward to seeing Laura.

When their car pulled into the driveway I ran to greet them.

"I'm so glad you're all here." I hugged Laura. She looked amazing. She still had some of the extra weight from her pregnancy but she glowed with vitality.

I leaned in and kissed Mark on the cheek and whispered a "thank you" meant for his ears only. He squeezed my hand in reply.

I turned my attention to more important matters and peeked under the blanket that bundled the baby Mark lovingly carried.

"She's absolutely beautiful." I could see she would have Mark's coloring but Laura's facial structure. She blinked at me and my heart melted. "May I hold her?"

Andrea was carefully handed off to me and we began to make our way around the house.

"She's the reason we took so long," Laura spoke and looked down at her daughter in my arms. "You're all content for your Auntie Jessie now, aren't you? But where was that for mommy an hour ago?" She threw an arm around my waist. "How are you Jes? You look great."

"So do you. And I am great."

"Honestly?"

"Honestly." I shifted the baby so that I had an arm free and pulled Laura close in a one armed hug. I could see Job approaching. "There's something I'll tell you later, only you have to promise you won't be too angry."

"Too angry?" She threw me a sideways look. "That means whatever you have to say will make me angry."

"Maybe a little." I grinned fanning the fire of her curiosity.

Job greeted Laura with a big hug and kiss before he shook Mark's hand and congratulated him on his daughter. He ran his hand down the side of my face in a gentle greeting.

"That's going to take some getting used to." Laura said in reference to Job's touch. "I still find it hard to believe that the two of you are finally at the same place."

"Believe it," Job said as he carefully lifted the baby from my arms. We had discussed children. Job wanted as many as God deemed to give us. I was a little wary about how undefined that number might be, but I definitely wanted more than one. "The game's about to start, Jes." He said in between the soft noises he was making to get Andrea to smile.

"Some things never change." Laura shook her head with a certain amount of good-natured disgust. She spoke to the baby as Job handed her back. "You're not interested in baseball are you?"

Andrea's coo had her mother pleading mercy from heaven.

The team captains were Job and Jimmy. The outcome of the game had been the only thing of the evening not carefully orchestrated. I played well, considering how rusty I was. I suffered a pang of fear that all our plans may have been for nothing when a ground ball took an unexpected hop and hit Job under his left eye, but the cut was not serious and play continued, both of us taking a little more care. Jimmy's team won by two runs.

After the game, I insisted that Laura leave her baby in the very capable care of her Grandma and dragged Laura into the house with me. We started up the stairs. Laura hung back in protest. "We can't go up there."

"Yes we can." I dragged her the rest of the way up and into the master bedroom.

"What's going on?"

"Not much." I shut the door behind her and headed for the closet where my dress hung. "I'm getting married."

Laura laughed. I held my dress up in front of me. It was a simple linen sheath in a light cream. My mother had argued when I had shunned the typical white dresses, but I did not want to look like a lace curtain going down the aisle.

"It's true?" Laura's eyes were wide with disbelief. "You're getting married? Today?"

"Yes. I said so didn't I?"

"But…but…to Job?"

"Who else?"

Looking staggered by the news, Laura sank onto the bed. I went and sat next to her. "Will you be my matron of honor?"

I could almost hear the gears clicking into place as she began to put things together. "Mark knew didn't he?"

"Who do you think is performing the ceremony?" I took hold of her hand and tried to redirect the way I sensed her thoughts were going. "Please, don't be too angry. My parents don't even know it's happening today. At least, I'm pretty sure they don't. It's hard to tell if they've really figured out why Michael and Catherine chose this weekend to visit, or if they still think it's because they wanted to tell them about the baby in person. And I don't know if they've connected anything with you and Mark being here. We're eloping, only we wanted everyone to be there when we did. And Job promised my dad…well, if we just eloped without telling anyone, I'm sure you can imagine how that would be received."

She continued to stare at me, not believing a word I was saying.

"Laura," I pulled her to her feet. "You've helped me do this countless times. Now I need you to do it once more. Please, will you be my maid of honor and help me get ready for my wedding?"

"Of course I will." She smiled through the tears that suddenly welled up in her eyes. "But first things first. What am I going to wear?"

Laura grimaced at the snugness in the waist of the dress I had chosen for her, but wore it without complaint and looked stunning all the same. Catherine managed to get Sarah upstairs without anyone seeing and, after her happy exclamation of surprise, the two of them had put on the dresses that matched Laura's.

They were simple sundresses in the softest butter yellow, linen. It was the same cut as mine, with the skirt falling in full folds just above the ankles.

My arms and feet were bare, and my hair was piled loosely on top of my head. The bouquet of yellow and white roses I would carry was carefully hidden in the cool of the cellar and would be retrieved just before we went outside.

"Jessie?" I heard my mother call from downstairs. Michael had sent her and my father in, right on cue.

"I'll be right down!" I called and took one last look in the mirror. I barely recognized the young woman before me. Her eyes shone, her cheeks were pink with excitement, and the smile on her face was full of hope.

I went first down the stairs.

"Jessie, why were you up –?" My mother's eyes widened and she gasped. "Today? Right now?"

"Is that okay?" I struggled on the sudden verge of tears.

"It's perfect." She hugged me tight.

Over her shoulder I saw my dad. He was just standing there looking at me. He had yet to say a word. I gave him what I knew to be a rather watery smile. His own looked a little wet around the edges too.

He stepped forward when my mother released me. "Are you sure you wouldn't rather go for ice cream?"

I laughed and cried at the same time as I let his arms surround me.

Michael knocked on the door, saving us from becoming maudlin, and took my mother to her seat. Laura, Catherine and Sarah had followed him out the door and now stood on the back porch waiting for their cue.

From just inside the back door, I observed the transformation of the yard that Michael had coordinated. A few chairs, enough for parents and those who could not easily stand, formed a short aisle up to the raised platform set up for the band. Mark would use it to address the crowd when signaled to do so. The ceremony would be short enough that everyone else could remain on their feet.

Rand and May had found their seats. I saw Rand take a handkerchief from May and dab his eyes. They beamed proudly as Job took his place at the end of the aisle.

David and Jimmy were standing next to Job already, and Michael took his place in the middle as soon as my mother was seated. They each wore the soft grey wool trousers and yellow shirts that had been selected for them with Mr. White's help. Job's shirt was the same cream linen as my dress. I could hardly take my eyes off him, even when my father stepped up beside me.

I could sense the excitement growing as people gradually became aware that something different was happening. They stopped what they were doing and began to gather around. I saw some of them leaning close and whispering to each other.

"Hello everyone! If I might have your attention please?" Mark took his place and waited for the hubbub to subside. "My name is Reverend Mark Newcomb, and it is my great pleasure to be here and to welcome you all. The last time I was in your beautiful town, it was also for a wedding. My own."

Mark waited as there were several "ah ha's" of recognition and gasps of comprehension.

"Most of you know my beautiful wife Laura. And in the past couple of hours, my daughter Andrea has charmed many of you."

There was general laughter and agreement.

Mark had their full attention. He held up his hands and the group settled. "I see some of you have already jumped to the correct conclusion, but for those of you who can't quite make the leap, it is my honor on behalf of Jessie Bingham and Job Nightingale, to welcome you to their elopement!"

There was a moment of silence before Mark's words sunk in. When they did, cheers and applause rose up from the onlookers. My heart rate increased, sending my blood pounding through my system. My father squeezed my hand as the band began to play *I Will Sing of my Redeemer.* Laura went down the steps of the porch followed by Catherine and Sarah. Each carried one white and one yellow rose. Then it was my turn.

The crowd stood as one when I stepped out onto the porch. I remember trying to smile at them, but I do not remember any faces but his. He looked so calm, so confident, standing there with just a hint of a smile. Any nerves that may have tried to linger, faded away.

I remember walking down the makeshift aisle and answering "I will," or "I do," as prompted. I remember the lantern light as it flickered in his eyes while he repeated his vows without wavering. And I remember a sudden bashfulness when Mark told Job he could kiss his bride. I had forgotten about that part.

I danced with my father, my father-in-law and every other gentleman present it seemed, young and old alike—and my husband. I said it over in my head, *my husband*, just because I could. It was close to midnight before the first guests began to depart, and after one o'clock in the morning by the time the last ones had gone. Never had the gathering gone that late.

Then it was time to say goodnight to our parents. There were a few last minute tidbits of advice whispered in my ear from my mother, which was bad enough, but when they also came from May, Mrs. White and even Laura, I was too embarrassed to look anyone in the eye.

Then, we were alone on the front veranda.

I fiddled self-consciously with the unfamiliar weight of the rings on my finger.

"Well, Mrs. Nightingale, was the day everything you hoped it would be?" Job took my hand and kissed the rings I had been twisting.

"Yes." I wrapped my arms around his waist and buried my face in his chest. I inhaled deeply the scent of him that was becoming familiar and comforting. "It was fun surprising everyone like that. I'm glad we did it this way."

"It certainly made planning the guest list easier." I chuckled at his observation. "I can't imagine how we would have fit the whole town in our little church," he said.

I groaned just trying to imagine it.

We entered the house together. I waited while Job made sure the front door was closed securely.

"Why don't you go upstairs?" He spoke over his shoulder, not quite looking at me. "I'll make sure everything is settled and be up in a moment."

"I'll help." I made the offer as a wave of uncertainty caused my heart to skip erratically before settling into a steady thump. "I don't mind."

"I can manage," he said and slid the lock into place.

My heart skipped again but not with anxiety. The door was never locked. I turned and climbed the stairs.

In the master bedroom, his room, our room, I discovered all the signs that our mothers had been there first. It seems Job and I had not been the only ones planning surprises.

The bed, with its fresh linens was turned down. Draped across the foot was a simple white cotton gown. The straps were narrow and the bodice was embroidered with tiny yellow and blue roses. I ran a trembling had over its delicate softness. An oil lamp on the dresser was lit and fluttered in the breeze that crept in through the open window. A gold illumination glinted off a flat rectangular object sitting on the dresser next to it. I saw a framed photograph. Intrigued, I went to examine it more closely.

The black and white image immediately transported me back twelve years. A six-year-old Jessie and an eight-year-old Job grinned into the camera lens. The picture had been taken on the bank of Miller's Creek about a week after Job and I had met in that same spot. I remember the day Rand took it and how difficult it had been to remain still for the pose. I just wanted to run and jump and play. There were still traces of the bruises around Job's eyes from the kick he had taken. Job and I had sat side by side on the bank. It had taken several tries but eventually I had been persuaded to keep still and Rand had gotten his photo.

I ran my fingers over the edge of the silver frame and could not help but remember how frustrating I had found it that Job's legs were long enough for his feet to completely submerse in the water while I could only touch it with my toes. I realized Job was like that about everything.

His feet were fully immersed in his faith, his family, life, me. I felt like I had only been skimming the surface of my life and realized that had changed forever. The promises I had made were those of a grown woman, not a child. Innocence would be given and taken willingly before God that night. There would be no shame or guilt in it. There would be no need for those recriminations. The good Lord had willed it.

It was awkward and perfect and amusing—at least in hindsight. Until that night, neither one of us had shared a bed on such an intimate level. Certainly as a young girl, Laura and I had slept in the same bed when at each other's houses, but it had been years since that had occurred. Sleeping next to Laura in that context could in no way compare to sleeping beside a large fully-grown man accustomed to sleeping on his own, and on whichever side of the bed he chose.

I remember the distinct impression that I was sliding. Falling. At the last second I managed to wake enough to realize that I was actually falling, or being pushed rather, right out of bed.

I twisted enough to get my hands and feet out to break my fall but not fast enough to prevent my left knee from connecting with the rail of the bed. I hit the floor with a thud and a grunt and grabbed the injured knee. Rolling from side to side and gritting my teeth in pain I felt my temper begin to simmer.

"Jes?" Job's sleepy whisper came a few moments later. His face appeared over the edge of the bed and hovered in shadow above me. "What are you doing down there?"

"Asking myself that same question." Carefully I stood and tested my knee. It did not appear to be permanently damaged. "Look, Pally, you need to pick a side and stay on it."

"What are you talking about?"

"I have been kicked, elbowed, almost strangled, and now pushed out of bed." I rubbed at the knee one more time for good measure. "You know I'm not at my best in the morning, even with enough sleep."

I sensed he was smiling but without enough light to give solid evidence to my case, I had to go with the innocence before guilt adage. To give him his due, he did an admirable job of keeping the laughter out of his voice. "I'm sorry. I'm not used to sharing."

Abruptly the ache in my knee shifted higher, to the vicinity of my heart. The thought of his sharing what we had shared together that night with anyone else, was enough to send me down on all fours again. I sat on the edge of the bed instead. It no longer mattered if he pushed me out of bed every night.

"Job?"

"Yeah?"

"Thank you."

"For what?"

"For not being used to sharing."

There was a brief moment of silence in which I fought the tears that threatened. I felt the bed shift followed by the warmth of his body as he knelt behind me. He pulled me to him so my back was against the solid warmth of his chest.

In sickness and in health, for better or for worse, for richer or poorer. I sometimes wonder if I had understood the true meaning of the words, if I would have had the courage to say them. I like to think so.

PART TWO

His wife said to him, "Are you still trying to maintain your integrity? Curse God and die."
Job 9:2 (*NLT*)

Twenty-two

December 1940

My shoes beat a steady rhythm on the ice. Tap, tap, tap.

Harder, with my heels this time. Tap, tap, tap.

Again, harder, and harder still. Tap. Tap. Crack!

Water seeped through the break in the frosted ice. It made a clear glass-like surface, allowing me to see the mix of twigs, stones, and brown muck of the creek bottom. In the summer, the mud would squeeze between my toes as I entered or exited the creek. I would laugh or squeal in disgust and wriggle all digits until the offending mess rinsed free.

I could not feel my toes.

I wished I could not feel more.

A lot of time had passed since that first encounter on the bank of Miller's Creek. I was no longer six. He was no longer eight. I sat in the same spot where we first met and had met together many times since that life-changing day. To say I *wanted* his legs to appear as he sat next to me, and for his feet to tap the icy surface next to mine, is inadequate. *Yearned, ached, needed*—all of these too failed to meet what it was inside me.

My thoughts turned to Cora Miller, and the speculation that her death had not been an accident. I wondered how old she might have been. Laura and I had spent several days one summer searching the local graveyard for her resting place in order to find out. We had failed to find it; something easily explained if Cora had been Catholic. Had Cora been older or younger than my nineteen years? Maybe the same? I supposed it made no difference as I contemplated what might have led her to such a desperate act. Laura had woven a rather tragic and romantic tale of lovers divided by a cruel fate only to be reunited in death. We had read *Romeo and Juliet* that year. I smiled in spite of what I was feeling as I pictured Laura gesturing in her grand melodramatic style. The smile disappeared quickly.

I knew what had driven Cora Miller to do it, if indeed it was not by accident that she had slipped beneath the crystalline waters of the creek. She had not really wanted to die; she only wanted to stop feeling. I know I did.

For so long, my life had been idyllic. Certainly, from the distance of memory, I know where the imperfections lie, but in the light of what had come to be, those days were perfect, innocent—adolescent.

Our week away was a time of growing together, emotionally, physically and spiritually. In the months before we married, we had often prayed together and not just to give thanks for the food set before us. Many times too, he would open his Bible and read to me a passage that he had read for the fourth or fifth time, but in which he had found a new level of understanding. His joy at the discovery was evident in the way he cradled the leather-bound volume close to his body. I thought I understood his devotion. I know I admired it. I did not know I would resent it.

However, Job was not just a prayer. He was a talker. He talked to God just as he would talk to me. At night, while preparing for bed, he would converse with God and tell Him how the day had gone. Job would speak of the concerns he had faced with a particular person or issue. "I know He knows," he told me on our second night away after I questioned him about what he was doing. "But I believe He likes for me to tell Him. That way we both know I'm not trying to keep secrets."

"Does He ever talk back?" I tried to imagine God talking to me. I believed, I prayed, but this personal, relational God, was someone I was just beginning to understand.

"Sometimes." His smile was remote as his thoughts turned inward for a moment. He shrugged before sliding under the covers of our hotel bed. "Sometimes He speaks through other people, or scriptures, or sometimes when I wake up, I know He's been talking to me while I sleep."

"In your dreams?"

His head turned on his pillow so we were nose to nose. "Yes, but more often it's just this feeling that He's as aware of me as I am of Him. That's what I sense most of the time."

It was a foreign concept for me to adjust to, along with the rest of married life. But we both did some adjusting and our existence settled into a comfortable pattern.

In the morning, Job went to supervise the milking with Pops and the other men. I would do chores in the house until mid-morning when I could grab some time for myself to write. I was working on a series of children's stories centered around a main character, Benny Bunny, but he had many animal friends with which to interact and for which I could develop story lines. I had written the first one in high school and decided to carry on the tales. Job, much to my surprise and delight, had taken to painting illustrations for them.

Lunchtime would bring my hungry husband up to the house and we would share the meal together. Sometimes my mother or his would stop by, or sometimes it was Sarah. After lunch, I would do laundry, or clean until I had to begin preparations for the dinner onslaught of hungry mouths. After the evening meal, Job would work in his office updating the ledgers for a couple of hours before he would return to the barns for a quick meeting with Pops about plans for the next day. One last check on the barns, and then he would return to the house.

In the comfort of routine and the fog of newly married bliss, weeks slipped away unnoticed. Christmas came and went in a winter flurry of family activities and events.

In January, David and Sarah announced they were going to have a baby in June. In February, Michael and Catherine actually did have a baby and made me an aunt first with the birth of their son, Lucas Michael. All the talk of babies made me wish that I had similar news to share, but each month the telltale sign arrived and I knew I had not conceived. I was still getting used to being a wife. The idea of becoming a mother so soon into our marriage was not something that preoccupied my every waking moment. I did not feel ready to give up the exclusive sanctuary that was my relationship with Job.

Job took a big step and hired Robert and Lewis, brothers and seasonal workers who, because of the drought, had come east looking for work. Job was setting into motion his dream of broadening the scope of the dairy to include the making of our own cheeses. For the first time in almost twenty years, Nightingale Farms was mortgaged and the future was full of hope and promise.

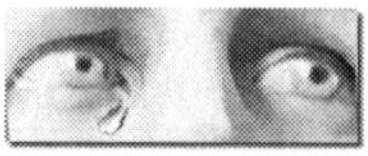

June 1941

It was the end of June before we knew it. David and Sarah were attempting to move into their newly completed house ahead of the arrival of their baby, and I eagerly awaited the approach of my nineteenth birthday.

I was helping Sarah pack up the final few items from their kitchen. I say helping, but the fact of the matter was that I doing all the work. Sarah was so huge and the day unseasonably warm that going up the stairs into the apartment was all she could manage. I was feeling hot and out of sorts myself.

"I can't believe how fast the time has passed." Sarah massaged her protruding belly. A sheen of perspiration had appeared on her forehead and upper lip. "It seems like only yesterday we were married."

"You were married the day before yesterday," I joked. "I was married yesterday."

Almost ten months. I now belonged to the club; the one to which all married women belonged. Membership requirements included knowing the answers to the perpetual questions of "Honey, have you seen my…?" and "What's wrong with what I'm wearing?"

"It's been good though. Hasn't it?"

"Yes." My face split into a smile as I paused in the process of wrapping a china cup in newspaper. "I don't ever remember being this happy."

The soft cry of alarm was not the response I had been expecting to my comment. I turned and found Sarah staring wide eyed at a pool of liquid under her chair.

"What does that mean?" I asked even though I knew the answer.

"We need to find David," she said calmly, but I could sense the panic circling.

"But—"

"Now!" Her grip on my arm almost snapped bone as a contraction took hold.

I managed to find someone to find David, and then called Doc Fisher, and Mrs. Fisher who assisted him with baby deliveries and other matters when needed. My phone call to the Doc had, via Margie Walters, been relayed to my father at the bank who relayed the information to my mother. My mother arrived just minutes after the doctor and his wife. My father followed, as did Job's parents. It was not their grandchild about to be born, but it may as well have been. We were all family.

"Any baby yet?" Job folded me in his arms when he arrived a couple of hours later.

"No." I squeezed him back. "I'm glad you're here."

"I brought some food for us all." He indicated the basket sitting just inside the door.

"That was thoughtful." I leaned over to pick up the basket intending to set out the food in the kitchen. I needed to do more than just listen to the muffled sounds from the bedroom. I felt restless, and not just because of the intensity of the moment. It was hot in the small apartment. The number of people in the room only added to the problem. I had the distinct feeling of confinement. That, combined with a lack of food and water was making me a little nauseous. It was not surprising then, that when I stood up, I was a little wobbly.

"Whoa!" Job reached out to grab my arm. "Easy, Jes."

I shook my head to clear it and offered a reassuring smile. "I just stood up too fast."

"Maybe you should sit down."

"No. I'm fine." Everyone was looking at me now. What was the big deal? "Really, I'm all right. I just need to eat something. Get some fresh air too."

"Jessie, sit." Job tried to turn me around

"I'm fine." I pulled away. I think I took three steps. It may have been only two. I do not remember anything until I woke up on the sofa with Doc Fisher checking my pulse and Job, along with everyone else, hovering anxiously nearby.

"There, Job, you see? She just fainted." The doctor smiled benignly at me and continued to count heartbeats.

"What happened?" I asked.

"You fainted." Job answered. He touched my shoulder seeking assurance and to reassure.

"What? Why?"

"Your husband tells me you haven't eaten much today." Doc Fisher switched from checking my pulse to feeling whatever it is they feel for when they prod your neck with their fingers. "Combined with the heat, it was more than likely just too much for your system. We'll do a complete exam just to be certain."

"Now?" I struggled to sit up. There was a room full of eyes looking at me. No way was I submitting to a doctor's exam in front of all of them. "I feel fine."

"Let's just be certain you stay that way." Doc Fisher gently pushed me back down. He called Mrs. Fisher to assist him and she sent everyone outside, including Job.

"Shouldn't you be in there with Sarah and David?" I tried one last time to get out of the thorough checking over I could see coming.

"Time enough yet," Mrs. Fisher smiled. I never knew her first name. Everyone called her Mrs. Fisher, even her husband—at least in public. I hoped he called her something more familiar when they were alone. I could not imagine Job addressing me as Mrs. Nightingale all the time.

I submitted quietly as the doctor "hemmed" and "haad" through the exam. I answered all his questions, despite the heat of embarrassment some of them brought to my face. Finally he smiled that friendly yet emotionally distant smile of his, gave me the prognosis and returned to David and Sarah.

"Well?" Job was the first to enter the room, once allowed to do so by Mrs. Fisher. He picked up my hand and squeezed.

"I'm fine." I avoided directly meeting his eyes by rubbing mine with my free hand. "I just overdid it today by not eating."

"Well let's get you something to eat."

We ate, and after a little more convincing that I would be fine, the attention finally returned to Sarah and David and the imminent arrival of their child. Job left to take care of the evening milking and I curled up and fell asleep on the sofa. It felt like only minutes that I slept before I awoke to find my mother sitting next to me.

She brushed my forehead with her hand. "How are you feeling?"

I thought about that for a moment and did a quick internal check. Everything felt normal. "Good." I sat up. "I feel good. What time is it?"

"It's after six."

"Really?" I questioned around a yawn. Then I remembered where we were and why we were there in the first place. "The baby! Is it here?"

"Yes." My mother's smile was serene. "A boy."

"Thomas Benjamin." My father beamed from the doorway. "He and Sarah are great. David however is a little worn out from pacing."

I snuck in to see mother and baby before heading home for the evening. I watched David and Sarah form a protective shield around Thomas as he slept in his mother's arms. Longing and inadequacy filled my gut. My lungs constricted and I took a deep steadying breath to ease the pressure. I needed to get back and talk to Job.

I encouraged my parents not to stay as they dropped me off in front of the yellow farm house. Job crossed the yard in our direction. He returned my parents' cheery wave as they drove down the lane to the road. I took my husband's hand when he reached my side and redirected him toward the woods and the path that led to the creek. I did not want to go inside just yet. There were things that needed telling first.

"So?" He swung our joined hands playfully as we walked.

"A boy." I smiled understanding his question. "Thomas Benjamin."

"Wonderful." He smile filled with delight. "Everyone doing well?"

I nodded and released his hand to wrap my arm around his waist and snuggle close.

"It's going to rain soon." His chest expanded as he inhaled the scent of the air.

Brief afternoon or evening thunderstorms were common this time of year. Often times, dark clouds would gather over the many valleys that characterized the countryside. The storms would blow through for an hour or two and move on. Sometimes it would rain on one side of the road and not the other depending on the position of the cloud overhead. Late summer it would rain for longer periods.

Despite the overcast sky, the air was warm, burdened with moisture waiting to be unloaded. The water of the creek felt delicious as we sat on the bank and, after removing our shoes, dangled our feet in the welcoming coolness.

His hand found the nape of my neck and he massaged gently. "Are you feeling better?"

"Yes. I had a sleep."

He lay back on the grass and pulled me down with him. I rested my head on his chest. In the short months of our marriage, I had become intimate with the strong, steady rhythm of his heart. It was slightly slower in tempo than mine, and most nights, as it lulled me to sleep, I would wait for the moment our cadences would match. It would never last for more than two or three beats, but as I drifted in the realm between wakefulness and sleeping, I could discern the moment when, in perfect synchronization the two would beat together. Now my heart was racing and my mind was having a difficult time keeping up.

"I'm going to have a baby." I spoke just above a whisper and waited.

"Yes." He kissed the top of my head. "When the time is right, we'll have our own."

"In January."

His hand on my neck stilled and I felt the skip of his heart as it accelerated to being on pace with mine. He did not say anything.

"Did you hear me?"

"Yes."

"You gonna say anything?"

"No."

I pushed up onto my elbow and looked down at him. His head was tilted back, eyes closed, and he was sporting the biggest dumbest grin I had ever seen. A suspicious moisture leaked from the corners of his eyes and ran down the side of his face into his hair.

"Job?" I had to laugh weakly at his foolish expression. "Say something. I'm beyond scared."

"I'm crazy scared too." He continued to grin foolishly, but at least his eyes were open and he was looking at me. "Isn't it great?"

He pulled me close and rolled over on top of me. I grunted in protest as we both gave in to ridiculous laughter. It was one thing to imagine what it would be like, to anticipate and want it. It was another to find out it would be.

"God is good, Jes." He pressed his face to my abdomen, and prayed for the Lord's will to be done in the life of our child.

Twenty-Three

June 1941

For three days the oppressive heat and humidity continued to build. Just blinking was enough to cause a sweat, and sleeping was near impossible. Tempers ran short and lethargy long. The storm became a constant and ominous presence looming in the not too far distance. Sporadic forks of lightening snaked sinuously across the sky while thunder rumbled in warning. This was just the prologue. When the maelstrom finally broke it would drive us from our Eden with an inequitable rage.

That third morning, I awoke to find the space next to me warm but empty. I sat up and looked around the room. Job was standing at the window, his silhouette barely visible through the lace that billowed in the breeze from the open window. I could hear the rain. I could feel the damp in the air. I shivered, chilled with drying perspiration. The temperature had dropped.

"Is something wrong?" I asked.

"I don't know." He shifted uneasily. "The rain is pretty heavy."

"We've had heavy rain before."

A flash lit up the sky revealing Job more clearly. He was partially dressed, wearing only his jeans. One arm stretched above his head to the top of the window while the other was bent at the elbow, hand in his back pocket. His forehead rested against the glass. It was too dark to see the clock, but I did not need to see it to know it was early to be out of bed, even for Job.

"Are you going out now?"

"I think I should." He turned from his stance at the window and opened a drawer to pull out a shirt. "Something isn't right."

Later that evening, I found him in the exact same pose, the only difference was location. He was leaning on the post of the front veranda when I found him. The men had returned to the bunkhouse after a subdued evening meal. I did not understand the mood, but I could not help being affected by it.

"Hey." I wrapped my arms around him from behind. I rested my forehead on that spot between his shoulder blades and breathed deeply finding comfort in his familiar scent.

"Hey, yourself."

"Tomorrow's the day." I brought up the subject that was sure to remove the brooding frown from his face, our baby. His face always lit up with the same silly grin when I mentioned him, or her. It took everything he had not to shout about it from the rooftop, but we decided to reveal the news to both sets of parents at the same time and avoid any issues of who told whom what and first. The most obvious way to accomplish this was to have them all over for Sunday dinner.

"Are you ready?" Job reached around and pulled me in front of him.

"I don't think so."

"We can wait a while yet. If you need to. It's still early."

I did not think I would ever get used to the idea that I would actually be a mother in just under seven months. "No. We have to tell them and sooner is better."

"It will be something happy in the midst of all this rain."

"Why are you so worried?" I looked out over the soaked lawns and paths. Water ran freely off buildings, down hill onto the driveway and towards the road. In 1927, a year before we had moved to Grand River Junction, a devastating flood had washed through Vermont carrying away the livelihoods and homes of many. Trains were knocked off tracks and the force of the water ripped iron bridges from their moorings as land, already soaked by a large rainfall, refused to accept any more water. Eighty-five people died and not just the landscape changed. This much rain, falling in such a short time would cause more than a few to walk the floor at night.

I felt his shrug. "Something's different. Off somehow."

"Did you talk to God?" I asked and he nodded. "He didn't ask you to build a boat did He?"

He laughed and shook his head.

"What did he say?"

The laughter faded. "Nothing."

His answer caught me unaware. Usually his response was a detailed explanation of what God was telling him and why.

"Well, it can't rain forever." I rubbed my hands up and down his back.

"I suppose not." He smiled down at me, but there was still worry behind his eyes.

In spite of my reasoning to the contrary, it did look as if it might indeed rain forever. The steady deluge eroded deep gullies in the drive and walkways. Animals and people grew edgy as paddock and fields turned to thick slippery masses of clinging muck. Job's concern for the small potato crop he had planted grew commensurate with the level of Miller's Creek.

The back field was low and bordered by the creek. A natural granite ridge formed the bank here and curved around the edge of the property. From the shape of the land, it was obvious that the creek had once been a much wider river that covered most of the field. Job had chosen the location for that exact reason. The soil was dark and fertile.

Now, however, because of the bizarre nature of the weather we were encountering, the location of the field no longer seemed ideal. The ridge of wall kept the water from spreading out in any direction but over the field. What were once clear and meandering waters, now combined with the runoff from the neighboring mountains to grow murky and turbulent and overflow the confines of the bank.

For a week, the rain fell unrelenting from the sky. I watched helplessly as Job waited hopelessly for most of his potatoes to succumb to the rising water. It would not have been so bad if, in the three days of reprieve that followed the rain, the sun had dried the ground, but the river continued to run high, fueled by rains up in the mountains. The days were warm again, but cloudy, without relief from the humidity. The odor of rotting vegetation pervaded everything.

Ten days after the first rain fell, I woke to find the bed next to me empty once again. I located Job seated on the steps of the front veranda, his head in his hands. His elbows rested on knees spread to accommodate the pail that sat on the steps between them.

I saw John, Robert and Lewis in the doorway of the new and partially built creamery. They cast uncertain glances towards the house where Job sat.

Pops appeared from within the milking barn, and seeing me on the veranda with Job, he encouraged the men to get back to work. I waited for them to disappear out of sight and sat down next to my husband. I slipped a hand under his shirt and rubbed his back. The muscles bunched tightly under the damp heat of his skin. I waited for him to speak.

"I don't understand, Jessie."

"Don't understand what?"

He reached into the pail and lifted out a soggy stem with what must have been a young potato. Now it was a squishy, blackened lump. "I've never heard of or seen anything like this before. Neither has Dad, or Pops, or anyone." He broke open the vegetable and showed me the equally black inside.

"What is it?" I switched to breathing through my mouth to avoid the stench that wafted in my direction. My sense of smell was uncommonly keen these days.

"Some kind of rot. And these are some of the ones that were in the higher part of the field."

"They're all like that?"

"All of them. There is not one salvageable potato in the entire field. And, I don't even know what it means for that field." His frustration got the better of him in that moment, and he flung the offending object across the lawn. Heedless of the residue covering his hands he plunged them into his hair and pulled it back from his face.

His hair was getting long. It covered his ears and collar. His mother would say it needed a cut, but I always liked it just a little longer than she considered respectable. I wiped a smear off his temple and wrapped my arms around his neck pulling him in tight.

"Did you get an answer?" I knew he would have been talking to God the whole time he was in the field.

"No." He managed to convey more than a measure of bewilderment in that one word. "I'm not sure there is one."

"If there is, you'll find it."

"Thanks. Having you believe in me means more than you know."

We sat in quiet comfort letting the soft buzz of activity pass by on the periphery of awareness. Thunder rumbled in the distance.

"What happens when it rains again?" I knew from the look of the sky it was inevitable.

"The corn should be fine. It's pretty sturdy." He looked out at the clouds hovering over the hills in the distance. "I'm praying this one blows over real quick."

“Is there anything I can do this afternoon to help?”

“Could you take a bath? You stink.”

My jaw dropped. It was not what I had been expecting. I saw the twitch of his lips.

“I’ve got news for you,” I said

“Yeah? What?”

“You stink more.”

Late that night, the shattering of glass jarred us awake. I felt myself yanked from the softness of our bed and shoved to the floor on the side furthest away from the window. My heart careened in time to the constant hard pelting sound of something coming through the window and bouncing off the hard wood of the floor.

“Stay down!” Job’s hand on my head prevented me from moving.

“What is it? What’s going on?” I could hear more glass breaking in other rooms of the house. “Who’s throwing rocks?”

“It’s hail!”

Lightening lit the room in a long suspended flash allowing me to see exactly to what Job referred. Hundreds of round pieces of ice the size of Job’s fist littered the floor of the room and more continued to follow, carried in by the constant rush of wind. Thunder added another voice to the melee.

“Stay here,” Job commanded. He crawled over, pulled the thick comforter from the chest at the end of our bed, and wrapped it around himself.

“Where are you going?”

“To close the curtains.”

In the warmer weather, we always opened the drapes once ready for bed. If closed, they were heavy enough to block any cooling breeze there might be. During the winter, their weight kept cold drafts at bay.

I heard a few yelps of pain as Job leapt over the bed and fought to close the curtains. The assault eased and I lifted my head to peer over the bed. It was difficult to see anything, but I could hear the rapid “whap-thunk” of the hail as it connected with the heavy drapery material before dropping to the floor. The strength of the wind caused the curtains to billow but their presence as a shield was holding.

“I think it’s easing up.” I heard from the direction of the window.

Another flash and clash.

“Yes, I can tell!”

The bed shook with his weight as Job jumped the distance from the window.

There was a lot of broken glass mixed with the ice. He peered down at me. "Was that sarcasm?"

The abrupt lack of clatter saved me from having to answer. It still rained outside but the pelting of hail stopped. The electricity was out, and because I was too afraid to move until Job lit a lantern, I stayed crouched beside the bed. Once we gained some light, we assessed the damage to the room. Other than the broken window and melting hail, it was relatively minor. The damage to Job was a little more extensive.

On his right cheek, a large purple welt darkened under a split in the skin that still trickled blood. Other round welts and bruises marred his chest and arms, and the instep of his left foot would probably need a new bandage soon. The deep gash in it had bled profusely. For now, the tightly wrapped foot remained protected inside a rubber boot and positioned under the kitchen table.

His were not the only feet planted on the floor in the kitchen. The room was full. Within minutes of the cessation of the hail Pops, John, Mitch, Robert, Rand, and May arrived. The only ones not there were Lewis, his wife Estela, and their son Alejandro. They stayed in town, in the apartment David and Sarah had vacated. With no privacy for a young married family in the bunkhouse, Lewis jumped at the chance to rent the space as soon as David and Sarah had moved. It meant a walk to work in the morning, but cutting across one of the fields shortened the distance.

May and I prepared a large pot of coffee and even larger breakfast on the wood stove while the others discussed the damage report from the various buildings on the property, at least what damage they could see with the available but limited lantern light. The worst damage was to the windows of the main house, our house. I had already swept up the glass, and the hail that had not yet melted, I tossed outside with the rest of it.

"John, you and Robert go into town later this morning and get some boards for the windows," Job said as he stuck his fork into the scrambled eggs his mother placed in front of him. "Ask Mr. Martin to order the glass too, since that could take a while. Come see me for the measurements before you leave."

"Yes sir," John answered with a nod.

"If you think of anything else we'll need before we go, just let us know," Robert said.

"There's the small window in the birthing barn," Pops offered.

"That can wait for now," Job responded around a mouthful of food.

The back door opened and Lewis stepped inside. He took off his hat and clutched it nervously in front of him. Mud clung to his boots and the bottoms of his pant legs. He shook his head. "It's bad."

"What now?" May asked of no one in particular and placed a mug of hot coffee in his hand.

"The corn." Lewis bobbed his head gratefully before swallowing a mouthful of the strong brew. "I was on my way here, see? Because of the storm an' all. I came through the field, 'cause it's faster. It's all broken."

"Broken?"

"Yeah, broken." He made a snapping gesture with one hand. "I ain't never seen nothing like it. The hail covered the ground and broke the plant stalks."

"All of it?" Rand asked.

"All what I could see."

Everyone looked to Job. He ran his hands through hair that already stood on end. If those hands were not quite as steady as they usually were, no one said anything. The cut on his cheek stood in stark contrast to the paleness under his tan. I knew he was shaken. Everyone in the room was in some way off balance.

"I'll go have a look, son. As soon as it's light." Rand volunteered.

"Thanks." He offered a small smile of appreciation to his father. "But I need to see it for myself."

Rand nodded his understanding and stood. Following his lead, the others made their way out of the house and down to the barn.

May took the plates I was clearing from my hands and put them in the sink. She directed me to the stairs. "Go get some more sleep," she said. "Use Job's old room."

I was too wound up to sleep. "I need to do something to help."

"Taking care of that baby is the most important thing right now." She gave me a hug. "I'll clean up here and when Estela comes, I'll have her help with putting something together for lunch."

"Job?" I wanted to make sure there was nothing he needed from me. He turned in my direction and although he looked at me, I knew he was picturing what might await him in the field. "Is there anything I can do?"

"Not at the moment. Thanks. Mom's right. Get some rest and I'll see you later." He waved absently and went out the back door.

I pushed aside my need to be needed and headed upstairs to the room that had been Job's right up until we married. It was across the hall from the master bedroom, and I could not help but stop and look in at where we had been sleeping. The bed was still unmade, the curtains fluttered slightly in the breeze coming through the broken window. The wind and rain had subsided. What had happened last night?

I entered the room and pushed aside the curtain. Just beyond the mountains in the distance, dawn was hinting at its arrival. It would be a beautiful day. The clouds were dissipating, leaving in their stead, a clear sky with the last few stars of the night. Their light would soon pale into nothingness when outdone by that of the sun. The uncharacteristic humidity that had weighed heavily in the air was gone, hinting at a more normal temperature, one that would be comfortably warm in the sun and just slightly cool in the shade. The kind of day Job loved.

The soft yellow of lantern light appeared in the milking barn, and I heard the first welcoming lows of the cows as they anticipated the relief of having full udders emptied. I pictured the men going through the routine of cleaning, feeding and milking. Normally I took comfort in the familiar sounds and activities.

I let the drape fall back into place and returned to Job's old room. I sat on the edge of the single bed and stared out the window. I do not know how long it was that I remained there unmoving, but it must have been some time for the sun had risen higher in the sky, enough to highlight the solitary figure walking through the far field. The corn, that had —was it only yesterday? —stood about a foot and a half high in straight orderly rows, now lay flat and lifeless at his feet. I knew in his heart Job was feeling as chaotic as the mess before him. How could he not? I was more than a little disoriented myself.

No longer able to stand the sight of Job walking amidst the devastation, I pulled the covers down and crawled beneath them. When I woke, the sun was high, although from the angle, I knew it was still morning.

"Hi," I said. The weight of an arm across my middle told me I was not alone.

"Hi."

"Is it bad?"

"There's nothing left to harvest. The oats are destroyed as well."

I tried to think of what it would mean for us, for the farm, but so much of it was outside my comprehension. I knew the basics of the financial side of things, but for a banker's daughter, my ignorance was shameful.

Job reluctantly explained what the events of the night would mean for us. It came down to the fact that without the corn and oats there would be no supplemental feed for the cows. We could plant more but the time for clearing the fields of the damaged plants and then replanting new seed would push the harvest time too late into the season. We would have to purchase feed from the co-op in town. On top of that, the bunkhouse needed a new roof, and the barns needed eight sheets of tin between them, damage only discovered in daylight. Combined with the glass needed for the house, the expense would be dear. We were not ready to sell cheese yet, and without the small income from the potatoes, the repair funds would have to come from the loan money set aside for wages. People would have to be let go.

The last ones hired were Robert and Lewis. I was deeply saddened at the thought of their having to leave. Lewis had brought with him his bride of five years, Estela, and their four-year-old son, Alejandro.

Alejo was an energetic child with the dark hair, eyes and olive complexion that was the genetic heritage of his mother's Spanish ancestry. I often heard his laughter from the backyard as he chased the barn cats that would dare to venture out into the open.

Estela had insisted on helping with the meals and household chores. Her family in Mexico was large and noisy, and she missed them. Helping me made her feel like she was part of a big family again. I also enjoyed watching Pops as he carefully tested the new and unfamiliar dishes Estela placed before him, or watching him slip Alejo a peppermint when Estela was not looking.

"I'll miss them too." Job buried his nose in the back of my neck.

"When will you tell them?"

"I'm not sure." He squeezed me tighter. "I would like them to stay for a week to help get things here back in order."

A soft knock at the door interrupted us and Job called for them to enter. It was Rand.

"I hate to disturb you, son." Rand spoke quietly. "There's a big tree threatening to come down across the creek. I think we need to get it moved before it damns things up and causes more trouble."

"OK. Sure." Job rubbed his eyes and yawned. "I'll be right there."

"I'll get Estela and we'll put together a lunch for you all to eat down there."

An hour later, Estela, Alejo, and I were on our way down to the creek. Alejo ran ahead, stretching legs cramped from being inside too long; of course in his case, five minutes was to long. I wondered if the child growing inside would be a boy or a girl. Would he or she have Job's eyes? I hoped whatever it would be, would not have my hair.

"Mister Job!" Alejo spied Job directing Robert as he maneuvered the tractor into position. It was clear they were going to hook it up to the tree leaning precariously over the swollen waters of the creek. Lewis waited with the chain that would wrap around the large maple.

"I want to fly!" Alejo flung himself at Job's legs.

Job obliged and scooped the boy up and spun him until they were both laughing and dizzy. He set the child down and with a soft swat on his behind, sent him running back toward Estela and myself.

"He is good with Alejandro, si?" Estela observed slyly.

"Si." I answered with a laugh. "He is very good with him."

"He will make a fine papa."

"I know he will."

"Hello ladies." Job greeted as we reached him. "How are you today Estela?"

"I'm fine Señor Job." She smiled sadly. "I fear your crop is not."

"No, it's not." He caught Alejo as he broke away from Estela's hand and made a dash for his father. The boy shrieked in delight as he was turned and held upside down. "Be sure to keep him close to the house for the next little while. The water's running pretty fast and some of the other trees along the banks look unstable."

"I understand." Estela took her squirming son firmly into her arms. What reprimand she spoke to Alejo was said in rapid Spanish, but it worked. He stopped wiggling and managed to stand next to his mother with only a few fidgets.

"Are you ready to eat?" I held up the basket of food prepared for them.

"As soon as Lewis gets that chain around the tree." Job turned and pointed to an area higher than the rest of the clearing. "Why don't you set up over there. It should be dry enough."

Alejo begged to be allowed to help his papa the entire time Estela and I were setting out the sandwiches and milk. Not until we were done eating did Job give the boy the task of ridding the clearing of the broken branches that had fallen during the storm and putting them in one big pile. With a feeling of importance, Alejo set off to do the job with great enthusiasm. Only after making certain the child was fully engaged in the chore, did Job, Robert and Lewis return to the problem of the tree.

The old maple died many years ago and the rushing water of the swollen creek had further undermined a decaying root system. The tree now threatened to fall and obstruct the natural flow of the water. The men would pull the tree away from the creek and onto the bank.

From where we sat, Estela and I could safely observe the progress and keep an eye on Alejo at the same time. We watched Robert climb into the tractor and wait for further instructions. Lewis called to his brother to start the tractor.

Robert carefully engaged the gears and the tractor began to creep forward. The chain tightened, and with the engine grinding the tractor began to pull the tree free from the earth. The ground was soft, slippery under the weight of the machine. The tires spun in an effort to gain some traction. With a lurch, they caught hold and just as abruptly, let go. The tractor slipped to one side, the tires spinning in futility. The change in angle shifted the tree. It drifted dangerously off course. Job's warning cry was lost in the protest of the tractor engine and the sound of roots as they were rendered apart.

Lewis realized the danger of where he was standing. He tried to run, but thick mud sucked his boots deep into the bank and trapped him.

I had seen death in the barns on more than one occasion when an animal died, and I would see it again; but I had never before felt its presence with the certainty I did as Lewis lay crushed beneath that old dead maple. The labored breaths he managed gurgled as blood filled his lungs, throat, mouth, and nose. It even trickled out of his ears. Robert cradled his brother's head in his lap and pleaded for him to hold on. Job was trying to turn the tractor around and re-attach the chain.

"Es." Lewis tried to turn his head to see his wife. She crouched down to make it easier for him to see her. In her arms a subdued Alejandro stared with wide-eyed fear and confusion.

"Estoy aqui mi vida." I am here, my life.

Lewis closed his eyes and waited for his own breathing to stop. We could do nothing but wait with him.

Twenty-Four

June 1941

Sheriff Brady and Doc Fisher arrived almost simultaneously. The sheriff would need a statement about the accident and Doc Fisher served as the county coroner. May had taken Estela and Alejandro inside. I did not want to go inside, instead I settled on the veranda swing. Rand sat next to me. Together we watched the sheriff and the doctor approach. Rand greeted both men with solemn handshakes.

"Mrs. Nightingale. Jes." Sheriff Brady doffed his hat to me. "Is it all right if I call you Jes?"

I had known the man for as long as I had been in Grand River Junction. On more than one occasion, I had danced with him at the summer gathering; and when Mr. Martin suspected someone was stealing penny candy from the open jar he kept on the counter next to his till at the general store, Sheriff Brady had hauled in anyone under the age of twelve for questioning. Mr. Martin had insisted.

I had been brought into the store and lined up with my brothers, Kenny, Job, and several others. I had been terrified even though I knew I was innocent. I remember Sheriff Brady seemed a little embarrassed by the whole thing. He tried to put me at ease with an awkward pat on the shoulder but it did not help. We all stood in silence for several very long minutes until a faint scuffling noise had us turning to look at the counter.

We watched in quiet fascination as a chipmunk stuffed its cheeks with sweet treats before disappearing over the counter and out through a crack in the corner where wall and floor met. Sheriff Brady turned to face us, a gleam of satisfaction in his eye. He walked over to the door and opened it. With a wink and a sweep of his arm he said, "You're all free to go."

This was bigger than chipmunks. I understood his need for clarity on the form of his address to me. I nodded consent to the informal, and Sheriff Brady took Rand's place next to me on the swing.

"Tell me what happened, Jessie." The Sheriff's prod was gentle.

I squeezed my eyes shut against the image of the tree falling on Lewis. I did not try to stop the tears that overflowed as I managed to sob and hiccup my way through the tragic event.

Job's truck appeared from out of the trees and slowly pulled onto the drive in front of the house just as I finished. In the bed of the truck, Robert sat next to his brother's body. I glanced toward the road and saw the wagon from Johnson's Funeral Home. Pulled by a pair of matching black and white Shires, it turned onto the driveway and made its way to where Job's truck stopped.

Mack Johnson set the brake on the wagon, not that it was necessary. After an initial toss of their heads, the two gleaming behemoths stood fast and firm. Cannon fire would not make them flinch.

The Sheriff thanked me and offered an awkward shoulder pat in comfort before making his way over to the wagon. Mack reached behind him and took a folded white sheet from the wagon bed then nimbly sprung from the wagon. He shook hands with the Sheriff and Doc Fisher. The few quiet words they exchanged, I could not hear from where I sat.

I could not bear to watch as they transferred Lewis's body from the truck to the wagon so I finally went inside. I heard May in the kitchen. She was talking softly to Alejo. I took the front stairs up, avoiding going through the kitchen, and went to Job's room.

Sedatives had brought a temporary relief to Estela's grief. I stood in the doorway of the room watching her sleep. Just hours before, in that same bed, Job and I discussed having to send the four of them—Estela, Lewis, Alejandro and Robert, home. Had it really only been hours ago?

I pulled the quilt from the end of the bed up over the sleeping widow. Widow. That was what she was now. It could have so easily have been me lying there in her place. I was both relieved and guilty that it was not. Seized with an irrational compulsion to assure myself of my husband's well being, I fled the room and hurried back downstairs.

In the kitchen, the mood was heavy. May was assuring Robert that the priest had been contacted and would perform the funeral. Job assured him the costs of the funeral would be covered. I went straight into his arms and was grateful when they closed tightly around me. It was not until later that night, as with every breath and touch we sought confirmation of life, did we voice the fear that had filled both of our hearts.

"If that tree had swung the other way—." I sobbed into his chest unable to finish the thought aloud.

"I keep thinking about Alejandro growing up without his father and how it could be you raising our baby alone." The hold on the control of the afternoon was finally lost as he allowed his own sorrow to flow.

Afterward, I watched and listened to each rise and fall of his chest and to each in and out of every breath. I watched him sleep, too afraid to close my eyes because he might not be there when I opened them.

Two days later, the small funeral service was held in St. Paul's Catholic Church on the other side of town. Lewis had attended it only briefly with his wife, son, and brother, but they had been faithful and well liked by the few who had gotten to know them. After the service, the simple oak casket Estela had selected for her husband's body was transported to the train station. Robert, Estela and Alejandro would accompany it back to Arizona for burial.

At the train station, Job handed Estela a white envelope. She protested after peering inside and tried to hand it back to Job.

"It's too much!" she whispered.

"It's not enough." Job pressed the money back in her hands.

"But the funeral. And the tickets." She shook her head in disbelief before placing her hand on Job's chest above his heart. "It is not your fault, Señor."

Job pressed the envelope back into her hands. "Please take it. Keep it for Alejo."

We waved a tearful goodbye to the three as they boarded the train.

That afternoon and evening, Job single handedly chopped the old maple to pieces.

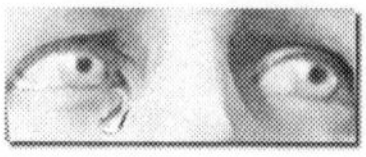

July 1941

It would be weeks before the atmosphere on the farm relaxed into anything that approached normal. Everyone had been walking around as though expecting another tragedy to befall us, but there was one day, an absolutely-ordinary-nothing-special kind of day, on which we all seemed to breathe a collective sigh of relief.

Perhaps it was because order had been restored to the place: windows and roofs were repaired, debris was cleared from the yards and surrounding paddocks, the fields dried out, and the creek subsided within the normal boundaries.

I felt the need for some company the morning of that ordinary day and went to visit Sarah and baby Thomas. I wanted to get in some baby practice. The more the better, as far as I was concerned.

Flashes of maternal inadequacy and abject fear rushed through my veins on a fairly regular and frequent basis. I called my mother and together we just dropped by. Sarah appeared so happy to see us I thought she could weep. "Finally, people I can actually understand when they answer me."

My mother decided the sanity of her grandson's mother was imminently more important than a visit with that same grandson. She volunteered me for baby watching for a couple of hours while she took Sarah to visit Mrs. White at the store.

"He's just been fed." Sarah was giving me a last few instructions as she pushed my mother out the door ahead of her. "He should sleep most of the time we're gone."

"Fine." I stood at the door just vacated by the two of them and watched as they hurried down the front walk.

"There are clean diapers in the top drawer of the dresser." Sarah paused, turned and took a few steps back toward the house. "You do know how to fold them, right?"

"Sure." No. So far I had avoided that actual chore itself, although I had observed it from a safe distance. It did not look that difficult. Besides, I was praying Thomas would prove his deep abiding love for his Auntie Jessie by showing remarkable restraint.

My mother grabbed Sarah's arm and pulled her down the walkway, and I went into the back bedroom. Thomas lay in his crib looking up at the mobile his parents had hung above it. His head turned when he heard my greeting. I got the "I-know-you-but-you're-not-my-mommy," look. That rapidly morphed into the "I-want-my-mommy" scrunch with a trembling bottom lip added for good measure, and ended by culminating in the bone chilling "Somebody-save-me-from-the-clutches-of-this-evil-woman" wail.

After ten minutes of that, I went from "It's-okay-sweet-baby-I'm-here," to "I-know-sweet-baby-I-want-my-mommy-too," and finally landed in the middle of "I-shouldn't-be-having-a-baby-I'll-be-a-terrible-mother."

I planted myself in the rocker with Thomas cradled carefully in my arms. Within seconds, he was asleep, and I relaxed with a huge sigh of relief.

As I watched my little nephew and listened to the occasional snuffling noises, my heart ached with how much love I had for him. I thought about Laura and the recent pictures she had sent of Andrea, now over a year old. I tried to imagine the chubby cherub tottering around on her sturdy legs.

Then there was my other nephew, Lucas, whom I had seen only once when Michael and Catherine had visited just after Thomas's birth. None of them—David and Sarah, Michael and Catherine, or Laura and Mark—had had any more experience with parenting than I did when they started, and none of them had injured or maimed a child yet. If the Bothers could raise children, certainly I could.

Besides, I had Job to parent with me, and I had complete trust in his abilities. The knot of trepidation that had resided next to the bubble of joy in my heart since the day I found out I was going to be a mother loosened a fraction.

My child watching duties ended without further mishap. Thomas showed his deep and abiding love for me by waiting for his mother to return before demanding a diaper change. I dropped my mother off and returned home. Instead of going straight to the house, I wandered down to the barns, stopping briefly to chat with a less gangly, more handsome James.

He was now a junior in high school and trying to decide on his plans for the future. All he knew was that he wanted to remain close to Grand River Junction. He and a certain Elizabeth Anne Alcott were quite serious about their feelings for each other.

I waved to Mitch and John as they turned the cows out after the afternoon milking and accepted a peppermint from Pops as we passed in the yard. I finally found Job in the back, sealing the cans of milk that would be shipped off to be bottled and placed on doorsteps all over the region. Just being near him lifted my mood.

I snuck up behind him and covered his eyes with my hands. "Guess who?" I demanded knowing it would be obvious.

"Midnight Mary!" he cried. "You've come back to me after all these years!"

"Nice guess, but wrong." I laughed and gave him a hug.

"Oh. It's only you." He sighed forlornly.

"What's that mean?"

"Nothing." He sighed again. "It's just that…I had hoped. Oh well…"

I gave his hands a playful swat as they reached for me. "Not so fast, Pally. Who's Midnight Mary?"

"Why do you want to know, Doll Face?" He attempted to grab me again.

"Because." I dodged him by putting a milk can between us.

"Because, why?"

"Job." I gave him a narrowed eyed glare.

"I'll tell you if you give me a kiss." He bargained.

"I'll give you a kiss if you tell me." I returned to which he laughed and lunged again.

I let him catch me but not kiss me.

"Midnight Mary was a cat." He said in soft mysterious tones.

"A cat?"

"Not just any cat." He stared down at me all serious and intent. "She was the fattest, meanest cat you ever laid eyes on. One day she just showed up, and a year later she just disappeared."

"What happened?"

"No one knows." He lowered his voice. "Nobody ever saw her again, but some say that when the moon is full and the midnight clear, you can hear her crying out in the woods."

"Did you ever hear it?" I was more than a little suspicious.

"Once." He nodded. "I'll never forget. It raised the hair on the back of my neck and sent shivers down my spine. It sounded like this."

Before he could inhale to demonstrate his meaning, the most unbelievable and creepy caterwauls filled the room. Both of us jumped a foot off the ground then stared wide eyed at each other. Gradually the sound of wailing turned into uncontrollable laughter. As one, we turned to the door.

Mitch, John and James were falling all over each other hooting and hollering. Pops flipped a peppermint into his mouth and grinned smugly. "Come on fellas." He pushed the candy into his cheek. "Someone best get to workin' 'round here."

They followed Pops, still laughing.

"Traitors!" Job yelled after them. "You're all fired!"

They laughed harder.

This is the day we were almost normal again, not the same, but able to feel lighthearted and hopeful, with the restoration of wounded confidence and belief in the future. The feeling lasted a week.

Twenty-Five

August 1941

It was early that August morning when John knocked frantically. Cool air hinting at the coming autumn. Job and I were awake but lingering. We had been marveling at the changes that were occurring in my body. What fascinated him most was the expanding of my waist and abdomen, indicating our child was growing steadily.

He had taken to whispering words to the baby that I could not quite hear, insisting it would be a girl. I refused to speculate. I had however, finally adjusted to the idea of being this child's mother, boy or girl. Not to say that every day was free of doubts and insecurities, but those things no longer overwhelmed.

"Who is that, my baby?" Job spoke to my belly when the first pounding sounded. "Why are they disturbing us this way?"

I pushed his head and hands away with a laugh and slid over to the edge of the bed.

"Stay, Jes. I'll go." Job slid over to his side as the banging came again.

"No, that's OK." I grabbed my robe. "I need to get up anyway."

"If you insist." Job lay back down with a smile.

The floor was cold and I was looking through the drawer for a pair of Job's wool socks to slip on when I heard the front door open followed by footsteps pounding up the stairs. I turned to look at Job who shrugged equally puzzled. We never locked our door but we did not have a need to. Nobody entered without knocking and waiting for a response. For someone to do so, especially at this early hour, indicated all was not right.

At the last second, the footsteps halted outside our open bedroom door. We could hear rapid breathing.

"Who is it?" Job called throwing back the bed covers.

"John."

"It's all right. Come in, John." I moved into his line of sight so he would know I meant it.

John took a cautious step into our doorway and stood there shaking. "I'm real sorry to come in like this, but there's trouble in the east field."

"It's all right." Job reached for his overalls and pulled them on over his pajama bottoms. "What sort of trouble."

"A real bad sort," John's voice shook with emotion. "Dead cows."

"Dead cows?" I could not have heard that correctly.

"How?" Job asked as he pulled on his shirt from the day before.

"Don't know for sure."

"Then tell me what you're not sure of." Job pushed when it seemed like the man was evading a direct answer.

"Looks like Fog Fever."

"I'll be right out," Job said. "Go get my father."

The rapid clomping of John's boots as he took the stairs more than one at a time indicated the gravity of the situation.

"Fog Fever?" I asked pulling a sweater from Job's dresser for him.

"It's bad, Jes." He tugged the sweater over his head. "It's like pneumonia for cows but worse. The don't really recover. If you startle them, they can drop dead right in front of you or linger for weeks. Most times they don't last more than twelve hours. Air gets caught under the skin over the ribs and brisket."

"How'd they get it?"

"Not sure if they have it yet." He disappeared into the closet only to reappear seconds later with the rifle he kept there. My heart sank at the sight of the gun.

I knew it was there. I knew Job owned it. His father had given it to him for Christmas a few years ago. The gun itself did not scare me, the presence of the gun in this situation did.

"Please, bring the other one from the study."

I nodded wordlessly.

"And the extra shells," He threw over his shoulder and raced from the house.

It took me slightly longer to dress than it had taken Job. I had to use one of his belts to keep up the jeans that I pulled on. I could no longer fasten them at all. I struggled with my burden of the extra rifle and shells, but I headed for the east field.

The others were standing motionless at the fence bordering the pasture. We joined them, and what I saw was indescribable. Almost a dozen cows lay dead or dying. Another dozen or so stood legs spread apart and panting. Their grunts echoed painfully through the predawn air.

"Give me your knife, Mitch." Job held out his hand for the sharp tool that was a constant presence on Mitch's belt.

Job entered the field and approached the carcass of our best milk producer. The rest of us stood in silence and watched as Job plunged the knife between two of the ribs and into a lung. If it was not Fog Fever, the lung would collapse when the knife was removed. It stayed firm, filled with fluid.

"You were right, John." Job wiped the blade on the leg of his overalls before returning it to Mitch. He took the rifle from my numb fingers and handed it to John while Rand loaded his. "Jessie, go up to the barns and check them for any sick animals. The rest of us will deal with this here."

From the look of how they were going to deal with things, I did not want to stay. I walked away quickly and left to separate the sick from the healthy. It would be a delicate task as those animals that appeared healthy could suddenly develop symptoms and collapse if forced to strenuous exertion. I was half-way to the Cottage when the first shot shattered the morning.

"How you doin'?" Pops found me what felt like hours later, but was only a few long minutes. I sat doubled over on a hay bale in the Cottage.

"Not too good." I lifted my face from my hands. The degree of their wetness told me my face was a mess. "How's Job?"

"Doin' what needs to be done." He sat next to me. "Any signs of it in the barns?"

"Not so far." I did not tell him I had not gotten beyond this point. "How many?"

"Too many." Pops ran a weary hand over his head causing his hair to stand up in white tufts. "All of 'em."

I could not breathe.

"Every one of 'em in that field."

"But that was thirty head!"

"They're checkin' the others now."

Outrage and disbelief propelled me toward the door. I needed to see for myself.

Pops, however, could still move quickly when the moment called for it—there just were not many he felt did. He took hold of my arm before I was able to slide the door half open.

"Don't go out there, Jes." His voice was soft, firm but pleading.

"I'm going." I did not look at him but at his hand on my arm. Slowly he released me.

"They've moved down further."

What I saw staggered me. Everywhere I turned, a cow lay dead, steam rising from the bulk of the still warm body. It smelled like a butcher shop. Job hurried over when he saw me.

"Go back to the house. This is no place for you right now."

"I'm staying."

"You don't need to be here." He softened his tone. "Please, don't fight me on this."

I looked carefully at him. Blood covered his feet and hands. There were flecks of it on his face, along with bits of other things I did not want to dwell on.

"I do need to be here." I resisted gently. "What happens to you, happens to me."

I extended my arm to Rand, who, after a brief nod from Job, handed me his rifle. This gun I recognized. It was old but well cared for. This gun was the one Job, Michael and David had used for target practice many times over the years. After taking a turn once, I pretended not to understand what the big excitement was. Instead, I played at being content to sit and poke fun at my brothers' attempts to match Job's skill. The truth was, firing it had scared me more than I was willing to admit to anyone. I had not picked up a gun since. There had been no need.

There were only two cows left standing. I carefully made my way over to the closest animal. It stood, legs spread, neck extended and covered in sweat. The whites of her eyes showed with the strain and terror of trying to breathe and not being able to do so. The foam around her nostrils indicated the stage to which the disease had advanced. I struggled for oxygen of my own and lifted the rifle.

The force of the shot jerked me back a step. I tasted blood on my tongue. It was my own. I had bitten the inside of my lip.

The animal before me seemed to take an age to fall, but her legs gradually buckled beneath the dead weight and she crumpled to the ground. The force of the landing pushed out what little air she had taken in. It left her body with a soft groan. I doubled over and vomited.

Out of the corner of my eye I saw Job take a step in my direction. With one hand I held him off, then wiped my mouth. On unsteady legs I made my way to the last cow. It was not as resigned to its fate as the first one and tried to move away but stumbled and went down. It took two shots, but I managed to dispatch her without throwing up.

We all stood in the sudden eerie quiet and surveyed the devastation. John was without his ever present smile as tears ran unheeded down his face. Mitch sent a forceful stream of brown tobacco juice to the ground then turned his back on the scene, and Pops, looking older than I had ever seen him, stood hands in his pockets and worried a peppermint with his last few remaining teeth. The most difficult person to look at was Mr. Nightingale.

To me, Rand always appeared larger than life. Now his tall, broad, and strong figure looked bent, almost frail. I found it disturbing. Abruptly, he straightened, his eyes fixed on a point out in the field.

Job stood amidst the carnage, arms outstretched and head tilted back. I watched dumbstruck, as he sank to his knees and began to pray.

"Gracious Father in Heaven," his words floated clearly to us. "You are merciful and great. Your goodness abounds even here. My life and livelihood are yours. Willingly, I trust them to your hands."

What was this? I did not see goodness in anything that had just happened. Every cow in the field lay dead, and it was not even mid morning.

Indignation, hot and fierce, replaced sadness and fear as I listened to my husband pour out praise and thanksgiving to God. When Rand kneeled beside him, I threw the rifle down and walked away.

I stoked the fire of anger the rest of the morning and through the afternoon. It burned hotter as I prepared the evening meal. After the morning's events, the roast I had been contemplating was out. It would be chicken or pork for quite awhile. By the time the group was seated at the kitchen table, I was ready to fight.

I listened as they discussed what the livestock hauler and several others had told them. He would have to make several trips to remove the many animal carcasses. Job's best option would be to dig a pit and burn them. It would take several days but it would help eliminate the risk of other diseases or problems.

We took hands and waited for Job to say the blessing on the meal. I refused to bow my head as once again he thanked God for His provision.

"How can you still thank God after today?" I demanded after his "Amen" had been echoed by his parents.

He looked at me with bewilderment.

"How can you sit there and proclaim His goodness?" I continued. "Especially when there is nothing good in what happened out there?"

"How can I not?" He acted like it was a reasonable question. "What happened out there today does not change who God is."

"Who is He?" I barely refrained from shouting as I pushed back from table. "Is He gracious and loving? Merciful? Where was His grace and mercy when Lewis died? Where was His love out in that field today? Or His bountiful blessing? He's taken everything, Job! Maybe you can thank Him for that, but I don't think I can."

"He has not taken everything!" Job also stood.

"What's left?"

"We still have food on the table and a roof over our heads."

"For how long? There are ten cows left. Ten out of sixty!"

"That's ten cows to be thankful for. And we can get more."

"With what money? If Lewis hadn't been killed, we would have had to let him and Robert go. With only ten cows, how can we continue to pay others?"

Too late, I remembered where we were and who was there. The "others" in question avoided looking directly at anyone, but I knew they were listening more closely now.

His frustration was evident in the way he pulled at his hair with both hands. They finally fell impotently to his sides. "Jessie, we still have friends and family that love us. We still have each other, and in a few months we will have our baby. If that's all we're left with, then that will be enough for me. That and the faith that I have that God has not, and will not desert me."

He left then, stating quietly that he would not return until late, as there were many things to take care of in order to begin the disposal of the herd. I do not know exactly what I felt as I took in my in-laws' tactfully lowered eyes, I just know that it was not good.

I ran upstairs and collapsed in a miserable heap on our bed, and eventually cried myself into an uneasy sleep. When I woke some time later, I felt childish and embarrassed. It was dark, and by the sounds floating up from downstairs, I knew I was not alone in the house.

The scent of *Calandre* told me that, if there were more than one person in the house, May had to be among them. The perfume had been a present to her one recent Christmas. Under the mixture of rose, sandalwood, and something else I could not name, I detected a whiff of smoke.

It was not heavy in the air but neither was it the comforting smell of fireplace or woodstove smoke. This smoke signified death. They were burning the carcasses already.

May was at the stove brewing a pot of coffee. The thermos next to the stove told me it was not the first of the night. A plate of sandwiches sat on the counter.

I stood in the doorway and watched as she instinctively made her way around the kitchen that had changed very little since it had been hers. I wondered briefly how she felt about it, and not just the kitchen. This place had been her home from the time she was my age. Now she and Rand knocked before entering.

"How are you holding up?" She must have sensed my presence.

"Not so good." I pushed away from the doorframe and retrieved the picnic basket from the floor. I set it on the table then moved to the counter where I began placing the sandwiches in the paper bag that I found waiting next to the plate.

"Jessie, my son loves you more than his own life." She came up behind me and wrapped her arms tightly around me. "There isn't anything he wouldn't do for you and that baby."

I squeezed back tears of shame. I did not want to embarrass myself further.

"But, you need to understand that his faith in God is what enables him to love like that. Don't ask him to doubt."

Without saying anything, for I had no reply to her underlying warning, I gathered the makeshift meal and made my way out the door to the back field.

Twenty-six

August 1941

The breeze carried the stench of burning cow flesh with it. I handed off the food to Pops who wrapped an arm around my shoulders briefly and inclined his head towards the tall cluster of pines off to the left. A form reclined against the base of a tree, down wind from the smoke.

I made my way over and eased myself down carefully next to him. Job stirred but did not wake. The light of the fire cast a soft orange glow that accentuated the hollows under his eyes. His jaw, now shaded with stubble, was tight with tension even in sleep. I buried my nose behind his ear and kissed his jaw. I do not believe it was wishful thinking to say that he relaxed slightly as he lifted his arm around my shoulders and I snuggled in.

He sighed deeply and I felt his lips press against the top of my head. "How long have you been here?"

"Just." I looked up into his eyes. In the flicker of the firelight they were deeper, darker. "How are you?"

"Tired." He leaned his head back against the trunk of the tree and shut his eyes. "So very tired. Today was probably the worst day of my life."

"I'm sorry I made it worse."

He sighed again. "I need you Jes."

"I know. I'm sorry about what I said to you earlier. I was angry and confused."

"And now?"

"I'm still both of those things. I don't understand any of this and it's scary, but I shouldn't have taken it out on you. I'm sorry."

"I'm sorry too." His hand came up and cradled my cheek. It was cool and felt nice against a face I knew was hot with shame. "I don't understand either. I still get no answers."

We sat in quiet for some time after that. Job had slipped his hand under the coat I wore and it now rested on my tummy.

I could not block out the stench of burning flesh that lingered in the air and that would cling tightly to our clothes and hair in the days that followed. His slow even breathing, broken only by the occasional deep sigh told me Job dozed lightly. I let my mind wander over the things that had happened and what might lie ahead of us. Gradually my thoughts centered and took me down a path that until now had remained hidden by the overgrowth of crazy events.

"Job?" I squeezed his hand that remained on my stomach.

"Mmm?" He shifted to find a more comfortable position but I would not allow it.

"Wake up. It's important."

"I'm awake."

"How much would buying new stock cost?" I waited while he thought about it and did some brief calculations in his head. He told me and I did some math of my own. "I have the money."

"What are you talking about?" He sat up and looked at me like I had sprouted horns.

"I have the money." I laughed. "Well, not that much but we could start again. Smaller."

"Did you rob your father's bank?"

"No, your father's. Job I've worked on this farm since I was fourteen years old. And a lot of these cows we're burning are Blizzard's offspring. And then I worked at Mrs. White's shop. All that money, I put in the bank. I used some of it for sure in New York and stuff, but I came home, we got married, and I forgot about it. It's still there."

"That's your money Jes."

"To use for what? I'm not going back to school. You share yours with me, so it's only right that this money is ours too."

It took a little more convincing, but eventually Job agreed to see things my way. After all, if he would not look at the money as ours, it was then my money to do with as I pleased. If he did not spend it, I would.

"I'll talk it over with Dad tomorrow and see what kind of plan we can work out." The tension in his body lessened with the words. It was as though having an actual physical task that would move us forward was enough to make the financial future less bleak.

"And I'll go and see my dad." I burrowed into his chest feeling more confident myself.

His hand returned instinctively to my lower abdomen and I pulled back with a jerk at the soft tickle.

"Don't." I laughed and pinched the skin at his ribs in retribution.

He grabbed my hand with a laugh of his own. "Don't what?"

"Don't tickle."

"I didn't."

"Yes you did."

"No, I didn't."

"Job."

"Jes." He looked straight at me.

"You really didn't tickle me?"

"No. I—"

"Ssh." I cut him off and froze. It was there again. Softer but more sustained. It was inside. The baby. I was feeling the baby move for the first time. It was thrilling and terrifying and amazing and real. I did not want to move in case it stopped.

"Jessie?"

I took Job's hand and placed it above the flutter in my womb. "Do you feel that?" I whispered.

"The baby? You can feel her?"

"Yes. Can you?"

He shook his head and smiled somewhat wistfully. "No. Not yet. What does it feel like."

I brushed my lips across his lightly. "Like that." I did it again and smiled. "When *he* moves, it feels something like that."

In that moment, surrounded by the soot and burning stench of what was supposed to have been the foundation of our life together, I did believe that there truly was much for which to be thankful. I did.

The next day Job began to search for new livestock, and I went to the bank to visit my father. We sat down for a discussion of finances and with reservation, he agreed with my plan to take out my money. He also suggested that I sit down with Job and learn the farm books. It would give me a better understanding where we stood with money and expenses, and allow Job to keep focused primarily on getting operations of the dairy going.

That evening I broached the subject to Job and the lessons began. I learned about feed costs, milk prices, wages, profits, and losses. The latter two were quickly becoming problematic after the losses of the past week. We were not totally penniless, but after meeting the financial responsibilities of the next couple of months, we would be close to it. We would just have enough to meet the basic needs. Keeping the men on the payroll could be managed sufficiently if, as we hoped, an infusion of new stock proved productive.

"Dad and I are going to an auction tomorrow," Job said as I closed the ledger and we prepared to go upstairs to bed. "We may be gone a few days so I'll need you to make sure the guys are paid."

"I can manage that," I smiled confidently and tapped the ledger in front of me. "All the amounts are right here."

"David will be expecting you at the bank. If there are any problems here, Pops will know what to do."

"I already miss you." I let him pull me up by the hand and out into the hallway.

"Me too." He stopped us at the base of the stairs. "This has to work Jes. Things can't continue to happen the way they have been."

"You're worried."

"Unsettled." He shrugged dismissively although I could see something more in his eyes.

"That's natural." I tugged on our still joined hands and took the first step up. "Things will work out. You'll see. Let's go pray about it."

Job and Rand left early that next morning and after waving as they drove away, I began to wander the farm. Smoke still drifted from the pit but the last of the carcasses had finally been placed. There was no wind, and the column of smoke and ash rose straight up in the air, reminding me of the story of the pillar of fire that God used to lead Moses and the Israelites through the desert toward the Promised Land. The night before, I had pushed my resentment aside and prayed with Job that our choices be guided by right motives. I prayed fervently now that this pillar of smoke would lead to a more promising future.

I watched as Pops and Mitch turned the ground of the field in which the destroyed cattle had been grazing. I saw John head to the milking barn with a bucket of lime and an armload of cloths. He would clean from the rafters down in preparation for the new residents that hopefully would arrive soon.

Two days later, I paid the men, carefully made the notation in the books, checked, and double-checked the balances. I was alone, and the house too quiet. I went in search of company.

May was not at home, and a quick call to my parents revealed that neither were they. I called Sarah and David. They were spending a quiet night at home with Thomas, and although they graciously invited me to visit, I declined. I called Laura to catch up, but she was on her way out to a ladies function at the church. I missed Job and felt sorry for myself.

I wandered back into the study and saw my typewriter sitting on the small desk in the corner. Job and I had placed it there as we laughed about me writing while he sat and did the books. I had not touched the machine in some time. There had been too much going on to even think about writing. Now it beckoned to me and I wondered if Laura would enjoy copies of my Benny Bunny stories to read to Andrea.

I went to the desk and pulled out the stories I had written and put them together with the illustrations Job had done. There were eight stories dealing with different themes. I would retype the stories and send them to Laura. The illustrations I would keep safe in the drawer for now.

I had three stories copied and a new one partially formed by the time I decided to quit. I hand wrote a note to Laura and sealed it along with two of the stories in a small package to mail to her the next day. Then, remembering my promise, I sealed the copy of the third story and one illustration in another envelope to mail to Professor Williamson. With that accomplished, I needed something else to do. I was avoiding going to bed. I snacked on some left over chicken, but it was dry and unappealing.

A flash of light from outside the window distracted me from my melancholy. I pulled aside the curtain and watched as a car crept past the main house and continued to the little one. It was my mother dropping May home. I let the curtain fall back into place. I would see if I could persuade one or both of them to chat for bit.

The phone on the wall rang just as I was about to open the door. I was torn between catching my mother before she left, or May before she settled in for the night, and answering the phone. A call at this time of night needed to be answered, even if I thought it was Laura calling back to finish our conversation from earlier.

"Hello?"

"Did I wake you?" His voice filtered through the line into my heart.

"No. I couldn't sleep without you."

"I was having the same problem, so I thought I would call and see if it helped any."

"Did it?"

"Too early to tell just yet." I could sense his smile. "How was your day?"

"Good." I smiled myself. "How was yours?"

"We should be home tomorrow."

"That soon?" I could not believe it. I expected them to be away for closer to a week.

"We could stay longer if you'd like?" He laughed.

"No!"

The auction had gone better than hoped. The new stock would arrive at the beginning of the next week. With the business taken care of, they were free to come home.

"Besides," Job laughed again. "You don't snore nearly as bad as my dad."

"I don't snore!" I protested. "Do I?"

"I love you. I'll see you tomorrow."

"Job!"

"Yeah?"

"I love you too."

Hope makes good company. With the prospect of Job's return and the positive outcome of the trip, I was able to sleep.

I was up bright and early, and eagerly headed off to inform Pops and the others about the phone call. The news seemed to cheer them, and work on readying the barns and fields resumed with renewed vigor.

On my way back to the house, I paused at the bullpen to admire Blizzard as he stood gleaming magnificently in the sun. His color had darkened over the years, but he was the picture of health. Blizzard, and Otto, the other bull, had not been in the field the day the cows had become ill. Both remained healthy but with the few remaining heifers still too young to breed, there had been very little for them to do to earn their keep.

Blizzard, with a strut reminiscent of his more youthful energy, made his way over and stuck his nose out for a pat. I crooned to him as I had when he was a baby and apologized for ignoring him lately.

"Don't let that animal fool ya," Pops said from behind me. "He's a mean 'un when he wants to be."

As if to confirm his words, Blizzard side stepped nervously. His eyes rolled revealing the whites and he snorted a challenge. I stepped back from the fence quickly.

"He was fine until you walked up," I joked to hide my dismay. "You have that affect on people."

"Ain't that the truth." Pops handed me a peppermint. "I'm thinking though, he's jealous because I'm the one's out here with you an' he's stuck in there."

"Are you serious?"

Pops patted my shoulder and flipped the peppermint in his mouth from one cheek to the other. "Just be careful 'round him."

"I will." A horn sounded and I looked down the drive. "They're early!"

"Looks like Blizzard ain't the only one that can't stand bein' apart from you."

I took off at a run as the truck reached the drive in front of the house and ignored Pops's comments about it not being dignified for a mother-to-be to carry herself that way. I knew Job would catch me as I flung myself at him and he did.

It was so good to feel him strong and vibrant. I found myself laughing for no reason but pure joy.

"I missed you," I whispered, before burying my nose in his neck.

"How are my girls?"

"I'm fine. And so is your son."

He laughed and set my feet on the ground. "Come and show me what you've been up to while I've been gone."

We walked hand in hand back to where Pops waited to shake Job's hand and learn about the new acquisitions.

"The new stock looks like a good bunch," Job said. "Strong. Healthy. A farmer just over the New Hampshire line passed away and his daughter and her husband were selling everything."

"They've been well cared for up 'til now then?" Pops asked. "No TB?"

"So it seems," Rand said and waved at May as she made her way across the yard. He called over his shoulder as he went to meet her. "They passed the vet inspection."

"They should be here the first of next week." Job looked around at the barns.

"We're ready for 'em." Pops answered Job's unspoken question before heading off to the milking barn for one last check.

"You look tired." I watched Job drop his small case on the floor at the foot of our bed.

"I am." He sat on the bed and pulled me onto his lap. "It's been a long couple of days. Dad and I drove all night. Now it's good to be home."

I pressed my lips to his forehead. "You feel warm. Are you sick?"

"A sore throat. Nothing that a little rest and some time with my wife won't cure."

"Why don't you sleep for a bit?" I stood up and pulled back the bed covers. "I'll wake you if we need you for anything."

"Will you stay for a while?" He pulled me close so he could press his face against my mid-section.

"Sure." I pushed him down on the bed and unlaced his boots. I pulled them off and swung his legs onto the bed. Before I could lay down next to him, Job was sound asleep. His cheeks were slightly flushed and there were dark circles under his eyes as he lay there breathing deeply and evenly, so I kissed his forehead and let him sleep.

When the time for the evening meal came and went and he still did not put in an appearance, I went to check on him. The sheets were tangled around his legs and the look of fever was still in his face. His skin was dry but hot to the touch.

I retrieved a couple of fever tablets from the bathroom and woke him so he could swallow them. I did it again, once more through the night, and by the next morning he was fine. His voice was a little rough and I insisted he continue to take it easy for the next few days. He did not resist the suggestion and stayed close to the house. By the time the truck containing our new assets arrived early Monday afternoon, he was back to normal and the incident forgotten.

We unloaded the cattle into the pen that had been set aside for them. As a precautionary measure, Job wanted to keep them separate for an extra day or two. This would allow a little more time for symptoms of any undetected diseases to appear. There were cows that would calve in a matter of weeks and cows ready to breed. They would be separated and those for breeding would be put in a field with Blizzard or Otto.

From the far side of the yard, Blizzard bellowed loud and long. Otto answered in similar fashion. While not as big as Blizzard, Otto was nonetheless a fine animal. He was younger, and when Blizzard's time had come, Otto would be the sole proprietor of the herd.

"They're eager to git goin'," Pops observed.

"Then we'll put them in the field tomorrow and not worry about waiting an extra day." Job rubbed the nose of a particularly curious animal. "Let's leave them to eat and calm down for the night."

I do not know if the cows calmed down at all that night, but I do know that Otto and Blizzard did not. They continued to bellow at each other at regular intervals.

With the new cattle, we had thirty head in total. Seven heifers, from our original herd, remained unaffected by the outbreak of Fog Fever. Three wet cows had been in the Cottage and were also clean. They had since dropped their calves; two were female. Out of the eighteen new cows, eight would calve over the course of the next couple of weeks and months. The other ten would go into a field with Otto. Milk production would not be what it was for quite some time but at least the farm would be producing again.

I sat atop the fence of a pen connected to the one that contained a very agitated Otto, and watched as Job opened the back gate to let the cows into the field. Mitch herded from inside the pen. Pops was in the milking barn with John, doing what I do not know. Blizzard was making a racket and rubbing up against the fence rails of his pen across the way. He would calm down once Otto and the cows were out of sight.

One of the cows Mitch was trying to shoo in the direction of the gate shied at something only she saw. Her sudden change in direction startled Otto and he jerked, bumping the fence close to where I sat. I jumped down quickly and stepped away from the fence at the same time a deafening crack echoed on the air. Job, Mitch and I turned in the direction of the noise.

A section of Blizzard's pen lay scattered on the ground in whitewashed splinters. Blizzard stood with his head tilted to one side as if to say, "Well, look at that!"

I cannot recollect all the details of what transpired next, but I do have certain indelible images tattooed on my memory. For instance, I clearly see Blizzard lifting his head and trumpeting his challenge before taking several steps through the broken fence and into the open yard. As well, I see John stepping outside of the milking barn, obviously curious about the noise. I hear Job and Mitch yelling frantic instructions to run. I see Pops, his arms waving wildly while standing in front of Blizzard, and I see John running madly in my direction. I remember Pops flying through the air like the rag doll that sat in lonely vigil on my childhood bed, at the same time John swung me off my feet and into his massive arms. Without breaking his stride, John headed for the nearest building—the Cottage. I remember thinking we were going to make it when he stumbled and faltered. The ground shook. Fifteen hundred pounds of bull was upon us.

I do not remember hitting the ground, but I will never forget the sight of Blizzard's massive hooves crushing John's skull. Everything went dark.

Twenty-seven

August 1941

Who is breathing in my ear?

I heard Job calling my name. He sounded too far away. So who was blowing into my ear?

I reached up to push whoever it was away.

"Don't move Jes!" The panic and urgency in Job's voice registered at the same time I realized my hand was pushing against a *something* and not a *someone.*

Blizzard.

I opened my eyes and could not have moved, even if I could get the thought from my head and into my petrified limbs. The morning sun was eclipsed by the bull's massive head while his legs were like four iron posts hemming me in.

He stood as a centurion, immoveable in his duty to protect. I carefully turned my head, seeking Job. I found John's lifeless body. I sobbed in distress.

"Jessie, it's okay. I'm over here." Job's voice came from the direction of the pen where Otto had been. I turned a little more until I could see him and Mitch standing behind the fence. They were using the feeble rails as protection.

"Are you hurt?" Job asked.

I did a mental inventory of what ached. My head hurt a little and my hip but I did not think I was injured beyond that.

"No," I swallowed back the need to scream.

"Good. That's good."

His smile tried for reassuring, but the pallor of his complexion and the tight lines at the side of his mouth betrayed the true level of his fear.

"Your dad can't shoot him, Job. Not without him falling on her." Mitch whispered.

"Jes, you have to get out from under him. He won't budge and he won't let us near you." Job sounded calm.

My mind was blank. I could not think about anything except Blizzard standing over me and nibbling on my hair. If he moved any of his feet, he could step on my arms or legs—or the baby.

The baby, the baby, the baby.

The chant repeated over and over as my heart kicked into a rhythm of matching pace.

"Talk to him Jessie," Job urged softly. "Just like you always do. He likes that."

I swallowed past the lump of terror in my throat. "Hi there, Blizzard." He tossed his head a little and shifted his feet dangerously close. "Easy boy. Easy now."

Carefully I lifted a hand and reached out for his nose. I continued talking until Blizzard lowered his head for a scratch. I kept talking and began to painfully and cautiously extricate myself from under the bull.

The journey to my feet seemed to take hours, but eventually I reached the goal. I took a few steps backward away from Blizzard. He followed. A couple steps to the side. He followed.

"Now what?" I asked in renewed panic.

"Try and get him to follow you into the Cottage." Job called softly.

The small barn was behind Blizzard. I would have to walk past the bull, and I realized with a wave of nausea, right over John. His face was unrecognizable, covered in dirt and sitting in a pool of blood.

"Don't look Jes," Job called softly. "Keep you eyes up and on the barn."

I can't. I did not think I spoke the words aloud but Job's encouragement made me believe I had.

"Yes, you can. One step at a time."

The first step was the most difficult but I managed it, and, once I maneuvered around John's body, it was surprisingly easy. Like a dog on a rope, Blizzard followed me into the birthing barn. I snatched up a flake of hay and led him into a stall. When certain he was occupied with eating, I slipped backwards out the stall door and dropped into place the piece of wood that would lock it.

The barn door was next.

The wooden bar was barely in place when Job's hands grabbed my shoulders and turned me to face him. I reached for him but he held me off and ran his hands over my face and arms. I pushed them away and kept reaching for him.

"Stop!" I shouted as we struggled against each other. I could not hold back any longer and I began to sob. That got his attention and got me what I wanted.

Job folded me close as he carried me to the front veranda and sat on the stairs with me. "I need to know if you're hurt Jes. Just let me check."

"I'm not." I refused to let go of my hold on his neck. "But John—"

"He's gone."

Incapable of anything more, I sat and sobbed.

"I've called the Doc." May sat down beside us and began to rub my back.

Mitch shouted from the yard. Pops was alive but badly hurt. Job made sure May had hold of me before he ran to where Mitch crouched over the older man. Rand joined them and together the three carried Pops into the house.

A minute later Job reappeared.

"Jessie, Pops is asking for you. He's pretty restless." He helped me to my feet. "He needs to see you're all right."

With May's help, I made my way into the room. I fell to my knees beside the sofa where Pops lay. Blood was everywhere, his ears, his nose and mouth. Only the bubbles that formed in the dark liquid on his lips attested to the fact that he still breathed.

I felt sick.

Guilty. I took his hand in mine and squeezed it. He squeezed back. His grip was strong, and I thought that was good. If he could hold my hand that tight, he would be fine.

"Jes?" My name was garbled as Pops tried the speak past the blood that was choking him.

"I'm all right." I lifted his hand to my lips. "I'm sorry, Pops. You warned me. I didn't listen and I'm sorry."

He tried to speak and only succeeded in coughing instead, spraying blood over my hands and face.

I ignored it.

I shushed him softly. "Don't talk. You need to rest to get better."

His grip grew fierce. He pulled my hand close and pressed it against his cheek. The bubbles at his lips stopped coming. His hand went slack in mine. I dropped my head to his chest, too spent to do more than let grief swallow me.

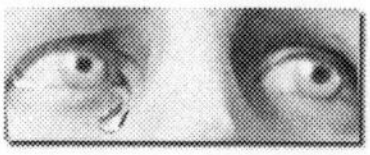

Doc Fischer, Sheriff Brady and Mack Johnson arrived again. From my place at the bedroom window, I sat looking down with numb detachment. I watched as Pops's body was laid next to John's in the back of the mortuary wagon. Internally, I felt flung off a cliff into a dark void. I could not see the bottom and did not know when I would reach it, if I ever would, or if I could survive it if I did. My mother stood at my side, encouraging me to get into bed and rest. Resting would not change anything, but I did not resist when she removed my clothes and helped me into my nightgown. As she pulled the bed covers up over my legs, I heard the jangle of the harness chains on the big black horses as Mack Johnson departed. I was cold.

There was a soft knock on the door and Job entered. I remember thinking it odd that he would knock on our bedroom door, but then, many things were not what they should have been that day.

"How is she?" Job asked as he came over to the bed

"Shaken." My mother rose to greet him. "How are you?"

"Shaken." He welcomed my mother's hug as he would that of his own mother. "Doc wants to take a look at Jes's head."

I looked beyond, to the door and noticed Doc standing just inside it.

"How's the head?" He made his way to the bedside and began to examine the tender lump on the side of my head.

"Hurts."

"And the rest of you?"

"Hurts." I shrugged and turned away.

"John fell on top of you?"

"I don't remember." I lied. If I said I did not remember, then maybe I would not.

"Well let's have a look-see."

I stared blindly at the ceiling as Doc looked into my eyes.

As he probed ribs and checked limbs, my mother and Job hovered anxiously nearby. They saw the small scrapes and bruises Doc Fisher discovered on my shoulder, and the rather large one spreading across my right hip. It was only as he began to palpate my abdomen that I looked at him.

"Any tenderness here?"

"No."

He searched my face for any hint of pain or a lie. He smiled and squeezed my hand. "I want you to take it very easy for the next few days. The baby is well protected in there but let's not take any unnecessary chances."

"Do I have to stay in bed?"

"For the rest of today at least." Doc Fisher pulled the comforter back up. "After that, no heavy work or exertion for a couple of weeks. If you don't listen, I will order you to bed."

"She'll listen." My mother stated as only mothers can.

I nodded, too heartsick to care about much about anything but closing my eyes and escaping. With one last pat on my arm and an order to call should anything change, Doc Fisher left followed by my mother.

Job knelt beside the bed and took my hand in his. "I'm so glad you're okay."

"Are you?" I whispered.

"I don't know what I am right now." He swallowed convulsively and I watched the myriad of emotions that crossed his face. He sighed and brought my hand up to his lips. "My mom and yours are going to stay for a while. There are some things I need to do, but then I'll be back."

I threaded my fingers in his hair and pulled his head down so it rested just under my chin. His shoulders began to shake and his breathing became raspy and unsteady. I could feel my chest growing damp with his hot tears. They matched the ones that slid down my face and onto the pillow. He prayed then, brokenly and quietly. He worshipped and asked for forgiveness. He sought understanding and answers. He laid his life before God, and then went to arrange to bury his friends.

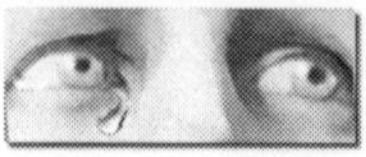

Two days later, two caskets were carried into and out of the church. The building was crowded and too warm. I was not able to rid myself of feeling confined and wanted nothing more than to be away from there, but I stood resolutely in the pew and sang *Nearer My God to Thee* along with everyone else.

Rand, who knew both men better than the pastor, spoke of what their lives had meant to those of us who knew them. Neither man had blood family of which we were aware. We were their family and we would miss them. That was enough.

From the church, we went to the graveside. John and Pops were buried in the small family cemetery on the farm. To call it a cemetery was exaggeration. Located on a rise in a pasture on the outer edge of the farm, there were, until that day, only two graves; Job's grandparents. The couple had been buried on the land from which they struggled to make a life.

Job took me there once, shortly after we first met those years ago. He had a certain curiosity about them, but he had not known either of them. It was not a place he felt compelled to visit regularly.

I stood at the edge of the hole that contained the simple casket in which Pops lay. In my pocket, my fingers worried the small, hard, round object hidden inside. I pulled it out and held it up to my nose. Peppermint, crisp and sweet filled my nostrils. I felt the soft flutter of the baby deep inside.

"Are you coming?" Job stood a few yards off. He looked so handsome in his dark suit. My body ached with the depth of my feelings for this man. He had lost weight.

"Yes." I closed my eyes and whispered another apology to the man who had been more than a friend and let the sugary orb fall into the grave.

At the house, I managed somehow to make small talk with those who had stayed. I felt as though something heavy was compressing my chest, making breathing and talking difficult. I often caught myself having to take slow deep breaths to counterbalance the shorter shallow ones that had become the pattern of the day. I lost track of Job until we stood side-by-side thanking people for coming. With every person who left, I sensed the tension leaving Job's body. I realized he was fighting to get through it just as much as I was. The utter absurdity of it tightened the resentment around my heart.

Now, I sat on the front veranda of the big yellow farmhouse, avoiding the last lingerers. It was unfair of me, but I had excused myself and slipped out. I could not force one more "It was so good of you to come," past my lips. The day was warm and full of color, a last tribute to summer and to lives that had ended. I was still cold. I had remained cold for days as recent events kept floating through my mind.

Blizzard still resided in the Cottage. It was the safest place to keep him, for his sake and ours. The eight cows expected to calve soon were in the milking barn, which, except for the three original cows of ours, had been empty. With only three cows to milk, it was easier to keep them in the barn at night and it was only necessary for one person to see to them in the morning.

Apart from a residual stiffness and a yellow-green bruise on my hip, I had no physical ill effects from what everyone called "a horrible accident." I had my own theory on the "accident" part, but it was easier to go with the crowd than say what I really thought.

I looked around to make sure the yard was empty. Carefully I stood and crept to the end of the veranda that was away from the main living room window. I climbed over the railing and dropped the short distance to the ground. From there, I ran around to the back, let myself into the empty kitchen, and took the stairs up the bedroom. I opened the closet.

The rifle rested in the corner, cleaned and ready for use. I stretched to the shelf above and felt around until my fingers bumped the box of shells purchased to replace the ones previously used. I slipped two into the pocket of my sweater and made my way back downstairs and out of the house.

I was midway across the yard before May spotted me. She called out, but I ignored her and picked up the pace. No one and nothing was going to stop me from doing what I had in my heart.

I reached the Cottage and barred the door from the inside. The barn was warm. Dust motes drifted in the rays of the afternoon sun that slanted in from the open windows and breaks in the wall slats. The familiar scents of straw and animals tickled my nose. Black flies buzzed and hovered over bits of manure that had fallen into the walkway during the mucking of the stalls. Blizzard was in one of those stalls.

He snorted a greeting and stuck his head over the door of the second stall on the right. I kept my distance, so he shifted to the far side of the enclosure and returned to munching on the bits of hay left over from the morning feed.

I withdrew one of the cartridges from my pocket and loaded the rifle. It was more difficult than I expected. My hands were shaking and tears obstructed my vision. I managed eventually to get the gun loaded, and I flipped the latch that released the stall door.

Blizzard was relaxed, his jaw moved rhythmically as he chewed. He tilted his head and looked at me with a clear dark eye. I could see myself reflected in the depths as I lifted the gun to my shoulder. I lowered it and readjusted my stance when I could not hold it steady.

The door behind me rattled and I jumped, almost pulling the trigger prematurely.

"Jessie? Open the door!" It was Job. No doubt May had informed him she had seen me, what I was carrying, and where I was going.

Blizzard threw his head back and his eyes rolled with menace. He let out a low agitated grunt. I brought the rifle up, all hesitancy gone. His eye met mine and he stilled. I dropped him where he stood then turned and left the stall without a backwards glance.

I lifted the bar and the barn door jerked open. Job stood there, pale and anxious. I held the rifle out to him and he took it. Without saying anything, I walked past him and those few that had gathered on the front veranda upon hearing the shot.

I climbed upstairs and crawled into bed under the quilts. I was cold.

I knew he was in the room. I heard him pause at his dresser. He began to speak and I thought it was to me until I heard the words.

"Please God," he pleaded. "I will leave tomorrow in your hands; just give me the strength to meet it."

I opened my eyes and saw him leaning against the tall dresser. He had changed out of his suit into old wool workpants held up by worn suspenders drawn up over a soft, long sleeved undershirt. The criss-cross they made on his back only served to emphasize the breadth of his shoulders; shoulders now slumped in defeat while his head rested heavily in his hands.

"Is everyone gone?" I asked.

He turned slowly and rubbed his hands over his face before forcing a smile. "Yes. You're still in your dress."

I watched him pull a sweater out of one of the drawers. "You look so tired. Why don't you just let someone else take care of things for a while?"

"I'll be fine. Besides there isn't much to do."

Not much except get rid of a fifteen hundred pound bull carcass.

He closed the drawer and paused without turning around. "What do you think we should do about next weekend?"

"What's next weekend?" I searched my mind for some plans that we had made. Then it struck me. Not only was it the annual barbeque, but it would be our one-year anniversary. What a way to end the year.

"What do you want to do?" I asked.

Just the thought of having all those prying eyes and ears made me shudder. It was bad enough that we had been the central topic for town gossip since the death of Lewis. Events like that did not happen every day in a small community like ours and when they did, especially to those with the community standing of the Nightingales, they kept the mongers going for longer than usual. Combined with the loss of our cattle, I knew the gossips must feel like a giddy group of six year olds on Christmas morning. The death of Pops and John would have been the candied cherry on top of one of Millie's ice cream sundaes.

Not that the intent behind all the talk was malicious, indeed many who discussed our recent misfortunes we counted among our friends. The concern and condolences they expressed were sincere; but there were always some who were less than so.

"I'm not certain what to do." Job sat on the bed and pulled the sweater over his head. "Pops loved the barbeque. He was looking forward to it as a time to forget the bad stuff and enjoy the good that was still here."

I smiled despite the moisture I felt gathering in the corners of my eyes. "He told me last year that he would give you until this year to make me happy. One year was all you were getting. He said, "When I asks if yer happy with that young bootstrap, you says y'ain't, I'm gonna throw you over my shoulder and run away with ya.'"

Job laughed at my imitation as much as the words. "He would have done it."

Despite the internal screaming going on at the thought of what it would mean to have the entire town out for the event—and make no mistake, this year they would all come—I took his hand in mine and spoke softly. "Let's do it."

Twenty-eight

September 1, 1941

Everywhere I went, I caught snatches of furtively whispered conversations. I did not need to hear the speculation fully to know it was there. It was in the awkward silences that fell when I approached small clusters of people, and it was there in the eyes that did not quite meet mine in spite of smiles of greeting. There were those however, who came with hearts of encouragement and support. They were the ones who had known Pops and John, the ones who understood exactly what had been lost. It was with them that we celebrated life. With them, we shared memories that brought laughter and tears, and moments of longing so sad and sweet my body ached.

Job and I fought to hold on to the last few moments of summer. We had just snuggled together for a dance when Mitch appeared and tapped Job on the shoulder. Job leaned closer to hear what Mitch whispered in his ear. I felt the muscles of Job's back tense beneath my hands.

"Go check it out and let me know." He said to Mitch before the man slipped away.

"What's happening?" I asked keeping my voice low.

"Some kids playing in the barn said a cow dropped her calf."

"It's early isn't it?"

"It's dead."

"The cow or the calf?"

"Calf."

"It's only one right? It happens, even I know that."

"It happens." He nodded. "But the kids said it looked odd."

"You can go if you want."

"Mitch can handle it." Job smiled down and me and kissed my nose. "I just want to stay here with you a little longer."

I tucked my head under his chin and allowed myself to relax against his warmth. Minutes later, he stopped moving to the music. He was looking over my shoulder. I turned to look.

Mitch hovered on the outer edge of the light provided by lanterns set around the dance area. He was nodding his head in answer to Job's unspoken question. I kept hold of Job's hand. The three of us hurried to the barn.

It was easy to find the section of the barn in which the dead calf lay. The kids that discovered it were still there looking on. They stood on bales of hay or balanced precariously on the wooden rails of the partition.

One little girl stood back by herself and sniffed quietly as tears ran down her face. I recognized her from church, Emma Pratt. She was not more than eight or nine. Her mother Audrey had been my Sunday School teacher when I was just a little younger than she. Her older brother was one of the boys hanging over the walls staring down with fascination. His name was Danny, or Daniel, as he was called loudly and frequently by his exasperated mother.

I called his name sharply as his mother did and ordered him to take his sister back to the main house.

Job and Mitch encouraged the others to depart and the barn emptied of the young spectators. I stepped up onto a recently vacated bale and peered down to where Job and Mitch now crouched and stared at a partially formed calf.

"I've never seen anything like it." Mitch scratched the neck of the confused cow that was licking the unmoving calf.

"I can't say that I have either." Job knelt to examine the calf more closely. "It looks like it just never finished forming."

Job asked me to fetch an old feed sack from the back of the building so we could wrap the calf and get it out of the way, before anymore children could see it. When I returned moments later, Job and Mitch were in a section two down from the previous one. They were both feeling the belly of another cow. The animal groaned softly and I could see the muscles tighten under her hide.

"It's too early right?" I asked.

"Uh huh." Mitch grunted as he pushed the animal aside in order to slip out and take the feed sack from me.

"What's happening?"

"I don't know," Job said. "Would you go get my dad? And see if—"

"'Allo?" Francois Paquette entered the barn. He was the veterinarian from just over the border in Quebec. He moved into the area three years ago when Dr. Case had retired to Massachusetts in order to be near his grandchildren. People needed a good veterinarian. Dr. Paquette was good. "Some kids say dere be a dead calve."

Mitch stepped from the stall into the walkway with the burlap wrapped calf in his arms.

"I'll go get your dad." I said.

"Eet iz a disease of a sexual nature," Francois explained to us what he believed to be the problem. "Like gonorrhea or syphilis. Dis type of ting can cause da calf to be mort-né, stillborn, or interrupt de growth before it is complete."

Infected cows would be useless. Even a bull bred to these cows could no longer be used for breeding, as it would spread the disease.

While Francoise examined each remaining cow seeking movement where Job could find none, I spoke aloud the dread in my heart. "What about the cows just put into the field with Otto? They wouldn't be affected, would they?"

"They came from the same herd." Rand spoke quietly. His eyes were on his son who waited for the laboring cow to deliver the front feet of its calf. "They could already be useless."

"And Otto?"

Rand ran a hand over his hair and sighed. He smiled at me, but it was grim.

I let my gaze wander to the far end of the barn where the three wet cows stood with their mouths in constant motion as they watched with curiosity the events unfolding before them. "Are they infected too?" I asked.

"They shouldn't be."

Francois believed we would know for sure over the next couple of weeks, but he would be wrong. It would not even take days. We knew before sunrise. Before the night was over, every cow that had arrived already bred, would drop her calf. None would ever draw breath.

Sometime in the middle of all the mess, I slipped into an empty area to sit and contemplate the implications of it. If all the new cattle were infected, that meant Otto was too. That meant no new calves or milking cows, and no more Otto—just seven original heifers, plus the two new calves, and three milking cows.

The income potential of the farm was limited to say the least. I last remember thinking I would have to hit the books the next day and re-evaluate expenses. I could predict that no matter how I looked at it, something, or rather somebody, would have to go. Even that might not be enough.

When I awoke, I was lying in a bed of straw with a blanket over me and Job curled around me. He was awake, the hand stroking my belly told me so.

"Can you feel him?" I asked.

"Sometimes I think I can, but it's probably wishful thinking." He turned me so that my head rested on his chest. "Besides, she's a girl."

I just smiled at our ongoing disagreement. "It seems like I'm getting bigger everyday."

"I love it." He kissed me as though to prove it. "I love you, Jessie of my heart."

Even as I returned his kiss, I knew I was crying. I could taste the salt of my tears on my own lips.

He pulled me tight against him. "Tell me what you're feeling."

"I'm sad. I'm just so very sad."

"I am too."

"And I'm confused and afraid. Tell me you're just as confused about all of this as I am?"

"I am, Jes. I don't know why any of this is happening. It doesn't make any sense. Every minute of everyday I try to figure it all out and I just can't. I ask God and I get nothing." I could hear the frustration in his voice. "But I can't lose faith either."

"I'm trying to keep mine, Job. I really am. It's just so difficult."

"I know."

"They think you must have done something to bring this upon yourself." The revelation was out of my mouth before I could stop it.

Earlier, I had overheard Francois discussing the matter with Rand and someone I did not recognize. The three men had been standing outside in the shadows of the barn and although I could tell it was Francois by his accent, and Rand by his size and voice, I was unable to distinguish clearly the features of the third man.

He was smoking, and as I passed by on a return trip to the barn with more feed sacks, he took a deep draw. The red glow from the end of the cigarette failed to illuminate eyes set deep into their sockets. His voice when he spoke was thin and gravelly, not a voice I remembered, but not one I would forget.

"So much tragedy in such a short time," rasped the voice. "It can only make a person wonder."

"Wonder what?" Rand asked.

I had the same question and slowed my approach. I kept my head lowered and eyes up.

"Oui," Francois responded to the third man. "I understand what you say. The young man must 'ave done some ting to cause this."

"That's ridiculous." Rand protested lowing his voice as I passed them. "I know my son and he's done nothing."

"Are you certain?" the third man said, exhaling a stream of foul smelling smoke.

"Yes."

"Really?" He drew the word out like a blade on a sharpening stone.

I could not hear Rand's response, as I had moved beyond the point of hearing clearly, and the blood rushing through my veins further impeded my auditory ability. I was enraged by the very idea that Job had done something to bring this upon himself, upon us.

My body shook as I entered the barn and handed the sacks to David who had come to help. He was wrapping the dead calves before placing them in a wheelbarrow and moving them outside.

Relieved of my obligation, I sat down in a quiet corner to calm down. I did not want Job to see me that upset. I knew that I could not put to voice what I had heard, and yet I began to reveal the information.

Job disengaged himself from my arms and sat up. He turned and looked down at me. "What did you just say?"

"I heard them talking. They think you did something to bring this down on yourself." I sat up too.

"Who is 'they'?"

"Francois, your father, and some man I didn't recognize."

"My father?" His brows drew together and he looked at me with so much hurt.

"No. I'm sorry. I said that wrong. Your Dad was there but he was defending you. He said he knew his son and that you haven't done anything to deserve this."

He relaxed only slightly. I could see his mind working over the information. His head shook in disbelief for a moment when his gaze locked on mine.

"What do you think, Jes?" He questioned softly. "Do you think I've done something to cause what's been happening?"

The intensity in his eyes told me how important my answer would be. The answer carried more weight than even the "I do," said one year earlier.

"No."

It was true. I could think of nothing that he had done or said that could have ever resulted in the mess of the last months. He gathered me close and we held on tight to each other.

"I just wish I could understand it."

"I wish I could too."

Job's chest rose and fell beneath my cheek as he sighed heavily. "These past few weeks have been the hardest of my life. I don't have the answers to why these things are happening, and I doubt I ever will."

"And you're okay with that?"

"No. But I can't let go of my anchor, Jes. I believe God is in control, even if I can't feel him. I know He loves me, and I will continue to be thankful for that as long as I live."

"Why?"

"Without God, there is nothing."

The simplicity with which he spoke his answer told me he considered it an absolute. It made me angry.

"I have you," I said.

"I'm just a man, Jes. If God is willing, I'll have a long life with you, but if that's not the way it unfolds, I want the assurance that the foundation you stand upon will not be moved. He should be the one you cling to because He will be there when I can't."

I could not say anything because I did not know what to say. A life without Job did just not seem possible. He had always been there, strong and steady from that summer when I was six and he was eight.

He had become my anchor, and the idea of that anchor giving way someday was terrifying.

The concept of putting God before Job was beyond my grasp. Despite the warmth of his body, I shivered.

"You're cold."

Job had misunderstood and I did not correct him. "Let's go up to the house. We have a lot of things to decide."

James was told that his part-time services were no longer required and he graciously understood; however, the little bit that saved us would not be enough.

There was also the continued expense of the of bank loan and Mitch's salary, and no income with which to pay either. Mitch offered to go as soon as he found another position. In the mean time, he would work for only room and board.

The solution seemed to be to sell the healthy heifers and use that money to purchase a few milking cows to go with the three we still had. It would not be much, but the small income would keep us afloat until we could get the ground steadied underneath us, we hoped.

Over the next few days the infected cattle and Otto were carted away for slaughter, the heifers were hauled away to auction, and Mitch announced he was headed to the northern part of the state.

"Up Highgate way." He muttered softly during his brief explanation.

"When do you leave?" Job asked solemnly.

"First light."

"We'll miss you." Job held out his hand to the man who was more than an employee.

"You call—and I'll be back here before the phone's on the hook." Mitch shook Job's hand.

"You take care of yourself," I said. I hugged Mitch making his ruddy face blush more.

"You too, Miss Jessie. And take care of that baby."

"I will."

He reached into the pocket of his coat and pulled out a small object. "This is for the little one. I was gonna wait until it were born but since I probably won't be here, you take it now."

He handed over the object.

The detail of the small wooden cow took my breath away. In the thick muscled neck and shoulders, and in the head held high, Mitch had captured a moment of grace and pride. The fine grain of the wood felt warm and alive in my hand.

"It's beautiful. Thank you."

Mitch ducked his head but I could tell my compliment had pleased him. He said a final goodbye and went to the bunkhouse for the last time.

The next night the barns burned down.

Twenty-nine

September 1941

It was Saturday, dull and cold. We were into September and fall arrives early in Vermont. The leaves were in the early stages of turning, and with the wind whipping about, many flew off their branches and skittered along the ground.

Job spent the day cleaning and adding fresh dry straw to the floor of the milking barn in preparation for the hopeful addition of several new cows. He did not break for lunch, and I did not disturb his labor. I spent most of the morning sleeping. I was not physically tired, but the emotional upheaval was exhausting. Sleep allowed me to escape the dark thoughts plaguing the majority of my waking hours. The farm had lost most of its life, and we mourned what was gone in order to make room for what we hoped would come.

The wind was screaming around me and I fought against its pull as I searched the farm for Job. I saw someone disappear around the corner of the barn. I called out but the wind stole my voice. I raced after the figure but when I turned the corner of the building he was gone. Why would he not wait? There he was again. I tried to run but something grabbed at my feet. "Who are you?" I tried calling but no sound came out.

I rounded the corner of the Cottage and came face to face with the figure. He was leaning against the barn, untouched by the howling wind that battered me around. He had no eyes, only dark shadowed sockets made deeper by the red glow of a cigarette as he drew on the slim pencil of tobacco. He exhaled slowly, the stream of smoke continuously expanding, enfolding me in its foul haze. The figure tossed the unfinished cigarette on the ground igniting the hay covering the ground at our feet. The acrid smoke burned my eyes and nose. He tipped his head back and laughed as a loud crack whipped across the night.

I sat up in bed.

My heart felt like it would beat its way out of my chest; my breath came in great gulps. A dream. It was a dream, albeit a bad one, but still, a dream.

"Jes?" Job sat up and placed a hand on my back.

"Yeah?"

"Did you hear that?"

"You heard something?" Maybe it had not all been a dream.

"Outside. It's hard to tell because of the wind but it sounded like something snapped."

"I thought I was dreaming. It was awful."

Job got up and pulled the curtain aside to peer out the window. "No, no, no!" He dropped the curtain and made a mad dash for the door. "Jessie, call the fire department now!"

I slid across the bed and over to the window. The orange glow peeking through the gap in the heavy drapes, told me what I would see before I parted them. The Cottage was almost completely engulfed in flames. Before I left the window and went downstairs to make the call to the fire department, I knew they would never arrive in time to save the building or its temporary occupants. That became a certainty when after picking up the hand piece, I realized the phone was dead. The winds must have knocked the line down somewhere.

I ran outside to let Job know that there would be no help coming from that quarter. I could hear the agonizing bellows of the trapped animals inside the barn. We had moved them into the Cottage because it was smaller and would be easier to maintain. Job was frantically searching for a way into the building to save them but the heat and smoke were keeping him at bay.

The wind kept changing the direction of the flames so one minute it looked like it was possible to gain entry from the main door but in a flash, the direction changed and the flames shot out of the openings at that end of the barn. I pulled Job back, leaned close, and yelled into his ear the information about the phone being out.

A screaming ball of flame streaked from a window of the Cottage and across the ground. Job leapt for it but missed. The partially ablaze barn cat ran straight into the milking barn where it collapsed in a writhing heap and set alight the clean, dry, freshly laid straw.

Job ran into the barn and vainly tried to stamp out the fires that were springing up. I joined him but the smoke became thick. I stumbled back, coughing and wiping tears from eyes that stung.

"Stay out!" Job yelled at me. I did not listen. I pulled the neck of my nightgown up over my mouth and nose, and ducked my head as I continued to try to extinguish the flames. It did not take long for Job to grab me and pull me out of the doomed building.

In the end, the barns were lost. The fire department had eventually arrived after someone in town had noticed the glow from the fire, but the only thing the small group of volunteers could do was to help ensure that the blaze did not spread to the house or creamery.

As the sun rose, both buildings collapsed in on themselves, one after the other. Flames died, leaving smoldering embers in their stead. The crowd of gawking onlookers had grown over the last couple of hours. Speculation threaded in and out as to the cause of the blaze, but it seemed that most agreed it was lightning, a freak accident, according to all but a few.

The question in my mind was not so much how, but why? It repeated over and over again like a needle skip on a phonograph record.

"Not much chance things will spread beyond the barns at this point." Wally Grant, the volunteer Fire Chief, placed a consoling hand on Job's shoulder. "The embers will be hot for a few days yet, so keep a watch."

"Thanks Wally." Job shook the man's hand automatically. His eyes never left the remains of the buildings.

"I'm just sorry we didn't get here sooner."

"Phones were down."

"Yeah, well, just the same." Wally turned to the other volunteers. "Come on, boys. Time to go home."

I knew the men who had arrived on the large red truck and watched as Mack Johnson, Francois Paquette, Sheriff Brady, and my father helped Wally roll up the hoses and pack up equipment. When the bell had rung long and loud in town, they had left the safety and comfort of their beds to rush to the aid of whoever needed it. My father had been stunned to realize Nightingale Farm was their destination.

Only once before could I remember him having to leave in the middle of the night to fight a fire, and it had been close to ten years since that had happened. The bright red, gasoline powered fire truck was a new purchase, and our little town was proud of moving up from a horse drawn steam wagon to the shiny vehicle. Some kids playing church in a barn just on the other side of town left some candles burning and set the wooden structure ablaze. The bell had sounded in town, and much like tonight, the team had rushed to the rescue.

It had all been very exciting and had made the front page of our little town paper, but, when a two-headed calf was born in the next township over, the incident was quickly forgotten. It would take more than an oddity of nature to have people forget the latest of tragedies to strike the Nightingale farm.

My father stopped and wrapped his arms tight around me. It was difficult not to let myself go and hold on forever, but I managed somehow to release him.

"Go get some rest. Take care of yourself and my grandbaby," he said, after planting a kiss on the top of my head.

"I'll see that she does." May wrapped a supportive arm around my shoulders and pulled me to her side.

I returned my father's last wave as the truck turned onto the main road in the direction of town. Rand, May, Job, and I were the only ones left standing in a dawn still hazy with lingering smoke. Job separated himself from us and limped slowly to stand in the yard between the two charred ruins. Marked with small burn holes left by burning cinders, his soot covered pajamas hung damp and limp on his form. At some point during the fight to get the fire under control, someone had given him a pair of his father's boots. Rand's feet were larger than Job's and the boots accommodated the bandages Doc Fisher had put on his burned feet.

My own feet had suffered a few cuts and scrapes and my nightgown, like Job's pajamas, was beyond salvage. I did not think I would ever get the smell of smoke out of my nostrils. I knew I would never get the sound of dying animals from my head.

I saw Job's hands reach for and take hold of the collar of his shirt. With a cry that was born in the center of his soul, he rent his shirt in two and flung it to the ground. Arms raised and chest bared, he fell to his knees, the ashes surrounding him serving as a burnt offering to God. From his knees, he fell prostrate on the ground.

And he worshipped.

Acknowledging that all he had was granted by God, and was God's to do with as He willed it, Job praised God.

My heart cried out against the injustice I saw before me. My heart raged with resentment at the sight of my husband lying in the dirt before a God who was supposed to love him, but now seemed to ignore him.

"Come inside, Jes." May took me by the shoulders and turned me toward the house. "Let's leave him and God time to work this out."

What purpose would that serve? God had already done all the working, and there was nothing left.

Again, May encouraged me to head upstairs and get clean. Too tired to argue, I was halfway up the stairs when I heard Rand speak. It was wrong to eavesdrop, but I could not help myself. I stopped to listen.

"I don't understand it, May," he said. "What could the boy have done to deserve this?"

"What do mean, what could he have done? He didn't do anything." May sounded matter of fact. I heard pans clanking and knew she was preparing to cook.

"He must have. Why else would God be punishing him this way?"

"Why do you think this is punishment?"

"Doesn't it feel that way to you?"

"You heard him yourself, Rand. Just now, outside." May's tone was shifting to incredulity. "He did not blame or question God about anything. He fell to the ground and praised Him. Praised Him!"

"There must be something he's done that he's not confessing."

"Rand Nightingale. In all these years as you've watched your son grow into a fine and godly man, have you ever known him not to confess or admit when he's done something wrong?"

There was a brief silence before Rand mumbled something too low for me to hear and then the kitchen door slammed. I heard a pan slam against the stove top.

Before I could think about what I was doing, I was standing in the doorway to the kitchen. "He hasn't done anything," I said fiercely.

May jumped and put a startled hand to her chest. "I know," she stated quietly. "Rand's faith is shaken. He needs to have everything make sense. He's trying to understand why this is happening."

"We all are."

"I'm sorry you overheard. Go and wash up now." She turned back to the stove. "I'll make breakfast. It's going to be a long day."

Lately it seemed that days were getting longer at a higher rate of frequency. I was not sure how much longer they could get.

I was only partly dressed when Job came in and stood in our bedroom doorway. He caught me examining my expanding middle. It amazed me to see how much I seemed to grow every day. While I could still tie my own shoes, bending over was not as easy as it had once been. I could now readily recognize the movement from inside my body. In that moment it gave me a point of hope on which to focus.

My eyes met his in the reflection of the mirror. His eyes, normally clear and bright, their dark depths always compelling, were dull with pain. His face was black, his hair flattened and grayed from the same ash that had covered my own. There were angry red welts along his forearms and the backs of his hands. I knew there were more I could not see: small burns like the few I had discovered on my own arms and back. They would blister and peel before healing.

Wordlessly I took him into the bathroom and locked the door behind us. I filled the sink with water and washed him head to foot. From there I took him into the bedroom and locked that door behind us. Food could wait, comfort could not.

Having your father as your banker has both pros and cons. The pros are that he loves you, and wants what is best for you, as well as knowing where you stand financially, and being able to provide informed and sound advice. The cons are that he loves you, and wants what is best for you, as well as knowing where you stand financially, and being able to provide informed and sound advice.

The advice was to take what little cash we had on hand and apply most of it to the outstanding debt, thereby reducing the payment amount. Job would find employment nearby that would bring in some money to pay off the last of the loan, so that when the spring arrived we could look at rebuilding. The bank would consider another loan to help in that area, once we repaid the first.

It was not a perfect solution, but barring further complications, we would manage.

Two weeks later, Job found a job.

"Yes, sir, I know." Job nodded when my father commented about the fact that he would be leaving his pregnant wife behind. "It's not ideal, but nothing about the situation is. However, I could make enough money by Christmas to pay off enough of the debt. I wouldn't have to go back in January when the baby is due. I could find something closer."

"And I wouldn't be alone." I jumped in to provide support, even though I just wanted to sit down and cry like a baby at the thought of his leaving. "You would all be here to keep a closer eye on me than you already do."

"Are you really all right with this?" My mothers normally clear blue eyes were filled with doubt. "The granite mines?"

"Yes." It was not really a lie. Job was doing what he felt he needed to do. Working in the granite and marble quarries was difficult and dangerous, and not just because of the risk of silicosis or tuberculosis. The constant tensions between laborers and mine owners had, on more than one occasion, led to violent strikes over wages and working conditions. At least the latest strike, in 1938, had not involved the calling in of the National Guard.

In addition, Job would be several hours away, working six days a week, and only able to come home periodically. Not ideal for our family situation, as my father was quick to point out on that Sunday afternoon when we all gathered together to discuss the matter, but, if I asked him not to go, Job would stay and find something else, even if it took twice as long to throw off the burden of debt.

I could not ask him to stay because it was important for him to do this.

Job even refused my father's offer of financial assistance. If things did not work out this way, he would take their help but only as a last resort.

Job's departure was set for two days time. I felt physically sick every time I thought of his leaving, which meant I always felt sick. He spent the first day getting his truck into shape for traveling.

I took my car into town to run errands, like picking up the ingredients for a special supper, and going to the bank to get money for his trip. I took a few minutes to visit with Sarah and Thomas. She gave me a few things for the baby that Thomas had outgrown, and I suddenly realized that Job and I had not even thought about getting a room ready.

I looked forward to having something to occupy my time while Job was away, and as I drove back to the farm, my mind began to play with the possibilities for Job's old room. There would not be much to change if we had a boy as I hoped. If we had a girl, as Job wanted, then it would need some redecorating.

Of course, there were other rooms in the upstairs, but Job's childhood room was right across the hall from ours. The plans would have to wait, for now anyway.

There was not an extra dollar in the budget for decorating. But it was fun to dream.

I wonder sometimes, if it was because my mind was occupied by something other than my driving, or if it was because of the afternoon fog that had rolled in with the light drizzle that had begun to fall; whatever the reason, I did not see the deer.

Thirty

September 1941

My world spun. When it stopped, I found myself staring into an ebony orb of glass. The orb blinked one, twice. I saw my tiny reflection in the darkness that slowly swallowed me.

I was cold. Someone had left the window open. I tried to move, to roll over and get under the warm blankets. The sharp pain that shot out from my shoulder brought reality back with the same sickening thud I had felt upon colliding with the deer.

My breath came in short panicked gasps and I struggled to calm myself. The windshield was broken, bits and pieces of the shattered glass were strewn everywhere, including over me. I did not know how long I had been unconscious. I took a deep breath and held it while I took inventory on what hurt where.

Nothing more than stiffness and a slight twinge in my right ankle where my legs were concerned. My heart leapt into my throat as instinctively I tried to cup my abdomen. Something was terribly wrong with my left arm. I could not move it, and the throbbing in my shoulder was growing unbearable. My right arm was fine and I used it to cradle the baby. My stomach was a little tender but I thought I felt the baby move and that provided a small measure of comfort. The left side of my face felt strange and I could not open my left eye. A brief exploration with my hand told me my eye was swollen shut, and my hand came away covered in blood. I turned my head to see if I could tell where I was and how I might extricate myself from the situation.

The doe had come through the windshield. Its head was next to mine, the black of its eye stared lifelessly out at me. The interior of the vehicle was dark red with the animal's blood. Glass from the windshield had slit the doe's throat causing the animal to bleed to death. I was covered in the blood. I started to retch. I needed out of the car, and I needed out now.

The car had come to rest in the ditch on the side of the road. It was tilted in such a way that in order to open the door, I had to fight against gravity. I used my left leg as a lever, and with as much care as I could manage, I pressed my lower leg against the door and slid my foot into the opening created. From there I grabbed hold of the steering wheel with my right hand and pulled myself around enough to slide my right foot down next to my left.

This meant that my left shoulder pressed against the car seat but I gritted my teeth and used my legs to push the heavy door open. I needed to shift, but with only one good arm it was easier to think about than to do. The door came back, smashing my legs because I forgot about my injured arm and failed in my attempt to stop the door before it swung back. I cried with pain and frustration.

I began to shiver and my teeth started chattering. I was wet from the drizzle and the rapidly congealing blood. I could just make out the roof of the main house ahead and to my left. That is where I wanted to be.

The car door opened unexpectedly and I looked up into the face of my mother-in-law. I began to sob uncontrollably.

"All right now, Jessie." Her voice was calm, soft and safe. It meant I was safe. She ran her hands over my head and arms. "I've got you now. You're going to be all right. I thought I would just take a walk down to get the mail. And it's a good thing I did, now isn't it? Can you tell me where you hurt?"

I wanted to, but I could do no more than shake my head and continue to cry. May continued to talk softly and calmly.

"Do your legs hurt,?"

A headshake no.

"Good that's good. What about your arms?"

Loud sobbing.

"Yes? Which one? The right?"

Another negative shake.

"OK, the left? The left one hurts?" She squeezed my fingers gently. "Here?"

I shook my head and with my good arm indicated my shoulder. I held my breath waiting for the hurt as she probed delicately. I sighed in relief when she was finished and managed to get control of myself.

"That's right. Just relax. It's nothing that can't be fixed easily enough." Her fingers began to probe my hairline and left temple. "It's just out of place. Remember when Mitch knocked his out that one time?"

May paused to see if I was listening and comprehending.

"Uh, huh." I managed the first intelligent sound beyond a sob.

"Rand popped it right back in. He can get yours too."

I remembered the incident. I began to cry again. The veins in Mitch's neck had just about exploded with the effort he exerted to keep from crying out when Rand forced the injured joint back into its socket.

"Hey now, it'll be so much better after that." May crouched in front of me. "You've got a mean cut on your head there, but I think most of the blood belongs to the animal and not you."

"I didn't see it. It was just there."

"I believe it, honey. Do you think you'll be good on your own for just a bit? I need to go and get somebody to help us back to the house."

I clutched her hand tightly.

"I won't be more than a minute. I promise." I refused to let go. I had begun to shake uncontrollably. "All right, Jessie. I won't go anywhere."

May reached past me into the car and sounded the horn long and loud. Job arrived minutes later followed by Rand, and I began to sob anew. He lifted me out of the car carefully and took a few steps in the direction of the house. Each movement jarred my shoulder and I could not catch my breath. I could feel myself sliding into darkness again.

When I regained consciousness, Rand was kneeling next to me. He had a hold of my left arm and was moving it around. The motion hurt but not as much as before. Rand had manipulated my shoulder back into place while I was unaware of what was happening. I was grateful for his judgment.

"It's all right now Jes," he soothed. "It's all done now. I bet it's starting to feel better already, right?"

I nodded and used my good hand to wipe away the tears that blurred my vision.

"I've got you now." Job picked me up again. "You're going to be fine. Everything will be all right." He continued to whisper those words all the way to the house, and as he did so, I believed for a little while that everything would indeed be all right. He had come and rescued me.

I was carried upstairs into our bathroom, and placed on very wobbly legs. May pushed the men out and ordered Job to call Doc Fisher and have him come. When she removed the wet and blood soaked clothing from my body, I could see the bruises running from my left shoulder down to my left hip. More disturbing was the red and purple half circle across the lower part of my abdomen.

I squeezed May's arm in dread. She looked in my eyes and did her best to hide the alarm in hers. We both knew that mark was a bad thing, but I think on some deeper level only she truly understood the ramifications of what we were both looking at.

"All right, honey, I need you to really focus for a minute. Can you do that for me?" She was kneeling in front of me and holding my hands.

"I'm cold." It was all I could think to say.

"I know. We'll get you warm in no time, but right now I need you to tell me if you hurt or feel any cramping near the baby."

"No."

"Really concentrate, Jessie." She gave my hands a slight shake. "It's important."

I closed my eyes and did as she asked. The bruise hurt a little and my back felt stiff, but I did not feel any cramps of any sort.

"Good, that's good." May wrapped a towel around my shoulders and sat me on the toilet.

She had just started the water running in the sink when there was a knock on the door followed by Job's voice stating his intention to come in.

"Doc Fisher's been out of town for the day," he informed his mother softly as he slid past her to kneel in front of me. "His wife says she expects him back any time now and as soon as she sees him, she'll send him over. I called Ben and Claire too. They're on the way."

"Well, we can at least clean that cut on her head for now and get her warm." May twisted excess water out of a towel she had soaked.

"How're you feeling?" Job rubbed his hands over mine.

"Fine." It was such a dumb thing to say, and so far from the truth. Weepy and frightened would have been more accurate. I just wanted to crawl into bed and have him hold me.

"Job, go get her something warm to put on." May stepped close and began to minister to the blood covering my face.

A minute later I had a death grip on her arm.

"Sorry, dear. I didn't mean to hurt you."

I could not respond. She looked from the cut into my eyes. I knew the moment she realized there was more going on than just the pain of having a gash cleaned. I saw it in the way the color left her cheeks and the way her eyes filled with tears as they met mine.

"Oh, Jessie." May pulled the towel off my shoulders and knelt to press it between my legs to stem the flow of blood that was spreading over the closed toilet seat and onto the floor. "Hold it tight, sweetheart. Hold the towel."

Thankfully, the spasm that took hold was brief.

"Hold the towel now and don't move." She grabbed my chin in her hands. "Do you understand me?"

I nodded mutely and she disappeared. I heard her speak to someone, and Job appeared in the doorway looking like I felt, scared witless. He dropped the flannel gown he held and slid across the floor to crouch in front of me.

I heard May shouting and feet running across hardwood and up the stairs.

Then my mother was there. Without saying a word, she grabbed up the gown, a second towel, and pushed Job aside. She pulled away the soiled towel and replaced it with the clean.

"Job, put this over her head." She shoved the gown into his hands.

She turned and tried for a smile. "Now Jes, lift your arms so Job can get your gown on."

I nodded automatically. I was beginning to disengage. It was like what I was watching was happening to a stranger.

I raised my arms as high as I could, which for the left was not high at all, and he pulled the garment over my head. I was caught up in Job's arms and he rushed down the stairs and out the front door. I caught a glimpse of my father behind the wheel of my parents' car at the same time Rand, who was standing holding the rear door open, turned and looked down the driveway.

The fire truck from town was barreling up the gravel drive, bells ringing to proclaim its arrival. Our town did not have an ambulance and May, in her wisdom, knew I would need to get to the hospital fast. The bright red vehicle with its gold leaf flourishes was the best way to do that.

Wally Grant was driving. He swung the engine around in the drive and stopped. Mack Johnson climbed out of the cab and took me in his arms. Job climbed into Mack's seat and Mack transferred me to Job's lap. Job repositioned the towel that had slipped. May passed him several more and shut the door.

They were waiting at the hospital, "they" being a lot of grim faced doctors and nurses. Job lowered me onto a gurney and someone wheeled me away into a starkly lit room to be poked and prodded. A bright light flashed in my eyes. There was a sharp sting in my arm and I fought the floating feeling that spread throughout my limbs. Snatches of conversation penetrated my semiconscious state. The last thing I remember was hoping they found that poor woman's baby that was lost.

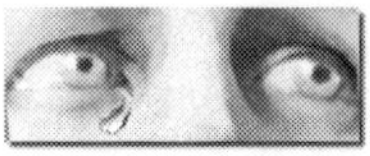

The room was dark. It smelled oddly unpleasant, and the window was wrong, not our bedroom. A light seeped under the closed door and gradually my eyes began to adjust enough to make out indistinguishable shapes. I had to go to the bathroom, urgently. I wanted to sit up but my body would not do what I asked of it. Every muscle twitch caused an ache. Someone had tied up my left arm, probably the same someone who had tucked the sheets in too tight for me to move my legs. It was all too constricting, too confusing. I heard the harsh in and out of my breathing. I was panicking.

"It's okay, Mrs. Nightingale." The voice was female and I automatically associated it with the cool hand that pressed against my cheek. In some recess of my mind, they were familiar. "I'm here. You're not alone."

I tried to speak, but my throat was too dry.

"Hold on. Close your eyes, I'm going to turn on a light." She sounded young but calm, in control, which helped me to settle back. I closed my eyes and heard the click of a lamp.

"Slowly now." The voice was speaking again. "Open your eyes."

Of course I opened them too quickly, which made me wince and blink against the light. I sipped greedily from the glass that pressed against my lips, the cool water a welcome relief to my parched mouth and throat. All too soon, it was taken away.

I put the nurse at about the same age as me, maybe a couple of years older. Her eyes were an unremarkable hazel but they were clear, bright and kind. Her hair was pulled back and, from what I could see under the starched cap she wore, was a dark blonde.

"I'm Nurse Robbins."

She smiled and it made her pretty. "How do you feel?"

"What happened? Why am I here?"

"Don't you remember?"

I shook my head and raised my hand to feel the bandages that wrapped around it. I remembered being in the car. There was a deer. And blood. Lots of blood. I squeezed my eyes shut, holding other images at bay.

"Where's Job?" I whispered. I could feel the panic returning.

"Your husband had to leave for a little while. He asked me to stay with you until he returned. He'll be here soon."

"I need to use the toilet."

"Of course." Nurse Robbins brought into my line of sight a white enamel pot that was flat and round.

"I'd rather get up."

"It's too soon."

I did not like it or the fact that I was dependent upon a perfect stranger to do something I had been doing by myself since the age of three. As the pot slid under my hips, I could no longer avoid looking down at my belly. While still rounded, it was in no way what it had been.

"Where did he go?" I wanted to know but I wanted more to distract myself. I could not face what I knew to be true.

"I'm just going to leave for a minute to get the doctor." Avoiding a direct answer, Nurse Robbins patted my arm and stepped back toward the door. "You'll be just fine for a moment."

I would not be fine for that moment, or any other. I let my hand slide over my belly and sought what I knew was no longer. There was no answering flutter or movement. It had been lost.

I was lost.

I pressed my hand against my eyes, trying to force the tears back in. If I started to cry, I might never stop.

"Mrs. Nightingale?"

I started at the deep the voice and tried to dash the tears away but they kept coming. I swiped at my runny nose and looked into a face that would have been austere if not for the sincerity of the pale gray eyes behind thin wire-rimmed spectacles. He could not have been older than thirty.

"I'm Dr. Peterson." He handed me a clean handkerchief from his own pocket. "How do you feel?"

It was only the second time I had been asked that question, but I already hated it.

"Tired." It was suddenly very true. I pressed the handkerchief against my eyes. The soft cloth was cool and soothing. Maybe if I closed my eyes and let the darkness come back, everything else would slip away.

"That's understandable. You lost a lot of blood."

"I lost my baby."

"Yes." His hand was warm and dry as it closed around mine. He offered no platitudes.

"Does Job know?"

"Yes."

"Where is he?"

Dr. Peterson released my hand and I heard a chair scrape across the floor. I opened my eyes to see him sitting next to my bed, his face almost level with mine. Again, he took my hand in his.

"Mrs. Nightingale, you've been in the hospital almost a week." His words did not make sense. I tried to follow as he continued. "Your baby girl was lost the night you came and for a while, I thought we would lose you too. We would have if the bleeding hadn't stopped. To be honest I'm still not sure how, or why it did."

A girl.

"Where is my husband?"

"He had to leave for a little while. He's been here the whole week though. In fact, there have been a lot of worried and ragged looking people here. You have a family that loves you very much."

I did not care. There was something not being said. "Where is Job?"

"The funeral for your baby was this afternoon."

Everything inside me hurt with wanting it not to be true. I rolled away from Dr. Peterson, ignoring the painful protest of my body as I did so. Someone in the room was wimpering. Me. I made those awful choked mewling sounds. I wanted them to stop.

"Why? I just want to understand why?" Fury, rage, frustration, and any number of other emotions with similar intent, boiled over.

"The car accident, Mrs. Nightingale."

Dr. Peterson, poor man, did not understand my question was not for him. How could he?

"Don't you remember?" He placed his hand on my arm and I tried to throw it off without thinking. I jerked my left arm hard enough to see stars. I fought the restraint, welcoming the physical pain as a companion for the emotional. It was not long before I was welcoming the oblivion and darkness of sedation.

Thirty-one

September 1941

The sharp and sudden sound of chair legs scraping across the floor made me jump. I opened my eyes and caught Job in the act of moving a chair closer to the bed. He stopped and stepped near instead.

"Hi." His lips moved in what I took to be a failed attempt at a smile. He looked very uncertain.

"Hi."

"I didn't mean to wake you." He still wore his suit, although his tie was gone and his shirt unbuttoned. His hair was rumpled in the manner that indicated his hands had pushed through it repeatedly. "How do you feel?"

I wanted to go back to the darkness. To sleep and forget.

His eyes were red-rimmed. They were no longer innocent and unguarded as they once had been on the bank of Miller's Creek, but then we were not as we had once been. We could never be again.

"You look tired." I turned the focus off myself.

"Yes." Something flickered in his eyes but was gone before I could read it. He reached across and took my hand in his. I took hold as if my life depended on it. *Tell me it was not my fault. Tell me you do not blame me. Tell me you love me. Tell me it will be all right.*

"Jes—"

A knock on the door interrupted what he was going to say.

Again, something passed through his eyes as he looked at me, but whatever it was went without voice. Nurse Robbins entered.

"Job, I just came in to—Oh, Mrs. Nightingale, you're awake." She appeared flustered that I should be so. She walked around Job to the head of the bed and fiddled with the tubes running to the bottle of whatever it was that I was attached to. "How do you feel?"

"Fine." We all knew I lied.

"Well, good." Her gaze flitted to where my hand still held onto Job's. "I'm just on my way home for my days off. I wanted to see if you or your husband needed anything before I left."

"I'm fine, thank you Emily," Job replied quietly.

Emily. I hated her. It was unreasonable, to be sure, but I knew I did. I hated the hospital too. I hated many things that day.

"When can I go home?" I sounded surly even to my own ears.

"Dr. Peterson will be able to answer that. He's on his way in." Nurse Robbins checked the dressing on my head. "Well, I'm glad you are feeling better, Mrs. Nightingale. I hope the doctor has good news for you."

"Thank you." Job replied for me when, after several seconds of awkward silence, it was obvious I would not.

Nurse Robbins' face flushed and her eyes dropped to look at the floor. She nodded, forced a smile and fled the room as Dr. Peterson entered.

I could go home as soon as I was able to walk about on my own. Yippee. What recovery there was left could be accomplished there. My shoulder would heal, and I would regain full use of it. I just had to be careful not to overdo things.

October 1941

It took two days before I could do more than get out of bed and sit in a chair. It took me several more before I could walk down the hallway unassisted. I still tired easily, and my mood and thoughts were so dark they barely reached morose, but I was getting better at faking it. At least I could go to the bathroom on my own.

The nights proved most difficult. During the day, I had an endless stream of visitors all asking the same question: "How do you feel?" They were all very eager for me to assure them I was fine. They chattered cheerily and inanely about the comings and goings of people we knew. I listened politely, or tried to, and when I was rude, no one acknowledged my churlishness as being anything more than exhaustion. Only one looked deeper.

I knew she had been watching me. I had been watching her watch me. I knew she knew I was lying every time I told someone I was fine. I would see her and my heart automatically kicked into a quicker, nervous cadence. Circumstances had, thus far, gone in my favor and I had been able to avoid a one-on-one session, but I knew that would change. She would see to it.

It happened the Sunday I was set to go home. Job was to come and get me that afternoon and I was not expecting visitors until I was back at the house; so, when my door opened, it caught me off guard.

I shut my eyes and pretended to sleep. I heard her footsteps cross the floor and stop by my bedside. The scent of her perfume drifted over me.

"Jessie Nightingale," her voice was soft but firm. "I can see the nervous pulse beating at your throat. I know you're awake.

I did not move.

"Ouch!" My eyes flew open in disbelief. She had pinched me. I shut them again, quickly.

"I did not fake a headache, skip church and drive myself out here just to have you ignore me." I knew from the tone of her voice, May was very displeased. "Look at me or so help me, I'll pinch you again."

My eyes snapped to hers.

"Now, tell me truthfully. How do you feel?"

"I'm fine. Truthfully." I looked away.

It is a funny word, feel. It implies something tangible, with shape and texture or form. Inside me, there was nothing of form. I knew I was unhappy, and there were so many intangibles contributing to that unhappiness. I did not know if I could find a way to touch them, to put words to them. I did not know if I was ready to.

"Jessie, I'm not leaving here until you look at me good and proper. I need to see what I think you've been lying about to the others."

"There, see?" I looked into her eyes and realized for the first time how very much like Job's they were. I saw the compassion in them, the understanding, and I finally acknowledged why being alone with this woman frightened me.

"Yes, I see," she said with quiet conviction. "And I'm just going to say this now so I know you've heard it. It's not your fault, Jes."

I turned my head and thought if I ignored the tears leaking out of the corners of my eyes, she would not notice them.

"I'll say it again when I think you need reminding. But for now, I won't push." She took my hand in one of hers and placed her other one against my cheek. With a gentle pressure, she turned my face back to her. "Don't keep it all locked inside too long. It won't go away and it'll only eat you inside out. You'll need to talk to someone and I'll be there if you need me, but I think you should talk to him. You need to talk to him. He needs to talk to you."

"I don't know the words," I whispered.

"Yes you do. Just tell him what's in your heart."

I could not tell anyone what was in there.

She left then, and I closed my eyes. It was exhausting keeping things bottled up, but I was glad to have had the confrontation done with. I was not ready to deal with the disorder inside me, but her understanding had been absorbed.

I was waiting for him when he arrived. I had dressed with the help of one of the day nurses. Nurse Robbins had been in several times but had maintained a professional distance.

While getting dressed I saw that my bruises were healing. The dark purples and blues had turned to yellows and greens. The swelling around my left eye was gone and the stitches in my hairline removed several days ago.

I could move my arm more although I could still not lift it over my head or pick up anything of substantial weight. It would remain in the sling for another three weeks.

My mind chewed over May's encouragement to talk to him. I wanted to. There were so many things I wanted to say. There were so many questions I wanted to ask. I wanted to ask the questions, but I did not really want the answers.

I did not hear him arrive, immersed in my thoughts as I was, but I sensed him.

"Hi." His smile was wounded and sad. I know because I felt that way too.

"Hi."

"We're all set to go if you're ready." He slipped a sheet of paper into his pocket. He still wore his Sunday suit. He must have come straight from church. I wondered if he passed May on her way back.

"I'm ready." I slid off the bed and he was immediately there to assist me should I need it. I shrugged off his hand.

"I'm sorry. Did I hurt you?"

"I can do it myself."

"I know. I just…Sorry." He shoved his hands in his jacket pockets, unsure what to do with them. Something he found in one had him pulling out his right hand. "Here. I kept this for you."

The tiny silver amphibian swam before my eyes as they threatened to spill the sudden tears that appeared.

"I thought I'd lost it." It was a tiny detail when compared to all that had happened, but the thought that I had lost my frog pendant had only added to my feelings of guilt and shame. I was glad to see it and offered a small olive branch. It was really more of a sliver.

"Thank you." I tried for a slight smile. "Could you put it on?"

I turned slightly so he could stand behind me, and used my good arm to gather my hair out of his way. He lifted the chain over my head and fastened it behind my neck. He buried his face in my nape and pressed his lips there, and for that brief moment I allowed myself the comfort of his touch.

"Jes," he whispered urgently.

"Don't." It sounded harsh even to my ears.

"Please, tell me what you're thinking?"

"I'm fine."

"Jessie—"

"Don't!" I turned to face him and put some distance between us.

"I'm sorry." He put his hands in his pockets and we stood there awkwardly, neither one of us knowing what to do or say next.

Dr. Peterson arrived. He was pushing a wheelchair. Job shook his hand in greeting and thanked him for everything he had done for both of us.

"Just doing my job, but you're welcome." He smiled and indicated the chair in front of him. "This is not usually my job but I wanted to stop by and wish both of you well."

I took a seat in the chair and waited for Job to retrieve my small suitcase. The three of us made our way to the hospital entrance where Dr. Peterson offered a few last words of advice about how to proceed at home. He assured Job that Doc Fisher could follow up with me there. Job shook his hand once more and we were alone.

The air outside was a startling change from inside the hospital. It was fresh, free from the smells of antiseptic and sickness. It was cold. I inhaled deeply and coughed and winced as the force hurt my shoulder.

"Are you all right?" Job was immediately by my side.

"I'm fine. The air's cold. That's all."

He looked around at the sky.

"It's going to snow soon." It was only just October but he was right. Winter came early to our corner of the world. That was what I had scented in the air.

"You're sure you're all right?" he asked again.

I took a deep breath and expelled it. I tried to remind myself of what I already knew. I was going to have to answer that question a lot, so I better get used to it.

"I'm fine. Really." I gave him an overly cheery smile.

He took deep a breath of his own and without another word, went to get the truck.

I let him help me into the vehicle without protest, mostly because I needed it, but also because I got the impression he was going to do it anyway. We were more awkward with each other that day than any before.

He climbed in on his side and slipped the truck in gear, but did not move forward. He stared out the windshield as though seeking something in the distance. I do not know if he found it, but after a long moment, he turned and smiled at me. It was sad around the edges, but it was a real smile.

"Let's go home." He rested his hand briefly on mine before easing the truck into motion.

I turned and stared blindly out the window. Thinking about what was—or was not—waiting for us at home was too much work. I let my head fall back against the seat and my mind go blank.

"Are you sleeping?"

"No."

"Laura would like you to call her when you're settled"

I nodded.

Pause.

"Your mother is willing to stay for a few days, if you need her to."

Another nod.

Longer pause.

"I made up my old room for now. Depending on how you feel about it, I thought I would stay there until you've healed more."

No nod.

Really long pause.

While not phrased as a question, I could sense there was one underlying his words. How did I feel about it? My head knew why he was doing it. He was afraid of hurting me in the night, should he roll the wrong way. In my heart, it was a different matter. It was a rejection. A rejection I believed, in some misguided way, I deserved, and yet…

I nodded.

The remainder of the ride was silent. Not until we had passed through town and were on the road that led to the farm, did I realize I was trembling. My stomach was roiling. I felt a bead of cold sweat trickle down between my shoulder blades. I tried breathing through my mouth to ease the nausea. I swallowed the bitter taste of bile.

I could see it as we got closer. The location of the accident. I could see the deer and hear the thud as my car hit it. I saw the blood, tasted it.

"I'm going to be sick," I said.

"What?"

"Stop. Now!"

He pulled the truck to the side of the road. I fell out the door as soon as I had it opened. Ignoring the pain in my arm, I doubled over, torn between the need to vomit and the intense desire not to. Need won.

I was down to dry heaves when I realized that Job was beside me, hand bracing my forehead. He was whispering comforting words of assurance.

I pushed away. I stumbled. I would have fallen had he not caught me.

"I'm trying to help Jes." He had a grip on both of my arms and bent to look at my face.

"You can't."

"Let me try."

I pulled away and sagged against the side of the truck. "You can't. No one can."

"How do you know?" He was shouting now. He had not spoken to me that way since the night of our engagement when I had been rude to my mother. "Talk to me!"

"Take me home," I whispered

"Jessie—"

"Take me home, or so help me I'll walk!"

He sighed with resignation. "Fine. I give up."

Please don't! I thought it, but could not say it.

The whole gang was there to greet us and came pouring out of the door and down the steps. "Oh great," I muttered under my breath as we drew up in front of the big yellow house.

"They care about you. About us." Job spoke quietly as he turned off the truck.

"I know." I felt chastised for my attitude.

My mother was there first and she hugged me as though it had been months and not yesterday since she had last seen me.

"How are you, honey?"

"Fine, Mom."

"You look a little pale." My dad observed as he kissed my forehead. I held my breath afraid he would notice the smell of vomit.

"I'm a little tired." I smiled weakly as he stepped back.

Rand was next and enveloped me in a gentle hug. "Glad you're home finally, girl."

"Thanks."

"Hey, sis." David gave me a brief hug. He whispered in my ear. "You look like a pile of manure."

I could not help it. I laughed. It sounded foreign. I had not laughed in forever, or so it seemed. I was just so grateful for the way he treated me. Normal. That is what he did for me. He made me feel normal, if only for an instant.

"Welcome home, Jes." Sarah flushed as she balanced a cheerful Thomas on her hip. "How are you?"

"Fine. Thank you." I avoided looking right at her and the baby.

I took a deep breath. Almost home free. If I could just get inside. I had taken the first step that would take me beyond her to the safety of the house when Thomas decided he had something to say.

"Ma!" the little cherub piped up. I doubt he was actually saying the word. He was too young yet, but he was vocalizing sounds. It would have been quite comical had my heart not stopped.

"Breathe," Job whispered for my benefit alone.

"I'm so sorry." Sarah looked like she wanted to cry. She looked beseechingly at David, at anyone. "He's just making noise."

"It's quite all right, Sarah." May's calm tone soothed frayed nerves. She took my hand and pulled me up the stairs. "Come on, dear. Let's get you inside where it's warm."

A half hour later, I wanted them all to go home. I had been made to sit in a chair that had been squeezed between my mother and Job. David and Sarah had left right away, saying that they needed to get Thomas down for his nap. I believe it was more that they wanted to get Thomas away from me. I was tired and beyond out of sorts. I wanted nothing more than to sit in a hot tub of water. I made no attempt to hide my yawn as the conversation around the table carried on with little or no input from me.

"Jessie, why don't you go upstairs and rest. We all understand."

My mother's words opened the floodgates and I felt the wetness of tears spilling over and running down my cheeks. It was like when I had been a little girl and had incurred some injury or hurt at the hands of my brothers. I had been able to refrain from crying until in the sympathetic arms of my mother.

The difference now was that there would be no kissing away of this hurt.

Job pushed his chair back and took my elbow as I rose from my seat. With a knee-jerk reaction, I pulled away sharply. The sudden silence at the table made me realize what I had done. I looked up into Job's face and watched the colour creep up the back of his neck. Immediately I felt the heat of shame in my own. Whatever I was feeling about him, about myself, or about the things that had happened, I knew he did not deserve that treatment.

Before he could do more than cast a self-conscious glance at the others still seated at the table, I reached out and took his hand in a fierce grip. It was a silent plea for him to look at me, to understand.

"Go on up," he whispered. He squeezed my hand before releasing it. "I'll just see your dad and my folks out, and then I'll come up."

I nodded and gave a huge inward sigh of relief. He had understood. I mumbled my excuses and left as quickly as I could.

Once upstairs, I took a moment to gather a clean nightgown and take it into the bathroom. I started the water running in the large claw foot tub and began to undress. I paused as I caught sight of myself in the mirror. The freckles across my nose stood out against the pallor of my skin. Before the accident, my face and figure had begun to round out. Now there were dark hollows under my eyes and in my cheeks. David was right. I did look like a pile of manure.

My hair was dull, in dire need of a wash. I pulled it away from where the stitches had been. The scab had just about disappeared leaving what would be a dark pink scar about two inches in length and just inside my hairline. I rubbed my fingers over the ridge of tender tissue. Eventually it would even out and fade. It was itchy but I refrained from the temptation to scratch. If I took off the scab, it might bleed. I was tired of bleeding.

My sweater and blouse fell to the floor next to my arm sling, and I stood looking at the mottled mess that was my shoulder. I rotated it gingerly. It was tender but bearable.

My skirt and tights followed the same course as my sweater and blouse. I closed my eyes and ran my hand over my front. For one brief moment, I allowed myself to yearn for that which I could no longer feel. Dr. Peterson had assured me that once my body healed, I would be able to conceive another child. It had been small consolation and of little consequence at the time.

I turned away from the mirror to shut off the water and froze. I had not heard the door open, but there in its frame he stood.

Here was a man who was intimately familiar with my body in a way no other was. Over the year of our marriage, I had found a certain satisfaction in the way his eyes would deepen in intensity as they followed me about a room. I had sought it, welcomed it, and found his desire delicious. In that moment, I felt naked.

A fierce frown darkened his brow and his jaw clenched. He swallowed convulsively. His eyes were inscrutable slits. He looked angry and my heart kicked into double time.

I grabbed a towel and held it as a meager shield in front of me. "I'm sorry." I apologized but did not know why. I bent down to shut off the water and once again stood in awkward discomfort.

Job approached until we were toe to toe. If there had been anywhere for me to go, I would have gone there.

With careful deliberation, he reached out and pulled the towel from my hands. Mortified, I made the instinctive and ineffectual move to cover myself with my arms. His fingers grasped my chin and forced my head up. I did not resist but neither did I meet his eyes, at least not until I felt the gentle caress at my temple.

I had to look to confirm that it was his touch I felt. It was so delicate. I watched his face as he looked at me. His gaze followed the same path his hand took as it lowered from my head to my shoulder. I felt his finger trace the outline of some of the remaining blotches. The muscles in his jaw flexed.

His hand lowered and hovered in the region of my navel. I began to tremble when I felt its warmth press against my flesh. Goose bumps spread across my skin. My ears were buzzing and I could not focus.

Gradually, Job went to his knees. He pressed his lips to my stomach in a kiss so gentle my heart hungered with it.

I was not the only one trembling. He turned his face and rested his cheek where his lips had been. His arms wrapped so tightly around me, I was forced to hold onto his head for balance.

"I was so scared."

I thought at first I imagined the words, so softly were they spoken. Then he said them again.

"I was so scared, Jes. For days you didn't move. You were so pale, so still. We can do this Jessie. We can get through this if we do it together." My fingers tightened in his hair. "For the first time, nothing feels solid. I'm searching for answers I don't know if I'll ever find. I'm confused and frustrated. And I'm angry."

"I know." I could not speak above a whisper. "I'm sorry."

Carefully, Job leaned back and looked up at me. "For what?"

I tipped my head back and focused on the ceiling trying to avoid looking at him, and keep my tears from spilling over. It took me a couple of tries but I finally managed to get the words out.

"For this." I indicated the bruises. My hand settled where his lips had been just moments before. "For this."

"Did you make that deer jump out in front of you?"

"No."

"Did you hit it on purpose?"

"No." I knew where he was going but guilt is more often than not, irrational, based on "What ifs," or "If onlys…." Mine was no different.

"Then what, Jessie? What are you sorry for?" He stood and framed my face with his hands. "I can play that game too. I'm sorry that marrying me has led to this much suffering for you, but I don't know how I could have changed anything. I keep trying to do what is best, what I think God would want me to do, and at every turn I fail. Do you want me to apologize for trying my best? I won't. Do you want me to apologize for doing everything I can to continue to serve God? I won't do that either. Do I feel awful about the fact that my best just doesn't seem to be good enough? Absolutely. I'm frustrated and confused and angry. I'm angry because every time I see those bruises on you and I think about what we lost—our daughter –"

I struggled to pull away from him.

He managed to hold onto my head without hurting me. "We lost our child and there was absolutely nothing I could do to change that. I was completely impotent, and that made me angry. Not you, not the accident, because that's what it was—an accident. I'm angry at my inability to protect you from anything that's happened."

A knock on the door prevented any further discussion. It would take me days to absorb and process his words and feelings, but for the moment, I was glad of the reprieve provided when my mother called out inquiring about my state of well-being. I turned the emotional lock that enabled me to put on the façade of relative normalcy, and called out that I was fine.

The door opened and my mother walked in.

"Sorry. I didn't realize you were in here." My mother said to Job. She flushed when she took in my state of undress and saw Job standing before me. She took a step backward to leave, but Job turned and stopped her.

"It's all right, Claire." He pulled her into the room. "Jessie needs some help getting into the bath. I was going to do it but I think it might be best if you stay."

He looked at me one last time before he slipped past my mother and was gone. I read in his eyes acceptance that the issue would not be resolved on that day and the promise that it would be—soon.

THIRTY-TWO

OCTOBER 1941

Job decided the time was not right for him to leave for the granite mines. Instead, he focused his attention on clearing the rubble from the burned out barns. At dawn, I would hear the axe or saw begin its rhythmic destruction. Periodically, Job would load up the back of his truck and haul the refuse away to some distant field. When he returned, the whack of the axe or rasp of the blade would start its repetitive refrain once again. With the aid of several lanterns, he worked well past dark. He worked alone and with feverish intensity, as though his physical labor could wrest the answers to his questions from the blackened ashes of what had been his past, present, and hope for the future. By the time he was done, only the foundation of the main barn remained. Constructed of large stones, it stood steadfastly in place despite the heat that had blackened it.

I was left alone to brood. My mother had stayed for several days and nights until she was certain I could handle basic tasks like getting dressed and bathing on my own. Her presence had served as a buffer between Job and me. As long as she was there, we avoided the awkwardness that existed between us when we were alone.

My mother shifted her schedule after those days, to arrive just before lunch. She would prepare food, which Job would eat standing up and so fast I am sure he did not have time to register what it was that passed his lips. My mother and I would eat quietly before I returned to my room to "rest," and she did the chores I ignored. Dinner was a brief and quiet affair between my husband and me.

"I'm going to be outside if you need me for anything," he would say before planting a benign kiss on my cheek. Job had moved back into our room over a week before but it was as though he remained across the hall.

For my part, I managed to smile and carry on as though I was not a mass of restless and swirling emotions. If I did get short tempered and snapped that I was fine every time someone forgot and asked me how I was doing, no one commented. They all went out of their way to avoid rippling the surface of the pond. All that is, but one.

May, it seemed, went out of her way to get in my way whenever the opportunity presented itself. She was not overt about it, but I knew. Then my mother began to notice.

November 1941

One particular evening, it was just the beginning of November by then, I watched from my bedroom window as large flakes of snow fell from the sky. They did not stay, disappearing into the charred ground of the main yard. Only the empty bunkhouse and never used creamery buildings stood as a reminder that this had once been an entity in which life had thrived. Earlier that afternoon, Job had taken what appeared to be the last load of debris away. It had taken over three weeks to clear it all. I wondered what he would find next to keep him out of the house. Would he now leave for the mines? The thought caused my stomach to drop. That anxiety, mixed with the knots of doubt, sadness and fear that settled in the middle of my chest, had become my constant companion.

I took a deep breath in an effort to slow my breathing and ease the constriction that increased by tiny increments each day. My cycle had started again, adding to my edginess. The sight of blood had set my heart racing in fear and confusion. Only when I recognized it for what it was, a sign that my body was healing itself and returning to normal, did the pounding in my chest ease and my breathing slow. Still, I was off balance, anxious, bordering on full-blown panic. I think that is why I made the mistake of leaving the haven of my room early that night.

On some evenings, like that night, our parents joined us for the evening meal. I usually waited until I heard Rand or my father arrive before leaving my room. The more people in attendance meant less time spent in close proximity to May. However, when I entered the kitchen and realized that my mother and May were the only two present and that the meal was still a short distance away from being ready, I did the only thing I could do. I asked, with great reluctance, if there was anything I could do to help.

"We're fine, Sweetheart." My mother threw a distracted smile over her shoulder before peeking in the oven to check the readiness of its contents. "You just sit and take it easy. We've got it covered."

I was only two steps into my cross to the table when May went to work.

"Oh, I don't know Claire." May's eyes pinned me to the floor where I stood. "I don't think it would hurt any if she helped a little."

"I'm sure it wouldn't, but there's no need yet for her to do anything too strenuous." My mother came and gave me a peck on the cheek and slight push toward the table. "There'll be plenty of time for that soon enough."

I almost made it to my seat before May fired her next shot.

"She has to start doing things for herself sometime."

"What does that mean?" My mother turned to face May in the universal hands-on-hips stance that spoke eloquently of battle readiness.

May answered the challenge.

"At every opportunity given, your daughter proclaims her wellness. I just think it's time we believe her and let her resume responsibility for her own home."

Like the fur on an angry dog's ruff, my mother bristled. "She's my daughter, and she's just been through a very traumatic experience. It's my job as her mother to see her through it."

"Well, I watched as my son went through the same traumatic experience. He's her husband. He should be allowed to see her through this."

"I don't see him doing that!" my mother replied. "He's never around and when he is, he never says much of anything to anyone, let alone Jes."

"Maybe that's because they're never left alone for less than a minute!" May pointed out forcefully.

A buzzing started in my ears. I clapped my hands over them in a futile attempt to block out the annoying sound.

"I suppose that's my fault?" My mother continued as though I were not there.

"No," May's denial was emphatic. "It is not."

"Then whose is it?"

"It's Jessie's."

I think I might have reacted to that had I not been preoccupied with getting the buzzing out of my head.

"Claire, how can those two deal with this if they're never allowed to?" May asked matter-of-factly. "Jessie has insisted she's fine, but if she is, then how come she goes out of her way to make sure she's never in the same room alone with him?"

"I do not!" My outrage was directed more at the truth of the statement than it was at the fact that May had stated it.

"You can deny it all you want, Jes." May waved her hand dismissively. "Just add it to the list of things you're in denial about."

"I don't know what you're talking about." I shot a beseeching look at my mother. She looked at the three of us as though she had never seen anything like us before.

"Oh yes." May's voice dripped with sarcasm. "That's right, you're *fine.* Your husband's livelihood is wiped out, you loose two dear friends, your first child and nearly your own life in the process, but you're *fine.* What could I have been thinking?"

My mother's gasp echoed mine. The buzzing was gaining power.

"Have you even grieved yet?"

"May." My mother spoke the name in warning.

I could feel the shaking start in my toes and work its way up. My knees, thighs, stomach, chest and hands, all tightened and shook.

"Why are you doing this?" I barely managed to whisper.

"Because I love you." May was calm. Maddeningly so. "Since the day I saw Rand juggling you and Job under his arms, you captured my heart. You faced everything head on. Oh sure, there were a few stumbles here and there and a couple of detours, but you always made your way. Now I think you're lost. We're all a little lost right now. None of us understand why things have happened the way they have, but you're trying to find your way on your own when you don't have to. I see what it's doing to my son. I don't like it."

"Then don't look!" I hissed.

"Jessie!" My mother's shock was more than evident. "May, I'm sorry. She doesn't know what she's saying."

May actually smiled. It made my blood go white hot. I loved this woman but I wanted to bash her face right in.

"It's nice to finally see some honest emotion."

"Get out!" I shouted. "Get out! Now!"

I stood, chest heaving as I tried to move air into and out of my lungs. My mother and May, stared at me with varying degrees of surprise. My mother looked concerned. May appeared more curious than anything, as though she were thinking, "Well, would you look at that?"

No one moved. Outside the wind howled eerily. Feet banged against the boards of the back porch seconds before the screen door hinges creaked. The inside door to the kitchen swung in and a blast of icy air followed Job inside.

"It's getting cold out there." He swiped at the few snow flakes that clung to his coat. His hands paused as he sensed the tension in the room. He surveyed his mother briefly, then mine before his gaze rested on me. "What's wrong? What's going on here?"

I could not stop the gut wrenching sob that took hold. I doubled over and wrapped my arms tightly around myself, trying to keep myself from flying apart. Even my skin hurt.

The outside door opened again and Rand stepped into the room followed closely by my father. Their conversation ceased when they took in the scene.

"I'll go run a hot bath." It was an odd statement from my mother. I found myself laughing almost hysterically through the haze of anger and grief and wishing that a hot bath was indeed the cure-all I was looking for.

"Stop." Job's voice allowed no disagreement. "What happened here?"

"We were trying to help." May spoke softly.

"It looks like you've helped enough for tonight." May had the grace to blush.

"There's no call to speak to your mother like that," Rand said sternly. "I don't know what's going on here, but I'm sure there's an explanation."

"My wife is over there sobbing because of something that was said or done." Job stood his ground firmly. "I won't have it in our house and I want you all to leave right now."

"Well let's find out what's wrong before you throw us out." My father tried to move by, but Job stepped up and met my father eye to eye. It was a strange moment to notice that Job stood a few inches taller than him. This was not a boy and a man facing off.

"Come, Ben," my mother stepped in before things became more heated. "Job's right. We'll come back tomorrow."

"No," Job spoke more quietly but nonetheless firmly. "This house is off limits to everyone until Jessie or I say so. He turned to his mother. "Everyone."

May nodded and made her way to her son. She raised her arm, resting her hand upon his cheek briefly. Job took her hand and kissed it.

"I know, mom," he said. "I know."

Then it was just the two of us, me, standing in the middle of our kitchen feeling as though I would never stop crying, and him watching with resolve. I was terrified to confront the overwhelming thoughts and emotions that had taken hold of me, and yet a tiny fraction of my consciousness was relieved.

He walked over to the table, pulled out a chair, took me by the shoulders and steered me in that direction. He sat down and tugged me onto his lap. He pressed my head down onto his shoulder before wrapping his arms around me. How I had missed the physical comfort of him.

"Jessie, we're going to do this. Now or later, but tonight we are going to talk about everything."

I nodded and clung tightly to him. For a little while words were not necessary. Eventually he rose from the chair and carried me upstairs to our bedroom.

He laid me down on the bed and removed my shoes. He slipped off his own and climbed in beside me taking care to pull the quilt over us both.

He was quiet for so long, I did not think he was going to say anything after all, but he took a deep breath and expelled it slowly, warming the back of my neck in the process.

"I was waiting for you to get home. Even though I was leaving, I was happy, really excited about things for the first time since the rain fell. I'm not sure why exactly, since the world seemed to be falling down around me, but I had my faith, you, and I had our baby on the way. I could lose everything and still be happy with those things."

I gripped his hands tightly. "I was planning how to decorate your old room—if we had a girl." My voice caught on the lump in my throat. Job held me tighter.

"My mom was on her way down to the mailbox." He continued his story allowing me time to gain a tenuous hold on my emotions. "I joked with her about not getting lost in the fog. She laughed and said she would have to be deprived of all her senses before she'd get lost on a walk she'd been doing since before I was born. With the fog, it was so quiet. Sounds didn't carry very well that day, Jes. I heard something but couldn't tell what it was so I ignored it. When I heard the car horn, I—" He cleared his throat and swallowed before continuing.

"I knew. In my heart, I knew. Something bad had happened again, only this time my life was going change in ways I could not imagine."

"I didn't see it." I forced myself to talk about it and once I did, I found the words would not stop. I told him what I could remember of the accident; the spinning, the deer's eye, and the blood. So much blood. He knew what happened after that.

"I held her Jes," he whispered. "Our daughter. She was so small. Perfect. She looked like the best of you and me. I told her we'd like to get to know her when we get to heaven and that we'd be waiting for that day."

I pressed my hands against my eyes. I could hear the anguish in his voice. I could feel it in my core. I turned to face him. His face was wet with tears I reached up to wipe away.

"I've never done anything as difficult as I did when I buried our daughter." Job said. "I was so afraid I would have to bury you next to her."

"I don't know how much more I can take." I said. "I don't know what is left to take."

Job kissed my forehead. "I wish I could tell you I understood what is going on, but I don't. I wish I could stop it all. I wish I knew what God is doing with all of this. I wish so many things, I don't know where to begin to look for answers."

"There aren't any." I stated, feeling the anger and rage that was always pressing. "And if there were, they wouldn't be good enough."

His silence told me he did not agree with my assessment. It said he still believed in God and believed that God is in control. I believed I resented God and that control. In many ways, it would have been easier if I could have entirely given up my belief in God. Then I could let go of my anger, confusion, and resentment. I could say that these things happened because they are just a part of life. They serve no purpose, there is no greater meaning in them other than they just are.

However, I did believe in God. I was angry, and resentful, and jealous of His position in my husband's life. I lacked any understanding about how God could do these things or allow them to happen, and I may not have liked the answers to those questions, even if I found them.

"I'm going to have to leave soon," Job said after long moments of quiet had passed.

My heart sank. We finally were connecting again and now he was talking about leaving.

"Why?" I asked. "There has to be another way."

"I wish there were." He sat up and rested his head in his hands. "There's nothing left. My dad has given me what he can afford. Your father paid the medical bills I couldn't. If I don't go, we'll lose the land and the house to the bank. Your dad has worked it so that as long as I'm paying something we'll hold on to it, but I have to work to do that. I put off going because I needed to know you were going to be all right. I needed to know we were."

I knelt behind him and wrapped my arms around his neck trying to absorb his strength. "When will you leave?"

"Day after tomorrow, if I can. I need to know you'll be all right."

"I will be because I have to be." I kissed the back of his neck seeking the intimacy I had missed. "I'm sorry I made it difficult for you. For us. I didn't know how to say what I was feeling. I didn't want to. I'm still afraid to feel it."

"Me too." He turned and buried his face in my neck. "If you say you need me to stay, I will. Even if it means losing the farm. You're more important to me than that."

A large part of me wanted to ask him to stay. I had been so lonely. An emotional state of my own making, to be sure, but I finally felt like we were together again. I was afraid of what I might feel if he left.

"I know that," I tried to hide the tears that were threatening again. I knew what losing the farm would do to him, no matter how willing he claimed to be to do just that. I still held on to remnants of my guilt. I did not want to add any more to it. "But you need to do this too."

"I'll be home for Thanksgiving, if I can."

"If you can't, I'll find a way to come to you."

Thirty-three

November 1941

I dealt with being alone by reaching out to my family. It did not ease the loneliness that still maintained its hold on my gut, but the days were passable.

I made a concerted effort to participate in daily life. I went shopping with my mother, had dinners with Rand and May, and forced myself to acknowledge the grief that I was just beginning to deal with.

"I miscarried twelve times before Job," May said one day while we were drying the dishes. We had been working side by side in quiet, each of us absorbed in our own thoughts. Her words shone a light on the affinity of those thoughts.

"I was never as far along as you were, but each time I felt that cramping… And then when the doctor said there would be no more—for a long time I found it hard to be thankful for the one I did have." She gripped the edge of the sink and closed her eyes momentarily. "I think that's what bothers me most—what I'll take to my grave regretting—those moments when I was ungrateful for that blessed baby boy."

I placed a hand over one of hers and realized she did understand, even more than my own mother. I wrapped my arms around her waist and let her see my anguish for the first time.

"How did you get over it?" I asked. I so earnestly wanted to know how to make it less than it was.

"I just got through it. One day at a time." She lifted her head and kissed my cheek. "That's all you need to do. Get through one day, then the next."

May's presence was something I no longer avoided after that. There were days when I actually sought her out. Not to talk, just so I could be in the same room with her. I also moved beyond my distress where little Thomas was concerned.

Sarah had come to visit the day Job left. I was wallowing and wandering, trying to decide what to with myself. I looked outside and saw a figure approaching. Sarah. She was carrying Thomas.

My heart lurched. I did not want to do what I knew was coming but what other choice did I have? It had been weeks since I had seen her or Thomas. It was not Sarah's fault that I would not hold my child, nor was it the fault of that wonderful baby boy. I could not continue to ignore them. I could not continue to nurse my envy and keep them apart from me.

I met them on the front steps.

Thomas and I gave each other a wary stare. His eyes were like my mother's, sky blue. His cheeks were rosy from the cold. He looked so much like David and yet, in him were parts of Sarah too. The best of both of us, Job had said about our daughter. I felt my heart tighten. Then Thomas smiled, a big drooling smile that crinkled his nose and eyes, and something inside me released.

"Hi. Jes. I wanted to…I hoped…I know…" Sarah stammered before stopping with a sigh. "I'm sorry."

"No. I'm sorry." I said and held open the door. "I should have called you before this. Come in."

The nights were the most difficult. The physical and emotional isolation caused a feeling of such desolation that I could not stay at the house by myself, and after a week, I moved back in with my parents.

I wanted Job. I needed to feel him, to hold him, to be with him. I could not sit still.

The disconnect was heavy. After Thanksgiving, when Job did not make it home, I found myself crying at the most inopportune times, fighting the urge to curl up in a corner and let the world fade away.

It happened when I was in the mercantile picking up some potatoes for my mother. Mr. Martin caught me standing in the aisle, tears streaming down my face and staring at a potato that had started to sprout.

Mr. Martin, took the offending vegetable from my hand.

"The bus for Barre leaves tomorrow morning at ten o'clock," he said with uncharacteristic kindness. "Shall I have them save you a seat?"

I nodded.

"It'll be busy, so get here early."

November 27, 1941

I was too keyed up to sleep. The elderly lady next to me picked up on my nervous energy and asked if I was meeting someone special.

"My husband," I answered and from there I found myself sharing some details of my life.

I never asked her name, and she never inquired after mine. Our brief friendship had its beginning and end on the bus ride, as is often the way between two travelers who sit side-by-side on route to mutual, or separate destinations. I was grateful however, for her kindness. It made the journey short.

As the bus pulled into the terminal in Barre, I scanned the small crowd waiting. It was a different group than what I would have found waiting for the bus in the Junction. The men looked more worn than their clothes. They had been hardened by hard labor.

Alighting from the bus, suitcase in hand, I was forced to move to the edge of the group. Now that I was here, I had no idea where to go. I stepped into the nearest shop and asked the clerk where I might find High Street and the address I was looking for. Although she had a slightly harried air about her, she took the time to point me in the right direction, and I began the fifteen minute walk to the house I was looking for.

It had seen better days, that was certain. The paint, what was left of it, had long since peeled and blistered. I believed it to have been white originally, but now it was a rather dingy gray. The screen door had a tear in it and hung precariously off kilter. The wooden steps leading up to that door were no better. Job had neglected to tell me the state of his living conditions.

Carefully, I navigated my way up and over the cracked and creaking boards. I knocked on the door, half afraid I would be the one to take it off the hinges.

"Coming!" a muffled voice from within called. I could not tell if it was male or female until the inside door swung back and revealed the source of the voice. On this, Job's description had not been remiss. Mrs. Grabaldi was the owner of the boarding house and was exactly as he said, a mixture of grandmother and worn out prostitute. Deep wrinkles around her mouth served as tributaries for the deep red lipstick that ran into them. Smoke from a cigarette clamped between those painted lips drifted up into her right eye forcing her to squint. "Yeah?" she said in her gravely voice as she wiped her hands on a small towel.

"Mrs. Grabaldi?"

Her squint became suspicious. "Depends. Whatcha want?"

"I'm looking for Job Nightingale."

Her eye opened and her gazed traveled from my head to my feet and back up. I tensed anxiously under her scrutiny. I wondered if I would pass, then wondered what it was I was hoping to pass.

"He's a married man."

"Yes, I know." I sighed a little in relief. She was being protective.

"Wife's got some boy's name. Jessie. Not Jessica. Just, Jessie."

"I'm his wife. I'm Jessie. Jessie Nightingale."

Another shrewd once over, this time with a raised eyebrow and a swift suck on the cigarette. "He know you was coming? He didn't tell me."

"No. It's a surprise. I wanted to see him."

"He ain't here." The woman took the cigarette out of her mouth long enough to stick it through the rip in the screen and knock the ash off the end.

I met her gaze briefly before looking away to blink back unexpected tears. I had not considered the possibility that he might not be at the house. What did I do now? I could not continue to stand on this woman's shabby porch and stare stupidly at her.

Something in my posture must have indicated my defeat, for Mrs. Grabaldi opened the screen door and indicated that I enter.

Like the trail of smoke from her cigarette, I followed the woman down a short dingy hallway. Wallpaper, faded by time, peeled in sections revealing layers of other paper faded by even more time. In contrast, the kitchen Mrs. Grabaldi led me into was clean and bright despite showing the same signs of age as the rest of the house.

With a flick of her hand, she indicated I should be seated at the table that was placed in the corner and butted against the walls on two sides. A crystal ashtray appeared ready to overflow and yet not an ash dared mar the surface of the scarred tabletop.

Moments later, she placed a cup of hot tea in front of me.

"Do you know when Job will be back?" I said before taking a cautious sip.

The tea was too strong and sweet, but it was fortifying. I would not complain in the face of her generosity.

"Couple hours I spect. 'Bout time for supper. Don't keep track. It's easier that way."

Mrs. Grabaldi shrugged before taking a seat for herself. Somehow she found room in the ashtray to snuff out the cigarette she held. Then, from somewhere in the folds of her apron, another appeared to take its place. The woman flicked her wrist and with a "ping", a flame appeared to light the slim white stick balanced precariously on her garish lips. I heard the metallic slick of the lighter lid clicking back into place and the flame was extinguished.

"Can't seem to give 'em up," she said after taking a deep drag. "Lord knows I've tried. It'd be easier that way."

Not sure how to respond, I took another sip of tea and gave a general murmur of understanding.

Smoke seemed to seep from every orifice of the rooming house owner—mouth, nose, ears. I could not help but think of a fire breathing dragon about to incinerate everything in its path. The image was dispelled when Mrs. Grabaldi coughed, a rattling hack from deep in her chest.

I felt an overwhelming sense of sadness. How had it come to this? Why did I find myself sitting across from a woman more worn out than her old house? Why did Job have to be living in that house with its stale air and grimy rooms, instead of at home, in our bright, airy farmhouse? Why had events or other greater powers conspired to bring us to this point?

I returned my cup to the saucer, and without warning I found my right hand grasped between both of Mrs. Grabaldi's. They were red and chapped. The index and middle fingers of her left hand were stained yellow. Startled, I looked at her and tried to pull away, but her grip was surprisingly strong.

"Faith," she said with a quiet conviction causing the cigarette to bounce up and down precariously on her lips.

"What does that mean?"

With a shrug she released my hand "Don't know. Don't care. It's easier that way."

She took another haul on the smoke before tapping the end over the ashtray. "I just say what I'm told, when I'm told."

I was confused. "You were told to say that? I don't understand."

"I don't myself. Stopped questioning long time ago."

I stared at her, waiting expectantly for her to expand her explanation. She took a drag and inhaled deeply. Her gaze penetrated the smoke she exhaled and locked on to mine.

"I got this relationship with God. We go 'round things quite mightily. But some things I quit banging my head against. Easier that way."

"I see." I did not, but I did understand difficulty with God.

Mrs. Grabaldi stood and pushed back her chair signaling an end to whatever it was we had been talking about.

"I don't normally let women upstairs. It's easier that way." She took my cup and brought it to the sink. "But you look a bit frayed around the edges, and since his roommate ain't around tonight, can't see no harm in it just this once. As long as you're discrete."

Mrs. Grabaldi was right. I did feel as though I was unraveling. She carefully studied the end of her cigarette for a moment before looking at me.

"By *discrete*, I mean the walls is thin and the bedsprings creak."

I buried my face in my hands and wished the floor would open up and swallow me whole. It would have been easier that way.

My face was still burning when Mrs. Grabaldi closed the bedroom door behind me.

She had escorted me up the stairs—the bedsprings were not the only things that creaked—and down the hallway to the left. We passed a small bathroom with black and white tiles on the floor and up the walls. It looked clean, for which I was grateful. There were two closed doors on the right and another on the left, which she had opened and ushered me into.

"That's his side, over there." Mrs. Grabaldi pointed to the far corner, by the window. "Sheets is clean this morning. Supper's at half past five. S'up to you if you come."

The room was unremarkable. The floorboards, once painted white, were scraped and worn grey. The small window was clean and framed by what appeared to have been once cheery pink curtains. It let in enough light to illuminate the tidy corner that belonged to Job.

The bed was made. It was really more of a cot, a narrow mattress on a metal frame with metal springs for support.

I thought of our big comfortable bed at home and the love that had gone in to making it. The small dresser, bleached by the sunlight from the window, revealed male toiletries arranged in an orderly fashion.

I walked over and ran a finger over Job's toothbrush, his comb. I picked up the soap and sniffed. The scent was familiar, as much a part of me as it was a part of him. Job's Sunday shoes rested neatly under the foot of the bed.

On the other side of the room, the bed was unmade. The clean sheets of the morning sat untouched on the bare mattress of the cot. Dirty clothes mixed with clean as they hung out of open dresser drawers or fell scattered about the top of the dresser and floor. If I had not been depressed before I entered the room, I was now.

I set my small suitcase down and took off my coat. Whatever else the house was, it was warm.

I eased myself down onto the bed slowly, the squeak of the bed-springs reminding me of Mrs. Grabaldi's advice. I could feel the heat returning to my face. Not since our return from our honeymoon when my mother pulled me aside seeking certain assurances, had I been so embarrassed.

I removed my boots and placed them just under the cot. I cringed as I swung my legs up and used my coat as a cover. How Job managed to sleep escaped my comprehension as much as did the fact that I slept.

I was overly warm. I could feel perspiration between my cheek and the hand it rested on. I tried to stretch but the object weighing me down prevented it. I turned my head and found Job. I could see the weight loss in the gauntness of his cheeks. His hair was long, the way I liked it but his mother did not. For what seemed endless moments, we absorbed each other.

"What?" I asked when he finally looked away.

"I didn't want to see you here."

"I'm sorry." My heart hurt.

"I'm happy though, that you are here." He took my hand in his and pressed it to his lips. I saw the moisture that filled his eyes escape and run unheeded down the side of his face.

"I just didn't want to see you here, in this place. I didn't want you to know this."

He gestured to the room around us, and the ache left my heart.

"I didn't tell you I was coming because I was afraid you would tell me not to."

"I would have. I'm glad you didn't."

"Really?"

His answer was to grab my head and take my mouth with his. This was what I came for, what I needed as much as breathing.

He had always been lean, but in a vital, athletic way. Lying next to him and running my hands over his ribs, I felt a marked difference. I rummaged around until I found his shirt and threw it on. I stood up to turn on the bedside lamp.

"Where are you going?" he yawned and grabbed for my ankle. Job had moved the mattress onto the floor after I had mumbled through my embarrassment, the explanation of why it needed to be.

"Turning on a light." I clicked the switch and ignored his protests over the sudden brightness.

I knelt back down and pulled back the sheet. "Stop it." I batted his hands away and ignored the hopeful glint in his eye. "I want to look at you."

"Okay, Doll Face," He spread his arms wide but his suggestive smile got lost in a grimace.

His skin was hot and dry under my touch. His stomach muscles were more defined, and his ribs and hipbones protruded alarmingly. The muscles of his arms were sinewy, made so by the difficult labor he was doing at the mines. There were nicks and cuts in various stages of healing along his forearms and hands.

"You've lost so much weight. Have you been sick?"

I tried to feel his forehead but he jerked away, evading my touch.

"Leave it, Jes."

There was a flush along his cheeks. I began to look closer. There was a rash hidden under his chest hair. He winced again as he crossed his arms in an effort to shield himself.

"How long have you had this?" I traced the edge of the rash with my finger.

"I don't know. A day or two. Thought I was just irritated by the dust. It happens."

He shivered and drew the sheet up. I pushed myself up and went to the dresser where I took out an undershirt and long underwear. A sweater, long pants, and wool socks followed.

I helped him dress, his lack of protest an indication of how poorly he felt. I could not help but notice the carefulness with which he moved.

"Where does it hurt?" I asked pausing to brush his hair off his face.

He gave me a rueful smile. "It seems like every muscle in my body has hurt since I've been here."

I tried to be as gentle as possible when I tugged the sweater over his head. "Is there a doctor nearby?"

"I'll be fine. Just lie down next to me until I warm up. I have to go back soon."

He reached for me but I easily avoided him. A sure sign there was more going on than either one of us understood.

"You're not going anywhere, except to a doctor or home with me." I pushed him back and he fell onto the mattress with a groan.

"Home," he sighed. "I've missed it. And you. So very much."

"Why didn't you tell me you were in pain? I wouldn't have, I mean we needn't have—"

"Yes, we did," he said quietly forestalling any further protests I might have offered.

"You're not in any shape to go back to work right now."

He gave a slight nod and let his eyes drift shut. "Tell Mrs. Grabaldi. She'll let one of the guys know and they can tell the foreman. Just let me hold you tonight. Tomorrow, if I don't feel better I'll go with you."

I had ignored his request and with the help of Mrs. Grabaldi and another man, bundled him into the truck. We probably should have gone to the hospital in Barre, but the sinking feeling lodged in my chest had me heading towards Grand River Junction and home.

Thirty-four

November 28, 1941

"Has anyone come to tell you anything?" Nurse Robbins asked.

I shook my head no.

"I'll see what I can find out for you and be right back."

Hers had been the first familiar face I had seen upon our arrival at the hospital. She had supervised the transfer of Job from the truck to the exam room with great competence. That was over an hour ago, and since then I had been sitting and waiting for word on Job's condition.

I jumped up when Dr. Peterson appeared.

"What's happening? Is Job all right?" I was afraid of the answer.

"He's hanging on." Dr. Peterson placed his hand on my shoulder and steered me back to the chair. He crouched in front of me and took my hands between his. "He's very sick, Mrs. Nightingale. His fever is dangerously high and the swelling around the joints has me concerned."

"Why? What do you think it is?"

"It's too soon to be certain. Would you like to call someone?"

I looked into his eyes and tried to comprehend the implication of this statement. When his gaze wavered and he glanced away, I understood.

"What is it?" I demanded.

"I really think you should call someone. It might be best if you had someone with you."

I looked at Nurse Robbins standing quietly behind the doctor. She avoided looking directly at me.

"Is he going to die?" The absurdity of the question almost drove me to laughter.

"I don't know anything for certain." Dr. Peterson squeezed my hand in a manner that was not as reassuring as was meant to be.

"Can I see him?"

"In a little while. We're getting him settled in a room," he said.

"I would like to call my parents. And Job's. I should call them too."

"I'll call them for you. If you'd like?" Nurse Robbins offered.

I accepted her offer. I knew if I heard my mother's or father's voices, I would lose control. I needed to maintain that.

I lost track of everything, even how much time passed before Dr. Peterson reappeared.

"How is he?" I sprang to my feet the moment I spotted the doctor coming down the hallway.

"He's hanging on." He took my arm. "Why don't you come with me?"

"What aren't you telling me?" I pulled back.

"Mrs. Nightingale, I wish I had something specific to tell you, truly I do." The doctor took off his glasses and rubbed his eyes. "I have a suspicion, but because of your husband's age, it just doesn't make sense."

"His age? He's twenty-one."

"I know. I think he has Rheumatic Fever, but it's usually a childhood illness."

"Rheumatic Fever?"

I had heard the name, but did not understand what the disease entailed. Before the day was over, I would learn more than I ever wanted.

I followed Dr. Peterson into a small examination room. Nurse Robbins was waiting to assist him. I suffered impatiently through the brief physical exam, which entailed answering more than one question about sore throats. Had I had one recently? Had Job?

I assured him I had not been sick with a sore throat or fever but could not answer for Job. "He's been away for weeks," I said pretending not to notice the poorly disguised curiosity from Nurse Robbins. "Over in Barre, working the mines. I took the bus out to meet him early this morning. Yesterday morning now, I guess. I noticed he wasn't feeling well and during the night he got worse. I know I should have taken him to the hospital in Barre, but I just wanted to get him home. We only made it here."

"I'm glad you did." Dr. Peterson stood in front of me. "Your husband's condition is a puzzle. I'm going to treat it as Rheumatic Fever since he has the major indicators, in spite of his age. His current physical state of exhaustion makes it worse of course."

"When can I see him?"

"I'll take you to him now."

I slid off the examination table. I was still oblivious to the true nature of what Job was battling. I had a feeling as the doctor placed his hands on my shoulders and looked me square in the eye, that would change.

"Remember, it's Job lying in that bed."

"I know that."

"Mrs. Nightingale—Jessie—your husband's case is severe."

I could feel the fear kick in, the quick jump of blood through my system.

"His joints are very swollen and extremely tender. It's difficult for him to move. There are bumps under his skin. These will ease eventually, but then there is the matter of his heart."

"His heart?"

"If he lives," he paused to make sure his words were sinking in. I nodded for him to continue. "His heart will, in all probability, be weakened."

"Just temporarily, right?"

"No," he said softly. "It will affect how he can live his life. His ability to do hard physical labor could well be diminished, now and in the future."

"*Could* be," I said seeking clarification.

"There really is no way of knowing until he begins to recover."

The "if he recovers," was implied.

"I need to see him." I thought maybe I could tell by looking at Job that Dr. Peterson was wrong. That he would wake up and smile and none of this would be happening. I refused to believe any of it.

Dr. Peterson nodded and ushered me through the door into Job's room. The only light seeped through where the drapes did not quite meet. There were three other beds in the room. All made up but empty. For that I was undeniably grateful.

During the time since our arrival at the hospital and the minute I walked into the room, a dramatic transformation had occurred. I tried to fit my mind around what I saw. Job's skin was full of bumps in various sizes. They contorted his features beyond the grimace of pain that came and went with great frequency. His elbows and wrists were red and enlarged. The rest of him was covered by a pristine sheet. I wanted to be anywhere but in that room. I mentally forced back inner cries of protest.

"How long?" I asked referring to more than just the signs of the disease. "How long will he be here?"

"I can't say really. Could be weeks or months," the doctor paused here. "Or days. He's fighting to survive."

I stood where I was for a long moment. Days. If he did not live. Finally I went to the bedside and pulled up a chair. I wanted to reach out and touch him but I was afraid, and not just of hurting him.

In sickness, and in health. For better or worse. Here was the sickness. I thought we had done the "worse," but was quickly discovering my mistake. If Job died, things would get a whole lot worse. If he lived, things would also migrate to that state. In all likelihood, Job would be left weakened, unable to do what he loved. He would hate that. Hate it, but accept it—the good Lord's will.

In my heart, I knew I could never love another man as I loved this one. As far as my limited experience went, there were not any more like him. Would my feelings for him change if he survived in some diminished capacity? He was more than his physical being, but what would watching him try to cope with limitations do to my feelings? To his?

Until death do us part. When I said those words, I believed with all the arrogance of youth that death lay far away, but I could feel its possibility in the bed in front of me. My life would end with his. Not physically, but it would be a death. I wondered which fate would be worse. Which could I survive better—a slow lingering illness that left his body, and my heart broken: or a death that came without any warning, giving no chance to consider it? How could anyone be ready for either?

I put my head down on the bed and closed my eyes. I listened to each breath I drew in and out and tried to match it with Job's breathing. I wanted him to smile at me, tell me everything would be all right. I did not care about the truth. I just wanted him to say the words. If he said them, maybe then, I could believe.

"Mrs. Nightingale?"

I lifted my head at the voice of Nurse Robbins.

"Your parents called. It seems the weather has forced them to turn back."

"Is it bad?" It had been snowing earlier, but not heavily.

The young nurse nodded. "It started to get heavy shortly after you arrived."

I pressed my fists against my eyes. "And Job's parents?"

"They said to tell you they love you, and are praying for you both, and will be here as soon as possible." She stepped further into the room. "I'm going on my break soon. Is there anything you need?"

I tried to focus my thoughts. It appeared as though no one was getting in or going out. "I'll need my bag from the truck. I'll go and get it in a little bit."

I waited for Nurse Robbins to leave. She still made me uneasy. Perhaps it was the way her gaze had lingered on Job, just a little too long. Maybe it was in the way she brushed back the hair from his forehead with the pretext of checking him for fever. I decided once again that I did not like her. I appreciated all she had done that day, but something made me edgy, suspicious. I put my head back down.

I did not want Job to die, but I could not understand what kept him holding on through it all. Why did he fight so strongly? If he railed at God, cursed him, I could understand. At least my anger towards God would be justified. God would have made Job lose faith. God would be guilty of wrongdoing, not Job as people suggested.

I did not rest for two days. I stayed awake, terrified each painful breath drawn would be his last, and yet, on some level, terrified they would go on forever. So I waited—for death or healing—either would end his suffering.

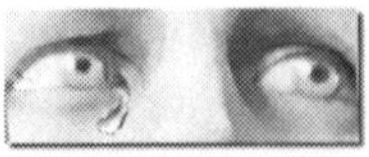

November 30, 1941

"Mrs. Nightingale, it would be best if you went with your parents," Dr. Peterson urged. "You need to keep well, for your sake and for your husband's."

"I'm not going anywhere." Especially not now. Not after what I had done, what I had said.

I stared out at the fresh white canvas that covered the ground. The sun bounced off all that white and hurt the eyes. I thought about how deceiving it was. Underneath the snow surface lay dirt and muck. The sun spoke of warmth, but a biting cold waited for those who ventured out.

"Jessie, my girl." My father's hand fell gently on my shoulder. "You should rest. You haven't slept or eaten since you arrived, according to the nurse."

The thought of food made me feel ill, the thought of leaving even more so. What if something happened and no one was there? What if the last words he heard from me were the terrible ones I had finally given voice to just last night?

"His fever is gone. The doctor says he's stable," my mother said reading my mind. "Your father, Rand and David will stay until we come back. I promise."

They had finally managed to make it. Rand, May, and my parents had arrived anxious and afraid. May had sobbed quietly at the sight of Job lying in the bed, but only for a few moments. She managed to take a steadying breath and pull herself together before easing into the chair next to her son. My mother had choked back tears of her own and pulled me in tight to her. My father had wrapped his arms around both of us, and Rand had stood beside the bed of his only son, bowed his head and let his anguish flow quietly. That was yesterday.

Today, they were all back, and this time David was with them. I wondered who was running the bank.

"Please, Jes? Go with your mother and May." My father ran his hand down the length of my braid. "I promise we'll call you later."

"Job's not going anywhere. He's in God's hands." I knew it was necessary for May to maintain the quiet air of confidence that her son would indeed be all right. Job's fever had broken during the night, and the relief May felt upon learning the news was a physical presence. I wished I could have felt the same.

"God's not here," I whispered to no one in particular.

I grabbed my coat and without a look back, I left the room.

My eyes watered from brightness, and cold. I knew it was not tears. I had cried them all out yesterday. Yesterday, when the betraying and hurtful words gushed from within. Yesterday, when Job woke up and heard those words.

Two agonizing days had passed. Days where I sat and watched the pain ripple across his face—pain that not even unconsciousness could subdue. With each moment that went by, my helplessness had grown. I had railed silently as I paced the room, unable to sit or stand still, torn between crying hysterically and trying to be stoic. When I finally reached desperation saturation, I decided to give Job's technique a try, and speak aloud to God. Maybe, even though God was not speaking to Job, He might be willing to listen, if I spoke on Job's behalf. Maybe I would hear Him as Job did.

I paced the room, trying to find the best way to begin. I became so worked up I finally went to window, braced my hands on either side and rested my head against the glass. I found the coolness stabilizing. The heavy snow had stopped sometime in the early evening. Now a few small flakes floated down to sparkle in the lights from the exterior of the building.

My breathing calmed, I began to focus my thoughts.

"Why are You doing this?" I started by accusing. "What could he have done to make You turn away like this? Why don't You let him feel you anymore? He believes in You still, and yet You ignore him. How can You? Why do You?"

I paused to regain a measure of control. "None of this makes sense. If we could…If I could understand. Why would You take away people that matter, why would You take away the animals…All those animals. And our baby! Why? Why? Now You allow this to happen to him, and I know in spite of this, despite all of it, he will offer You his heart."

I sobbed out my turmoil.

If God were going to continue to do all these things, the least He could do was not ignore Job. "Well, I'm not Job, and I'm not sure what I believe anymore! I'll tell You what I think though. I think Job might be better off without you!"

I knew my thoughts were wrong. They were a betrayal, a breach of the trust Job placed in me by allowing me to share in his relationship with God. Yet, I could not stop them.

"I don't want him to die. I don't. But if he did, he wouldn't be around for You to torment anymore. If he walked away from You and died, it would all end. All this bad stuff would end because he wouldn't be here for you to kick around. That's what I wish he would do."

"Foolish," the word came from behind me with surprising force.

I turned to find Job awake. His chest rose and fell in agitation, or pain. I could not tell the difference any more. Shame heated my face and held me still. How much had he overheard?

"Should we only take the good and not the bad?" He turned his head slightly, his eyes pleading with me to understand what he was saying.

I suppressed my urge to scream. It would solve nothing. I could not argue with him. Where God was concerned, there was no argument. God *was.*

I hung my head, refusing to meet his gaze. The moment stretched between us. I watched my tears splash onto the floor at my feet, amazed that I had any left to shed. I refused to wipe them off my face. Eventually,

I did look up, and found he was asleep. The wetness of his lashes testified to the hurt my words had caused.

Now, I waited for my eyes to adjust to the glare off the snow, and started my trudge down the road.

Thirty-five

December 5, 1941

"I'm going for a walk," I announced in the archway to the living room. I had been walking a lot the last few days. I would never be able to out distance my thoughts though, no matter how far I went.

"You're not too tired?" My mother looked up from the shirt onto which she was sewing a button.

I shook my head.

"I slept in the car." It had been just a short nap, but it had been enough to make it difficult to think about going to bed yet.

"Would you like company?" My mother put down the shirt and stood. May was upstairs "resting" in David and Michael's old room. Her staying would make it easier in the morning when the three of us returned to the hospital. I had heard the muffled crying.

"No." I tried to smile in order to ease the sharpness of my tone. "I just need some air."

I always needed air. There did not seem to be enough oxygen to diminish the suffocating feeling buoyed by my self-loathing.

"Don't be too late."

I nodded as I wrapped a scarf around my neck. I pretended not to see the worry she pretended not to feel. Six days had followed the same routine. My father, Rand and David sat with Job throughout the night, their vigil a silent one of support and empathy. My mother, May, and I, would arrive in the morning for the day shift. My mother and May would sit quietly in the corner, chatting about everything and nothing.

They worked on cross-stitching or mending. Job, when he was awake, uttered not a word. I took up position on an empty bed, alternating between lying and staring out the window, or lying and staring at Job, who stared back. Each of us waged our own private thought war. Tomorrow loomed before me, filled with more of the same.

I shut the front door behind me and pulled on a wool hat. The night was clear and still. No clouds hid the moon or the stars that kept it company. It was too cold to snow. Without clear direction or purpose, I went down the walk and turned toward Main Street.

The shops were closed. A few lights burned in the apartments above them. Christmas was only a few weeks away and from the looks of things, the town had begun to string the decorations.

I passed Millie's Ice Cream Parlour. Not much ice cream moving these days. I wondered where her milk was coming from since it was no longer the Nightingale farm. White's Apparel had a light on in the back. I wondered if it was Mr. or Mrs. White who was working late. Probably both. It was time to go over inventory and find out what could be sale listed for Christmas.

I was tempted to go in and say hello. I felt distanced from them lately. Since the trouble on the farm, the occasions for me to see them were few. They had made a couple of visits out to the hospital, and Mrs. White had provided several meals for us, but still I did not stop. The part of me that held back, the part that was afraid, was too fragile to have wounds poked at. Mrs. White was good at cleaning out wounds.

A few doors down was the General Mercantile. Kenny Martin stood just inside the opening to the alley that ran alongside the store. He leaned against the wall, one foot propped up behind him. I might have walked right on by without seeing him if he had not picked that moment to light a cigarette.

The quick burst of light caught me off guard and I started.

"Hey Jes," Kenny said quietly.

"Hi Kenny." I took a steadying breath. "You startled me."

"I apologize. I thought you must have seen me."

He sounded sincere. I nodded my acknowledgement. "You home for a visit?"

"Something like that." He flashed a quick smile.

Uncertain of what else to say, I stood awkwardly. "How do you like New York?"

"It's a great city."

"Yes, it is."

"That's right, you were there for a little bit."

"At school."

"You came back and got married." He took a pull on the cigarette and smiled. "Don't need to ask who."

I said nothing.

"Sorry to hear about your troubles."

"Thanks." I did not want to know what Kenny might have to say of those. "I should be getting home soon. I hope you have a pleasant visit."

He gave a derisive snort. "Sure. Thanks. There's nothing like a visit with Daddy."

I did not have a response. Kenny always clashed with his father. As children we were all aware of Mr. Martin's no-nonsense character.

"Sorry. You have enough problems of your own without my adding any."

He pushed away from the wall and grimaced in distaste at the cigarette. With a flick he tossed it and put his hands in his pockets. "Remember the chipmunk incident?"

I smiled. "Hard to forget."

"Yeah," he laughed. "You know, even after my dad caught the thing, candy kept disappearing from the jar. He plugged every hole he could find, but still, every morning candy would be missing. The confused look on his face was always so satisfying. Almost as satisfying as I found that candy. I never understood why he didn't put a lid on the jar."

We shared a moment of wishes and wistfulness. We had been friends once. We had run up and down these streets, in and out of these shops without a care in the world.

"Jessie?"

"Yes?"

"I'm sorry."

His look was direct, never wavering. I knew to what he referred.

I nodded my acceptance, looking away as his image blurred through tears that welled up.

"Hey, now. Don't cry," he said softly. His hand hovered in mid air, indecision holding it there. Should he wipe my tears or should he not? He pulled a handkerchief from his back pocket. Decision made. "Here."

"I'm sorry," I said and wiped my face. "I seem to do this all the time lately."

"Seems like you've got reason." He stepped close and squeezed my arm. "I know I'm probably the last person you'd expect this from, but if you want to talk, I'm not doing anything right now."

Suddenly I was crying again. Uncontrollably.

Muttering words of comfort, Kenny pulled me down the alley and through the door into the backroom of the store. Crates of dry goods were stacked on top of each other, and shelves of cans and jars lined the walls. He ushered me over to a large crate and together we sat.

Maybe it was because he was so far removed from my problems, or maybe it was because I needed to do it, but I unburdened myself to Kenny Martin like I could not do to any other, and for his part, Kenny listened without comment or criticism. He offered no suggestions of how I should proceed, no insight into the how or why. He held my hand and rubbed my back as I spoke, and when I was done, he wrapped his arms around me and let me cry some more.

"It's all right. I won't melt if I get wet," he said after I apologized for soaking his shirt.

"Wizard of Oz, right?" I smiled and sniffed.

"Yeah, but I'm really more the Tin Man sort. No heart."

I managed a short laugh and a sniffed. "Better get the oil can out. You might not melt, but rust is a definite possibility."

He smiled and looked away briefly before growing serious. He took a deep breath. "I meant it Jes. I'm sorry for the way I treated you."

"I know."

"The thing is, I really liked you."

I was a little stunned by his revelation.

"Then why?"

He shrugged. "Because I knew you would never like me back. Not really."

I looked up into his face.

He was still pretty, just more hard looking. The scar on his lip was a testament to simpler days. Now, I understood why Jennifer had been his friend. We had all wanted the same things. We still did. I reached out and traced the thin line with my finger.

"You have a heart," I whispered.

I leaned up to press a kiss to his cheek. When he shifted and his lips met mine, I should have pulled away. *Should* have.

My emotional bruises craved the tenderness. It was wrong, and I am absolutely without excuse, for in the moment before the kiss, in the moment when he hesitated and time was suspended long enough for me to recognize what was going to happen, I made a choice. A bad one. The bleakness of that decision would keep me from revealing it to anyone. I never spoke a word of it. Not until now. This is the moment that would keep me from finding absolute happiness in my life. This moment is my great regret.

He was vibrant and strong, a solid presence beneath my hands. And he was untouched by what was going on in my life. I clung to that for support. It was a long moment before it registered that something was different. I tasted tobacco. With dizzying speed, the ramifications of what I was doing, and with whom I was doing it, penetrated. I shoved him away and took a gasping breath. The horror I felt must have shown on my face as I stared at him.

"It's all right," he said with quiet urgency. "Don't panic. It was just a kiss. It doesn't mean anything."

He was right. It did not mean anything, and yet it meant everything. In spite of his words, I did panic.

"I have to go." I pressed a hand to my mouth, willing desperately for the taste of him to be gone.

"Don't." He made a grab for me. "Don't do something you'll regret."

I twisted, evading his hands "It's too late for that."

"Don't make it worse."

Worse?

"Move." I tried to shove him out of my way to get to the door. He was too strong so I stepped away from him and began to plead. "Please, please, let me go. Please, I can't stay here!"

"I promise you can go, if you'll listen. Just for a minute."

I shifted from one foot to the other, my agitation too great to contain. "Why? Why did you do that? Why did I do that?"

"Please Jessie? I'm begging you."

I could only bang the heels of my hands against my forehead.

"I'm leaving first thing in the morning. I promise I'll never be back here. Not ever again. You will never see me. When you walk out that door, this never happened."

It did. It did. It did!

He took hold of my arms and gave me a sharp shake. "This. Did. Not. Happen."

I grew still and stared back at him. For long moments we stood and stared at each other. I watched as his face softened. I saw the remorse, the begging of forgiveness, the uncertainty. I saw the resolve and understood what he implied. My betrayal would stay locked in this dark little store room. He would not speak of this to anyone. It was mine to do with as I wanted.

I jerked my head in what must have passed for agreement, for Kenny stood aside and opened the door.

I fled.

I ran down the street. I ran, blind to everything. The wind was cold against my face and pulled wildly at my hair. My lungs ached to the point of bursting but still I ran. I thought I heard my name called, but I ran from it.

I was running to escape my failure. Once again I had let Job down. Would I never stop? How could I have done what I just did? In that one instant, I had robbed Job of everything he valued on this earth. For that one instant, he had nothing, not even his wife. He did not know it, but I did. What did I do now? I too lost everything in that one instant and God had not done it. God had not stopped me, but neither had He made me. I had acted. I had made that choice. In my need to be comforted, I had picked the source of that comfort. I could not have made a choice that was more wrong.

I kept my legs pumping in a futile attempt to flee that which relentlessly pursued and threatened to paralyze. My body, my mind, and my soul burned. My body burned from physical exertion, my mind from an overload of fear and guilt, and my soul—my soul was hot with my disgrace.

The descent of awareness was swift and abrupt. I skidded to a halt. The creek. I had run to Miller's Creek. I was back at the beginning. The moon was bright, the bluish light bouncing off the snow making it possible to see clearly the surrounding trees, the sparkle of the partly frozen water.

I doubled over, hands on knees, and with loud sobs of despair I fought to pull air into starving lungs. I could feel the trickle of cold sweat as it slid down my face and neck. I closed my eyes against the sting. Inside I laughed with irony and hysteria. It had begun here, how fitting it should end here.

That is how I came to be seated on the bank of a partially frozen creek, pondering the fate of Cora Miller and comparing it with my own; wondering how it would feel if I let myself slip beneath the icy surface. Was I capable? Could I do just that? A part of me wanted to do it, believed I should do it. Another part of me just *wanted*. I was angry because

I could not let go of that last grain of something that prevented me from sliding off the bank and into the water. How had Cora Miller done it?

With force I brought my heel down against the ice, smashing an opening and sending my foot into the frigid waters up to my ankle. I kept it submerged as long as I could, which was only seconds, before the freezing temperature had the bones in my leg aching all the way to my hip. I tried to pull my foot out and only succeeded in soaking the other.

"Jessie!"

My name, spoken with such alarm, had me jumping out of my skin. The quick movement threw off my balance. Until I started to slip downwards toward the creek, I did not realize just how precarious my position was. I tried to back-pedal, using my heels to try and gain some leverage. They failed to grab and I slipped lower on the bank. I flipped over, instinctively clawing for a hold, desperately trying to pull myself away from the water. I was losing the battle.

"Grab the scarf, Jessie!"

I looked up and saw Mrs. White. What was Mrs. White doing at the creek? It was strange since I had been thinking about her earlier. The thoughts spun through my head.

She was kneeling a few feet away, her eyes wide with terror. In the moonlight, her skin had a bluish tinge. Her arms were extended towards me. "Jessie, please grab the scarf!"

With a jerk, I slid a few more inches, my legs entering the water up to my knees.

We both cried out in alarm.

Instinctively I reached for the end of the wool scarf lying inches from my hand. To grab it, I would have to let go of my tenuous grip on the snow. If I missed, I would slide into the creek. At the rate I was slipping, however, I was going to end up there anyway.

I held my breath and took a tight hold on the lifeline extended to me. When my body shifted down the icy bank, I gripped it in both hands. It did not help, and I went into the creek only to have my slide to certain death come to a jarring halt as my feet hit the bottom.

Mrs. White and I stared at each other. The absurdity of it struck me hard and I felt an hysterical bubble of laughter begin deep in my gut. I could not stop it. The laughter and the cold made me too weak to do anything but stand with my feet planted in the muddy floor of the creek and shake. This close to the bank, the water only came up to my thighs.

With an angry growl, Mrs. White sat on her heels and dug in, fighting the drag of my weight. "Help me, Jessie," she ordered. I tried to lever myself up the slippery bank as she expended a groan of effort and straightened out her legs to pull. "This is not funny! Stop laughing."

Somehow I managed to climb-crawl up the scarf, hand over hand and found myself lying on top of the other woman. Her arms went around me and I was safe, or so I thought.

Mrs. White was angry. Mad angry. She shook with it, almost as violently as I did from the cold. I felt it vibrate through her as together we got to our feet.

Both of us were rubbery around the knees. I knew I was, and from the way she swayed, I took it as a pretty good indicator that she was also. She squeezed my arm in a vice like grip and without a word, marched me in the direction of the farm house, at least as much of a march as either of us could manage.

My feet were absolutely numb, and I worked hard to keep up with her. I slipped once and was ruthlessly yanked back up. I knew better than to say anything, but as we left the woods and started across the yard toward the big yellow house, I hesitated.

No warm glow of light from the windows beckoned. No sounds of laughter or music from the radio floated out to connect the inside world to the outside. It was a house meant for such things. I wondered if it would ever hold them again. Would my mistake make it impossible?

I fell to my knees, unable to stand under the emotional burden.

"No!" Mrs. White grabbed my coat from behind. With a Herculean effort she hefted me up and shoved me several feet in front of her. "You do not get to do this."

"It's not what you think." I panted and I held up my hands to ward off another manhandling as she bore down on me.

"How do you know what I'm thinking?"

"I just do."

Her glare and step towards me with arm raised told me that was not a good enough answer. I backed up and tried again.

"I know because, at first it was."

"Was what?"

"What you're thinking it was."

My admission appeared to throw her off guard. Her arms dropped to her sides and her shoulders sagged slightly. I could read the unspoken question in the puzzled look that accompanied the small shake of her head. *Why?*

My choice was made. I was never going to expose to the light what was locked in that shabby little storeroom.

I shrugged and told what truth I could. "I thought about it. Sliding under the ice. I thought I wanted it. But I didn't. I Don't. Not really. All I want is for the things that have happened, to not *be*. I'm afraid of what can still happen. If I died, they wouldn't."

Mrs. White gasped in shock. She opened her mouth to say something but I held up a hand and cut her off.

"But I couldn't. I can't, and I don't understand why exactly. I realized it just before you shouted. You scared me, and I slipped, and you know the rest."

I could tell she did not believe me, not totally. She ran her hands over her face and gave her body a shake. The anger appeared to be replaced by sadness. She released a muffled sob then took a deep fortifying breath.

"I'll drive you back to town."

Thirty-six

December 6, 1941

I was not allowed out of anyone's sight.

Not even to warm up in the tub. Mrs. White told my mother about seeing me run past the store and calling after me. She said she was about to let it go, there was a lot to do for the inventory, but something had urged her to follow me, so she locked up and drove out to the farm where she found my footprints leading to the creek. She told my mother about what she suspected, and about what I had said. I did not feel the need to clarify any of the details. I do not think I would have been believed if I had.

Without protest, I endured the supervision and lack of privacy as they set up camp in my room. I was not going anywhere anyway, except back to the hospital, the absolute last place I wanted to go. I may not have wanted to die, but that did not stop me from wishing to be swallowed by some behemoth or whale, like Jonah, and be spat out on the distant shores of some far away land.

My mother, May, and Mrs. White, cried with varying degrees of distress and disappointment.

For once I did not cry. I repeatedly expressed how sorry I was, but it did no good. I believe they knew there was something I was not telling them. I knew I never would.

Now, as I walked in a somber procession down the hall of the hospital toward Job's room, I was faced with how my father would react. Then there was Job.

How could I ever look him in the face again? I could not even meet my own eyes in the mirror. Raising my head took more self-respect than I knew how or where to find.

A large lump had taken up residence just under my rib cage. It made holding down food almost impossible. The closer we drew to Job's room, the closer I came to embarrassing myself.

I stopped abruptly, just short of opening the door.

May bumped into my mother, who in turn, bumped into me. It might have been comical had the situation not been so angst ridden. I fought to stay conscious. I panted; in and out, short shallow breaths through my mouth. I could feel the bile rising in the back of my throat and swallowed it down. My mother gave me a look that questioned my odd behavior.

"Mrs. Nightingale!"

May and I both turned at the name. It was Dr. Peterson.

"My apologies," he laughed ruefully and jog-walked toward us. "I mean to speak with Jessie."

"Is something wrong?" I tried not to let dread take hold. I was having enough trouble holding myself together without any more bad news.

"No." He smiled and gestured for me to precede him down the hallway a few steps.

Once we had separated ourselves enough to avoid being overheard, he continued. "Mrs. Nightingale, Jessie, your husband's condition has stabilized quite well these last several days. He's still in quite a bit of pain, and has residual swelling, but I believe he's out of danger."

I closed my eyes and exhaled a huge sigh of relief. Job would not die. Nothing I had done would change that.

"Of course I can't be certain of the damage done to his heart, but we may not be able to ascertain that for some time."

"I understand." It had been explained to me on more than one occasion. "So what's changed?"

"I can't see any reason to keep him here any longer."

"You're saying he can go home? When?"

"Today if you'd like."

I was stunned. This was unexpected. "I just thought he would have to stay for much longer."

"I don't see why that would be necessary, as long as he takes it easy and avoids exerting himself for a few more weeks. Of course we'll give him something to manage the pain for the first little while."

"Does Job know?"

"He's sleeping still. But I wanted to let you know as soon as you came in."

No more coming to the hospital. We could go home.

Then what?

"He wishes he'd never been born," I spoke the words aloud to no one in particular. I do not remember making the conscious decision to say them, but then they were out, and there was no taking them back.

It was lunchtime, and the family, minus Job, gathered around the kitchen table in the big yellow farmhouse. Job was sleeping again. The journey home had proved to be quite an effort for him. Rand and David moved a bed into the office, and relegated the desk to the living room while May and Sarah dusted and warmed the house to a comfortable temperature.

My parents and I had waited at the hospital until Job woke up and was ready to leave. He had been encouraged to sit up for the first time and even attempted a few very painful steps. It was a gut wrenching experience to see a once vital man reduced to such a weakened state. I had seen infants just learning to walk who were steadier on their feet.

On the drive home, I sat in the back seat with Job and my thoughts. Job's eyes were closed, but I knew he did not sleep. My mother attempted to make cheery conversation until she got tired of one-syllable answers from me, and nothing at all from Job. I know she felt the occasion called for a more encouraging atmosphere.

Eventually Job had been settled into his temporary room and the rest of us had sat and pretended to eat, but I could not get my last conversation with Job out of my head. It had been our only conversation since the day I said the things I should not have. It had left me unsettled.

We were alone in the hospital room, finally. My father was bringing the car up to the door, and my mother was getting last minute instructions for Job's home care—a task I should have seen to, but was more than happy to pass on to someone else. I used the time to consider what I had done and what I wanted. I did not know how things would be once we got Job home, but I knew how I wanted it to be. I wanted it back the way it was. Reality stipulated that impossibility.

Job's eyes had closed and I thought he was dozing, until he spoke.

"I wish I'd never been born," he whispered.

I turned from my position by the window. He was staring at the ceiling. Silent tears ran down the sides of his face.

My heart broke at the despair I sensed in him. That the first words he should speak in seven days were a wish for his non-existence, stirred something deep down inside. How much more would he feel that way if he knew?

"I was so afraid this would happen."

Now my heart jumped into my throat. Did he know? Had someone, Mrs. White maybe, seen something and figured out why I was in such a desperate state of mind? I was terrified at what I would see when he looked at me.

"Everything was so good," he choked. "Everything we had. My biggest fear was that some day I would wake up and it would all be gone. As if it never existed and I would be left wondering what happened. But if I'd never been born, if I'd never existed, then none of it would have happened. We would never have met, and you would not be going through this. You would be married to someone else, having a great life somewhere. You wouldn't have lost a child. You wouldn't be so sad."

I would not have betrayed him.

"You don't know that." It was something I had found myself wondering. What would my life be like if we had not met. Would my life be any better? Somehow I did not think so. I probably would have found a way to mess that up too.

"I wish I could die," he continued, ignoring my words. "At least then it would be over. Then I wouldn't have to keep feeling it."

That, I understood. It was what I had wanted on the bank of the creek. It was what my mother, May and Mrs. White all misunderstood. I did not want to take my life. Neither did Job. I just did not want to continue to feel what I was feeling.

I wanted it to go away.

"You're getting better," I said addressing the physical pain and leaving alone the fact that I could do nothing for his mental and spiritual agony. "You're coming home."

"For how long?"

I looked at him in confusion. "How long what?"

"How long will we be able to stay at home?"

"For good. You're coming home for good."

He turned and met my look. I wanted to turn away, but forced myself to hold still.

"This hospital stay is going to mean more bills. Bills we can't pay. The house will have to go. The land, the house, it's all gone now."

It was true. There really would be nothing left once we managed to pay off the hospital debt. Job had not been gone long enough to make a dent in the bank loan. It was so unfair.

"They're not gone yet." Where had that come from? Had I really said something that had a hint of the possible behind it?

"No. You're right." He sighed. With effort, his hand reached for mine. "I know this is difficult, beyond anything we could have imagined. But I'm glad you're here."

I could not hold his gaze any longer. I found myself staring at our joined hands. The voices in my head were screaming in contradiction. *He wouldn't be glad if he knew. Tell him and he'll forgive you. Tell him and it will be you who loses everything! Tell him and it will kill him.*

"Jes?" He squeezed my hand. "What's wrong?"

I shook my head and reached behind me to pull a chair closer. I sat and pressed my cheek against the back of his hand. It was cool against my heated skin. "Nothing. I'm here and I'm not going anywhere."

"What did you say?"

It was May, who spoke first, pulling me back to the table and the present. She carefully lowered her fork to her plate and waited. Everyone waited.

"He wants to not exist."

"That doesn't make any sense," my father said.

"Yes it does," I disagreed quietly. "If he didn't exist, then none of the things that happened these past few months would have happened."

"Excuse me." May was pale, and the hand she pressed to her mouth visibly trembled. She disappeared in the direction of the bathroom. I recognized the look on her face. I had felt that way for quite some time, even more in the last almost twenty-four hours.

No one commented.

We heard the sound of water running in the sink. The toilet flushed a few minutes later, and, moments after that, a still pale but steadier May returned to her seat at the table. She pushed her plate away and then stared down at her hands.

"I'll speak to the boy," Rand said quietly and May gave a slight nod. He turned to me. "What else did he say?"

"That's it." I shrugged. "He wants to understand God's purpose. He feels he deserves answers." I believed he deserved them.

"If he's not careful with what he says, he risks a great deal more than he's lost." There was a warning in Rand's voice and it got my back up.

"It's like we talked about last night, Rand. There has to be a reason why all this is happening now. Why it's all come at once," my father joined the discussion.

"You were talking about this last night?" I questioned. My father nodded.

"In Job's room?" May asked.

"Oh, Ben," my mother sounded dismayed. "Why?"

"He was sleeping," Rand said before my father could do more than shrug. "And we were just trying to figure out the purpose for all of this. We figured if we could find the answers then we could help him. I can't stand seeing my boy like that."

"Don't you think we've tried to find the answers?" I demanded. "Don't you think we've asked ourselves the same questions?"

"Jessie, Sweetheart," my father started. "That's not it at all. It's just that sometimes when people are in the middle of a mess like this, they can't see beyond it."

"Do you have an answer? Do any of you? If so, please share it." How dare they imply that we were not seeking answers to those questions; that Job was not trying with every fiber of his being to find them.

"We're not claiming to have the answers. Right, Ben?" Rand turned to my father who nodded his agreement. "It just seems to me that maybe God is punishing him."

"Punishing him? For what?" I asked. "For living his life according to what he believes God wants? For falling on his face in worship when the farm burned down around him? For what is he being punished?"

"That's too strong a word." Rand shook his head. "Correcting is more like it."

"He hasn't done anything wrong!"

"Jessie." My mother placed a hand on my arm, but I shook it off.

"Are you on their side?'

"It's not about sides," she said.

"It's not? Then somebody better explain to me what it's about, when even his own father believes he's done something wrong."

"Not wrong exactly." It was Rand's turn to get defensive. "I just think God is trying to get his attention about something."

"God is trying to get his attention?" I shook my head in disbelief. "Really? How much more of Job's attention could he get? Even now, Job clings to the belief that God is in control."

"Jessie," my father's tone held reprimand.

"No, Dad." I stood and stared at them all. "All of you know Job. You know his heart."

"Yes, we do," Rand agreed. "But maybe there's something he's done. Something we can't see. Something between him and God, and God's trying to get him to see it."

If there were someone who had done something to confess, if there were anyone keeping something from God, it was I, but all of this had started before my transgression. Maybe if God was trying to get anyone's attention, it was mine.

"He hasn't done anything!" I shouted.

"Jessie, please just hear me out," Rand kept his voice calm.

I sat back down and motioned for him to continue.

"No one's perfect."

"Bible says that," I agreed.

"Not even Job."

I nodded in concession.

"He's my son and I know what kind of life he lives, I just believe God is correcting him about something, and he keeps resisting. If he quit fighting and just admitted what it is he's hiding, he'd find the peace he's looking for."

If Job had indeed done something, had committed a sin not confessed before God, there would be tremendous truth in Rand's words. *If.*

"I'm afraid if he let's this get the better of him, he might say something that can't be unsaid," Rand finished.

"What are you afraid I'll say, Dad?" Job asked from the entrance to the kitchen.

None of us had seen Job arrive. He was breathing as though he had exerted a great deal of energy, and indeed, it would have taken that, and a lot more determination, to get into the borrowed wheelchair. His forehead gleamed with sweat. I worried it might be the fever returning. Maybe he had left the hospital too soon.

"Dad?"

"You should be in bed," Rand said.

"You should believe in me."

"He does. We do." May jumped in trying to placate Job.

"It sounds like you believe I deserve this," Job said ignoring his mother and concentrating on his father's words.

"These things that keep happening, there's something about them. There's got to be a reason for it, and you're no different than anyone else God might try to correct."

"You're right. I'm not. Except that I'm your son."

Rand had the grace to blush. Even my father looked slightly chastened around the edges. May visibly paled and my mother avoided looking directly at anyone.

"Your father doesn't mean that the way it sounded," May tried to sooth some of the tension.

"I know," Job sighed. He inched the wheelchair further into the room. "But you know this, I don't believe these things happened because of something I did or didn't do. I'm still the same person you believed in when things were good. I haven't changed, but because circumstances have, you believe the worst. If you can tell me what it is I've done to bring this on myself, I'll gladly seek forgiveness. Just tell me what to confess and I will. However, I won't admit to something I didn't do."

If I expected more from my father, I was to be disappointed.

"God doesn't punish anyone who doesn't deserve it." He spoke calmly but his exasperation was evident. "He doesn't suddenly forget who He is and start confusing justice with mercy. You need to be careful you don't accuse God of anything like that. You need to listen to what we're saying. We just want you to be happy again."

"God may not punish those who don't deserve it, but He doesn't always punish those who do." Job's temper was getting the better of him. The color in his cheeks was high. "I see people living very successful and happy lives who have no belief in God. It seems to me that they have it easy. It seems to me, that people who love God suffer more than most."

The back door opened and David, who had gone to check on Sarah and Thomas, entered followed by Jimmy and a blast of cold air.

"Whew!" David said with a swipe of his hair. "Those are some big flakes falling. Look who I brought with me."

"It's a great night out there," Jimmy laughed, brushing off his own head. "Calm and quiet."

David paused in the action of taking off his coat. "What's going on?"

Jimmy looked up and surveyed the room. The smile left his face as he felt the mood.

Job turned to David. "Do you think I've done this to myself?"

David did not pretend to misunderstand. He folded his coat over his arms with a sigh. "You know how it must look."

"All right then, tell me," Job demanded. "Tell me where my sin is. I believe in God's justice. I recognize his power. I also know what I have not done."

"What do you want from us?" David asked, his voice rising quickly to meet Job's.

"From you, I want nothing." Job opened his hands and spread them wide showing there was nothing in them. "From God, I want an answer. I want Him to answer, but He's silent. I don't know what to do from here. I want someone on my side. I need someone to fight with me."

"You need to be careful with your attitude," my father's reprimand was sharp, a tone I had never heard before.

"I would walk down the street naked if it would prove I'm innocent of whatever it is you think I might have done, except that would probably just make me look more guilty," Job said, ignoring my father. "All I want is to have it be the way it was between me and God. I have to find some way to make that happen."

"Then think hard!" David could not contain his bafflement. "There has to be something you haven't thought to confess. What about something in your relationship with Jessie?"

"No." Job denied with conviction.

I held my breath and my tongue lest I reveal something that would be my undoing.

"You forget," David spoke ominously. "I know just how long you two kept your relationship a secret."

"If you knew, then it wasn't a secret, was it? And I don't like what you're implying about your sister."

"What about with Emily? Are you sure you didn't encourage her?"

"Emily? Who's Emily?" Job appeared genuinely confused.

"Emily. At the hospital," David clarified. "The nurse."

"I've only ever hit one person," Job said quietly. "You make me want to make it two."

"Fine. I apologize, but if you want things to improve, you need to repent. If you devote yourself to God completely, you'll find the peace you're looking for. There must be something standing in the way of that."

"There is not." Job closed his eyes, dejection evident in every bit of his body. "And I'm not going to make up something in order to please you or anyone else!"

"Please, Son," Rand pleaded. "Think about your future."

"I am thinking about it. What kind of future do you think I'll have if I lie and confess to something I'm not guilty of doing."

"Do you expect to be forgiven without asking for it? Without at least acknowledging that you need to be?" My father was angry. "Think about somebody beside yourself. Think about what you're putting Jessie through. What kind of future are you going to give her? You need to quit talking and do something."

"Dad!" I could not sit through any of it much longer.

"I'm sorry Jessie." My father stood and paced. "No. No, I'm not. Your husband insists on speaking to us like we don't know what we're talking about."

"That's not it at all," Job denied. "I just wish you would believe me. I want you to stand with me and not against me."

"We are with you." David said. "We want you to get better. We want you to be happy. We want you to have your relationship with God restored. I just don't think it's going to happen, unless you figure out what it is that you've done and ask forgiveness for it."

"I have nothing that is not confessed and forgiven," Job responded. "And do you know what else? I believe God will redeem me. What I know about God tells me he will."

"Jessie, you speak to him," David folded his arms and hung his head with a shake. "I've done what I know to do. I'm through."

Rand stood and clapped a hand on my father's shoulder. "Come Ben," he said. "Let's all take a break. We could use one."

I remained seated as the others stood and stretched muscles stiff from sitting too long.

I wanted so much to tell Job they were wrong. I did not feel qualified to do so.

I looked at him, uncertain of what I should do. Job was watching Jimmy who was leaning unobtrusively against the door through which he had just recently entered.

"What about you?" Job said to the younger man. His words made everyone stop and turn to look at Jimmy. "You've not said anything, but I'm sure you've got an opinion."

Jimmy looked around him as though seeking permission to speak. When no one did anything to prevent him from doing so, he crossed the room to Job and sat. "You don't have to talk, and I know you've got no reason to listen to me. I ain't as smart as you, and your dad, or Jes's Dad, or even David. I don't have the same experience. And, even though you treat me like I am, I'm not family, not really, but that doesn't mean I don't have something to say that might prove helpful."

Job shrugged and Jimmy continued.

"I disagree with the others," he said. "I don't believe that what you're going through is because of something you've done."

"You don't?" Job sounded skeptical.

"No," Jimmy responded ignoring or not understanding the tone of Job's question. "God doesn't do wrong things. He's God, right? So, I think He's is trying to get your attention to keep you from doing something that you haven't done yet. Something you might regret."

"Jimmy," I wanted to stop him. I could see where he was going. Nowhere. I wanted to spare Job from having to listen to this type of talk once again.

"It's all right Jes," Job said. "It's not going to change anything."

"That's just what I'm getting at," Jimmy jumped on Job's words. "God don't answer to anyone, especially not a human being. You profess your innocence over and over. You demand God proves it. I think you're being too familiar and that's a dangerous path."

Jimmy stood and began to pace, his agitation evident in the restless wandering.

"You told me once that God talked to you." He looked to Job for confirmation. Job nodded. "Sometimes it was dreams, or sometimes some other way, but you communicated with Him. Now, He's not talking to you, at least not the way you think He should. But, I think God is still talking to you, only He's doing it through these trials. He wants to help you. You just need to ask Him to show you what you can't see and then promise not to do what you're doing or whatever it is you might do."

Jimmy stopped pacing and waited expectantly. Job refused to look at the younger man. He glanced at me briefly before gazing over my shoulder and out the window once more.

"I don't think you have to do something to bring bad things down on yourself," Jimmy stated when he realized there was no response coming from Job. "But instead of protesting how unfair it is, you should accept it as God trying to stop you doing something you might do. You can't stand against God, and the longer you try, the worse it's gonna get."

Job nodded, but not in agreement. It said, "I know where you stand now, and you're no different from the rest."

He tried to turn the chair but his strength was disappearing rapidly.

My own legs were unsteady as I stood and made my way around the table. I asked my mother and May to help Job to the den, making it very clear when my father and Rand stood, that they were not welcome.

"Jessie, we're just concerned about you both," my father said when the others were out of the room. "What does the future hold for you if Job continues in this manner?"

"What does the future hold for any of us?" I argued. "Can anyone really know for certain? It seems to me, the only one who knows what will happen, is the only One who has yet to comment on the situation."

"You're starting to sound like Job," David said.

I laughed with as much scorn as I could muster. "He's been nothing but a good friend to you, more like a brother, and you stand among his condemners. Go home to your family and leave me with what's left of mine."

"We're not condemning him," Rand said over murmurs of protest and disbelief.

"You're not helping him. None of you believe him. You've even made me doubt him."

"That was never our intent," my father said.

"It doesn't matter anymore," I said having reached my limit. "It's enough for the night."

I turned and left them, not waiting to see if they stayed or not.

Together, with May and my mother's assistance, we helped Job sit on the edge of the bed and swing his legs up. I brushed the hair out of his eyes and off his face where it clung in damp strands.

I turned to my mother, prepared to plead for her understanding. "Would you please make sure everyone leaves?"

I could see the words of protest form in her mind, but she chose not to speak them. "Is there anything you need before we go?"

"No. We'll be fine. We'll see you sometime tomorrow. I promise." I added the last because I knew what it had taken for her to agree to go without protest. I owed her that affirmation.

She placed a kiss on Job's forehead in the same manner she had done over the years with Michael, David, and me. "I'm glad you exist," she said to him. "Even with all that's come and gone, and what might come."

"Can I get you anything?" I asked Job as I pulled the quilt up and tucked it around his legs. "Are you hungry? You didn't eat much today. There's chocolate cake your mother made."

He had not eaten much in the ten days he was in the hospital. I would not have believed he had any weight left to loose, but the pounds had fallen away, accentuating the swollen joints of legs and arms. The nodules under the skin were receding and his face, in spite of the shadows, was looking more like his own.

"A glass of milk maybe."

"I'll get it," May said and disappeared, returning momentarily. I watched as she helped her son drink from the glass.

"Don't be too hard on your dad," she whispered. "He only wants good things for you. He wants you to have what you had before. He's afraid."

Job snorted but did not say anything.

"It's true," May continued quietly. "He's afraid of losing you. He's afraid that he's wrong, that all this is truly happening for no reason. If he accepts that, then he has to deal with the fact that it doesn't matter how good a person is, how strong his faith, trials are inevitable."

She was more composed than she had been earlier. I wondered about that. I wondered where both she and my mother found the strength to keep from getting sucked into the mire that, as of late, was an enemy continuously slurping at my mind. Was it their faith? Was it experience gained through time? Or, was it a character trait, born in their nature? What was it that provided them the momentum to keep going day after day? Maybe they did it just because there was no other choice. I was beginning to recognize there were few options left for me either.

Thirty-seven

December 6, 1941

"Do you believe them?"

I thought he had fallen asleep. After May and my mother had left, I sat in the armchair next to the bed and stayed until his eyes closed and his breathing regulated. He had caught me trying to slip quietly from the room.

"Do you think I've done something and God is trying to punish me?"

I sagged against the wall near the door. My finger found a small tear in the seam of the cabbage rose wallpaper. May had hung the cheery paper years ago. Job and I had tried to help but had only gotten under foot. With a frustrated but gentle hand on our heads, she had pushed us out the door and told us to see if someone else needed our help. I wished I knew the words to say that would help Job.

"Jes?"

I thought about my answer a few moments longer. Just as Job considered what his experience of God had taught him, I thought about what my experience of Job had shown me.

"No." I did not look up, afraid he would see what I was hiding. "I don't think you've left anything hidden from God."

"Then what?" He must have sensed the hesitancy in my answer.

I struggled for words, finally giving up and pressing my head to the wall. "I can't make any sense of it."

"Maybe there's no sense to be made."

I heard the bed creak as he shifted. I lifted my head at his hiss of pain. "I'm innocent of any wrong doing, Jes. That's where I'm making my stand. If I'm not, then may God take me."

"Please, Job." I begged, for what I do not know.

"I know what kind of relationship I had with Him before all this." He ignored my plea. "I know how blessed I was to have that. I know how blessed I was to have the life I did. Every day, I tried to make sure I kept nothing from Him. I worked hard to live a life that would demonstrate my commitment to His service. Now, all I have to show for it is the doubt of those I love and respect the most. But even worse—worse than all of that—is the silence."

I could pinpoint the exact day that Job believed God stopped communing with him. The day the rain fell, that was when the silence began for Job. I began to wonder about my own silence. When had it begun to grow quiet between God and me? Long before the rain, that was certain. But the silence was my doing. I had stopped talking. Stopped seeking. I did not know if I wanted to mend the matter. I did not know how.

"I'm so tired, Jes."

"I know."

"My whole body hurts. All the time. But it doesn't even come close to the ache inside."

I could hear it in his voice.

"I've done nothing to bring this on myself. No matter what anyone says."

"Their intentions are good."

"Good intentions." He said it as though testing the words for balance and weight. "We both know where they end up."

I could not gauge his mood. There were too many emotions hidden in his dark eyes.

"I don't think I've ever heard you sound so....so—" I could not find the right descriptive.

"I've never had reason to sound so *so.*" He waited until he was sure he had my attention. The sudden flash of temper I saw in his eyes told me one thing; he was certain about what he was going to say next.

"I'll tell you what I told David. What I told them all in the hospital last night after you left," he continued. "I have never lied to or mislead anyone for my own benefit. I don't hang out with people like that. Not even in Barre, where everyone was out to get what they could to make things better for themselves, no matter what they had to do. I haven't mistreated anyone who worked for me or withheld payment for work done. I've paid a fair wage for the job. I've always gone out of my way to ensure the land and the animals were never abused, and I've tried to be as generous as I could with those who had less. I've opened my home to this community even when I knew they were looking at me and wondering what I'd done to deserve what was happening.

"I've done all that and not expected anything in return. I've never been one to put my faith in things I could get. I've not taken them for granted either, but I've never put my faith in what I had because I've known it would never last beyond this lifetime."

His face softened, but remained no less fierce. "I've never looked with want at another woman, and I have never encouraged another woman to think there could be anything romantic between us. I've never even considered it. I know Emily feels something for me, or thinks she does, but I have never given her reason to believe those feelings were welcome. I have never thought about returning those feelings. Not once, because I don't want them from, or want to give them to, anyone but you. It's always been that way for me."

In the pause he took to form his next thoughts, I prayed fervently that I would not be sick and wished for the ability to sink through the floor. I thought about what he said about Nurse Robbins. Like Job, I did not have feelings for Kenny. I did not want him to have feelings for me. I was not sure I even liked him. And yet, in a single moment, I had opened myself up for something irreconcilable to anything I had ever thought or felt. Would it have been possible for Job to do the same? Maybe. Would he have done it? I did not believe it.

He was looking at me intently. "You believe me, don't you?"

"Yes." I looked away unable to hold his gaze for too long. I feared he would somehow be able to see what I had done. I was afraid something in my face or posture would give me away.

"There's something else then," he said quietly. "What?"

He waited until I finally looked at him again. I searched his face as he had done mine. Could I tell him? Should I? I could see the question in his eyes. I watched it shift through different phases: compassionate concern, speculation, and denial.

I crossed to the bed and sat, gently pressing my hand against the side of his face. I leaned in and pressed my lips against his, and lied.

"There's nothing," I whispered. "Nothing else."

He tilted his head and smiled a small crooked smile. To me it said he did not quite believe, but he would not push. He looked beyond me to the window and outside. I knew when he spoke next, it was not to me, not really.

"I'll take the pain," he said. "I'll take it all, whatever is thrown at me, but not because I believe I'm being corrected or punished. I'll take it because it makes me depend on God more. I'll let go of everything else and accept whatever comes, even if it means giving up my life."

He closed his eyes and let his body relax as much as he could. I brushed the hair back from his face before taking his hand in mine.

"I have only ever worshipped God," he continued. "I've done what I could to keep Him first and foremost in my life. I know sometimes it's been hard for you to understand, but that's the way it had to be. It's the way it still is, and until God Himself proves the truth of what I've just said, I'm through talking."

What was left to talk about? Everyone had had their say. The only thing left was to wait and see what God would do.

He closed his eyes and it did not take long for him to fall asleep. For long moments I watched as his breathing slowed and evened out. The depth of my feelings for him pushed up and overwhelmed. I felt insignificant, dwarfed by my despondence. I wiped the tears off my face, tears I did not realize were falling until they landed on our joined hands, and I crept out of the room.

For a moment I stood just inside the door to the kitchen. Dust danced in the afternoon sun that angled in through the windows and cast the room into a contrasting pattern of light and shadow. I pictured what had been. I saw Rand seated at the head of the table, the Farmer's Almanac in his hand. May was at the stove, apron tied around her waist and a light dusting of flour across her left cheek. Pops, John, and Mitch tucked cloth napkins in the necks of their shirts in eager anticipation of the meal to come, while Job and I snuck a kiss in the hallway.

I turned and let memories fade into the shadows.

Upstairs, our room was just as I had left it. The bed made. My nightgown lay at the foot of the bed. It was the one from my wedding night. An entire lifetime ago.

I sat on the edge of the bed and held the nightgown. The cotton had softened with washing but the blue and yellow embroidered roses remained bright against the white background. I stared down at the garment and hated it. Hated what it stood for. I grasped the bodice in both hands and pulled. It ripped right down the middle.

What did I do from here?

I dropped the torn nightgown onto the floor and stood. As I did so, I caught sight of a stranger in the mirror above the dresser.

Physically the resemblance was mine, but the eyes I did not recognize. They were haunted. Hollow. Empty. There was no trace of the hope-filled young girl who once stood in this spot. She had looked to the future with such eagerness and innocence. I had erased her existence. I did not know the woman before me.

Job's straight razor rested on the dresser, next to the picture taken at Miller's Creek when I was six and he was eight. I picked up the sharp blade and turned it over in my hand. I slid my finger along it for a short distance. A thin line of red appeared on the pad of my finger. With the razor in one hand, I took hold of my braid with the other, and with a savage slice, I hacked off my hair. Freed from the confines of the braid, the hair that remained on my head sprang out in an uneven bob.

I placed the severed braid next to the photograph and took one last look at the glassy eyed stranger. Tomorrow a different woman, one I would have to take the time to get to know, would replace her. Today I would grieve for the girl that had been lost. I bent to retrieve the pieces of the torn nightgown and kept them with me as I crawled onto the bed and shut my eyes.

My stomach rumbled. I was hungry and the lack of sun told me I slept well into the evening. I stuck my head under the water of the sink in an effort to smooth down my shortened hair and surveyed the results. Not too bad even if it was curlier than I realized it would be.

My stomach gurgled again letting me know that I needed to fill it, so I went to take care of that before waking Job to make him eat.

Nothing appealed to my appetite, in spite of the demand to be appeased. I went to the breadbox and pulled a hunk off the loaf inside. I tried a glass of milk next and thought I felt improved. I went to look at the mail somebody had placed on the table—it had been quite some time since I opened any of it and a rather thick stack had accumulated. I spied a note on the table next to the mail and read it over quickly. May had knocked but gotten no answer so she left a stew. I took the lid off the white enamel pot resting on the side of the stove and inhaled. Within seconds I realized the milk was not going to stay down and ran to the bathroom.

Was I getting sick? Would that be what came next? I rinsed my mouth and washed my face. Maybe it was guilt. I carried a lot of that in the middle of my gut since the night before. Had it really only been the night before? The thought made me feel nauseous again. I put my head down and took deep steadying breaths.

I examined my face in the mirror and pinched some color back into my cheeks. Inexplicably, I found my mind jumping from thought to thought, never staying long enough to allow one to form fully. I grew uneasy as I stood staring at my reflection. I sensed something different in the house. It was not a smell or sound, and nothing had been out of place. Still, something brushed against the edge of my awareness. The hair on my arms and at the nape of my neck stood on end. Full of dread, I flew to the makeshift bedroom.

Job was just as I left him, almost. A sheen of perspiration covered his face, but it did not look like fever. Just to be certain I went to him and pressed my hand against his cheek. Warm, but not alarmingly so. Still, something about his countenance was different. A slight frown furrowed his brow and he twitched in his sleep, but he did not look restless. I brushed back the damp tendrils that clung to his forehead and whispered his name.

The crease between his eyebrows deepened and his head tilted as though listening to something. It had been some time since, but I had seen that look before. He was listening, but not to *something,* to *Someone.*

The urge to flee was powerful, my body hummed with it. My hands clenched so tightly my fingernails left deep crescent crevices in my palms. I was intruding, an outsider spying on a private moment between two lovers.

I was hot, suffocating. Without thought to where I was going or why, I grabbed a coat and hat, stuffed my feet into boots, and slipped out the front door. I stood and absorbed the cold damp air as it hit my face and neck. It smelled fresh, clean, and very different from the hospital smell that seemed imprinted on my skin. It reminded me I was alive, a feeling I had forgotten, or rather tried to forget. I did not know what to do with it now. I was afraid to feel it.

I took the stairs of the wide veranda two at a time and started across the yard; the yard that had once seen every manner of life before it had been reduced to a dark scar on the ground. The pure white that covered the darkness was deceiving. If someone were to remove it, to scrape it back, they would see the ruin underneath. I was like that.

The foundation stones of the milking barn remained solidly in place, although blackened by the fire. Job was like that. He had been burned, but his foundation remained.

My foundation had fallen apart in an instant. If worlds could collide and crumble in a matter of seconds, imagine what could happen if given more time. I pushed aside the feelings of failure, tucked my head down and pointed myself in a direction away from the creek.

The temperature had dropped. A thin crust had formed on the snow. It crunched beneath my weight. I settled into a steady rhythm and began counting my steps. I soon lost track as my focus turned inward. Threads of thoughts unraveled themselves.

I believed Job when he protested his innocence. I lived with him. I knew what was in his heart. He expressed it so clearly every night when he laid his life open before God, even on the nights he believed God to be withholding his presence.

But why?

That was the question. I did not know if there was an answer. I did not know if I wanted it, or if it would matter if I got it. I did not know what I wanted, I just *wanted*. Where did I find the answer to that?

I tripped and sprawled headlong across the ground. I lay still, momentarily disoriented.

In front of my nose was a stone marker, the white marble almost invisible in the snow. A few inches more and my head would have connected with it. I was in the small family cemetery. I had not been there since we buried Pops and John.

Grief, warm and thick spread out from my heart and for several moments I lay in the snow, hoping to cool the rush of emotion.

Gradually, I pushed myself to my knees and began to brush myself off. I cannot say what made me pause, only that I did pause. Filled with trepidation, I turned to see what I tripped over. The grave marker was small, about five inches thick and not much more off the ground. I had not seen it before. I reached out and carefully brushed the snow from the stone. There was no date, and only one word engraved on the pure white marble.

FAITH.

He had named our daughter Faith.

I ran my cold fingers over the letters. Outwardly, for those who chose to believe it, it would seem as though Job buried his faith the day he buried his child. Nothing could be further from the truth. His response to those who doubted him lay etched in stone, a blatant act of defiance. A permanent testament.

I could not scream or cry. In silent fury I stood. Why did God ask so much of us? As a child, I believed. It was a simple faith, a sure belief that God loved me.

Now I felt like a rug hanging on a line, beaten until all the dirt and dust fell away. I supposed what happened next would be up to me, but I did not know if I could find faith again. I did not know how to find it, or if I wanted to find it.

During my courtship with Job, I felt a renewal of desire to understand who God is. I wanted to love him the way Job did. I wanted that passion, but now that seemed so far away. Perhaps, like the Biblical Thomas, just being told something *is*, was not enough. Perhaps I needed something tangible of which to take hold.

Would I never find peace? Would I never have the answers to anything? Right now I wanted that peace, but could I have it without the answers? How did I begin to satisfy the persistent want?

I was resentful. Looking at the small white headstone sent sadness through to my bones, leaving me lost. Disillusionment was foremost in my heart. How could I choose to believe that God was in control of everything, even the bad stuff? How could I find the faith to trust that control in the face of such apparent chaos?

In my mind, I heard my mother's voice from my childhood. "Because I said so," she would answer after I posed the "why" question one too many times. It was not a satisfying answer in any manner, and yet I understood I pushed too far. "Because I said so," was the only answer I would get. I would obey my mother, but my head and heart stirred in rebellion.

Now, it felt as though the small rectangle of marble was a "Because I said so," from God. The only choice left was obedience. What would that entail? I thought I knew, but doubted my willingness to take that action.

I got up from my knees and took the first step toward home.

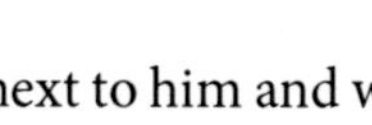

I sat on the edge of the bed next to him and waited. He was sleeping now. The frown was gone, replaced by a serenity I wished could be absorbed through the skin. His lashes were wet as though he had been crying.

I swallowed my anxiety and touched my hand to his face.

His eyes opened and I saw the life in them. He smiled at me, the first real smile I had seen from him in a long time.

"Hi," I said.

"Hi.," he said.

"Did you get your answers?"

"No." His smile became serious and he shook his head. He took my hand in his and pressed a kiss into my palm. "At least not the ones I thought I wanted."

I watched as his eyes skimmed over my face and hair. He looked at me a long while. His hand reached out and tugged gently on the strands of my shortened locks.

"And you? Did you find any?"

I shook my head, unable to speak past the lump in my throat.

He pulled my head down to his chest and I clung to him in spite of the discomfort I knew he felt. I buried my nose in his chest and breathed deeply. The odors of sweat and hospital filled my nostrils. He needed a bath, but underneath was his familiar scent. I turned my head and lifted it enough to kiss him. *God forgive me! How could I have wanted something different, even for a second?*

He must have sensed my desperation, for he pulled back and searched my face.

I looked away, attempting to avoid his gaze. He carefully turned my face back to him and waited until I looked him in the eye.

"Tonight I saw God. It was only a glimpse, but that's all I could take, and He allowed it. Not because I demanded it, but because He chose it." He traced first my eyebrows, then my nose and mouth with his fingertip. "It was a reminder, one I needed, that I serve Him for who He is and not because of what He can do for me. After that, everything else is nothing—everything, even justification. So whatever it is, whatever you think you've done, let it go."

I tried to protest but he would not hear it. He drew my head forward and placed a kiss on my temple. "There's nothing you need to say, Jes."

I broke down and started to sob. I did not deserve it. Not any of it.

"We're going to be all right." he said when I was finally quiet.

He said the words and I believed them. I believed the truth of them in spite of the doubts and insecurities still struggling for room in my head and heart.

My act of obedience, my faith, would be in the words I heard from Job knowing they came from God. Not having answers to many of the questions that still plagued me in the moments of the day was something I would need to come to terms with.

"You'll stay for a while?" he asked with a yawn.

"Yes." I sat up carefully. "But first you need to eat something."

"What is there?"

Inwardly I sighed and resigned myself to the churning in my gut.

"You mother brought stew."

Thirty-eight

December 7, 1941

What followed in our lives after that night would find Job's words to be true, for although it was not an easy future—and there were many times I battled against fear and uncertainty—it was a good future, an abundant future that is now an abundant past.

That night, after eating, Job wanted to get out of bed. He said he wanted to feel more like himself and less like a patient. I was glad to help him into the bathtub and wash all traces of the hospital away. I sat with him while he read aloud from his Bible until eventually, in the early morning hours, I fell asleep in the armchair next to his bed.

I awoke to the sounds and smells of breakfast cooking. I stretched and moaned at the stiffness in my body caused by sleeping in the chair.

"Morning, Doll Face." Job smiled from his place by the window. Someone had helped him into the wheelchair. "You slept late."

"I'm still tired." I yawned and stretched.

He looked relaxed, at peace, very different from recent past days. I felt it too, although I still experienced twinges of severe remorse that made my breath hitch and my stomach churn.

"You look like you, Pally," I said and sniffed the air. "Who's here?"

"My parents."

I sighed heavily. After the conversations of the previous evening, I was afraid of what the day might hold. The uncertainty came winging back. My stomach lurched. I felt a clammy sweat on the back of my neck and forehead.

"What's wrong?" Job asked. "You went pale."

"Nothing. I just—I'm worried about what they'll have to say this morning."

"I'm not." Job's gaze wandered out the window to the empty snow covered yard.

"Why?"

His shoulders lifted in a slight shrug.

"They were wrong in what they believed about me. They'll know that soon enough, and things will change. They can't help but change. How they look at me, how they look at God—even at themselves—it will be different." He turned a considering look at me. "We've already changed because of this, and it will continue to change us. I can't let my hurt over their opinions stand in the way of where we're going. I've prayed for them, for forgiveness for them. They'll have to forgive themselves, which will be much more difficult than accepting mine or God's."

I was learning that truth myself. I doubted if self-forgiveness was even possible for certain things. I wondered if it should be.

The sounds of people arriving floated in from the direction of the kitchen, my parents from the voices.

"I don't want to go in there," I said. I stood and pressed my lips to the top of his head.

"I do." He lifted his arms carefully and wrapped them around my waist. He buried his face in my midriff. "It's a new day, Jes. There are new promises."

Rand sat at the table absently shuffling the mail still there from the night before. My father stood gazing out the window of the back door, his hands in the pockets of his Sunday suit. My mother was halfway across the floor, the bowls in her hand telling me she was about to set the table. They all looked in our direction when I pushed Job through the doorway. For long moments nobody said anything.

"I cut off my hair once too," May finally spoke into the awkwardness. She stood by the stove, wooden spoon in hand as she stirred a pot of porridge.

"I went blonde," my mother said.

"Truly?" May gave my mother a curious study. "I can't picture it."

Neither could I.

"It was," my father hesitated looking for the right word, "definitely interesting." My mother threw him the look she gave him when she wanted him to know they would be talking in private later.

Self-consciously I lifted smoothed down my hair. "It needs some evening out," I stated the obvious.

"I'll do it after we eat," my mother came over and wrapped her arms around me.

I squeezed back tightly, absorbing as much of her comfort as I could in the brief embrace.

"For now," she continued and pulled out a chair, "you two sit and we'll get food underway before we leave for church."

Once we were seated at the table, Job opened the conversation with a statement that put my father and Rand at a loss for words.

"God wants you to know you've been forgiven," he said quietly but directly.

The two men looked about to protest the need for that statement. Rand was the first to look away. His body sagged and he covered his face with his hands. His shoulders shook with silent remorse.

The color rose up the back of my father's neck and spread across his cheeks. I saw the muscles of his jaw clench and the grip on his spoon tighten. My mother reached across and massaged his hand gently until he released the utensil. Slowly he placed his hands in his lap and bowed his head.

"So what now?" he asked quietly submitting to weight of truth in Job's words.

"I'm really not certain," Job answered. "I guess we look at things realistically, financially, and see what we have to do to make sure that all our obligations are taken care of."

"How can I help?"

I knew I should be listening, but the relief of moving forward finally was enough for me. There would be no more recriminations, no more speculation and no more accusations. Job was restored to God, a state accepted by everyone.

I let the conversation proceed without me and picked at my cereal. The scent of cinnamon wafted up and enticed me to take a spoonful, and then, as discreetly as possible I spit the contents into my napkin and waited for the nausea to pass. I needed a distraction and reached for the mail.

Slowly I slid one envelope after another off the top of the pile to the bottom. Twice, I went through the pile before one letter in particular caught my attention. I turned it over in my hands several times before sliding my finger into the corner of the seal and tearing it open. A slip of paper floated out from between the folds of the letter and landed face down on the table. As I reached for it, I noticed the elegant flourish at the bottom of the letter. Professor Williamson.

I scanned the page and then read it again, being careful to make sure I understood his words correctly. I flipped the letter off the top and looked at the sheets of legal documents underneath. I tried to read what they said, but my heart was pounding so hard, and there were so many words, I could not distinguish one from another. I gave my head a shake, read Professor Williamson's letter once more, and then turned over the paper slip that had fallen out.

I sat and stared at the check in my hand. It was not a large sum, but it was more money than I had seen in months.

"I believe I can hold them off until January," I heard my father say. "So that will give you a small reprieve."

"Would this be enough to hold them off for any longer than that?" I slid the check across the table to my father.

"What is this?" He picked it up and turned it over, looking for what I do not know.

"It's a check." I stated.

"I see that," he sighed in exasperation. "Where did it come from?"

"A publisher."

"A publisher? Of what?"

"Of books."

"Whose books?"

"Mine."

"Yours?"

I nodded, my exasperation growing beyond his. "Is it enough?"

"Is what enough?"

"The amount! To hold off the bank!" my voice raised in frustration.

"Yes, I believe so," my father looked perplexed. "But why do you have it?"

"Ben, catch up," my mother ordered. She was smiling as she turned to me. "That's wonderful Jessie. Congratulations."

"They want Job's illustrations too." I could feel myself beaming as I looked at him. He was right. This was a new day with new promises. "They want to pay you for your paintings."

"The ones I did for your stories?" He frowned in confusion.

"And they're asking for more," I nodded.

That moment I let myself believe Job's words about a new day and new promise. While my faith remained cocooned, I could feel the metamorphosis begin. I felt the shift in the wanting, but when the Japanese dropped their bombs on Pearl Harbor that same day, the belief in a new promise dimmed to almost utter darkness.

President Roosevelt declared the country at war and it seemed that we spent every waking moment listening to the radio.

It was impossible to go anywhere and not see or hear the call to arms. Patriotic outrage and fear propelled many into actions previously outside the realm of comprehension. And, though it would hardly seem fair, this turmoil, this devastation, served as further impetus for our restoration. For many the world had tilted on its axis, but mine was just beginning to right itself.

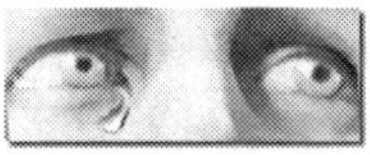

February 1942

After weeks spent huddled around the radio, listening and praying as the highest human powers made preparations to send our country into battle, I declared a small war of my own and pulled the plug on what I viewed as an intrusion into our home—no more radio, at least for one entire sunrise to sunrise period. On top of that, the house was off limits to everyone, no one in or out except Job and me.

The next day we sat on the front veranda. It was a misty day, the mild temperature causing snow to melt and fall from the eaves of the roof in a steady drip. Job had managed to make it out and onto the porch swing without use of the wheel chair. He was breathing a little hard, his forehead damp with the effort, but the accomplishment put a smile on his face. I tucked the heavy quilt around us both and snuggled next to him.

I was still feeling unwell and the desire to sleep, especially on a lazy day like this one, was overpowering. With world events taking priority, I managed to hide the state of my health quite easily, but as the frequency and severity of the bouts of sickness increased, and it grew more difficult to pull myself out of bed in the morning, I doubted how much longer I could keep it up. Attributing it to stress would only go so far.

Job still napped in the afternoon and when he did, I was able to slip upstairs and do the same. On those days it was easier to manage without embarrassing myself, and I continued to push away my fear that something was terribly wrong. I told myself it would go away. I wondered about how much longer I could do that, and then pushed that thought away also.

"You probably shouldn't be out here too long," I said on a yawn.

"Mm. It feels good though."

I nodded my agreement.

We sat, curled together and listened to the cadence of the drips from the roof and trees. My body relaxed as the natural music lulled me into a light doze.

The slam of a vehicle door gave me a jolt, and I sat up to find Job waving at a man as he climbed down from his truck. In the bed of the truck were milk cans. I figured there to be a dozen.

"Hello there!" The man called.

"Hello," Job returned. "Welcome."

The man smiled and waved. He paused and looked over his shoulder and across the yard at the silent creamery.

"Who is that?" I whispered. He looked familiar, but I could not quite place him.

"Donovan March." Job answered. "From the other side of the Junction."

"March? Gerry's dad?"

"Yes."

Gerald was the same age as my brother Michael. His mother had died when Gerry was very young. Even though I did not know him well, I remember him for more than the fact that he had a decent arm and often played center field during the baseball game at the summer gatherings. I remember him because he is the one who first made me aware that sometimes parents die. Gerald was a shorter, but no less lanky version of his father.

Donovan March's long strides covered the ground rapidly despite the slow even pace he took on his way to us. He stopped at the base of the veranda steps and propped a foot on the bottom level before leaning against the railing. He was somewhere in his mid sixties I guessed, it was hard to tell, his face was browned and weathered by years of outdoor living. He had just the hint of a paunch through the middle.

"Job. Missus." Donovan March shifted his cap by way of greeting.

"Mr. March, how are you sir?" Job shifted to push his self off the swing and stand.

"Don't get up," Donovan said. "I hear you been sick."

Job nodded.

"Well, you look like you've rounded the bend," Donovan continued, the slightest hint of an Irish brogue more pronounced with each word. "Glad I am to see it too."

"Thank you." Job said.

"Heard about the other. The barns and such." His eyes flickered in my direction before dropping to the ground briefly. His head lifted turning toward the creamery once more. He adjusted the cap again, smoothing down the full head of salt and pepper hair underneath before settling the head cover. "I see the creamery over there. Looks like new, still."

"It's never been used," Job responded. "Never had the chance."

"Now, that's why I've come. See?" He indicated his truck and the milk cans residing in the back. "I got a load of milk here. I'm trying to run it down to the co-op."

The co-op had been started it 1919 by a group of farmers up in Cabot. Farmers from within a hundred miles could bring their excess milk and have it made into butter. Any further away and the milk would spoil before arriving at the creamery. Grand River Junction was just outside the limit, but the March dairy, on the north side of the Junction, was inside by half a mile. The co-op had proved successful enough to survive even the depression.

"You're a bit out of your way," Job observed leaning forward, interest evident in his posture.

"Aye, I was on my way, but then I got to thinking," Donovan came up the steps to stand and look across the yard. "My Gerald's gone and signed up for the army. Wants to go and kill himself some Nazis. Can't say I blame the boy. His cousin barely survived Pearl Harbor. Well, Gerry's leaving in the next little while. Don't know when he'll return."

Neither Job nor I knew what to say in the heavy silence. We could hear the implied "if" in the older man's voice. I tried to link Gerry's enlisting with the unused creamery and could not, so I waited with Job for Donovan March to make the connection.

"I don't wanna be away his last days here, and I can't afford to let the milk go useless."

"You'd like to use the creamery." Job stated.

Donovan March turned and gave Job a direct look. "Yes. Yes I would," he said. "An' not just me. We've been talking, me and a few from around. None us of like to make that drive, especially in the winter. Some days it's just nigh impossible."

"It'll have to be cleaned out," I said. "We've been storing a few things in there."

After the fire, we moved some equipment and other supplies into the empty building to keep them out of the elements. No one had been in or out of the place since.

"Gerry said he'd help before he leaves. He can be here first thing in the morning," Donovan responded. "Won't be much earned at first, but a little something's better than naught. You just tell us what to do an' we'll do it."

"I think we can work out an arrangement." Job nodded and this time succeeded in pushing to his feet. He stuck out his hand and Donovan March met him with a handshake.

"You're a good man, Job. Everyone 'round these parts knows it and they've all heard what's happened here. You wait. Come spring you'll have barns again, and they'll be full." With a last tip of his cap in my direction, Donovan March took the veranda stairs with one long stride, crossed the distance to his truck and disappeared down the drive.

I looked at Job holding onto the railing to keep him upright.

"You're not ready for that kind of work yet." I said.

"I know," he carefully made his way back to the swing.

"You're getting better but you can't do long days. And we don't even know the state of your heart."

"I'll tell them what to do and let them do it." He turned to me and smiled. "As for the state of my heart? It's pretty full right now."

I breathed through the hitch in my chest and returned the smile. I reminded myself that God had said we would be all right.

True to his word, Donovan and Gerry arrived early the next morning. I looked at the clock on the dresser and realized it was late, almost ten o'clock. The voices outside told me there were people working. I lay there and listened. It sounded almost like I remembered, only without the sound of cows.

I threw back the covers and sat on the edge of the bed, breathing deeply until my stomach settled. I was not getting better.

From the window, I could see activity in the vicinity of the creamery. Donovan was directing a man I did not know to move some empty milk cans away from the entrance. Rand was talking to another man I did not recognize. I heard the front door slam and looked down in time to see Gerry piggybacking Job across the yard. A boy of about twelve or thirteen followed, dragging the borrowed wheelchair behind him. I held my breath as Gerry lost his footing. I thought he would go down and take Job with him. Laughter floated up to where I stood as Gerry managed to keep upright and continue on to the creamery. It came as some surprise when I burst into tears.

The more I tried to stem the flow of emotion, the more difficult it became, and the harder I cried the sicker I felt. I flew to the bathroom, and emerged sometime later with the realization I could no longer put off what I dreaded. I would go see Doc Fisher this afternoon, while Job was either busy or napping.

Thirty-nine

February 1942

Doc Fisher was with a patient.

The presence of Emma and Nathan Pratt lead me to believe it was their mother, Audrey, who was in with the doctor. She had been Audrey Skeels when she had taught Sunday School. I was still was very fond of her.

I admired her easy way with people and her open friendly nature. Her oldest, Daniel, was the boy out at the farm this morning. I recognized him when I went out to see the progress being made in the creamery. Nathan, the youngest, was two. Their father Simon Pratt died just after Nathan's birth. He had worked in the bank with my father. One moment Simon Pratt had been standing in his place, serving Mrs. Martin. He clutched his head suddenly and just like that he was dead on the floor.

I was in New York at the time and did not return for the funeral, but I do remember feeling a sense of loss at the sudden passing of the man with the round spectacles and easy sense of humor. After I returned to the Junction, I noticed that even though Audrey Pratt smiled and her children ran and played with other children, there was a difference in all of them. An air of sadness would creep into the corners of their eyes, or sometimes I could see it in the slight slip of a smile, as though in those moments they were thinking of their father. Emma wore that burden today. It was present in the tension of her mouth as the young girl struggled to hold onto the squirming toddler. My entrance caused a much needed distraction.

"Hi Emma," I said and sat down next to her.

"Hello, Missus Jessie," she responded quietly. Her bottom lip trembled.

Nathan held his arms out and grinned at me.

"May I?" I asked the young girl who nodded with relief and relinquished the wiggly bundle of energy.

With only a slight pang of residual resentment, I cooed and made faces at Nathan who grinned around fists tucked into his mouth. He spied the little silver frog dangling from the chain around my neck and clapped his hands with delight.

"Gog!" he crowed.

"That's right, frog." I laughed shifting him so his grab just missed the chain.

"He likes frogs," Emma said solemnly.

"I do too."

"I think they're icky."

"Some of them are," I chuckled knowing Emma would not understand my amusement. "But this one's special. Mr. Job gave it to me."

Emma stared at the little frog. "My momma said Mr. Job was very sick."

"Yes. He was."

"Did he die?"

"No," I answered gently. "He's getting better."

"My papa died." Emma's eyes swam with tears. She looked like her father, with his white blond hair and pale blue eyes.

"I know. I'm very sorry about that."

Nathan, finding his efforts to reach the frog thwarted, squirmed to be released. I set him down and watched as he made his way to the coffee table and the colorful magazines.

"My momma's sick." Emma's whisper was barely audible. "It's the cancer."

Inside, my heart broke for this little girl. Her tiny body vibrated with fear and uncertainty. Her words explained the haunted look I saw in Daniel's face this morning. I had originally attributed it to the fact that Gerry was heading off to war in a few days. While Donovan March had not much use for church, Gerald showed up on more than the occasional Sunday, and even more regularly after Simon Pratt had died. Gerald's bond with Daniel had no doubt grown out of a shared understanding of grief.

Now, faced with losing his mother and his almost big brother, Daniel was certain to be feeling as terrified as his sister.

"How do you know?" I finally asked. "That your momma's sick?"

"I heard her talking to Mrs. Pike," Emma said. "She's scared about what's going to happen to us. We ain't got no one to go to."

"Gook!" Nathan chose that moment to demand attention.

Emma looked at Nathan and the magazine he held. She turned to me anxiety written all over face. "He likes books," she said.

I took the proffered magazine from Nathan who beamed up at me, drool and bits of something clinging to his chin. The magazine was months old. It bore a photo of Nazis Goebbels and Goering on the cover. The little boy had eaten a good portion of the corner.

"Yes, Emma," I agreed. "I can see how much."

I winked at her and it seemed as though I picked the right tone. Her thin shoulders relaxed and she smiled.

The examining room opened, and Audrey Pratt was ushered out by Doc Fisher. Many considered her plain, but I always thought her a pretty woman. She was about fifteen years older than me with features that were fine and crisp. She had a light overbite when she smiled and her hazel eyes were fringed by thick dark lashes. Her skin was clear and unmarked; at least that is how I remembered it, but as I looked closely, I saw signs that she was indeed sick.

The yellow tinge under her skin told me her liver was affected by the cancer. During Job's stay at the hospital, I passed a room in which a yellow man lay in a bed. I asked Doctor Peterson how a man turned yellow and Dr. Peterson explained about the man's liver failure due to cancer. He had not lived to see the next day. It was not a future I wished for this woman whom I admired.

Audrey looked like she had been crying. Doc Fisher squeezed her hand in a reassuring manner that failed in intent. When Audrey turned and saw me sitting next to Emma she stopped short and stammered a greeting.

"Hello Mrs. Pratt," I returned. "Emma was just telling me how much Nathan likes books."

"Gook!" Nathan said again. He reached for the tattered magazine.

"Oh Nathan," Audrey sighed. "What have you done?"

The boy ran to his mother who scooped him up and hugged him close. I took note of the extra squeeze she gave him as she buried her face in his neck.

"Emma, weren't you watching him?"

"It's my fault," I placed a hand on Emma's shoulder. "I let him go."

"How's Job doing?" She asked as Emma crossed over and clung to her mother.

"He gets a little bit better with each day. I just hope he doesn't overdo it this afternoon."

"I know Danny went over with Gerald, but I didn't quite get the reason for it."

"It looks like we're opening up the creamery," I explained including Doc Fisher in the conversation. "I'm not sure how it will work but at this point, there really isn't anything to lose."

"Having something to keep him busy will be good for your husband," Doc Fisher said. "Just keep an eye out for any signs of shortness of breath or chest pain."

"Well, I really should be going," Audrey said adjusting Nathan on her hip. "I need to get this one home for a nap and Emma could probably use a snack."

"Mrs. Pratt, may I stop by sometime for a visit?" I listened to the inner compulsion driving me to ask the question.

The woman was caught off guard and appeared at a momentary loss for words. "Please, call me Audrey," she said. "And yes. A visit would be nice. Thank you. And Doctor Fisher, I'll replace the magazine."

"Mrs. Pratt, it's an outdated issue." The doctor took the magazine and held it up. "I think young Nathan showed remarkable restraint, all things considered. Another inch and he would have taken off Goering's head. If only it were that easy to rid the world of Nazis."

There were a few more polite comments about the state of the war and the world, before the Pratts left and Doc turned to me.

"Well, Mrs. Nightingale, what seems to be the problem." He held the door for me, waiting until I passed through before closing it quietly.

"I'm sick," I stated.

Hearing the words out loud had me feeling even more so. I was suddenly very frightened. What if it was, as Emma had phrased it, Panic, fear, resentment, anger at the unfairness of that thought, unsettled my stomach.

When my body had calmed down enough to enable me to set aside the waste bucket Doc Fisher handed me just in time, I endured the exam and answered the doctor's questions, even the most personal. My mind stirred the pot of anger at God. How could he test my faith this soon?

He had to know how precarious my footing was. Why would he do this to me? To Job?

By the time the doctor had finished poking and prodding, I had worked myself up into another bout of sick, but since my stomach was empty, I only succeeded in heaving myself sore.

"Take a few deep breaths, my dear," Doc fisher handed me a damp cloth and another glass of water. "You're getting yourself all worked up."

He waited while I wiped my face, rinsed my mouth and did the recommended breathing.

"Better?" he asked.

"Yes," I croaked.

The doctor pulled up a chair and looked at me where I sat. He rested a hand on my knee in a manner that said what he was about to say, was serious. He sighed deeply, first puffing out his cheeks, then pursing his lips.

"It's serious, isn't it?" I whispered.

"Yes, it is."

"Just tell me."

He did, and I threw up.

Spring 1942

I managed to hide the diagnosis for far longer than I expected. With all the commotion going on, no one paid attention to me. Even Job was lost in it, and there was a lot to get lost in.

Construction on the new milking barn was underway. We had cows that needed a home as once again, the world's conflict provided for our rebuilding. A man clear across the state, over by Middlebury, heard about our troubles from someone passing through the area. This man's wife was gone, his daughter married and moved to Burlington and his son preferred to fight rather than farm. With no one, and no will left to pursue the dairy farming, the man decided to give away the animals and move closer to his grandchildren. He showed up a week to the day after Donovan March did, unloaded a truckload of cows, said he would be back in another week with a few more, and left. I never learned his name, but true to his word, a week later another load of cows plus one bull stood in the paddock. Now, the herd of thirty waited for shelter while a barn raising was underway.

My father had managed to keep the bank away with the money from the publishing contract, and the promise of more where that came from. An intense and furiously fast planning session between Rand, Job, David, and my father resulted in a business plan for the co-op and dairy. My father presented the plan to the bank with an offer to secure the money for building materials himself. The bank accepted the offer four days ago, and once the word got out that Job needed a new barn, the whirlwind had begun.

The weather continued mild so three days ago people from all over the county converged with tools and food. The house was full to overflowing and the barn would be completed today.

They had built on the existing foundation. Stones, blackened by fire, supported fresh beams and planks waiting for paint. Spring would be soon enough for that.

Job, at times, forgot he was still recovering from a serious illness and would find himself without wind or legs. I worried he pushed himself too hard, too soon, but his return to joy was such a relief, I lacked the real desire to contain him. However, my need to move cautiously, to protect myself emotionally, tempered my enthusiasm.

In spite of it all, my heart remained bruised. It could not, and would not, be fixed at the same rate that a barn was built, but I was learning to redirect the want by listening. I paid more attention to the thoughts that entered my mind when I was alone and still, and I spent much time alone and still, in the days since my trip to see Doc Fisher.

I began to distinguish between the thoughts born and sustained by hurt, and the less self-destructive ones—the ones I hoped were from a different place.

Hearing God speak was too new for me to know it was what it was, but I prayed for clearer understanding and the knowledge to act in accordance with those thoughts. To my astonishment, I found myself gaining that understanding. I wanted more.

I found the confidence to act in spite of the fear that would forever be my personal battle to overcome in my efforts to live each day in abundance. By accepting the fear, but never acceding to it, I lived the life I sought. The knot of my regret served as a reminder of how close I came to being something other than what I was meant to be; so, when my breath hitched with memory, and my heart stuttered with remorse,

I acknowledged my stupidity, cried the necessary tears, accepted it, and looked beyond it.

The resentment for the lack of clear understanding about those things that transpired, I quickly blotted up whenever it threatened to seep through. I needed to trust God was in control no matter how scary it was to let go of my own; something that became easier when I realized just how little control I owned, especially over my own body.

My body had betrayed me, at least that is how I originally looked at what happened.

In the days and weeks that passed after the loss of our Faith, I convinced myself, there would be no children for me. I was certain I did not deserve them, and even more convinced I did not want them, so when Dr. Peterson said it would be possible to try again after my body healed, I did not believe. I felt positive I was damaged more than anyone indicated, that they were too afraid to say anything because of my fragile state. Indeed, the very idea of having another baby filled me with an unreasonable dread.

As well, there was the fundamental issue of creating a life. Except for the one night in a tired old boarding house in Barre, not since my accident had Job and I shared a bed for anything more than sleeping. I had needed time to heal and then Job was too ill, but, when Daniel Pratt discovered me leaning against the far side of the bunkhouse, drawing in great gulps of air, the speculation on his pale face made me realize I could no longer deny the truth of Doc Fisher's words. I was pregnant.

I moved quickly to grab hold of the young boy's arm before he could alert anyone about where I was or what I was doing. "It's not what you think."

"You sick?"

"No, I'm not." I said quietly and firmly.

His eyes darted to the spot on the ground that indicated otherwise.

"Okay, yes, I'm sick, but not in the way you think."

"Sick is sick," Daniel said.

"Not when it's a baby."

"You're having a baby?"

"Sh," I peeked around the corner of the building. I thought I timed my visit to the creamery just right, but the smell of the building sent me running. The bunkhouse and the outhouse serving the bunkhouse, were the closest sources of refuge. I did not need to be pregnant to feel sick at the thought of heading over to the second building.

"You're having a baby?" Daniel asked again his expression skeptical.

"Yes," I sighed. "But you can't tell anyone."

"Why not? Ain't you happy about it?"

"Aren't you," I corrected automatically as I heard his mother do with regularity.

"I don't feel one way or t'other," Daniel said with a shrug "Ain't me having the baby."

"Isn't," I corrected again.

"Isn't what?"

"Isn't me having the baby."

"You just said it was."

I started to laugh, which made him suspicious. I pulled myself together.

"I'm too terrified to be happy." I eased my grip on his arm and took a deep breath as my stomach lurched at the thought.

"Why? Mamma had three of us." His face clouded over at the thought of his mother. "Does Mr. Job know?"

"Not yet, but I'm going to tell him."

"Tell him now."

"It's not that easy."

"It ain't that hard," the boy argued.

"It's not that hard."

"That's what I said," Daniel bumped the heel of his palm against his forehead in a gesture that maligned my sanity. "It's just words you have to say. You said them to me."

How could I explain what I could not understand? It was so much more than the words, but Daniel was right. I had already said them. I could say them again. I think.

Before I could stop him Daniel broke free from my grasp and stepped around the corner. "Mister Job!" he called. "Missus Jessie needs you."

"Daniel, stop." I snuck a peek and saw Job lift his head. Just outside the creamery door, he was in the act of sitting down in his chair. Rand was helping him.

Everyone was there, waiting. It was lunchtime and it looked like all the men were taking the break together. Even those working on the barn were gathering to make the trip to the house. At Daniel's words, every eye turned in our direction.

Job pushed himself up even as his father tried to make him sit. The progress of Job's recovery was evidenced when he pushed past his father without too much difficulty. He started across the muddy yard toward Daniel.

"Where is she?" Job called and to which Daniel pointed. "What's wrong?"

"I'm here," I said and stepped out. "I'm fine. Stay there."

I carefully made my way over to where he now stood, half way between the creamery and the bunkhouse. Rand stood a few feet behind Job. Daniel trailed closely behind me. I looked around and saw that people were watching with undisguised curiosity. I turned and glared childishly at Daniel, who glared right back.

"What's going on?" Job asked observing the look between us. "Are you all right?"

"I'm fine."

"Are not," Daniel jumped in.

I bit my tongue, refusing to allow the conversation to spiral into a juvenile debate.

"Jessie?" Job prompted.

I hesitated. Daniel did not.

"She's gonna have a baby," he said watching closely for Job's reaction.

"What?" Job shook his head.

"She's gonna have a baby!" Daniel said loud enough this time for his words to carry across the open yard. My father, standing on the bottom step of the front veranda of the house, dropped his hammer. My mother, standing at the door of the house waiting for him, let the screen door slam behind her.

In a sudden moment of clarity, I gained great empathy for David and Michael, and for what they endured through our growing up years by having me as a younger sibling.

I lunged for the boy who danced out of reach.

"Is it true?" Job put himself between me and the object of my ill will.

I saw movement out of the corner of my eye. May appeared in the doorway of the house. I saw her lips move although she spoke too softly for me to hear. My mother said something back and when May's hands flew to cover a very audible gasp, it was not difficult to guess what was said.

I stomped in frustration. "Can we not have this conversation here?"

"Is it true?" Job ignored my request and repeated his question.

"Job," I pleaded.

"Jes." He was unmoved.

"Fine." I said through clenched teeth.

I turned to the onlookers.

"Yes!" I shouted. "Yes, I'm going to have a baby. We're going to have a baby."

I turned back to Job. "Happy now?"

"Yes," he answered calmly, quietly. "But you're not."

"No! No, I'm not!" I wrapped my arms around my waist. "I want to be, but what if something happens? I don't know if I can do it again."

"Stop for minute." He reached out and gave me a gentle shake. "Look around."

I did. I saw the faces of friends and family. People I had known all my life.

"Now, close your eyes and listen," he instructed.

I did. I heard the wind through the trees. I heard the jangle of tool belts and the shifting of feet. Somebody coughed. Someone else sniffled. A cow lowed deep and long, answered by another—a mother and calf. In the distance a dog barked and a car drove past the lane way. There was life here, life renewed more quickly than it had been taken. There was promise in it. Sustenance.

"It will be different this time, Jes." Job wrapped his arms around me and I clung to him.

Epilogue

Today

Job died quietly in his sleep two years ago last week. I crawled into bed next to him that night and settled down to listen while he prayed and told God all that had transpired that day. I added my own accounting of things, as had become our way, but it was different that night. There was an energy in the air, an expectancy. I reached out and squeezed Job's hand, told him I loved him and waited while he returned the same. I thanked him for our life and for our children.

Time had shifted our faces and grayed our hair, but the eyes were the same as I remember when I was six and he was eight. I waited until his breathing became regular before allowing my sorrow take me down and under. By morning, Job was gone, and I had found the place that accepted it was my lot to remain, to walk with that pebble in my shoe for a time, for some purpose, until my life also will end.

My body and my God tell me that time draws near, and so I fight against the days to get these words down, words I hope will ease the burdens of another, words that will explain that while what happened could not be changed, we were changed by it. Grief cannot be removed, and in this world death cannot be undone.

But he was right, that day in the middle of the yard. Life would definitely be different. It was so abundantly full, difficult and joyous, lean and rich, and frightening. But that afternoon, standing in a muddy yard, surrounded by the love of family, friends and community, I accepted something that made it easier to find the peace that eased the want.

I conceded that the answers I sought so badly, I would probably never attain, and that maybe having them was not as important as I believed. It was how I chose to live without them that would matter more. I understood answers only matter in this life. In the next, if it is as promised, they will not matter at all.

ABOUT THE AUTHOR

Caroline Way was born in Portland, Oregon, raised in St. John's, Newfoundland until high school, when her family moved to Ontario. Currently she lives in Hamilton, Ontario, where she received her B.A. in Drama from McMaster University. From there she went on to obtain an M.A. in Communication from Regent University in Virginia Beach, VA, where she studied film making and screenwriting.

Once an active member of community theatre in both Ontario and Virginia, Caroline has always enjoyed exploring the "how" and "why" questions of the characters she portrayed, directed and created.

Caroline was also a member of the *Act One: Screenwriting for Hollywood* inaugural class of '99, and is an associate member of *The World Guild,* in Canada. Caroline has worked on many types of productions, from television commercials to feature films, in a variety of capacities. She has written and directed two of her own short films as well as a documentary for the town of Pickering, Ontario, and instructional video for the Ontario Principals' Council. Currently, Caroline has a day job as an Executive Assistant.

Confessions From a Farmer's Wife is her first novel.

Lightning Source UK Ltd.
Milton Keynes UK
UKOW050209070612

193907UK00003B/78/P

9 781937 573089